SINS OF THE FATHER

A rich elderly man, Rupert Moncrieff, is beaten to death in the silence of his West Country waterside mansion. His extended family are still living beneath his roof, each with their own motive for murder. And in this world of darkness and dysfunction are the artefacts and memories of atrocities in colonial Kenya that are returning to haunt them all . . . At the heart of the murder investigation is DS Jimmy Suttle who, along with his estranged wife Lizzie, is fighting his own demons after the abduction and death of their young daughter, Grace. Two deaths and two investigations. Two individuals tested to the limit, exploring the damage that human beings can inflict upon one another. Not simply in torture camps in the Kenyan bush, but much, much closer to home . . .

Books by Graham Hurley
Published by Ulverscroft:

THE PERFECT SOLDIER

THE D/I JOE FARADAY SERIES:
ANGELS PASSING
DEADLIGHT
BLOOD AND HONEY
ONE UNDER
THE PRICE OF DARKNESS
HAPPY DAYS

THE D/S JIMMY SUTTLE SERIES:
WESTERN APPROACHES
TOUCHING DISTANCE

GRAHAM HURLEY

SINS OF THE FATHER

Complete and Unabridged

CHARNWOOD
Leicester

First published in Great Britain in 2014 by
Orion Books
an imprint of The Orion Publishing Group Ltd
London

First Charnwood Edition
published 2016
by arrangement with
The Orion Publishing Group Ltd
An Hachette UK Company
London

A catalogue record for this book is available
from the British Library.

ISBN 978–1–4448–3068–2

Published by
F. A. Thorpe (Publishing)
Anstey, Leicestershire

Set by Words & Graphics Ltd.
Anstey, Leicestershire
Printed and bound in Great Britain by
T. J. International Ltd., Padstow, Cornwall

This book is printed on acid-free paper

For
Diana Warren-Holland
1940–2014

All of humanity's problems stem from man's inability to sit quietly in a room alone.

Blaise Pascal

Prelude

'Full lips. Freckles. Soft brown eyes. Plus a sudden smile like a note of music: unexpected, harsh, atonal. Scary hair too. Another clue.'

This from an email recovered from Claire Dillon's hard disk after the seizure of her PC. Claire had evidently been in contact with one of the men who'd drifted across her path, and had offered a brief glimpse of the person she thought she was before the darkness enveloped her forever. A copy had gone to Jimmy Suttle, courtesy of an ex-colleague on the Pompey Major Crime Team, and Suttle had shared it with Lizzie, who'd printed it out.

Alive, this woman had perplexed family, friends, occasional lovers and a small army of recce troops from the mental health establishment. She had looks, talent. She plainly knew how to write. She could even put herself inside her smile and recognise how crazy she was, how brittle, how lost among the razor-edged shards of someone she might once have dimly remembered.

Dead, though, she'd left nothing but media headlines and a scalding grief. The headlines — what she'd done — had come and gone in less than a week, but the grief knotted and thickened as Lizzie struggled to get this woman into focus.

Only last week, with Claire's self-description

1

etched on her brain, Lizzie had insisted on seeing the photos from the post-mortem. Suttle thought it was a lousy idea, but Lizzie was way past listening to anyone else and in the end Jimmy's mate on the enquiry had taken the case file to the photocopier and obliged with a selection of shots. Two of them were head and shoulders on the gleaming slab and told Lizzie nothing she didn't already know. In death it was rare to smile, but the rest was exactly the way Claire Dillon had described herself: *Full lips. Freckles. Soft brown eyes. Scary hair too. Another clue.*

Was this the face of evil? On balance, Lizzie thought not. Which didn't help at all.

★ ★ ★

As for Jimmy Suttle, that interminable summer — blessed by the best weather he could remember — passed in a blur. He felt totally adrift, an object in deepest space. Much of what had once masqueraded as real life no longer meant anything to him. He ate little, drank less, seldom returned social calls, walled himself away. When colleagues at work began to worry about how thin he'd got, and how gaunt, he blamed it on the pile of stuff he was having to do at home, not just the house but the garden as well. It was a lie, of course. But that didn't matter either.

Chantry Cottage, for sale since late spring, finally went to a couple moving down from the West Midlands. The estate agent said the guy had been a jobbing builder all his life. He'd have the roof sorted in weeks, ditto the windows, though decent central heating might take a while longer.

The sale went through in early October. Suttle, mercifully busy on a complex murder enquiry in Barnstaple, had neglected to find anywhere else to live, and it wasn't until a week before exchange of contracts that he started asking around. On the phone to Lizzie, conversations that were happening less and less often, he assured her that he had the matter in hand. He'd made calls to a couple of estate agents in Exmouth. There were loads of properties on the market. Two more lies.

In the end, with the buyers due to exchange the following day, he was saved by one of the younger civvy inputters in the Major Incident Room, a woman called Angie. Her granny had died. She'd been living alone in a flat overlooking the seafront in Exmouth. The place apparently had brilliant views as well as parking. Might D/S Suttle be interested?

The two of them went down to Exmouth that night. The Beacon turned out to be a picturesque terrace of tall Regency houses straddling a rise several hundred yards back from the seafront. Angie had the key. The property lay near the top of the hill. To the rear was a big church, its tower visible for miles around. Out front, with the remains of a sunset still pinking the clouds over the estuary, the view looked more than promising.

There were four bells beside the shabbiness of

the front door. Granny had lived on the third floor. Angie and Suttle let themselves into the gloom of the shared hall. The creaking stairs went on for ever. Behind the door on the second floor someone with hearing difficulties was listening to the local weather forecast. Rain and strong winds by dawn. The front clearing through by midday.

Making a mental note, Suttle followed Angie up two more flights of stairs. She had a moment's difficulty with the key to Flat 3, but then they were inside. The tiny entrance hall was in semi-darkness. There was that lingering smell of cooking oil and over-boiled vegetables Suttle recognised from a trillion witness interviews: solitary lives buoyed only by lap-top meals in front of the telly and the odd sudoku to warm the rest of your brain.

Angie was trying to find the switch for the hall light. Suttle stepped past her, wanting more of the sunset.

The front room was dominated by a huge bay window. Beyond lay the darkening coast, which seemed to go on for ever. Way out in the far distance the arm of the bay was already pricked with lights. Closer was the mouth of the river and the long curl of salt marsh he recognised from expeditions with Lizzie and Grace when they'd still been a family. A cloud of gulls pursued a trawler pushing towards the dock. A line of bigger vessels stirred at their moorings. The water, from here, had a luminescence he'd only ever seen in photograph galleries. It looked like velvet.

'We can get rid of all this. Don't panic.'

'Rid of all what?' Suttle was still staring at the view.

'All Granny's stuff. Christ, it's a museum.'

Suttle at last looked around. Angie was gesturing at the furniture, a neat half-circle of matching armchairs in threadbare chintz drawn up in front of the electric fire.

'And Jesus, take a look at these. I've no idea why she'd buy stuff like this.'

She was gazing at the pictures on the wall: clumsy, lifeless watercolours in fading blues and yellows. Flowers. Beach scenes. A stick-like child astride what might have been a donkey.

Suttle shrugged. The pictures, like the rest of the folksy bric-a-brac that littered the room, had probably come from half a lifetime of bring-and-buy sales, but he didn't care. What mattered was the view.

'Look,' he said. 'Just look.'

★   ★   ★

Afterwards he took Angie for a thank-you drink at a pub down the road. He hadn't touched a beer for weeks but the last half-hour had unlocked something deep in his head. After the suffocating chill of Chantry Cottage — the windows that never closed properly, the damp, the constant *drip-drip* of water — Flat 3 had been a release. The view dominated everything. It was so theatrical, so laden with water and light and the promise of constant change. It shook your feathers. It pulled you out of yourself. From

5

there, on his new perch, he could practically touch the weather. Rain and strong winds by dawn, he thought. The front clearing through by midday.

Angie had settled for a soda and lime. For reasons Suttle recognised only too well, she was reluctant to look him in the eye. She knows, he thought. Just like everyone else knows. You do your best to hunker down, ride out the storm, pretend nothing has happened, but what you never take into account is other people. They want so much to help you. And they always know best.

'I'm serious about Granny's stuff,' she said. 'A couple of trips to Ikea, you won't recognise the place.'

Suttle studied her a moment, then shook his head. Mentally, days ago, he'd already consigned everything he owned in Chantry Cottage to some house clearance guy with limitless patience and a biggish white van.

'Fuck Ikea,' he said softly. 'You know what that flat reminds me of? My mum's. When I was a kid.'

'Exactly. That's why you need Ikea.'

'Wrong. Just now I'm no one. I need nothing.' He reached for his glass. 'Cheers.'

1

SUNDAY, 8 DECEMBER 2013

Suttle was on the beach when he took the call. D/I Carole Houghton, as wedded to quiet Sunday mornings as he was.

'We have a situation,' she said at once. 'You're going to love this.'

Suttle turned his back on the scouring wind, cupping the phone to his ear. The beach was empty at this time in the morning but his borrowed dog seemed to have spotted company half a mile away.

'Skip,' he yelled. 'Come here.'

The dog ignored him. It belonged to a young Polish couple who occupied the flat above Suttle's, and he took it out first thing on Sundays to give them a lie-in. A couple of hours at the right state of the tide would take him miles along the gleaming beach, emptying his head of everything but the chill blast of wind off the sea, and interludes like these had become increasingly precious. Now he ran, conscious that the rest of his day suddenly belonged to someone else. His boss, as it happened, had a great deal of time for dogs but absolutely no patience with crap excuses. You kept dogs on leads. Much the way you led your Major Crime team.

D/I Houghton restricted her briefing to the barest details: posh house in Topsham, an incident rung in an hour or so ago, a visit within minutes from a uniformed patrol, and now a long list of calls she was making on behalf of Detective Superintendent Malcolm Nandy.

'Operation *Amber*,' she said briskly. 'Suspicious death doesn't do it justice. Enjoy, eh?'

★ ★ ★

Topsham was a pretty village five miles upstream from Exmouth. Centuries of commerce had settled comfortably on the merchants, shipwrights and assorted gentlefolk who'd turned a bustling trading post into a sought-after riverside postcode. The trophy address in the village was The Strand, a street of handsome Dutch-style houses that overlooked the water downstream from the quay. These properties, as Suttle had once gathered from Lizzie, went for deeply serious money, and the pick of them all lay at the very end of the street where the tarmac suddenly gave way to a breathtaking view of the estuary: miles of silver-grey water framed by the gentle green swell of the Haldon Hills.

Suttle nosed his Impreza through the open gate. Crime scenes were always badged by SOC vans and metres of blue and white tape, and this one was no different. Thanks to Skip, Suttle was a late addition to the carnival.

Nandy emerged from the house, deep in conversation with D/I Houghton. The Detective Superintendent was a lean veteran in his late forties with a greying fuzz of close-cropped hair and a legendary reputation for seizing every investigation by the throat. In Nandy's view, most of the pieces fell into position within a day or two if you gave the evidential bag a good shake. Beyond that, if you weren't looking at a result, you were probably into something altogether more troublesome.

Just now he was tallying the boxes he wanted Houghton to tick. Scene parameters. Time parameters. Search parameters for the Territorial Aid Group. CCTV. Automatic number-plate recognition. House to house. Each new ask drew a cursory nod from the D/I, and Suttle guessed she'd actioned much of this stuff already. Major crime investigations, like riding a bike or flying a 747, came naturally after a while. Especially if you were as savvy and proactive as Carole Houghton.

Nandy had finished. He tapped his watch, shot Suttle a murderous look, checked an ever-growing list of unanswered calls on his smartphone and headed for his car.

For the first time Suttle noticed the name of the house, engraved on a slab of slate beside the big wooden gates.

'Magharibi?' he queried.

'I gather it's African, Jimmy. Christ knows what it means.'

D/I Houghton was a big woman with tinted glasses and a mass of artfully permed hair, and like Nandy she had a million things to do elsewhere. The makings of a squad were racing in from various corners of Devon and Cornwall and she needed to be at the Middlemoor headquarters to set up the Major Incident

Room. The first team briefing could wait until this evening, but for now she wanted Suttle to get himself up to speed.

'You'll find Luke inside. He's doing a flash intel search.' She was looking pointedly at the salt stains on the bottoms of Suttle's jeans, at the sand on his runners. 'There's a pile of forensic suits in the SOC van. Help yourself.'

She dug in her pocket for her phone and left without saying goodbye. Suttle watched her climb into the Range Rover she used for towing her horsebox and then turned back to the house.

It looked Edwardian, maybe a decade or two older, a slightly forbidding essay in red tiles and greying stucco with a multitude of lead-light windows and a sturdy front door with iron studs that badly needed painting. It was the kind of house that promised countless rooms inside, a twilight world, deeply private, somewhere you might lose yourself for weeks on end and not see another soul. Suttle listened to himself. Was he making this stuff up? Probably not, he thought. The best jobs happen in the shadows.

He was still wrestling with the forensic one-piece when D/C Luke Golding appeared. He was small — five six, five seven — and as ever the suit engulfed him. He and Suttle had been working together for a couple of years and for a time the relationship had floated on the shared acknowledgement that life, in the round, was a richly bonkers proposition. At first Suttle had gladly signed up to this proposition, enjoying Golding's astonishing talent for surfing the madness that lay at the heart of so many investigations. But now, after what had happened in the summer, he knew different. Your own life could come close to killing you. In places where it really mattered.

'Well?' Suttle nodded at the house. Treading plates were visible through the open door, disappearing into the gloom of the hall beyond.

Golding loosened the hood of the suit and tilted his face to the wind. With his boyishness and sudden grin he could almost pass for a teenager, an assumption that some of the rougher trade had lived to regret.

'Guy's in his eighties,' he said. 'Or was.'

'Name?'

'Moncrieff. Rupert.'

'So what happened?'

'Someone set about him. Big time.'

Moncrieff, he said, appeared to have been poorly for a while. A mild stroke had affected his mobility, and he'd spent much of the last year in and out of bed. He shared the house with two of his kids — a woman in her sixties and a younger son. The son, whose name was Neil, had rung the incident in, the call logged at 09.02.

'How did he die?'

'Stab and slash wounds. Plus something special for afters.'

Golding watched Suttle slip on his bootees then led the way inside. There was a smell of furniture polish. The gloom of the long panelled hall was splintered by cold shards of winter sunlight on the parquet floor. Doors were open down the hall, and from every room came the

11

ticking of clocks. Suttle paused to listen, wondering what happened when the hour came round and some of them chimed. A chorus of insects, he thought. Feasting on time.

'Are you interested or what?' Golding was waiting at the end of the corridor. Another open door.

Suttle joined him. Golding stood aside.

The bedroom seemed to double as a study. One of the walls was lined with bookshelves, and the antique desk in the big bay window commanded a view across the garden to the water beyond. Suttle was still trying to remember the name of the stately white birds pecking at the acres of gleaming mud when Golding drew his attention to the bed in the corner masked by the suited figure of the CSI. He was deep in conversation with the Crime Scene Manager, a guy called Robin whom Suttle had last met at the Barnstaple job.

'How's it going?' This from Golding.

The CSM broke off, offering Suttle a nod of recognition. 'Fine. We'll be through here by close of play. Tomorrow we'll start on the rest of the house.'

'Matey?' Golding nodded at the bed.

'The pathologist's due any minute. Driving down from Exmoor.'

He stepped aside and for the first time Suttle saw the figure collapsed against the nest of pillows. The wrecked face had been slashed to the bone, the ribbons of flesh hanging from his cheeks and chin still dusted with white stubble. Blood had fountained over the pillows and duvet

12

from deep wounds to his throat. His head sagged to one side, nearly dislocated from his body, and there was a look in the startling blueness of his eyes that spoke of incomprehension as well as terror. Transfer this tableau to an art gallery, thought Suttle, and the queues would stretch around the block.

'What's that?' He'd spotted an object on the pillow. The material looked rough, maybe jute. More blood.

'It's a sack. The son who phoned this in found it over the old boy's head. Two eye holes. Crude as you like.'

'What was it doing on his head?'

'No idea.'

'Weapon?'

'In the corner.' The CSM indicated a neat pile of evidence bags stacked on the carpet.

Suttle knelt beside them. The machete had to be a couple of feet long, the tarnished blade swelling out from a wooden handle. There were roughly carved markings on the handle, and blood had already congealed where the steel bedded into the wood. A leather scabbard occupied another evidence bag, neatly tagged with date and time.

Suttle got to his feet again and looked around. One of the walls, bare of bookcases, was hung with primitive tapestries. Skinny native women with gourds on their heads. Palm trees. Mountains. A dark green smudge of forest below the treeline. Elsewhere was a line of native shields, animal skin stretched tight over wooden framework. The best of them was carefully patterned in reds and blacks, another gust of Africa.

'It's Masai.' The CSM again.

'How do you know?'

'We took a safari last year. Kenya. The missus wanted to bring one back.' He pulled a face. 'No chance.'

Suttle nodded, his gaze returning to the machete. 'This belongs to the house? Part of the collection?'

'Yeah.' Golding this time. 'Neil, the son, ID'd it. There are two of them. They both belonged to his dad.'

'So where is he now? This Neil?'

'Heavitree nick. Waiting for us.'

★ ★ ★

Lizzie Suttle was late for her meeting in Gunwharf. A girl from the publishing house had phoned on Friday. Simon Horobin was attending a reception in Portsmouth's new Mary Rose Museum at noon and would very much appreciate an hour or so of her time beforehand. Just a coffee and a chat and a chance to take stock. Nothing ominous.

Nothing ominous. Lizzie's blood had iced at the phrase. Back in Devon, eighteen months ago, she'd played a major role in an armed siege transmitted live on TV. Half the nation had awaited developments at Chantry Cottage, where a bunch of psychotics had taken both her and Jimmy hostage at gunpoint. The men in blue, mercifully, had finally done the business,

14

and in the tumult of the weeks to come Lizzie had signed a six-figure deal with a leading London publisher.

Her husband had been a key member of the squad that had nailed the bad guys. She herself had spent four long hours contemplating a messy death. There were links — richly sensational — to the war in Afghanistan. The book couldn't fail.

But alas it had. Failed to behave. Failed to make it beyond a first feeble chapter. Failed to become the passport to the kind of life she'd always dreamed about. For months she'd been fending off increasingly alarmed enquiries from both her agent and her editor at the publisher. Its publicity department was whipping up a storm. Pre-sale subs into the likes of Waterstones were deeply promising. TV companies were already queuing up to option the story. So where was the fucking book?

She'd only ever met Simon Horobin once in her life. He headed the editorial side of the company. At the press conference to announce the deal, more than a year ago, he'd pumped her hand, given her a hug and told the world they were looking at the biggest thing to hit publishing in a very long time. After that, silence.

Now he occupied a corner table in the café-bar. She'd chosen the Waterfront Café because even on a Sunday morning it would be reliably full. She could hide her shame in the swirl of other people's conversation. With luck she could be away within the hour.

Horobin got up and extended a hand. No hug this time.

'Coffee?'

'Sure. I'll have a latte.'

Horobin waved her into a seat. He was a short, slightly dumpy figure. The last time she'd seen him he'd gone for the bookish and slightly tweedy look. Now, despite a visible paunch, he'd submitted himself to a greying razor cut, designer jeans, an uncomfortably tight denim shirt and a sprinking of estuarial vowels. If it was meant as a makeover, thought Lizzie, it didn't work.

Waiting for the latte, Horobin tried to attempt small talk, but Lizzie saved him the trouble. No point in avoiding the obvious.

'The book's not happening,' she said.

'At all?'

'At all.'

'Why not?'

'I don't know. Stuff?' She was watching a family battling the wind on the boardwalk outside. 'I just can't do it.'

Horobin nodded, seeming to understand.

'I saw you on TV back in August,' he said at last. 'That press conference. The one about Gracie. The one the police organised.'

Nobody called her daughter Gracie. She eyed him for a moment.

'And?'

'I thought you were amazing. Real composure. That must have taken some doing.'

'It did.'

'And afterwards?'

16

'Horrible. Horrible beyond belief.'

'Right . . . ' Something seemed to have brightened in his face. Lizzie could see it in his eyes.

'My agent says you'll be wanting the advance back,' she said. 'Have I got that right?'

'You have.'

'The full thirty thousand?'

'I'm afraid so. Unless you think there's still a chance.'

'No way.' She shook her head. 'What I thought was there has gone. I just can't find it. I had a plan. I've always had a plan. This one seemed foolproof. Jimmy's mates in the Job. Access to the guys in prison. Military contacts in the Marines. What drove those men to do what they did. It had bestseller written all over it. Then . . . ' She made the vaguest gesture, both hands, resignation writ large.

'But you started?'

'I did. I gave it a month or two, just to get my breath back after all that bloody trauma at the cottage. Then it was Christmas. My husband and I . . . there were issues for sure but we were getting on top of them.'

'Issues to do with the book?'

'Yes, in part. Jimmy was never that keen on lining his mates up for me to have a little chat. I'd somehow assumed that would just happen, but a girl can get these things wrong. You go through a thing like that, have a bunch of nutters with a gun to your head, the cavalry lined up outside, and afterwards you assume the men in blue will be happy to talk. Wrong. Some of the key guys on the case didn't want to know. They'd toss me little bits and pieces — leavings really, stuff I could have got from the press cuttings — but there was no way they were going to let me close. That was a problem. I was starting to write fiction. I was starting to make it up. Hopeless.' Her hands again, shaping the big hole where a book should have been.

'What about the guys they put away?'

'One of them was dead. Even my reach doesn't extend that far.'

'And the other two?'

'They were on remand at first. Then banged up for life. I went through their solicitors. That was another thing. One of them wanted serious money. The other one had had enough.'

'Of what?'

'Everything. Afghanistan. What happened to him afterwards. Me. The lot. The closest I got to him was a phone conversation with a prison visitor who'd had an encounter or two. She said he'd turned his face to the wall. Apparently it happens all the time. She called it zombie land.'

'Nice title.' The interest was back in his eyes.

'Thanks. But I'm not really helping, am I?'

'*Au contraire*.' He leaned forward, frowning now, a man with something important on his mind. 'Be honest with me?'

'Yes.'

'Will it *ever* happen? The Devon book?'

'No.'

'Good. That makes things simpler.'

'Does it?'

'Yes.'

'I pay you back the thirty thousand? We call it quits?'

'Not necessarily.'

'You mean there's a way out of this?'

Her own interest had quickened. The last ten minutes had been as embarrassing and shameful as she'd expected. Now he seemed to be offering some kind of deal.

'What happened back in the summer . . . ' he said slowly. 'We were all with you. Everyone I know who followed that story. We felt for you.'

'We're not talking Devon, right?'

'Of course not. I don't know how much bad luck one person can expect but you seem to have copped everything.'

'Copped' sat uncomfortably in the sentence. He must have picked it up from his kids, Lizzie thought. Or some shit TV series.

'What happened in the summer was in a different league,' she said quietly. 'What happened in the summer turns you into someone else.'

'That's well put.'

'Thank you.'

'Tell me more.'

'Why?'

'Because it might save you a lot of money.'

Lizzie held his gaze. He's talking about the advance, she told herself. 'So how does that work?'

'You write a book about it. You explore the way it happened. You look for answers.'

'There are none.'

19

'How do you know?'

'I've looked already. Had one or two conversations.'

She briefly outlined the doors she'd knocked on, the people she'd met, the questions she'd asked, the answers she'd discounted. Faced with what had happened, people either lied for their own peace of mind or simply turned away. Zombie land, she confirmed.

'But you're still interested?'

'Of course I'm still interested. It changed my life. It *is* my bloody life.'

'Then I suggest you start all over again. Get inside what happened. Tease out every detail. Go for multi POV.'

'POV?'

'Point of view. A tragedy like yours touches dozens of people. They each have their own story.'

Lizzie sat back for a moment and nodded. A psychoanalyst she'd contacted in her darkest moments had said something similar. To properly recover you have to *understand*, she'd said. Only then can you begin to put yourself back together again.

'Writing as narrative therapy? Is that what we're talking about?'

'Exactly. But something else too. The best books are inspirational. They take us to somewhere very bleak. They force us to confront the unimaginable. And then the journey takes a different turn. We all need to feel better about ourselves. You can make that happen. As long as the story's right.'

As long as the story's right. More than a year ago Lizzie had thought four hours looking down the barrel of a gun in Chantry Cottage had the makings of a pretty good story. Now this.

'We're talking personal here,' she said. 'Deeply, deeply personal. You *do* realise that?'

'Of course. That's why I'm suggesting it. Before, you were in the hands of others. This time the story belongs to you. It's your property. From where I'm sitting that earns you the right to a lot of conversations. People won't refuse you. Trust me. I know they won't. Not if you do it right.'

The silence stretched and stretched. Lizzie had long forgotten about her promised latte. When it finally appeared, she pushed it to one side. How come this man had beaten her to the obvious? How come it took an overweight London publisher to tease just a glimpse of salvation from the purgatory of the last four months?

'Forty thousand,' he said. 'And that's just the advance.'

'To do what?'

'To explore what happened. To make it real. To share it with us. And to hunt for some kind of answer. I'll need to fix the small print with your agent, but that's the basic offer. Seventy-five thousand words. World rights. Plus TV, film and audio.'

'What's the deadline?'

'Thirtieth of April'

'That's impossible.'

'It's not. This book writes itself. The deadline

21

gives us time to meet the obvious pub date.'

'Which is?'

'August the 24th.' The smile was back. 'That's the first anniversary, isn't it?'

★ ★ ★

Neil Moncrieff was already in the biggest of the interview rooms at Heavitree police station when Suttle and Luke Golding arrived. Someone had fetched him a coffee from the machine down the corridor, and he sat in the throw of light from the high window behind him, a tall hunched figure casting a long shadow over the scuffed table.

Suttle did the introductions before dispatching Golding for more coffees.

Moncrieff watched the D/C dig in his pocket for coins and then leave the room. 'What sort of person would do a thing like that?' he asked. His voice was light, barely a whisper, and there was a hint of a lisp.

'Good question, Mr Moncrieff.' Suttle slipped into the chair opposite. 'That's what we're here to find out.'

Moncrieff nodded. Suttle judged him to be in his late thirties. The scarlet remains of a long-ago attack of acne had cratered the paleness of his face, which was partly curtained by a lank fall of hair, and there was something about the way he held himself that suggested extreme apprehension. Bad things had happened. And there was maybe worse to come.

Suttle offered his sympathies. No one's day

should start with finding their father hacked to death. Moncrieff said nothing. He was wearing jeans and a white sweatshirt. The sweatshirt looked box-fresh and sported a striking yellow symbol Suttle had seen somewhere else.

'Camino de Compostela.' Moncrieff had registered Suttle's interest. 'It's the pilgrim route to north-west Spain.'

'You've done it? Walked it?'

'Last year. Four hundred kilometres in ten days.'

Suttle nodded in approval. He and Lizzie had visited Santiago de Compostela years ago, spending half a day in the huge plaza in front of the cathedral, watching pilgrims like Moncrieff celebrating the end of their journeys.

Golding was back with the coffees. He gave one to Moncrieff and settled beside Suttle, opening his notebook, but Suttle was still in the plaza, still watching the pilgrims, still feeling the warmth of the July sunshine on his upturned face. Afterwards, he and Lizzie had taken a coach to La Coruña, a journey north through the mountains that had delivered them to a tiny hotel room with glimpses of the marina and the sea beyond. They'd stayed a couple of nights and barely got out of bed. Another life, he thought. Another planet.

'What time did you get home this morning, Mr Moncrieff?' Golding had decided to take the lead.

'Around nine.'

'And what did you find?'

'Nothing to begin with. I was sweaty after the

ride back. I was muddy too. So I had a shower.'

'Your father was spending a lot of time in bed. Is that right?'

'Yes. He had a stroke a while ago. He tired easily.'

'It affected him badly? This stroke?'

'Yes and no. His memory wasn't what it was and he had difficulty walking, but his speech was fine. He could hold a conversation, read the paper, all that.'

'So did you check on him? Before you took the shower?'

'No.'

'OK.' Golding scribbled himself a note. 'So what happened next?'

'I got out of the shower. Got dressed. Then went through . . . ' His voice began to falter and he looked around the room as if to summon help.

'Through to where, Mr Moncrieff?'

'Through to my father's bedroom. He was there in the bed. Blood everywhere. It was horrible. I can't explain. Just horrible. He had that thing on his head. Ghastly.'

'You're talking about the hood?'

'Yes.'

'You're saying it was on his head?'

'Yes.'

'So what did you do?'

'I took it off. I needed to be sure.'

'About what?'

'That he was really dead.'

'You touched him? You felt for a pulse?'

'Yes. He wasn't breathing but he was still

24

warm. That's when I phoned 999.' He gulped. 'And you came.'

Suttle gave him a moment or two to compose himself. Then he leaned forward over the table. 'I know this isn't easy for you, Mr Moncrieff, but we need to know more about your father.'

Moncrieff nodded, said he understood.

'So when did you last see him alive?'

'Yesterday. Before I went out.'

'Were you looking after him?'

'We both were. Me and Hils.'

Hilary, he explained, was his stepsister, his father's only child from his first marriage. Suttle was scribbling himself a note. Hilary Moncrieff had been contacted on her mobile. She should be in Topsham by now.

Golding wanted to know more about yesterday. The uniformed officer who responded to the treble nine had already told him that both Hilary and Neil had spent the night away.

'You told us this morning you'd just come back from Exmouth. Is that right?'

Moncrieff nodded. Hils, he explained, had started a string quartet a couple of years back, four musicians with a shared love of chamber music. Last night they'd played a concert in the hall behind the Baptist church in Exmouth.

'Many people turn up?' Suttle this time.

'Couple of dozen. A disappointment to be honest.'

'And afterwards?'

'We went for a curry.'

'And then what?'

For the first time Moncrieff faltered. His head

25

went down. His long fingers explored one of the deeper scars beneath his ear.

'Hils stayed with her cellist friend,' he said at last. 'He lives in Exmouth.'

'And you?'

'I stayed with someone else.'

Golding asked for names and contact details. The cellist was Lawrence Tidyman with an address — Moncrieff thought — somewhere at the back of the town. Moncrieff had stayed with a woman called Roz McIntyre who had a ground-floor flat in Victoria Road.

'You'll be checking all this out?' Moncrieff appeared to be surprised.

'Of course. Strictly for the purposes of elimination.'

'Elimination?' The word brought a flicker of alarm. 'Then maybe I ought to explain.'

'Explain what, Mr Moncrieff?'

'About my father's friend.'

'Friend?' Golding was staring at him. 'You're telling me there was someone else in the house?'

'Yes.'

'Who?'

'A black guy. A stranger really. He just turned up at the beginning of this week. He said he knew my father.'

'And was that true?'

'It seems so. My father was happy to have him around. In fact they spent a lot of time together.'

Suttle and Golding exchanged glances. The phrase 'early arrest' would bring a very big smile to Mr Nandy's face.

26

It fell to Golding to voice the obvious question: 'Why didn't you tell us about this guy earlier?'

'You didn't ask.'

'But he was with your father last night?'

'He must have been.'

'And by the time you got back this morning he'd gone?'

'Yes.'

Another pause. Another exchange of glances. Amazing.

'So does this stranger have a name?' Suttle this time.

Moncrieff shook his head. 'I'm afraid not.'

'No name?'

'Not that he'd tell us.'

'No details? No clue where he'd come from?'

'Nothing.'

'Didn't you ask?'

'Of course we did.'

'And?'

'He'd just laugh. And then go back to sitting with my father. They got on well, really well. He made my father laugh. That wasn't easy.'

'You say he was a friend of your father? Had they met before?'

'I'm afraid I don't know.'

'But they might have done?'

'Yes.'

Suttle shook his head. Hopeless. Vagueness on legs.

Golding pressed him harder: 'Exactly when did this man turn up?'

'On Monday. In the afternoon.'

'Was he driving? Was he on foot?'

'I assume he was on foot. He never mentioned a car and we never saw one.'

'And he was with you all week?'

'Yes.'

'At whose invitation?'

'My father's. He made all the decisions. It was his house. No matter how sick he was.'

'You gave this man a bedroom?'

'Yes. We're spoiled for choice.'

'Did he go out at all?'

'No. He spent most of his time with my father.'

'You cooked for him? Fed him?'

'Yes. He took his meals on a tray. With my father.'

'And you say he was still there yesterday? When you left?'

'Yes. He said he'd keep an eye on my father until we got back.'

'Still no name?'

'No.'

'And when you finally got back? This morning? He'd definitely gone?'

'Yes.'

'You looked for him? You're sure?'

'Yes. I shouted. I called out.'

'But did you look? Did you do a physical search? It's a big house, Mr Moncrieff. We need to be sure.'

'Of course.'

'And?'

'He'd gone.'

Suttle was already on the phone to Carole

28

Houghton. She needed to rouse the photofit guy at Middlemoor.

He covered the phone while she made the call. 'You can describe this man? Picture what he looks like?'

'I think so.'

'Try.'

'Medium height. Thin. Skinny really. Very black — '

Suttle gestured for him to stop. Houghton was back on the phone. The photofit technician would be available within the hour. Maybe Suttle could run Moncrieff up to Middlemoor.

'Is this kosher?' she asked. 'You believe him?'

'I don't know, boss. That's a conversation we ought to be having later.'

Houghton ended the conversation without saying goodbye. Golding wanted to know more about the machete and the hood. Were these items that Moncrieff had seen before?

'Yes. They both belonged to my father.'

'He kept them on display? Somewhere obvious? Somewhere you could see them?'

'They were on his bedroom wall.'

'The hood as well?'

'Yes.' He swallowed hard, reached for the edge of the table. 'My father was crazy about Africa. It was the love of his life.'

'Does that explain the name of the house? Magharibi?'

He offered them a thin smile. 'In Swahili it means 'sunset'.'

★　★　★

Lizzie spent lunchtime at her mum's place in Anchorage Park, a boxy three-bedroomed house on a tiny patch of garden uncomfortably close to the roar of traffic down Portsmouth's Eastern Road. Lizzie had adopted the bigger of the two spare bedrooms as her own, grateful for regular meals and the occasional evening in front of the TV.

Her estrangement from Jimmy after the disastrous move to Chantry Cottage had been difficult for both women. Lizzie's mum had done her best to help repair the marriage and by the summer the relationship appeared to be on the mend. Jimmy would make the journey up from Devon whenever his weekend leaves permitted, and by August the three of them — Lizzie, Suttle and daughter Grace — were practically inseparable. Chantry Cottage was at last attracting interest, and after the place was sold they could all make a brand-new start. Then came the kite festival on Southsea Common, after which all bets were off.

Now Lizzie was pondering Simon Horobin's offer. In truth, returning the thirty-grand advance wouldn't be a huge problem. She'd deposited the money in her bank account, blown a couple of thousand on clothes, two interviews with a psychoanalyst, plus a course of rather disappointing reflexology sessions, but the rest remained intact, and the fact that she was working, pulling down a decent wage at the Pompey *News*, would quickly make up the difference.

But that wasn't the point. Her abject failure to

deliver had wounded her deeply. It spoke of a loss of nerve that she'd only ever associated with lesser mortals. Lizzie Hodson was better than that, as a number of journalistic scoops amply confirmed.

No, what really tempted her was something else, something that Horobin had detected, something that she'd maybe been hiding from herself. Since August, if nothing else, she'd become a world-class authority on grief. How it swamps you. How it numbs you. How it robs you of all the compass bearings, all the assumptions you'd once taken for granted.

Only recently she'd decided that grief had a form and a presence. In strip cartoons or fantasy movies it was an evil-coloured gunk that oozed from an alien spaceship and devoured everything in its path. In her many nightmares it was the lesbian PT teacher who'd always scared her shitless at school. To stand in front of this woman and try and find the words to explain yourself was to truly know how vulnerable and how helpless you could be. That was what grief did. It paralysed you. It rendered you speechless. It robbed you of every option except submission. Jimmy knew that. She'd seen it in his face the handful of times they'd met since. You became a stranger to everyone. Including yourself. Because you'd utterly failed in the one job that was of any real importance. And because after that nothing made much sense any more.

So maybe, just maybe, Horobin's offer might at last mark a bend in the road. In the school of second chances she might at last get the opportunity to turn rage and blind helplessness into something else.

Like what? She lay on the bed, staring up at the single crack in the ceiling, the duvet tucked up around her chin, knowing she had no idea. More and more, hiding away like this, she was letting life treat her like the child she'd lost. She closed her eyes, summoning for the millionth time her last glimpse of Grace at the kite festival, the shot that Jimmy had caught on his mobile, the one the police had used at the press conference and later distributed to the media. Sun-browned legs. Pink sandals. The flower-patterned dress Lizzie's mum had bought her only the previous week. And that sweet, sweet grin.

Don't worry, mum. I'll be back in a minute.

2

Hilary Moncrieff turned up at Heavitree in the early afternoon. She'd driven straight to Topsham from Exmouth after getting the call about her father and parked her car out in the road. The scene guard, a uniformed constable, had been deep in conversation with the Crime Scene Manager and so she'd stepped past him and entered the house. By now the pathologist had arrived and was in conference with the Crime Scene Investigator about the photos she needed of the body. They were talking in the bedroom when Hilary appeared at the open door. The sight of her father's face, according to the CSI, had sent her running to the nearby bathroom. Afterwards she'd asked to be left alone for a while. An hour or so later, it was boyfriend Lawrence who'd driven her to Heavitree.

Now she sat in the interview room recently vacated by her step-brother. She was a bulky woman, perhaps a stone overweight. Her greying hair was cut in a style Suttle always associated with a certain kind of magistrate — simple, almost severe — and her eyes were a pale blue behind the heavy-rimmed glasses. Her face was bare of make-up and she wore a single gold ring on the third finger of her left hand. Suttle judged her age to be early sixties. After the trauma of seeing her father's wrecked face, she appeared to have composed herself.

Nandy had been on the phone twice in the last half-hour. After a briefing from Luke Golding he wanted a great deal more on the mystery guest Hilary and Neil had left to look after their father. Golding was still over at the Major Incident Room, helping plot how best to pursue this investigative windfall.

Suttle slid into the chair opposite Hilary and offered her his warrant card. She scarcely noticed it. Instead she was staring at Suttle.

'I know you from somewhere,' she said.

'I don't think so.' Suttle shook his head.

'No, I do.' She was frowning now. 'It'll come back to me.'

Suttle wanted to know about the visitor who'd so suddenly stepped into their lives. 'Neil says he was black.'

'That's right.'

'Someone you'd never seen before.'

'That's also right.'

'So who saw him first?'

'Neil did. It was Monday evening. By the time I got back he was sitting in Pa's bedroom, chatting away nineteen to the dozen.'

'You got the impression they knew each other?'

'I got the impression they liked each other. It may not be the same thing.'

'But there has to be a link, surely?'

'You'd think so.'

'You don't know?'

'No.'

'You didn't ask?'

'Of course I did. Neil did too.'

'And?'

'Pa liked playing games. Liked keeping us guessing. That was his style in pretty much everything. A stranger walks in. No one has a clue who he is. He won't give us a name. Just says he knows Pa, or knows *about* Pa. That makes my father very happy. Especially because the guy's African. Africa is over there. Africa is something none of the rest of us knows anything about. Pa? He was in love with the place. Any friend of Africa was a friend of Pa's. *The big over there.* That was his phrase.'

'So no clues at all about this man?'

'Only one. He had good French. He spoke to Pa in French most of the time. His English was OK but his French was better.'

'You think he came from French-speaking Africa?'

'That would make sense.'

Suttle scribbled himself a note. Senegal? Mali? Somewhere else? His geography was letting him down. Then he thought of Didier Drogba and looked up again.

'Ivory Coast?'

'Could be.'

'But you can't be sure?'

'No.'

'You didn't see a passport? Didn't ask for one?'

'No to both. We don't work for the Border Agency.'

'You didn't take any photos? Him and your dad? One for the album?'

'Alas, no.'

Suttle nodded. He'd driven Neil Moncrieff across to Middlemoor and he'd already be starting work on a photofit, but there was no harm in a second opinion. 'OK. So describe this guy.'

Hilary paused, summoning an effort of memory. She thought late twenties, early thirties. Slight, on the thin side, but good-looking, animated, with a wonderful smile. Except for his eyes.

'He had the eyes of a reptile,' she said. 'A crocodile or a snake. Yellow eyes. Eyes that watched you all the time.'

'Neil said he stayed in the house.'

'Yes. He really made himself at home.'

'He had luggage?'

'A single bag. Brown leather. Tassels. Big shiny locks. Very African.'

'Flight tags?'

'None. I checked.'

'What was he wearing when he turned up?'

She frowned. Her recall was meticulous.

'Levi's,' she said. 'White T-shirt. Leather jacket. Nice scarf. The guy had taste. Except for the gold necklace — ' the smile was mirthless ' — and the fake Guccis.'

'Did you ask him *why* he'd come? Just arrived like that?'

'Of course.'

'And?'

'He wouldn't say. He'd turn every question

36

into a joke. Then he'd run back to Pa. Pa knew he was upsetting us. He loved that.'

'Upsetting you how?'

'He had us on the end of a string. That was very Pa. A couple of times I heard them laughing about it.'

'You speak French?'

'Yes.'

'And your father's French was good?'

'*Impec*. My father spoke a million languages. It was part of his charm. He could wind you up in French, Spanish, German, Italian, even Russian. Languages were made for Pa. He built a whole career on them.'

Suttle nodded. He wanted to get back to the mystery visitor who'd so suddenly descended on the house.

'Did you expect to find him there when you got back this morning?'

'That was the deal. He'd keep an eye on Pa so I could stay over at Lawrence's.'

'So what time did you leave the house last night?'

'Gone five. I drove. Neil left earlier on his bike.'

'Why the bike? Why didn't he travel with you?'

'I imagine because he wanted to keep his options open. He might decide to come back after the concert. He might not.'

'So why didn't he?'

'Because he had too much to drink. We went out for a meal afterwards and I bought a bottle of Italian red. Neil drank most of it. My fault, if you're asking. My little brother did me a big

37

favour with all his video stuff and that was my thank you.' She paused. 'He'd have told you all this, surely?'

Suttle ignored the question. He was still trying to imagine the scene back in the house, the ageing invalid and his surprise African visitor tucked up together.

'Your father was happy to be left with this man? You're sure about that?'

He broke off to answer his phone. Nandy again. Suttle got up with a murmured apology and left the interview room. Nandy wanted to know what progress he was making.

'None, sir. Except the guy spoke good French. We might start looking at West Africa.'

'We need a name, son.'

'We haven't got one.'

'That's nonsense. Everyone's got a name. Ask her again.'

'I did, sir. I have done. Three times. No name.'

'Press her harder.'

'Yes, sir. But she might decide to get herself lawyered up. Do we really need that?'

Nandy didn't answer. Suttle could hear voices in the background. One of them was Carole Houghton.

Then Nandy was back. 'Five o'clock, son. Team briefing. Major Incident Room. And you'd better bring something better than this horse shit.'

Suttle gazed at the phone a moment, then stepped back into the room, aware of Hilary watching him as he sat down again. He was trying to pick up the threads of their

38

conversation when she leaned forward.

'You were the guy who lost his child,' she said softly. 'Back in the summer. It was all over the news, the papers, everywhere.'

'Is that right?' Suttle held her gaze.

'Definitely.' She nodded. 'You've lost a bit of weight since then but I'd swear it was you.'

Suttle shrugged. He didn't know what to say. This had happened before, especially when the headlines were still fresh, but lately he'd managed to ghost himself into the shadows.

Hilary was still watching him, waiting for a reaction. Finally, she settled back in the chair. 'Your poor wife,' she said. 'What she must have gone through.'

★ ★ ★

Lizzie found the address among the notes she'd kept while she still had the energy to ask a question or two. Mr and Mrs H. T. Dillon lived in the eastern corner of the city where the trophy villas of Craneswater gave way to something a little more modest. She'd only seen them once, at the Coroner's inquest, and her attempts to engage them in the beginnings of a conversation had come to absolutely nothing. She remembered the father as a harassed fifty-something, flushed face, high blood pressure, best suit and tie, determined to extricate himself and his wife from the courtroom at the earliest possible opportunity. The last thing he wanted to do was discuss his lunatic daughter.

Number 35 Selsey Avenue was a three-storey

terraced property with bay windows and a tiny front garden. The curtains were already drawn in the room downstairs and Lizzie caught a shadow as someone got to their feet to check who'd pulled up outside. Instinctively, she ducked her head in the gloom of her ancient Peugeot, not at all sure what the next half-hour might bring. If she was to meet this challenge then she had to be certain that people would talk. And Claire's parents, given what their daughter had done, were a very good place to start.

She watched the shadow behind the curtain disappear again and gave herself a minute or two before reaching for her notebook and getting out of the car. Lizzie Hodson. You might remember the name. Grace's mum. Just popped round for a little chat.

She pushed through the gate, sensing already that this couple would be waiting for her. Maybe the clever thing would be to simply ignore her. Pretend they were out. Pretend that nothing had ever happened. Pretend that two lives hadn't been snuffed out barely four months ago.

The front door swung open at her second knock. It was the father. She recognised the slight stoop, the big face. He'd been drinking. She could smell it. Maybe whisky. For a moment he stared at her, swaying slightly as if the wind had got up. Then he took a step forward, his forefinger in her face.

'We knew it would be you. Knew it. Had to happen. Can't leave it alone, eh?'

Lizzie, startled, abandoned the little speech she'd prepared. Grace was dead, for Christ's

40

sake. Meet fire with fire.

'Excuse me. Is your wife in? Someone sane I can talk to?'

'Go away. We don't want you here. We don't need any of this. Go. Just bugger off.'

He forced the words out between gritted teeth, a man seconds away from losing it completely, then Lizzie became aware of another figure — his wife, Claire's mum — standing in the hall behind him. Lizzie took a step forward, wondering whether it might be possible to force her way in, but that would have made her as mad as their shipwrecked daughter, and in any case the figure at the door wasn't moving.

'Hop it.' He might have been talking to a dog. 'Just get in that little car of yours and *go*.'

Lizzie ignored him. Among the litter of pens in her bag she found one of the cards she used at work. She scribbled a number on the back, checking it in the spill of light from the open door.

'What's that? What do you think you're doing?'

The father made a lunge for the card and lost his balance, reaching out for the support of the door jamb. Lizzie seized her moment, stepping past him. His wife hadn't moved. She seemed neither surprised nor alarmed.

'I'm sorry,' she murmured. 'He shouldn't be like this.'

Lizzie said it didn't matter. The man was roaring now. Before he made it back down the hall, she had slipped the card to his wife. 'My home number's on the back,' she said. 'Can you phone me tonight?'

The woman stared at her a moment. Then came a tiny nod before Lizzie ducked a second lunge. Mad, she thought grimly, making for the open door and the safety of the darkness beyond. No wonder.

★　★　★

Suttle was a minute or two early for the team briefing at Middlemoor. *Amber*, according to his latest update on the phone from Luke Golding, had pulled together a squad of twenty-seven officers. A dozen of them were already gathered in the Major Incident Room, little knots of seasoned detectives anticipating a decent whack of overtime. Early December was near-perfect for a promising job like this. A couple of weeks sorting out multiple lines of enquiry, and Christmas would practically pay for itself.

Suttle found Luke Golding in an office down the corridor. The young D/C had his mobile to his ear, evidently waiting for someone to answer.

Suttle wanted to know about Nandy. Would he be chairing the squad meet? Or was that down to Carole Houghton?

'Nandy,' he said. 'At boiling point.'

'How come?'

'Border Agency.' Golding gestured at the phone. 'Apparently those guys don't get out of bed on Sundays. No wonder they keep losing all those asylos.'

Nandy, he said, had decided to run with Suttle's belief that the mystery guest may have come from one of the French-speaking African countries. In short order he'd dispatched the troops to scour airline bookings, track down six months' worth of CCTV at Heathrow and Gatwick and press the immigration honchos about whatever details they could pass on with regard to French-speaking black incomers. All this in a bid — maybe — to come up with a photo or a screen grab that might just trigger an ID from Moncrieff's kids and thus kick open an important investigative door. Suttle could see the point.

Golding thought it was pissing in the wind. Too much data. Not enough bodies. He gave up on the phone call, checked his watch and got to his feet.

'Good luck, skip,' he said. 'Nandy tells me you're on first. Nothing personal, but I think he's after blood.'

'Whose?'

'Yours.'

The threat went over Suttle's head. 'Skip' he liked. 'Skip' was what sergeants used to be called back in Pompey. The day Golding had driven over to Exmouth for a Sunday morning of recreational dog walking was the day Suttle became — in Luke's book — 'skip'.

The team meeting started minutes later. Suttle had never seen the room so full: civvy inputters perched on their desks, detectives up from Cornwall renewing old acquaintances, a pile of overnight bags stacked in a corner near the door. Topsham, he thought, was exactly the kind of moneyed community that would expect — and receive — Rolls-Royce policing. And here was the living proof.

Nandy offered a few gruff words of welcome and then, to Suttle's immense relief, turned to the Crime Scene Manager. *Amber*'s Senior Investigating Officer wanted to know what the crime scene had told him.

The CSM consulted his notepad. A flash search first thing, he said, had revealed no obvious signs of forced entry. Unusually for premises of this size there was no alarm system or cameras, but none of the windows had been forced and neither had the lock on the front door been tampered with. So the assumption had to be that *Amber* was dealing with someone who had a house key.

Golding's raised hand drew a nod from Nandy.

'There's access to the house through a door in the garage,' he said. 'I noticed a combination lock first thing this morning.'

'Thank you.' The CSM shot Golding a look. 'I was coming to that. The same applies. If you knew the combination there wouldn't be a problem.'

Nandy nodded. He wanted to know what else the flash search had revealed.

'This is a big property. We're talking six bedrooms including Moncrieff's, three bathrooms, huge kitchen, dining room, separate study, utility rooms, box rooms, all sorts.'

'The state of the place?'

'It needs a bit of TLC. This isn't a guy who spends money. We found correspondence with a

44

couple of estate agents on the desk in his bedroom. It may be that he was planning to sell up.'

This appeared to be news to Nandy. He glanced sideways at Carole Houghton, and then asked the CSM about Moncrieff himself. The pathologist had spent a couple of hours at the scene. Any early clues on time of death?

'She's talking roughly a three-hour window. Rigor hadn't set in. Anywhere between six and nine.'

'And nine's when the son turned up?'

'Yes, sir.'

For the benefit of the squad the CSM briefly described the state of the body and produced a sheaf of photos for circulation. Hands reached for the carnage that had once been Moncrieff's face. One of the inputters put her hand to her mouth and turned away.

The CSM hadn't finished.

'Something we need to be aware of is the presence of a hood over the guy's head when the body was found. Add the fact that he was hacked to death with a machete and we might be looking at some kind of tribal thing. It seems the guy had links to Africa. Some kind of blood debt? That might be worth exploring.'

Nandy nodded. He wanted to know about the rooms beyond Moncrieff's bedroom.

'It's early days, sir, but there are definitely traces of blood in the hall outside and on the stairs. My guess is it has to be blood from the victim, carried out of the bedroom. The splatter patterns were all over the bedding, the wall, the carpet — everywhere. There's no obvious indication that he fought back. We don't think his attacker would have been injured.'

'And upstairs?'

'Blood residues in a shower in the biggest of the bathrooms. We'll have the drain sump out by tomorrow, but I'm guessing the attacker had a wash. Very wise under the circumstances.'

More photos were circulating among the assembled squad. The machete. The hood. One of the D/Cs asked about the machete's handle.

'It's wooden, obviously. Crudely carved patterns. We're thinking it was some kind of souvenir.'

'I meant prints.'

'Nothing. It was either wiped clean or the guy was wearing gloves.'

Nandy wanted to move on. Computers?

'Three PCs, sir. We think one of them was the victim's. The others belonged to the daughter and the son. We seized the lot.'

'Laptops?'

'No. We took a couple of smartphones off the daughter and the son. It might be worth saying the son was really upset.'

'About the phone?'

'About his dad.' He frowned. 'I think.'

The note of caution drew a ripple of laughter from the room. These were men and women schooled in never taking anything at face value. Suttle found himself thinking about his own interview with Neil Moncrieff. The man had been anxious, certainly. But genuinely upset? He wasn't so sure.

The CSM was finishing. First thing tomorrow he'd be putting another CSI on the job. With luck, they'd have boshed everything worthwhile in the property by midweek. The Territorial Aid Group had already searched the garden, which was sizeable, but found nothing. Unless something unforeseen came up, the daughter and son could definitely have their house back by the weekend.

Nandy nodded. Carole Houghton had appointed a Family Liaison Officer called Wendy Atkins. It was her job to get alongside the daughter and son and shepherd them through the coming weeks. In her view, how were they coping?

'OK, sir. The way I read it, the one who's really suffering is the daughter. It might just be shock. That was a pretty horrible scene.'

'How about Neil?'

'He's hard to read, sir. Very withdrawn. I went up to Middlemoor when he was putting together the photofit but I couldn't really get through. He's very tense — you can feel it.'

'Is the photofit ready?' Nandy was looking at Carole.

'Yes, sir.'

'And has Hilary seen it? Like I asked?'

'Yes.'

'And?'

'She seems happy. We'll have copies ready for the press conference tomorrow. Scans are going out with the media release as we speak.'

Mention of a photofit had stirred audible interest among the watching faces. Nandy was

47

eyeing Suttle. Your turn, son.

Suttle played a weak hand as best he could. A black stranger had appeared from nowhere at the start of the week. No one — with the possible exception of the victim — knew where he came from or what his name was. He'd stayed all week in one of the spare bedrooms and spent a lot of his time at Moncrieff's bedside. They may have known each other before, or maybe not, but according to both Hilary and Neil they'd certainly got on. Big time.

The D/S in charge of the Outside Enquiry team raised a hand. 'Did this guy go out at all?'

'Apparently not.'

'So no one else saw him?'

'No.'

'No one visiting the house? Postman? DHL? No one like that?'

'No.'

'Neighbours?'

'No.'

'So we've got nothing on him? Nothing at *all*?'

'He speaks good French. Better than English. But that's as far as it goes.'

Carole was circulating with copies of the photofit. Then came a shake of a head, an exchange of glances, even a hint of laughter. Maybe Nandy had been right, Suttle thought. The guy doesn't exist. This was horse shit.

A copy of the photofit came his way. He studied the face for a long moment. Bony, trace of a goatee beard, high hairline, hooded eyes and a smile too big to be anything but fake. As a specimen of compositional guesswork, it was undoubtedly a masterpiece. Whether it had anything to do with real life was another question entirely.

It was Carole Houghton who voiced the obvious: 'How far should we take this, sir?'

'As far as we can. We can't afford to ignore it. Just now it's all we've got.'

'Apart from the son and daughter.'

'Indeed.'

Heads nodded round the room. Detectives had already checked the alibis for Hilary and Neil, and both were kosher. Hilary had spent the night tucked up with her cellist friend while Roz McIntyre had confirmed that Neil had kipped on her sofa. Barring an intervention from someone else with access to the house, that left the face in the photofit.

'We're already talking to the airlines and the immigration people,' Nandy said. 'Tomorrow I want house to house across the village. Every address, every door. There aren't a lot of our African brethren in Topsham. If the guy exists at all, he must have left at some point. In which case *someone* must have seen him.'

Carole Houghton wanted to know whether he'd turned up by car. Suttle said he thought not. He'd asked the question and both Hilary and Neil had said no.

'We're probably talking public transport then, or taxi. Unless he had a mate.'

Nandy nodded. He wanted the photofit distributed to the train and bus people and to all the local taxi firms. Topsham station was covered by CCTV, as were the bigger mainline stations in

Exeter. He wanted all footage seized and viewed. Ditto video from ANPR cameras within a twenty-five-mile radius. More priority actions for tomorrow.

He paused, struck by another thought, and turned to Suttle.

'You say our African friend had a bedroom of his own?'

'Yes, sir.'

'We know which one?'

'Yes. It's at the back of the house, upstairs, river views.'

'Great.' He was looking at the CSM now. 'Bosh it for fingerprints. Then look for a match in Moncrieff's bedroom. Eliminate the son's and the daughter's prints, and the chances are the guy might really exist. Yeah?'

The CSM nodded and wrote himself a note.

Nandy was already back with Suttle. 'What else have you got for us?'

'I talked to the woman, Hilary, at length, sir. My impression is they didn't get on.'

'Who didn't?'

'She and her dad. Neil was the same. He didn't like him at all.'

'Any particular reason?'

'According to Hilary, the man was difficult. Demanding. She said he was a control freak, always had been.'

'We're talking more than one marriage?'

'Two. Hilary came along when he was still at Oxford. The mother was a fellow student. She divorced him several years later. By that time he was back from National Service.'

50

'Where?' Nandy's interest had quickened.

'Back in England, obviously.'

'I meant where did he do his National Service?'

'I didn't ask, sir. I'm sorry.'

'Find out, will you?'

Suttle nodded.

Nandy wanted to know more about the way the house by the river worked. Or didn't.

'Didn't is closer, sir. This was a guy who was seriously rich and made sure they knew it, but he kept them on short rations. He paid Hilary an allowance for the housekeeping and bunged her a couple of extra quid when times got rough. She says it was the same with Neil. Board and lodging were free, but beyond that it was up to them.'

'Don't these people have jobs?'

'No. Hilary has recently come out of a marriage. She's a qualified accountant. Her husband was an entrepreneur. She helped him run an antiques business, which did well, but then he sold up and ploughed everything into a fancy restaurant. She told him from the start it was a crazy thing to do — horrible timing, rubbish location, big issues over the menu and the chef — but it seems he wasn't the kind of bloke to listen. In the end he declared himself bankrupt and went off with a waitress who was half his age, so Hilary was left with nothing. I'm not sure she was fussed about losing her husband, but her only option was to move in with Dad. Bit of a nightmare, the way she tells it.'

'When did all this happen?'

51

'About a year ago. By that time Moncrieff wasn't in the best of health. So it fell to her to keep an eye on him.'

'That was her idea?'

'His.'

'Does she have kids of her own?'

'One. His name's Kennan. He's twenty-three.'

'Local?'

'He's living in Spain. She says he fled there after uni. Couldn't face coming home with Mum and Dad at each other's throats. He's still out there trying to make it as a musician.'

Nandy nodded, then told the Outside Enquiries D/S to TIE Hilary's husband. TIE stood for trace, interview, eliminate. Maybe the guy held a grudge against the family. Maybe he'd appealed for funds to fend off bankruptcy and been refused. Maybe he knew the combination on the door from the garage. Definitely worth further investigation.

Nandy turned back to Suttle. He wanted to know more about Neil Moncrieff. Where did he belong in the family pecking order?

'He comes from Moncrieff's second marriage, sir. The old man found himself a German mistress and never took the trouble to keep it a secret, which is why Hilary's mum divorced him. That makes Neil Hilary's half-brother. I get the feeling she's always mothered him. She says he's very vulnerable, really shy. He bailed out of a degree course years ago and has been a bit of a basket case ever since.'

'So where's his real mother?'

'She died when he was fifteen.'

52

'So he's been living with his dad these last few years?'

'Yes, but hiding away. Since Hilary moved in she's been trying to chivvy him along. Apparently he has two passions: video and cycling.' He flipped a page on his notes. 'He's mad about birds too. That's where the video comes in.'

The mention of video sparked fresh interest. Nandy wanted to know more.

Suttle recounted what little he knew: that Neil had acquired a couple of cameras and some editing software, and that he was currently involved in some kind of birding project, taking advantage of his own perch on the riverside.

Nandy nodded, his attention on other areas. He'd already told Houghton to get production orders on mobile and landline billing for Moncrieff and his two children, plus every relevant bank account. He had a couple of D/Cs trawling Facebook, Twitter and a handful of other social media sites for further lines of enquiry. But it was the news that Hilary was a qualified accountant that had really nailed his attention. The victim had been loaded. His kids hadn't much liked him. Hilary would know exactly what he'd been worth. Rich pickings, if you were looking for a motive.

He summed up the shape of *Amber's* next twenty-four hours, underlined the importance of scaring up possible leads with the photofit, then turned back to Suttle. The majority of killings came from within a family or a relationship, he repeated. They spoke of disappointment, impatience, anger and then rage. By Suttle's account the little household by the river appeared to have been richly dysfunctional. Time to apply a little extra pressure.

'So where's the son now? Neil? Remind me.'

'Exmouth, sir. Staying with his blind girl-friend.'

'And Hilary? She's with the cellist bloke?'

'Yes.'

'Talk to them again. Find out more about Rupert Moncrieff. We need to follow the money.' For the first time a ghost of a smile. 'Never bloody fails.'

★ ★ ★

Lizzie was asleep in front of the TV when her mother woke her up to take the call. She'd been dreaming about Chantry Cottage. For once the sun had been shining. The back door to the garden was open, there was a risotto on the stove, and she could hear Jimmy chasing Grace through the buttercups in the lushness of the uncut grass. Laughter, she thought, and the promise of a decent bottle of red once Grace had gone to sleep.

'It's for you.' Her mother was offering the cordless. 'A Mrs Dillon.'

Lizzie rubbed the sleep from her eyes as the dream began to fade and took the phone.

It was Claire's mother. Her voice was no more than a whisper.

'Howard's gone to bed,' she said. 'I hope it's not too late.'

Lizzie struggled upright on the sofa. Her mum

had been watching the mid-evening news. Bitter fighting in South Sudan. Apprehension, pre-Xmas, about sales on the high street.

Mrs Dillon was apologising for her husband. He was under a lot of stress. Since the summer they'd been fighting ghosts. Under the circumstances she felt they owed Lizzie some kind of explanation. There was no way Howard would agree but she was happy to meet somewhere quiet for a private chat. Might that help?

'It would.' Lizzie was reaching for a pen. 'Would tomorrow be OK? Do you mind if I call you?'

'Not at all. Howard's out all day so you can phone any time. My name's Jo, by the way.'

'Thanks.' Lizzie wrote down the mobile number. 'I'll be in touch.'

The phone went dead and Lizzie stared at it a moment, wondering whether this was the moment to put a call through to Jimmy. Buttercups, she thought. And laughter.

★ ★ ★

It was Golding who dragged Suttle to the pub. Since the summer Luke had been sharing a boxy newbuild on a featureless development on the outskirts of Exeter with a leggy Irish redhead he'd met in a club on one of his wilder excursions. He claimed she'd drunk him off the dance floor, scooped him up, emptied him into a cab and spent the next day tending his bursting head in the comfort of a basement flat she occupied round the corner from the big hospital at Wonford.

It had taken him several weeks to work out what turned him on about her, but once she confessed to being a nurse in A & E he knew that all his fantasies had come true. She had a body to die for and a huge appetite for recreational sex. She had no objections to doing the ironing and her interest in the small print of his working day seemed totally unfeigned. She also had a passion for Italian food and turned out a succession of inventive pasta dishes without ever consulting a recipe. In every corner of her busy life she had a rare ability to busk her way to a result. She also made him laugh.

She was waiting for them in the pub. Suttle had met her a number of times before. She reminded him of a good friend called Eamonn Lenahan who'd been a locum registrar in A & E and whom — as it turned out — she'd known by reputation. The two of them, Suttle had decided, might have been brother and sister. The same irrepressible optimism. The same acknowledgement that most of the world was on the road to perdition. The same glad acceptance that there was fuck all anyone could do about it. Lenahan had died the previous year after a fall at Chantry Cottage. Suttle missed him badly.

'Another Guinness?' Suttle nodded at her empty glass. Guinness was code for a large red wine, preferably Pinot Noir. Oona drank nothing else.

Suttle settled on a bar stool and waited for service. He liked being with this couple. They had an easiness he could dimly remember in his own marriage, an unspoken delight in each other's presence. Lately he'd taken to warning Golding off the odd solo excursion to city-centre clubs to see what might be about. If he was still up for the odd one-nighter, he told him, then he should think very hard about what he might lose. Men were drawn to this woman by the raw scent of someone very rare. Enjoy. And appreciate.

Oona was asking about the Topsham job. She'd caught a mention of the killing on the radio on the drive down to the pub. Sunday was no time to meet your maker.

'Why not?'

'He's busy, you eejit.' She gestured upwards. 'Yer poor slaughtered man's up there waiting for the place to open. Won't get booked in until tomorrow.'

Golding rolled his eyes. He was still tallying the finer details of the crime scene when the barman arrived. The lad did his best to ignore the more graphic bits of Golding's description but Oona seemed untroubled. She must see stuff like this every working day, Suttle thought. Maybe the Pinot Noir helped.

She wanted to know where the investigation was heading next. Was this the usual family fuck-up or something more exotic? Her eyes were on Suttle, the deepest green.

'Good question.' He pushed one of the Stellas in Golding's direction. 'What do you think, son?'

'I think he had it coming.'

'That's judgemental.' Oona looked reproving. 'Does this guy have a wife?'

'Two. Both dead.'

'Machete jobs? Both down to the husband?' She put her hand on Suttle's thigh. 'Is this an outbreak of conscience, my sweet boy? Might we be thinking suicide?'

Suttle choked on his lager. Mad idea. Wiping his chin, he realised it was the first time he'd laughed all day. Oona hadn't finished.

'That one's for free. Simple but elegant. The guy topped himself. Tell your boss I'm available if he needs more details. This is a harsh old world but who needs fucking detectives?'

★   ★   ★

Afterwards, famished, they drove into the city for a curry. Golding had lifelong rights on a prime corner table in a restaurant in Heavitree, the fraying sleeve on the woolly cardigan that was Exeter. A couple of months ago, with Oona looking on, he'd seen off a trio of drunks threatening to demolish the place after a quarrel over the bill. He'd shepherded them into the street, warned them they were on a nicking for ingratitude and bad language, and returned to several rounds of Baileys on the house.

Tonight Oona did the ordering. Poppadoms and onion chutney for starters. Chicken bhuna. Lamb dansak. A medley of veggie sides. She knew it by heart.

Over pints of Cobra and yet more Pinot Noir the talk strayed to the next holiday. Oona fancied Rome; Golding said the Pope wouldn't be interested. He was up for Acapulco. She hated all that burrito muck. Then, aware that Suttle appeared to have no destination in mind, Oona changed the subject.

Her hand slipped over Suttle's. She gave it a squeeze. 'We've been having a little talk about your lovely self.' She nodded at Golding. 'Yer man and me.'

'And?'

'We think it's time for a woman in your life.'

'I've got one.'

'You haven't. You never see her. You never even *talk* about her, not the way I'm hearing it. That's unnecessary. Life is life, my sweet boy. Expect nothing but grief. In the meantime, take a risk or two.'

'Risk?' Suttle was lost.

'We have an idea. Golden bollocks here calls it a plan. To be frank, I think that's a bit grand.'

'Golden bollocks' was new. Golding was looking into his Cobra.

Oona hadn't finished. 'There's a lady we think you ought to meet.'

'Forget it.'

'That's less than grateful, Mr Suttle. You need to do better. *Carpe diem*. Seize the fucking day.'

'My days are busy. You might have noticed.' Suttle was aware of how defensive he was sounding, and how ungrateful. 'Listen. Maybe — '

'We mean it. And we have someone in mind.'

'Who?'

'No clues. Rules of the house. Just say yes.'

'I can't.'

'Nod then. Give me a smile. *Any* fucking thing. You'll make my lover's day.'

Suttle stared at her for a moment. The curry had arrived but he ignored it. Job-wise Luke Golding had a reputation for seizing the initiative but he'd yet to take charge of Suttle's private life.

'I'll give it some thought,' he said stonily. 'I'll let you know.'

'Please do, my sweet one.' Her hand was on his thigh again. 'It's my birthday tomorrow. GB has fixed up a little treat. It involves tickets. He's bought three.' She kissed him on the lips. 'And you know what, my lovely? The third one's for you.'

'GB?'

'Golden bollocks.'

3

MONDAY, 9 DECEMBER 2013

Lizzie was at work at half seven. The Portsmouth *News* operated from premises in the north of the city and she was at her desk in the near-empty newsroom in time to call the editor before he convened the morning prospects meet.

'Have you got ten minutes?' she asked. 'Like now?'

'Is this important?'

'For me it is . . . yes.'

Lizzie made her way to his office. Mark Boulton was in his mid-thirties, a front-line reporter who'd elbowed his way to the editor's chair with alarming ease. Thanks to a brutal year-long fitness regime he seemed to have weathered the tensions of the job with some success, but lately his ever-shrinking platoon of journalists had noticed signs of strain. In common with the rest of the regional press, *News* sales figures were heading south. When you started bigging up the digital edition, free to anyone with a tablet, you knew you were in trouble.

The office door was open. Boulton was on the phone. He waved her into one of the seats across the desk while he finished his conversation.

'Dickheads,' he muttered, putting down the phone. 'What have you got for me?'

'Nothing. I'm afraid it's personal.'

'Should I be worried?'

'I'm not sure.'

She quickly outlined the offer she'd got from Simon Horobin after hitting the rocks with the first commission. She'd thought about it overnight and she was due to test the waters in the shape of a meet with Claire Dillon's mother later in the day. The delivery deadline was really tight, but given the right kind of access and a clear run she thought it might be possible.

'You've given up with the Devon book?'

'Yes.'

'So what makes you think you'll finish this one?'

'Because it matters more.'

Boulton nodded. The events of the summer had been huge for the paper, not least because the missing child's mum was the lead feature writer on the News. Having the inside track on a big national story had done Boulton's career no harm at all and he'd predictably milked it for all it was worth. But he'd been caring too, protecting Lizzie from the worst of the London tabloid boys, and she'd been deeply appreciative.

'You're sure you want to do it?' Boulton was watching her carefully.

'Yes.'

'No qualms? No cans? No worms?'

'Lots of cans. Lots of worms. That's the whole point. I want to find out exactly how this thing could ever have happened.'

'Why?'

'Because I want to know who killed my daughter.'

Boulton raised an eyebrow. Then he offered a tiny nod of applause. 'Neatly put.'

'I mean it.'

'I'm sure you do. So how are you going to make this thing fly?'

It was a good question, shrewd, typically blunt. Lizzie began to talk about the sheer number of individuals Grace's story would have touched — cops in the first place, media people, social workers — anyone, in short, who'd come into contact with Claire Dillon.

For once Boulton appeared to be giving Lizzie his undivided attention.

'Are you angry? Is that where this comes from?'

'I was, but I'm not sure that's the right word any more.'

'You feel let down?'

'Yes. That's much closer.'

'You want to give the system a kicking? Find out where it failed?'

'Yes.'

'So it never happens again?'

'That's a big ask.'

'Sure. But who cares? Something like this kicks off and you need to do something about it. A good wallow would be the easy way. But that's not we're talking here . . . am I right?'

'Christ, no. I couldn't think of anything worse.'

Boulton nodded, his eyes straying to an

63

incoming email on his PC. Lizzie was impressed. In less than a minute this man seemed to have caught the essence of what she'd be trying to do. Not a weepie. Not a hatchet job. Not an act of revenge. Just an honest attempt to tease a little sense — and maybe a few lessons — from the traumas of the last five months.

'Call it a detective story,' she said. 'That comes pretty close.'

'Sure. So what do you want from me?'

'Four months' leave.'

'Unpaid, right?'

'Of course. And a job to come back to. Might that be possible?'

'Anything's possible, you know that.' He was frowning now, trying to frame some kind of response, and for a moment Lizzie thought she'd blown it. Too hurried. Too pushy. Too me-me. She was wrong. 'In principle there isn't a problem,' he said. 'In fact I think it's a brilliant thing to do. We'd need serialisation rights, first bite at the apple, plus a big piece from you on the eve of publication. Do I hear a yes?'

'I'll have to talk to my agent.'

'Do that.' The frown again. 'And you're telling me the other book's really history?'

'Yes. My fault. I couldn't hack it.'

'That's very honest.'

'Yeah . . . and it's true too.'

She grinned at this little moment of self-revelation, then got to her feet. She needed to be out of the office before Boulton changed his mind. She was at the door before he called her back.

'I liked the line about the detective story,' he said. 'Just for the record.'

★   ★   ★

Suttle left the flat in bright sunshine and walked to his first interview. He'd conferenced with Carole Houghton on the phone first thing and she'd agreed there was no point him driving into Exeter only to turn round again. Neil Moncrieff was still with his new friend in Exmouth, and *Amber* needed to know a great deal more about life beside the river.

Victoria Road lay within earshot of the beach. Gulls wheeled overhead, and Suttle could hear the rasp of a high tide on the launching slip at the end of the road.

It was a woman who came to the door. She was middle-aged and attractive with a mass of black curls threaded with grey and a wide dimpled smile only partly masked by a pair of dark glasses. She was wearing a pair of tracksuit bottoms and a red and white Exeter City shirt. A yellow Labrador appeared between her legs, nose tilted up towards Suttle, but disappeared inside again at a whispered word of command. Suttle was about to offer his warrant card but realised there was probably no point. This woman was indeed blind.

You must be the policeman.' She held the door wide open. 'Neil said you'd be along.'

'Is he here?'

'No. He's gone to the shop for milk. Back soon.'

'But you're Roz McIntyre?'

'I am.'

She turned back into the house and led the way into the ground-floor flat. The narrow hall was occupied by a new-looking tandem, but she slipped past with a confidence that took Suttle by surprise, her outstretched fingers mapping the contours of the bike. A rubber duck's head, yellow with big black cartoon eyes, was fixed to the front handlebars, and she gave it a playful squeeze — *parp-parp* — as she went by.

'That was Neil's idea. He put it on.'

Suttle paused and did the same. The second *parp-parp* drew a chuckle from Roz.

'I'd offer you coffee but it would have to be black. Shall we wait for Neil?'

The living room was the victim of a landlord looking for maximum income from the property. The tiny space was dominated by a sofa, an audio stack on a low table and a collapsible chair that looked like it might have come off the beach. Roz's taste in music stretched from the Rolling Stones through Paul Simon to Mozart and Verdi. The rugs on the polished floorboards looked Turkish or maybe Afghan, and, absorbing the lived-in spareness of the room, Suttle thought at once of Eamonn Lenahan. No TV. Big black and white landscapes on the wall. Warmth from the hiss of a gas fire. Seagulls on the soundtrack outside. Perfect.

The Labrador was curled on a blanket in the corner. It seemed to be asleep already.

'What's his name?'

'She. I call her Beanbag.'

'Why?'

'Because I can lie all over her and she doesn't throw a wobbly.'

She ducked her head, and then looked up again.

'I'm blind,' she said. 'It's quite a recent thing but Beanbag has been my salvation. She and the tandem in the hall.'

Cycling, she said, had always been a passion of hers, but once her sight had gone there was no way she could pedal solo. Tandems were really expensive, but the local paper had done a little feature, and the Rotary club had kicked off an appeal with a hefty contribution. The new bike had cost a fortune, but what she'd also needed was someone on the front.

'That's how I met Neil.' She was smiling. 'There was a follow-up piece in the paper and he was nice enough to volunteer.'

'When was this?'

'During the summer. He'd come down a couple of times during the week and we'd go out for a spin. He's a lovely man, very gentle. He's like Beanbag. He takes care of me.'

'And you still cycle together?'

'Yes.'

Suttle had turned his attention to one of the nicely framed black and white photos on the back wall, a shot of the wideness of the river falling away to the distant smudge of Exmouth. There were birds everywhere: waders pecking at the mudflats, a raft of what looked like Canada geese bobbing in the tideway, the lone silhouette of a sentry heron, sharp-edged against the light, waiting patiently to stab a passing meal. Then he realised he'd seen this same view before. Only yesterday.

'These photos,' he said. 'Where did they come from?'

'Neil gave them to me for my birthday.' She sounded like a child. 'I'd love to be able to see them but listening to Neil is just as good.'

'He describes them?'

'Yes. And every time is different. Different birds. Different weather. Different things happening. He's very inventive, Neil. You've no idea how much that helps.'

Suttle said nothing. Then he asked whether he did the same thing when they went cycling on the tandem, describing what he could see, what she was missing.

'Of course. That's the whole point.'

'And do you believe him?'

'It doesn't matter whether I believe him. If it's enough to fill my mind with pictures, that's all I ask for. That and the smells and the sounds, especially along the seafront. Believe it or not, I can tell you the state of the tide just by listening. When I first went blind I thought it was the end of the world, but you adapt. It's amazing. It's better than amazing. Some days it can be rather magical.'

She wanted to know the reason for this second visit. Two other men had come round yesterday, asking her about Saturday night. She thought she'd told them everything they needed to know.

'You did. I'm really after Neil.'

'I see.' At last she felt her way past the sofa

and settled in the beach chair. Then she gestured around. 'It's nice to have him here. I can't believe what happened to his father. He's really upset, poor lamb. You can sense it.'

Suttle was eyeing the door that led back to the tiny hall. He needed to get a fix on how it might have been on Saturday night.

'How many bedrooms do you have?'

'Just the one. Mine.'

'So Neil slept here, on the sofa, while you were next door?'

'That's right. I found a bottle of wine for us before he settled down. It was nice to relax him.'

'Does he often stay the night?'

'Never.'

'So this was the first time?'

'Yes.'

'And you say he was tense?'

'He's always tense. I tell him he tries too hard. He needs to please. All the time.'

'Is that such a bad thing?'

'Of course not. I love it. But he should think of himself too. Maybe tense is the wrong word. Nervous. How does that sound?'

Suttle didn't answer. He wanted to know about Neil's bike. The tandem filled the hall. Where had he left his bike on Saturday night?

'In the back garden. I can lock the gate.'

'Did you hear him leave on Sunday morning?'

'No.' She shook her head. 'I'm afraid the wine got the better of me. By the time I got up he'd gone.'

'When was that?'

'About ten. I told the two men yesterday. I was

surprised because we always go to church on Sundays. Neil normally comes to pick me up.'

'So why didn't he stay?'

'I don't know. Maybe he was worried about his father.'

'Did he worry a lot about his father?'

'Yes. I think he did.'

'You'd know, surely.'

'Then yes.' She nodded this time. 'He did.'

'Why?'

'That's something you should ask him.'

Suttle looked at her for a moment, saying nothing. She seemed unflustered.

'Who lives upstairs?'

'A couple of young girls. They're a bit noisy but it's nice to know someone's around if you need them.'

'And they were here on Saturday night?'

'Not until very late. Neil had gone to bed. Me too. I didn't even hear them come in.'

'And Sunday morning?'

'Nothing. They always sleep late on Sundays. By that time Neil had phoned. He was in a bit of a state, as you might imagine.'

'What did he say?'

'He told me what had happened to his father. He said he wouldn't be able to stay in the house for a bit. That's when I said he should come back here.'

'Anything else?'

'Yes. He said his laptop had gone.'

'Gone?'

'Yes. I think he meant stolen.' She looked up at Suttle and took off her glasses. Her eyes were a milky shade of blue. 'Have you found out who did it yet? That terrible thing?'

* * *

Neil Moncrieff returned several minutes later. Roz made coffee and then departed with the dog for a walk on the seafront. She seemed to have a natural sense of tact, for which Suttle was grateful.

Neil sat on the sofa, his hands carefully crossed in his lap, his body erect, his eyes narrowed against the blaze of low sunlight through the front window. He might have been a candidate for an interview. Which in a way he was.

'Roz tells me you've lost your laptop.'

'That's true. It's gone. I thought I'd mentioned it.'

'We can't find any trace in the scene logs.' Suttle nodded at his mobile. 'I just checked.'

'Oh dear . . . ' There was something close to panic in Neil's eyes. 'That must be my fault.'

'Did you tell any of our guys?'

'Obviously not.'

'When did you last see it?'

'Saturday afternoon. I keep it on the desk in my bedroom. I didn't realise it had gone until I got home on Sunday morning.'

Suttle nodded. 'You told me you went to your bedroom first. Before you checked on your father.'

'Yes.'

'And that was when you realised the laptop had gone?'

71

'Yes. It was brand new. HP ZBook. I'd only had it a month or two.'

'So where do you think it went?'

'I've no idea.'

'But you're still telling me that your father's visitor had also gone?'

'Yes.'

'So it must have been him, mustn't it? Had the thing away?'

Neil shrugged. It sounded logical but he had no proof. All he knew was that his precious laptop had disappeared.

'What did you use it for? What was on there?'

'Mainly video rushes. That's why I went for the spec. You need loads of RAM. The ZBook gives you plenty.'

'You've got editing software?'

'Yes.'

'So you've lost that too?'

'No. I've still got the software disks but all the rushes have gone. Plus the masters of the material I cut. All I've got left is the stuff I shot at Hils' concert. But without the laptop I can't do anything.'

Suttle made a note. Then he looked up. 'Roz tells me you take her to church every Sunday.'

'That's true. I do.'

'In the morning?'

'Yes. She worships at Holy Trinity.'

Suttle nodded. Holy Trinity lay behind his flat on the Beacon, a big handsome Victorian church visible from miles around.

'So you cycle down to Exmouth every Sunday morning to take her to church? Is that right?'

72

'Yes.'

'But last Sunday you were already at her house.' He frowned. 'So why go home?'

'Because I was worried about my father.'

'Worried how?'

'Worried because both Hils and I had left him.'

'But he had his friend with him. His African friend.'

'Of course. But we still didn't know who this man was.' He plucked at his jeans. 'The truth is I should have gone back the previous night, after the restaurant. That's what I should have done.'

'Why?'

'Because . . . ' his eyes closed ' . . . none of this might ever have happened.'

Suttle made a note. The silence stretched and stretched. Finally Suttle leaned forward. 'You told me yesterday you had a shower as soon as you got back on Sunday morning.'

'That's right.'

'Which bathroom did you use?'

'The closest one. The one next door to my bedroom. My father kept the big bathroom for himself. He didn't like anyone else using it, even after he'd given up with the stairs.'

'I don't understand.'

'After the stroke Hilary had a bathroom put in on the ground floor. She offered to install one of those stairlifts but he wouldn't hear of it. So he used the new bathroom but still insisted no one touched the other one upstairs. I didn't really care and neither did Hils. Hot water is hot water. Though he even rationed that.'

The boiler, Neil said, had never really been big enough for what the house needed. Hils always wanted to leave the immersion heater on full blast but that was something else his father forbade.

'So you took your shower on Sunday morning in the small bathroom? Are you sure I've got that right?'

'Yes.'

Suttle made himself a note. The CSI had found traces of blood in the big upstairs bathroom, which evidently belonged to Moncrieff. Not the one that Neil had used.

'You used the word *forbade* just now, Neil.'

'Yes.'

'That's strong, very strong. Are you sure it's appropriate?'

'Utterly.' He stared at Suttle, seeming to wrestle with some inner decision. Then he abruptly leaned forward, his elbows on his knees. 'My father was a monster. You had to live with him to appreciate that, but it's true. He was a monster and a bully, and before you try and trap me with one of those clever questions, I hated him. God knows what happened in that house when we were away, but you know something? I'm glad. I'm really glad. Why? Because that man deserved it.'

There was colour in his face at last. He tilted his head back and stared up at the ceiling. Suttle could feel the force of his anger. He's been wanting to get this off his chest for years, he thought. Maybe all his life. Only now, in a very different setting, did he appear to feel at home.

Thank God, he seemed to be saying, for this new woman in his life. Roz had been right to detect rough water between father and son. Only the blind see.

'Tell me more, Neil,' Suttle said softly.

'About what?'

'About your father. I understand he did National Service.'

'That's right. He did.'

'Where?'

'In Kenya.'

'Tell me what you know about that.'

Neil nodded, nearly in control again, fighting to compose his thoughts.

'The way I understand it, he was at Oxford,' he said at last. 'He read modern languages. Hils has the best expression. She says he had the gift of tongues. He was quick, a jackdaw really, always robbing other people's nests. When it came to real life it could be anything — a woman, someone else's wife, someone else's business idea — it didn't matter, anything to help him on his way. Languages were just an extension of that. He'd settle briefly in a country, help himself to the language, use it for his own ends, impress people with his fluency, then move on. My father had no ties, no loyalties and no conscience. He did what suited him. And fuck everyone else.'

His voice had risen again, and Suttle caught the first faint hint of hysteria. The way his fingers kept mapping the scars on his ruined face. The way he rocked his thin body back and forth. This man, he thought, was on the edge.

'And Kenya?' Suttle laid aside his notepad. 'Where did that fit in all this?'

'He was out there in the 50s. There was an insurgency going on, a kind of rebellion against the British. The rebels were called the Mau Mau. They were Kikuyu. It was all a big tribal thing. Very ugly.' He bit his lip, turned his head away, tried to get the sunshine out of his eyes. 'You should talk to Hils about this. She knows more than I do.'

'I'm talking to you, Neil.'

'Right. You're right. All I'm saying is my father was very good at languages, and the army took advantage of that and put him through some kind of course and sent him out to Kenya.'

'Speaking Kikuyu? Swahili? Whatever it is?'

'I assume so. That's the kind of man he was. And in a way he never came back. Not literally. I think he did a couple of years out there. That was his National Service. Hils says he got close to the Pathé people, acted as an interpreter, helped them shoot their newsreels. Then his National Service was over and he was back in the UK and he had to find a job.'

'So what did he do? After the army?'

'Hils says he worked with Pathé first. Then he moved on. My father was exceptionally intelligent but he was more than just brainy. I've always seen him as an animal. He could smell the future coming down the tracks — newsreels, television, *pictures* — and he wanted to be part of it. In the end he chose advertising. Which I suppose is where the money came from. In a way he was a visionary. Hils says he never got a single decision wrong — not in his own terms, not in business, not in his private life. This is a man, like I say, who just helped himself. Which is what makes it so unforgivable.'

'Says who?'

'Me. Hils. Anyone he was supposed to love. Hopeless. And cruel. And selfish. And now this . . . ' He turned away again. There were tears in his eyes.

'How long have you lived with him?'

'Seventeen years.'

'Why didn't you live somewhere else?'

'I should have done. I tried to. But it was beyond me.'

He was staring at the window, his face a mask. For a long moment there was silence. Then he explained how he'd won himself a place at Bristol University to read modern history. He'd struggled the first year, he said, living in a student residence block on campus, but the second year was worse. He had no friends. He was hopeless with women. He was far too shy to join the merry-go-round of parties on Saturday nights and so he'd stayed in his basement bedsit in one of the scruffier parts of Clifton, keeping his head down, reading book after book until one academic assignment blurred meaninglessly into another and nothing made much sense any more. In the end one of the library assistants in the history faculty, scenting trouble, had suggested a visit to a service run for the benefit of students who — for whatever reason — had ceased to cope.

'I was a basket case,' he said. 'I could have got

a first-class degree in maladjustment. They put me on a course of counselling, one to one, and I'd spend hours with this woman trying to find a fancy name for whatever I was suffering from. Alienation? Bipolar disorder? Anomie? It was all nonsense. The truth was I was lonely. And a bit lost.'

And so he went home. No money. No degree. No prospects. Just the house by the river with its silence and its freezing rooms, and the looming presence of a man he'd learned to fear.

'*Fear?* You mean that?'

'You're not looking at someone brave. I'm a coward at heart. I'm weak and feeble and easily frightened. I'm also very easily upset. Which was my father's speciality.'

Back in the house by the river, dimly remembering a suggestion from his counsellor at university, he decided to write a big historical novel. His father was keeping him on short rations — school food, the occasional beer, a trickle of pocket money as long as he sorted out the laundry and did the shopping — but by now he was realistic enough to know that this was probably all he could expect from life in any kind of material sense. And so he spent several months casting round for a suitable theme.

'What did you chose?'

'I settled on the Exe, on the river. It ran past my bedroom window. That river was my salvation. It kept me sane.'

He plotted out a story called *Downstream*. He wanted to create a big tapestry of a book, a novel

78

that would flow — like the river — through the ages. Families interlinked by the developing plot. Pockets of drama on the high moorland where the river rose. Quarrels over trade and inheritance. Rumours of inbreeding in the more isolated communities. The arrival of the Exeter Ship Canal and the wealthy merchants who had transformed Topsham. And glimpses of a thousand other characters, who'd slip in and out of the narrative.

'You started this epic?'

'I wrote three chapters.'

'Were you pleased with them?'

'I was. Very. Pathetic, isn't it?'

'Why?'

'Because I gave them to my father. I suppose I wanted to show him what I could really do, what I could really achieve, just left to myself.'

'And?'

'He lit the fire with them. I found them in the grate in the little living room he used. Hils called it the snug. That did it for me. Something died.'

'Did he ever mention the book at all?'

'Never. Not once. It was as if I'd never dreamed the thing up, never started it. If you want the truth I think he thought it was a pointless thing to do. He was probably ashamed of me. He used to call me his spotty little girl. Either that or it was just the usual.'

'The usual?'

'He wanted to hurt me. Probably needed to hurt me. Because that was the kind of animal he was.'

He was still staring out of the window. The

sunshine, now filtered by the curtain, no longer troubled him.

'So did you carry on writing?'

'No. That's when I started getting interested in the clocks. My father had this collection. Some of them are really valuable. You need to look after them. After a while I started to understand how they worked and what you needed to do to make sure they kept good time. I suppose I was trying to make myself useful. Maybe I was trying to please him.'

'And did it work?'

'No.' He shook his head. 'Nothing worked. He was an impossible man to reach.'

Neil mused about Africa again. His father had fallen in love with it that first time in Kenya. He'd heard since that this often happened. They fell into the pace of life, the upcountry climate, the fertility of the place, the vividness of the colours, the strange sense of homecoming that seemed to settle on your soul.

'He went back?'

'Often. He'd made contacts out there, more women probably. When we were kids he'd be up in London most of the time or over in Europe on business, but then he'd cut himself loose and disappear and turn up again months later, very brown and very noisy. It was a plugging-in thing. He needed to recharge.'

'He went alone?'

'Always.'

'Your mother . . . ?'

'Never.'

'Tell me about her.'

80

Neil stared at him for a long moment and then shook his head. 'I can't.'

'Why not.'

'Because she deserved better.'

'Than your father?'

'Yes. The truth is my mother had the hardest time of all.'

'How come?'

'I don't want to talk about it.'

'I understand she's dead.'

'That's true.'

'So what happened?'

Neil looked away, biting his lip, then shook his head. 'I told you. I don't want to talk about it.'

'Why not?'

'Because I don't. OK?'

A hot spark of defiance hung between them. Suttle let the silence stretch. Neil, to his surprise, smothered a yawn. Enough, he seemed to be saying. Then he stiffened a moment, distracted by another thought.

'You want to know what kind of man my father was? You really want to know?'

Suttle nodded, gestured for him to carry on.

'This last year or so he hadn't been that well. He was confused sometimes. And he couldn't get about any more, not like he used to. Anyway, he asked Hils to look for someone to come in and give him a good massage. Hils asked around and found a woman from Woodbury. Her name's Erin. She's a vegan and jogs every day and runs some kind of alternative therapy clinic. Lots of candles and body oils and chanting. She's an attractive woman.'

'And?'

'My father loved her. He booked her three times a week. Mondays, Wednesdays, Fridays. She'd turn up in her little 2CV, and the bedroom door would close and she'd do my father's bidding.'

'What do you mean?'

'Whatever he wanted.'

'How do you know?'

'Because he was that kind of man and because he paid her a fortune. Hils kept an eye on his accounts. My father loved that. He loved her to know he was mega-rich and she could do nothing about it. Erin was just another way of getting at us. I've told you already. He took what he wanted — needed — and the rest of us could go hang.'

'What kind of money are we talking?'

'Four-figure cheques. On a weekly basis.'

'What else do you know about this woman?'

'She lives with some kind of car mechanic. Woodbury.'

'You have contact details?'

'Ask Hils. She knows everything.'

Neil shifted his weight on the sofa. He looked almost pleased with himself. He'd let Suttle into the most private of worlds and thought he'd done it justice.

'My father was an animal,' he repeated with the faintest smile. 'You reap what you sow.'

4

Lizzie spotted Claire Dillon's mother the moment she walked in. The Continental Café lay at the heart of Portsmouth's busy student area, surrounded by a non-stop swirl of traffic. It served good coffee and a variety of light lunches and was a popular meeting place for both students and university staff. At this time of day, barely half ten, it was nearly empty.

Jo had found herself a table wedged against one of the big plate-glass windows in the far corner. A coffee at her elbow, she was staring with a fierce intensity at her iPad.

Lizzie shed her coat and dropped into the other seat.

'You work at the university?' she asked.

For the first time Jo looked up. She was a tall woman, middle-aged, slightly hunched, and had dressed with some care: neat grey suit, simple blouse, single loop of pearls.

'I do.' She nodded at the tablet. 'For my sins.'

'Lecturer?'

'Careers advice.' She closed the iPad. 'It used to be an easy gig. Now I'm not so sure.'

The jobs market, she said, had never been tougher. Graduates with any of the fluffier degrees — media studies, publishing, leisure management — were expected to work for

83

nothing, while kids looking for proper jobs were joining an ever lengthier queue. Either way, secure employment was fast becoming a thing of the past.

'We've been lucky. Two of our own kids have made it. One's a medic, the other took a law degree. Fingers crossed, they're on their way.'

'Which only leaves Claire.'

'Right.' She held Lizzie's gaze for a moment and then extended a hand. 'I should have said a proper hello. This is long overdue. I'm glad you've come.'

Lizzie took her hand. 'So am I. Do you want something to eat?'

'No, thanks. Get yourself a coffee. Then we'll talk.'

Lizzie fetched a latte from the counter. She hadn't expected someone so organised, so sure of herself. By the time she got back to the table, the iPad had been stowed away.

'Where do you want to start?' Jo said.

'Your call. I'll do the listening.'

'Fine.' She gazed out of the window for a moment, composing herself. 'Youngest of three girls. Very pretty. Not very bright. Low self-esteem. Problems with boys. Then with men. Are you getting the picture?' She reached for her bag and produced a set of photos. 'I dug these out this morning. After Howard had gone to work.'

'Does he know you're meeting me?'

'No. He's a jobbing solicitor. His world runs on tramlines. In Howard's book going off-piste is a hanging offence.'

84

'This is going off-piste?'

'Of course.'

'Why?'

'He'll think it exposes us to risk. Howard doesn't do risk. Close the doors. Lock the windows. Keep the world in its proper place.'

'Didn't work though, did it?'

'Sadly not.' She nodded at the photos. 'What do you think?'

Lizzie was leafing through the shots. Her mother was right. Even as a teenager, Claire Dillon had been a stunner: freckles, lovely smile, full mouth, a hint of mischief in the playful tilt of her head. One of the later photos caught Lizzie's attention. It hadn't been obvious in the shots from the post-mortem.

'This is a tattoo? On her neck?'

'Yes.'

'For real? Not just a transfer?'

Lizzie looked again. Claire must have been sixteen, maybe slightly older. Beneath her left ear she sported a small blue-winged figure.

'It looks like an angel.'

'It is. Was. Howard went through the roof. He said it was the last straw. I wasn't too pleased either. A girl that pretty? You can imagine.'

'But why an angel?'

Jo reached for the photo and stared at it for a moment. 'She was still at school at the time. Sixth-form college up at Havant. The previous year she'd got herself involved with this older guy. He was married, of course. Kids. The lot.'

'And?'

'They had an affair. We didn't know much

about it at the time. Only that she was out a lot in the evenings.'

'So what happened?'

'She fell pregnant. She tried to hide it at first, but after a couple of months it became obvious. Sick in the mornings. Moodiness. Tears. Howard was oblivious, sweet man, but you don't put on that kind of weight on what my sparrow daughter was eating.'

'You confronted her?'

'Of course I did. To be honest, I think it was long overdue. She'd been waiting for me to say something for weeks. Probably longer. It all came out. How he was going to leave his wife. How they were going to find somewhere abroad. How they'd start a new life. All nonsense, of course. The moment she told him about the baby, he dumped her.'

'What did this guy do?'

'He was a teacher. At her old school. Should he have known better? Of course he bloody should. Was I surprised? Not at all.'

'And Claire?'

'She was heartbroken. She couldn't believe it. First this lovely man in her life, a real man, not a boy. Then the baby. Then — *bam* — that's it, thank you and goodnight. I've thought a lot about him since, what he did to Claire, how she happened to cross his path, the impact he must have made, how naive she was, how vulnerable, how fucking *innocent*. Bastard.'

'And the baby?'

'I arranged an abortion. Claire hadn't got a clue what to do. Her father thought she'd gone in for a screening procedure. You've no idea how easy it is to fool a man. To this day he still doesn't know.'

'Was that wise?'

'It was necessary. There was enough going on between them as it was. She was skipping classes. Behind with her project work. Out all hours with lover boy. Claire pregnant would have done it for him. Knowing Howard, he'd have killed them both.'

Lizzie's gaze returned to another photo, before Claire got the tattoo. It must have been high summer. She was up on one elbow on a plaid blanket in the sunshine, toying with the remains of a picnic. Grass stretched beyond towards an encircling line of trees. Topless, she had a lovely body and the scarlet thong left little to the imagination. Did the new man in her life take this shot? Was this where they went to get to know each other, to make love, to plan a new future together?

'She had the abortion?'

'She did. Horrible. Horrible for her and horrible, if you're asking, for me too. It damaged her. You could see it. She was wounded. She couldn't understand what had happened. Only that part of her had been taken away. And I don't mean the baby.'

'But before all this, before she took up with this guy, had she been . . . ?' Lizzie struggled to find the right word.

'Odd?'

'Yes, thank you. Odd. I suppose by that I mean different.'

'No, you don't. Odd's good. It's code for mad, and I suppose it's the question I should have been asking myself. But in situations like that you don't. You can't imagine your own daughter having any kind of psychiatric problem. That's not the way it works. You're asking me if I saw it coming — all the other stuff that followed — and the answer is no, I didn't. I blamed the man she fell in love with. I blamed Claire for being so trusting, so bloody naive. I blamed me and Howard. I even blamed Claire's sisters for making such a success of their lives. But not for a second did I think she was clinically insane. Clinically insane didn't belong in our family.'

Clinically insane. Lizzie stared at her coffee. Such a neat way of packaging the nightmare of the last four months. Everything in life must have an explanation, she thought. *Clinically insane.*

'When did she get the tattoo?'

'A couple of weeks after the abortion.'

'And the angel is the baby she lost?'

'That's what I thought. At first.'

'But you were wrong?'

'Yes. When I asked she shook her head. The angel was the father. That's who she really missed.'

Lizzie stared at her. Outside in the street an ambulance swept past. Blue lights. Two-tones. 'That's mad,' she said softly. 'Totally bonkers.'

★   ★   ★

Jimmy Suttle was at the Major Incident Room by late morning. A hour and a half with Neil

88

Moncrieff had made him a great deal wiser about the riverside family which had so dramatically imploded.

Nandy and D/I Carole Houghton were sharing an office down the corridor from the MIR. Only Houghton was in residence. Suttle pushed at the open door and stepped in. Houghton had the phone held away from her ear. Nandy, Suttle thought. At full throttle.

Finally the conversation came to an end. Houghton was starting to look knackered, but just now she had the broadest grin on her face.

'You want the good news or the good news? We've got hits on the black guy. The man exists.'

The photofit, she explained, had triggered a handful of sightings. A taxi driver had taken a call on Sunday morning from a mobile. A guy with a very foreign accent needed picking up outside the Co-op in Topsham.

'Why the Co-op?'

'They've got cab cards in their window.'

'What time was this?'

'Just gone seven in the morning. When he got there the guy was waiting. Perfect fit. Same build. Same face. Leather jacket. White T-shirt. Fancy leather bag. The lot.'

'Where did the cabbie take him?'

'He wanted to go to the train station in Exeter. St David's. He paid with a fifty-pound note. The cabbie asked for something smaller but he said he hadn't got it. The cabbie had to go into the station to get change. That's one of the reasons he remembered the guy so well.'

'Did he see him buy a ticket?'

'No, but I imagine we can assume he did.'

'Did the guy mention where he might be going? In the cab?'

'No.'

Suttle nodded. St David's was the biggest of the Exeter stations. From there you could access the entire country: London, Birmingham, Manchester, Leeds, even Scotland.

'There's decent CCTV at St David's.'

'In hand, Jimmy. Be patient. First Great Western are in for a treat. Nandy's all over them. A look at the CCTV tapes. A bid to interview the guy on the ticket counter. He's even trying to trace the fifty-pound note. Apparently it was new.'

'When do we hear about the CCTV?'

'Imminently.'

'Excellent.'

Suttle helped himself to a seat at the desk. Then he dug inside his briefcase and slid an envelope across the desk.

'What's that?'

'A receipt for a new laptop. I got it from Neil Moncrieff.'

He briefly explained about the missing ZBook. Maybe someone should be talking to the cabbie again in case he'd noticed it. ZBooks weren't small, and Neil Moncrieff had bought a case to go with it.

'Fancy floral print. Moncrieff says you couldn't miss it.'

Houghton got out the receipt and gave it her full attention. 'That's more than two grand,' she said. 'This is a guy living on nothing. Where did he find that kind of money?'

'Very good question, boss.'

Houghton's phone trilled. Her hand reached out. Nandy again. Any word on the CCTV?

'No, sir. You'll be the first to know. We've checked out Hilary's ex-husband, by the way. The one who went bankrupt. He was in Glasgow over the weekend. And the alibi's kosher.'

Houghton rang off, glanced at her watch and got to her feet.

Suttle hadn't finished. 'One other thing, boss.'

He told her about the masseuse, the vegan from Woodbury with the oils and the dancing fingertips and God knows what else. She'd been a regular caller at the house by the river for at least the last six months and — in Suttle's opinion — deserved a visit.

'Agreed, Jimmy.' Houghton was heading for the door. 'Take Luke with you. Give her a spin.'

*   *   *

At the Café Continental a mid-morning coffee had stretched to an early lunch. To the surprise of both Lizzie and Jo Dillon, they found themselves on the same side, trapped in the path of an oncoming disaster.

Claire, still grieving, had managed to scrape a place at Leeds Metropolitan University on some kind of media production course, the details of which escaped even her mother.

'She never talked about it, never told us a thing, never showed the slightest flicker of excitement. To be absolutely frank, both Howard

91

and I were relieved to get her out of the house. Especially Howard. Just the word university was enough for him. She'd obviously got over whatever was wrong. She was obviously a human being again. And she was on her way.'

'Really?'

'Absolutely not. We didn't realise at first, but I went up there halfway through the first term, just to check how things were working out. I've been around universities and students for years now and I like to think I can recognise when there's a problem. We were together for a long weekend. She had a nice room in a big block, lots of other students around. It wasn't anything grand, but if you were looking for the first real place you could call your own, it was perfect. I met a couple of her new mates, who seemed pretty normal, and we all went out for a Chinese on the Saturday night. That's when I noticed how much she was drinking. She was just throwing it back, and what worried me was the fact that it didn't seem to affect her. One of her mates made a bit of a joke about it. 'That's Claire,' she said. 'Mad as you like.' At the time I put it down to freshers' frenzy, just a rite-of-passage thing, but it wasn't that at all. Not remotely.'

Towards the end of the first year, she said, Claire's eldest sister had a baby, a sweet little treasure called Freya. Howard, to Jo's surprise, was delighted.

'He wanted to host a big party in London at Fiona and Jake's place. I never realised the dynastic thing was so important to him but he definitely believed we'd all hit an important bend in the road and ought to celebrate. Anna was still up in Glasgow, doing her stretch as a junior doctor, and naturally he wanted his two other girls at the party to wet the baby's head. Anna was definitely up for it but Claire wasn't at all keen. That should have rung an alarm, but sadly you always miss the obvious.'

In the end Claire took the train to London from Leeds, but she was a ghost at the feast and later that same evening Jo found her slumped in the back garden, her arms clamped tightly around herself, her back against the garden shed.

'She was shivering fit to bust. It was May, for God's sake. It wasn't cold, but there she was, white as a sheet, rocking from side to side, moaning to herself. I thought at first it was something really awful but I was wrong.'

'Ketamine?'

'Yes. How did you guess?'

'I did a feature recently. Here — ' she nodded out at the street ' — it's the student drug of choice just now. Cheap. Effective. But often cut with all kinds of other rubbish. Did she recover?'

'She did. And, more to the point, we kept it to ourselves. When Fee asked I just said it was something she'd eaten on the train. Claire was grateful for that. She even gave me a kiss when I saw her off at King's Cross.'

'You think it was seeing the baby?'

'I'm sure it was. Claire always regarded herself as the runt of the litter. She was the pick of the girls when it came to looks but in every other respect she'd pretty much given up. Men? Her degree course? Her sheer inability to relate? She thought she was useless at all the important stuff, all the stuff that really *mattered*. She came back for the summer and did her best to hold down a job in a bar in Gunwharf. They were good to her there — they sensed something wasn't right and they did their level best to help — but she was her own worst enemy. She lasted three weeks. Then she just walked out. When I asked why, she said she couldn't cope. The customers, the orders, the change, even the swipe card she had to use to access the till: it was all beyond her. This was a girl, a woman, who should have been in her prime. A girl with half-decent A levels. A girl on a *university* course, for God's sake'

Lizzie made a note of the bar. Jo hadn't finished. The second year Claire moved into a student house up in Leeds, sharing with three other girls and a French student called Alain. He made a play for her early on and they enjoyed the beginnings of a relationship before he sussed what was really going on in her head.

'He moved out. Did a runner. She was that bad.'

'You met this man?'

'I did. I was up there again just before Christmas. Claire didn't want to come home and I wanted to know why. He was decent enough to get in touch through one of the other girls and we had a drink. I quizzed him pretty hard, like you would, but all he could talk about were her voices.'

'Voices?'

'In her head. He thought she'd lost it

completely. The word he used was *extraterrestrial*.' She repeated the word with a French heavy accent. 'I wasn't over-impressed at the time but later I realised how close he'd come to what was going on. She was beyond reach. She was imagining things that weren't there. I wasn't around long enough to see it for myself but apparently there were times when she'd become totally incoherent. This wasn't ketamine any more. The psychiatrists call it word salad. It's supposed to be a marker.'

'For what?'

'Schizophrenia.'

Lizzie had heard the diagnosis before — at the Coroner's Court when she'd attended Grace's inquest. By that time it had grown to paranoid schizophrenia. Naturally she'd googled the condition but had been in no state to make sense of the words on the page. Hallucinatory delusions? Perseveration? Neologisms? A give-away symptom known as clang? She'd backed out of the website knowing only that schizophrenia builds a wall between yourself and the rest of the world. Only now, listening to Claire's mum, could she begin to picture the bricks going up, course by course, squeezing out the daylight, throwing the longest, the darkest of shadows.

'She got her degree?'

'No chance. In the third year you have to come up with a project, get it approved and then complete it. We're talking a twenty-minute video. It's a test of whether you've spent the last three years listening or not and it pretty much counts for everything. Claire, bless her, came up with something no one understood. One of her mates told me it had to do with a blog she'd started. The blog was off the planet. I read some of it. It was really well written but it was totally weird. Stuff about children living in the roof space above her bedroom. How they talked to her. What they got up to. How one of them was learning to fly. Just nonsense. According to her course tutor, Claire wanted the video to be the key to this blog, a kind of visual aid. She got as far as approaching a local junior school for kids willing to perform for her and it was then that the alarm bells went off. The course tutor, who was pretty broad-minded, was horrified. He'd seen it too.'

'Seen what?'

'How mad she was. How much she needed help.'

Claire had dropped out of Leeds halfway through that final term. Her project had crashed and burned, and two sessions with a counsellor on campus had done nothing to quieten the voices in her head. She took the Megabus south and turned up on Jo's doorstep in early May.

'It was strange how normal she looked. In a way that was a blessing because I'd kept most of this stuff from Howard because I knew he'd never be able to cope. She could be a real little actress. She knew what people were thinking and she absolutely hated it. If she could find her way back to a room of her own — four walls and a door that locked — she was happy. As it turned out I could do that for her. It wasn't much but it was all she seemed to need.'

'Did you look for help?'

'That sounds like an accusation.'

'It isn't. Believe me.'

Jo accepted the reassurance with the faintest nod. Then she bent into the conversation again.

'I made enquiries. Of course I did. We have the full range of services down here on campus and I knew who to talk to. But the more people you talk to in this field, the wider variety of answers you get. You meet practitioners who talk about bipolar condition or schizophrenia or some other personality disorder, and they all seem convinced that their diagnosis is the right one. I guess that's human nature, and it's a tricky field, but it seemed very hit and miss to me. Especially when all these diagnoses lead to medication. The last thing I wanted was a zombie daughter on medication in the attic.'

'So what did you do?'

'Nothing. I fed her. I talked to her. I bought her a new telly and a new laptop. And I tried to make her life as normal as possible.'

'And Howard? Your husband?'

'I think he was in denial. Most of the time he told himself she was still up in Leeds.'

'So where are we now? Time-wise?'

Jo paused, counting back on her fingers. 'This was 2011. Early summer. Two and a bit years ago.'

Lizzie nodded. Two and a bit years ago she was living in a semi-derelict cottage in the depths of East Devon. It was driving her crazy but she still had a husband, and she still had a daughter. At the time, if she was honest, they were both

97

mixed blessings. She missed the job she'd given up in Pompey and could find no solace in a whingeing child and a winter of incessant rain. But both, looking back, were infinitely preferable to the place this woman's daughter had taken her.

'So what happened next?' she asked.

Jo didn't answer. She was writing a name and a phone number on the back of a card. She passed it across.

'Call me whenever you like,' she said. 'It hasn't been a pleasure but I'm glad we've met at last.'

'Me too.'

'You mean that?'

'I do.'

'Good. Because I've lost a daughter as well. Not just once but twice.'

Lizzie watched her get to her feet and reach for her coat. It was raining outside and the traffic was a blur through the window. Lizzie turned the card over. She could make no sense of the handwriting.

'His name's Steve Dalgety,' Jo said. 'I took the liberty of phoning him this morning. If you want the truth about Claire, you should be talking to him as well.'

5

Suttle and Golding talked about Oona's birthday on the way out to Woodbury. Suttle had thought about the invite overnight and needed to know more.

'Does this woman have a name?'

'Of course she has a name.'

'So what makes you so sure we should meet?'

'Because she wants to and you need to.'

'How can she want to if she doesn't know me?'

'Your reputation goes before you, skip. There's a long line of women out there just waiting for the phone to ring.'

'Are we talking someone from the Job?'

'We might be.'

'Then the answer's no. I can't do it. Won't do it. End of.' They were rolling through the outskirts of Woodbury, looking for the masseuse's address.

Golding was gazing at his smartphone. Then he grinned.

'I'm not sure that's an option, skip.'

'Why not?'

'Oona just texted me.' He gestured at the phone. 'The lady's on for tonight.'

$\star$ $\star$ $\star$

Open Road was the business that belonged to Erin's partner. Suttle had got the contact details from Hilary Moncrieff, who was gladdened by the news that Neil had pointed Suttle in Erin's direction. She confirmed that the masseuse had brought a little sunshine to her father's life and wasn't the least bothered by the idea that her services might have extended to something altogether more personal.

'To be honest, I'd be amazed if he didn't come on to her. My father was a goat. He always knew exactly what he was after. And, given the state of him, money would make it a lot easier.'

'Neil's talking about four-figure cheques.'

'He's right. You should ask her about it.'

Erin's partner was called Tim Stone. He ran his business from a converted barn on farmland to the north of the village. Golding bumped the Fiesta to a halt outside the big open doors. To the side of the barn was an untidy line of camper vans, most of them VWs badly in need of attention. Inside, flat on his back beneath a jacked-up split-screen camper, was a figure in overalls and a black beanie.

'Mr Stone?' Suttle crouched beside him and held out his warrant card. The man squinted at it against the light. Even the beanie had seen better days.

'What's all this, then?'

He wriggled out from under the van and stamped the cold from his feet, wiping his hands on his overalls.

'We'd like a word with Erin.'

'What about?'

'That's not your business.'

'No? I fucking hope not.' He led the way outside. Fifty metres away, tucked into the shelter of the hedge, was a Portakabin chocked up on breeze blocks. The windows were curtained against the winter chill and there seemed to be a light on inside.

'She calls it her consulting room,' he grunted. 'Some fucking stretch, eh?'

He turned on his heel and went back to the camper van. Suttle and Golding exchanged glances and headed for the Portakabin. A rusting 2CV was parked on the far side. Suttle paused and studied it a moment. Neil had mentioned a Citroën. This was obviously it.

Suttle stepped forward and knocked on the door. The woman who opened it was wearing the sort of black leotard that Suttle had last seen in a porn movie. She was small and well made with a big open face and lots of cleavage. A lingering tan suggested a recent holiday. Party time for Moncrieff, Suttle thought.

'Erin?'

'That's me.'

'CID.' He flashed her his warrant card. Golding did the same. Suttle shepherded him into the muggy warmth inside with a muttered warning to behave himself. Erin cupped her hands round a mug of something hot she'd been drinking.

'What's this about?' The same question without the attitude. 'You guys want mint tea? Decaf? You must be freezing.'

Golding settled for mint tea. Suttle declined.

101

Even in his lowest moments he'd never descended to flavoured water.

While Erin busied herself with the kettle, Suttle took a look around. The treatment table looked as if it might have come off a skip: scuffs everywhere, a makeshift repair on the wonkiest of the legs and taped-up tears where the stuffing threatened to spill out of the bulging mock-leather. At the far end of the Portkabin was a glass-fronted cabinet, clumsily repainted, full of small phials of what looked like oils. Another trophy from the municipal tip, thought Suttle.

Erin was asking whether Golding fancied a candle or two.

'Why?'

'Just for warmth. The lights are on a dimmer. Warmth is a state of mind. Candles always help. Here.' She passed him a mug of mint tea.

Golding studied it. 'Do I get sugar?'

'Afraid not.' She had a lovely smile. 'Any chance you might tell me why you're here?'

Suttle took a seat. He wanted to know about a man called Rupert Moncrieff. He understood he'd been a patient of hers.

'Still is,' she said at once. 'Lovely man.'

Her answer stopped Suttle in his tracks. Did she ever watch TV? Read the papers? Take a look at her iPad?

'No to all three. Pollution's one thing, global warming another, but the media is even worse. Believe all that crap and you'll take years off your life.'

'I'm afraid Moncrieff's dead.'

102

'Really?' She seemed genuinely amazed. 'When? How?'

Suttle explained. There was something in her face that hinted of disappointment rather than distress. Someone had closed down the mother lode and she wasn't best pleased.

'Killed? That's hard to believe.'

'I don't think suicide's an option.' This from Golding. 'You want to see the pictures?'

'No, thank you.'

Suttle let her take a sip or two from her mug. GREASE MONKEYS DO IT BETTER. Red letters against chipped white china. Then he asked her when she'd last seen Moncrieff.

'Three weeks ago. I've been away. Came back a couple of days ago. Still decompressing.'

'Somewhere nice?' This from Golding.

'Lovely.'

'Like where?'

'India. This time of year I always go to an ashram in Uttar Pradesh. The kind of spirituality, the kind of peace, money can't buy. You want the contact details? Do yourself a favour. Here . . . '

Golding ignored the proffered pen.

Suttle took up the running. 'We need to talk about money.'

'Good. I get paid for this?'

'Sadly not. How much do you normally charge?'

'For what?'

'Massage.'

'Forty pounds an hour. Depending.'

'On what?'

103

'On the clients. And what they're after. Some people have specific requests. Issues with their shoulders or their joints. Physical difficulties they want me to resolve. This area is full of old people. I've got nothing against that — they pay my wages — but sometimes it can creep above forty quid.'

'And Moncrieff?'

'Moncrieff had issues with everything. Where do you want me to start?'

'Start with how much he paid you.'

'Depended on the session. But never more than eighty. Maybe ninety.'

'That's for an hour?'

'Yes.'

'So top whack? For a whole session?'

'Two hundred. Absolute max. Why?'

'His daughter looks after the chequebook. She says he'd pay you over a thousand.'

'This is Hilary?'

'Yes.'

'I've met her. Seriously uptight. She could do with a massage too.'

'That's not what I'm asking. How come the discrepancy?'

She looked from one face to another. 'I know what you're thinking, and you're wrong.'

'What are we thinking?' Golding this time, transfixed.

'You're thinking I shagged the man witless every time we met. You're thinking he gave me a little list of what turned him on, we agreed a price, and off we went. Am I close?'

'That's our question. You're telling us it's not

true?' Golding was bracing himself for a major disappointment.

'I'm afraid so. Moncrieff had issues with his todger. He couldn't get it up.'

'Did you ever try and help him?'

'That's client confidentiality. I'm not at liberty to tell you.'

'The guy's dead.'

'Sure. And that's a shame. I actually liked him, believe it or not.'

'Why do you say that? Didn't everyone else?'

'Christ no. Have you talked to Hilary? And her weed of a brother? Welcome to the Addams family. Those people give dysfunction a bad name. Rupert used to tell me about them.'

'So you got on? You and Rupert?'

'Of course we did, and that's because we had to. There's nothing more intimate than my kind of massage. If you don't mean it, it doesn't work.'

'And if it doesn't work?'

'You don't get paid. No, Mr Moncrieff and I were the best of friends. Apart from anything else, he trusted me.'

'In what sense?'

'With his money. The cheques were always way over the top because he wanted me to cash them at the bank, take my fee and bring back the balance next time. He couldn't make it out of the house any more so little me ran his errands.'

'Why didn't he ask Hilary? Or Neil?'

'Because he didn't trust them. Or that's what he said.'

Golding was doing the sums. 'Three times a week? Have we got that right?'

'Sometimes. Not always.'

'So on a good week he'd be getting out — what — two and a half grand in readies?'

'Yes. And always in fifties.'

'Fifty-pound notes?'

'Yeah. And if possible they had to be new. Otherwise he'd throw a moody.'

'You complied?'

'Of course I did. How is a girl supposed to say no?'

Suttle scribbled himself a note. This was more evidence that Moncrieff's African friend existed. The foreign guy in the taxi had paid with a fifty. Plus Scenes of Crime had now matched fingerprints in Moncrieff's bedroom to lifts from the bedroom the African had allegedly used.

Golding wanted to know where Moncrieff kept the money.

'I'm guessing he had little stash holes.'

'Like where?'

Erin shrugged, said she didn't know.

Golding didn't believe her. 'Client confidentiality?'

She looked at him, that smile again. 'OK, just the one.'

She described a piece of wooden sculpture holding up one end of a line of books. She said it looked like a big black witch doctor in a very bad mood. The inside had been hollowed out. It was a bit of a guess, but she thought there might be eight grand inside, minimum.

'Why would he need that kind of money?'

'I never asked. If you've got it, I suppose you use it.'

'On what?'

'I've no idea. Maybe he liked counting it at night. You'd be amazed at what old people get up to.'

This was going nowhere. Suttle changed the subject. 'Moncrieff must have trusted you,' he said. 'Did you get the impression he'd made any serious enemies? Did he ever talk about stuff like that? In business, maybe? Or in his private life?'

For the first time she appeared to take the question seriously. Moncrieff, she said, was the most alpha male she'd ever met: bossy, controlling, always convinced he knew best. 'He was vain too. This was a man who could never pass a mirror.'

'Even after the stroke?'

'Especially after the stroke. He wanted to check he'd still got it. All I had to say was yes. You want to see him in the flesh?'

Suttle nodded. What he'd seen in the bedroom yesterday had been a poor guide to what he must have looked like.

Erin fetched her phone. She'd taken a selfie with him a couple of weeks back. Suttle found himself looking at a man who could have passed for someone ten years younger: strong chin slightly uptilted, full head of hair, tiny gold ring in one earlobe. His face and bare chest were deeply tanned, and Erin had her spare arm around his shoulders. He looked like a pirate recently retired after a run of good pickings.

There wasn't a hint of a stroke in the broadness of his smile.

'He had a sunlamp?'

'Of course he did. He was addicted to UV. I told him how dangerous that can be, but he didn't care. At that age you can't be arsed with other people's advice. Shit happens, yeah?'

Suttle began to understand why she'd liked him. In their separate ways they were both buccaneers. Moncrieff had made a fortune in the world of international advertising while she was scratching a living in the wilds of East Devon, but they seemed to share the same assumption that things would always work out. Might this kind of optimism have prompted Moncrieff to bung her an extra grand from time to time? Suttle wasn't sure.

Golding wanted to know about other visitors to the house.

'There weren't any. Not while I was there.'

'No one from the village? Friends he might have made?'

'He didn't have any friends. He didn't want any. He thought friends were a burden. This guy was a solitary. He once told me the best thing about the village was the view from his garden.'

'South?'

'Exactly. He'd turned his back on everyone else. Didn't like them. Didn't need them. Plug in the UV lamp and this was one happy man.' She paused, staring at Golding. 'I've got that wrong. A couple turned up back in the spring. Might have been April. Might have been May.'

'Friends of his?'

'I doubt it. When I arrived, they were screaming at each other.'

'Really?' Suttle reached for his pad.

'Yeah. These people weren't young. The woman had to be eighty at least, though it's always hard to judge, isn't it? With Africans?'

'You're telling me they were black?'

'Yeah. The woman, certainly. The other one was a man, younger. Coffee coloured. They could have been mother and son. Easily.'

'They went when you arrived?'

'They did.'

'Was anyone else around?'

'I don't think so.'

'Did he talk about these people afterwards?'

'Only to say good riddance.'

'Was he upset?'

'Not at all. You haven't been listening to me. This is a man who doesn't do upset.'

'Didn't.'

'Right. And wouldn't. And you know why? Because being upset, in his little head, would have been a mark of weakness. And that's something else he didn't do.'

Suttle went back to the African couple. He wanted a full description and some kind of date. Erin did her best with both. The descriptions were close to useless. Date-wise, the first week in May was the best she could manage. Then she grinned.

'You're going to like this,' she said. 'I was the one who showed them out. They wanted to know a good place to stay. Handy. Not too expensive. I suggested the George and Dragon out by Dart's

109

Farm. You might check there, yeah?'

Suttle made a note of the address and checked his watch. The George and Dragon was a pub on the main road with rooms attached. Time to get back to the Major Incident Room. He got to his feet. Golding didn't move.

'One more question,' he said. 'Where were you on Saturdaynight?'

'This Saturday night?'

'This Saturday night.'

She thought for a moment, and then the grin returned.

'That's easy. Jet-lagged under my pissed boyfriend. Ask him on your way out. He might even remember.'

★   ★   ★

Nandy was at the MIR by the time Suttle and Golding returned. Suttle could only guess what had put the smile on his face.

'We've got hits on the CCTV at the station?'

'We have, son. Our man hopped on the 09.05.'

'London? Manchester? Bristol?'

'Plymouth. The bloke on duty remembered all the fuss about sorting change for the cabbie. He issued the ticket to a black guy. And guess what? He paid with another fifty-quid note.'

'Bingo.'

Nandy led the way into the office he was sharing with the D/I. Golding had peeled off to brief the SOC team about Moncrieff's hidey-holes. At the very least they would be able to take a look at the wooden statue.

110

'So what next, sir?'

Nandy was already scrolling through the latest wave of emails. One caught his attention. Ignoring Suttle's question, he turned to Carole Houghton. 'Those Diversity people in Plymouth. Have they come back yet?'

'No. I left a message. They're both out on some awareness thing.'

'Ring them again. Give them a shake.'

Houghton shot Suttle a look and reached for her mobile. The number didn't answer.

Nandy had something else on his mind. He was looking at Suttle. 'The woman Hilary,' he said, 'Moncrieff's daughter, she wants another word.'

'Who with, sir?'

'You.'

'About what?'

'That's the whole point. She won't say.' He nodded towards the door. 'Wendy's got the address where she's staying. It's in the village somewhere. Quick time, yeah?'

Suttle went back to the MIR. A gaggle of detectives had formed a loose queue at the desk of the D/S in charge of Outside Enquiries, waiting to be assigned fresh actions. Nandy was clearly revving up the Major Crimes machine.

Wendy Atkins, *Amber*'s Family Liaison Officer, had squatter's rights on another desk in the far corner. The moment she saw Suttle she beckoned him over.

'You need to talk to Hilary,' she said at once.

'So I understand.'

'She's not happy.'

'I'm not surprised. The state of her father when she arrived at the scene?'

'I think she handled that. It's something else. You talked to Neil, am I right?'

'I did, yes.'

'This morning?'

'Yes.'

'Then you and she need a little chat.'

Suttle studied her a moment. Being a FLO was never an easy gig. While you were tasked to look after family members adrift in a domestic catastrophe, you were also eyes and ears for the operation's SIO, in this case Nandy. Striking the right balance could be a real trial, and there was always the possibility that Wendy Atkins had gone native.

Suttle wanted to know more about how Hilary was coping.

'She's OK. She's a strong woman. I'm getting the message that this wasn't a nice house to live in, but she seems to have buckled down and made the best of it.'

'And now?'

'Now's different. The way I read it there's only her and Neil left. Naturally she's feeling protective. I get the feeling one body's quite enough.'

'What does that mean?'

'Go and talk to her.'

Suttle wondered whether to take Luke Golding with him but decided against it. This morning, talking to Neil, it had been far easier to unlock him one to one. Or that was what he'd thought at the time.

Hilary was staying in a narrow terraced house in one of the Topsham streets that climbed away from the river. Late afternoon, the sun was dying over the hills across the river, and Suttle paused by the water to enjoy a raft of what he thought might be widgeon. Watching them drift upriver on the tide, he thought of Faraday, his old boss in Pompey. He'd been a serious birder since the dawn of time, and Suttle had a dim recollection that he might have been down this way. Photos of avocets? Talk of some North American orphan blown east beneath the jet stream? He couldn't remember the details, but there was no doubt that Faraday had loved the area. A man of taste, he thought, heading up the hill.

His knock drew Hilary to the door. She'd clearly been expecting him. Suttle wondered whether Wendy had phoned ahead.

'Come in.' She held the door open. 'I'm through here.'

She directed him into a small cluttered room at the front of the property. A nest of family photographs stood on the windowsill. Many of the shots featured children. Suttle stared at them a moment, his eyes narrowed against the afternoon sunshine.

'You talked to Neil this morning.' Hilary couldn't hide her anger. 'He phoned me the minute you left. In tears.'

'How come?'

'You upset him. And I'm not sure that was

113

either necessary or kind.'

Kind? Suttle blinked in disbelief. According to the FLO, Hilary had gone back to using her maiden name.

'This is a murder investigation, Mrs Moncrieff. Your father has been killed. It's my job — our job — to work out why and how that might have happened. We need to get close to people like yourself and Neil. We need to understand what made your family tick.'

'Why?'

'Is that a serious question?'

'Of course it is.'

'Then I'll give you a serious answer. Most murder victims knew their killers. They were either friends or lovers or family. That's where we start.'

'Are you suggesting we're under suspicion? Because that's what Neil believes.'

'No. I'm telling you we go through a process of elimination. And that's exactly where we are now. No smoke. No mirrors. Just a whole load of questions that just might be uncomfortable. For that you have my sympathy. But don't think I'm here to apologise.'

'You think that's what I want?'

'I don't have a clue what you want and I'm not sure you do either. Something terrible has happened, something truly appalling. The least you owe your father is to show a little patience and a little understanding. Life can be evil. And you're talking to someone who knows.'

They were standing toe to toe. He looked her in the eye, not conceding an inch, until the fight went out of her. Her hand strayed briefly to her face. Her eyes were shiny.

'I'm sorry,' she said. 'I apologise. It must have been awful.'

'What must?'

'Losing your child like that.'

'It's got nothing to do with my child. Bad things happen. You live with it. Life moves on.'

'Yes, I expect it does. You're right. We should sit down. Try and be human beings again.'

She turned on her heel and left the room. *Bad things happen? Life moves on?* If only, Suttle thought.

He sank into the leather armchair beside the window. In the depths of the house he heard the fall of water into a kettle. The last few months he'd done his best to resist the dozens of images that haunted his dreams, but the intimacy of some of the photos on the windowsill brought them flooding back.

Grace in Lizzie's arms at a farm gate, her tiny hand reaching for a horse on the other side. Grace naked in the shallows on a hot day on Southsea beach. Grace trying to blow out four candles on her last ever birthday, the softness of her cheeks ballooning with the effort.

Suttle closed his eyes, fighting the memories. Grace had invited half a dozen of her best friends to the party and Suttle had taken the day off to drive over from East Devon and play Dad. Lizzie had got hold of an amateur magician, and Suttle could still hear his daughter's shriek of laughter when he produced a small brown hamster from the depths of nowhere. The hamster had been a present, Grace's first pet, and she'd treasured it.

Three days after the funeral it had fallen to Suttle to set the creature free. He'd taken it to Grace's favourite walk on Hilsea Lines, an area of woodland at the north of the city, muttering the only prayer he could remember as the quivering creature scampered away into the undergrowth.

O Lord, defend us in our weakness, protect us in our hour of need, grant us succour and eternal peace. Fat chance, Suttle thought, burying his head in his hands.

Hilary returned within minutes. She was carrying two mugs.

'It's tea, I'm afraid.' She sounded brisk again. 'We're out of coffee.'

Suttle nodded woodenly at the other armchair. He said he wanted to get back to Neil. He needed to know what had really sparked his outburst on the phone.

Hilary eyed him for a moment. Then she settled in the chair, warming her hands on the mug. Her voice was softer.

'Whatever you said to him really hit the spot. If I may say so, that's clever on your part.'

'No, it's not. He did most of the talking.'

'Did he?' She seemed genuinely surprised.

'Yes. I didn't want to get in his face but I didn't have to. He had a lot to say.'

'Really? That's rare, believe me. He was ranting on the phone. He never does that either.'

Shaken by the call, she'd cut the conversation short and driven down to Exmouth. Roz was still

116

out with the dog; Neil was on the sofa, distraught.

'He's a sensitive soul, my little brother, but I've never seen him like that.'

'Like what?'

'He was in bits. He couldn't control himself. At one point he was threatening to jump off the sea wall at the end of the road, and he's terrified of the water.'

Suttle nodded, said nothing. He wanted to ask her about Erin, about the money Moncrieff had hidden away, about what might lie behind the sessions with the masseuse, about whether or not he had really been planning to sell the house, but he knew — for now — that it was wiser to let her talk.

'Why is Neil so frightened?' he said softly.

'Because of him. Because of my father. Because of the man he was. And because of lots else.'

'I get the impression he bullied Neil.'

'That's true. Neil was always an easy target, even when he was young. He was the one at the back of the herd, limping along. Pa couldn't resist it. Just picked him off. I was around quite a lot at the time, even though I was married by then. It was horrible to watch.'

'How did Neil cope?'

'He didn't. He just hid himself away. The crab under the stone. Serious withdrawal. I'm sure any psychiatrist would have a name for it.'

'What about his mum? Where was she in all this?'

'Nowhere. Not to begin with. She was

German, a real high-flyer, an account executive Pa met on his travels abroad. Her name was Inge. She was a real catch. Beautiful. Intelligent. Multilingual. And still single. Pa helped himself, of course, and they had a long affair before he decided to drag her back to the cave and make a wife of her.'

'He was still married at the time?'

'No. My mum had seen the light and left. Pa never bothered to hide the women he was seeing. I think she gave him some kind of ultimatum, but Pa probably thought she was joking. Either way, she divorced him.'

'And Inge?'

'She became wife number two. She was much stronger than my mum. She carried on working for a start, and I get the feeling she was probably more successful than Pa, which would certainly have been a challenge, but then she got pregnant and Pa convinced her to give up work. He had a much smaller house in the village at the time. Mum and I lived in a flat around the corner.'

'The baby was Neil?'

'No. The baby was stillborn. That was a real tragedy, and I'm not sure Inge ever got over it. I think she regarded herself as a failure. It certainly knocked her confidence because she never went back to work. So Pa had his way again.'

Neil, she said, was born the following year. He grew up in the shadow of his father, and as he got older it became obvious, at least to Moncrieff, that he was far too sensitive to bear his father's weight of expectation.

'Pa really belonged in the Middle Ages,' she said. 'He had this dynastic thing. He wanted a son in his own mould, a perfect replica, someone he could trust to carry the Moncrieff genes on to the next generation. Neil never measured up, never wanted to. That's what's dictated the shape of their relationship ever since. Disappointment — occasionally rage — on the one hand, blind fear on the other.'

'And Inge? She couldn't help?'

'No. Pa ground her down. You could see it. Her looks began to go. She started drinking. And in the end she became just another of his cast-offs. Neil worshipped her, maybe because they'd become fellow victims, fellow prey. I think he did his best to protect her when it got really ugly, but that was never going to work. Pa was a steamroller. Once he'd done with them he flattened them both.'

'They divorced?'

'They didn't have to. She died before that could ever happen.'

Her body, she said, had never been found. Inge was returning to her native Munich to spend a little pre-Christmas time with her family. She'd decided to take the ferry and then a series of trains from Cherbourg, which seemed an odd decision. The last anyone saw of her was a shadow on deck towards midnight. When the woman sharing her cabin reported her absence, a search of the ship revealed nothing. Only later, when the police failed to find any evidence of train tickets in her bag, did the authorities conclude that she'd deliberately

119

thrown herself overboard.

'In mid-Channel?'

'Yes.'

'In the middle of winter?'

'Yes. Early December. This time of year.'

'Was this something she'd planned all along?'

'Yes, it must have been.'

Suttle sat back, trying to imagine the icy shock of the water and the lights of the ferry slowly disappearing into the darkness. Of all the deaths you might wish on yourself, this would have been especially unforgiving.

'Why did she do it?'

'I think she still loved him.'

'How do you know?'

'She left a letter in her bag. To Pa. The Coroner read it out at the inquest.'

'What did it say?'

'I can't remember, not exactly, but it boiled down to an apology. She'd let my father down. She'd never been good enough for him. She was deeply, deeply sorry. Can you believe that?'

'No.'

'Neither could we. Especially Neil. To tell you the truth, I don't think he's ever got over it. As far as he's concerned, Pa killed his mum. He'll take that to his grave.'

'And you think he has a point?'

'I do, yes.'

Suttle nodded, remembering his session with Neil only this morning. No wonder he hadn't been prepared to talk about his mother. That was a door that led to nowhere but darkness. Rupert Moncrieff was a man whose son believed him to be a murderer. *You reap what you sow*, he thought. Neil's very words.

'I need to ask you about your father's massage sessions,' he said. 'I think we may have got to the bottom of the money thing.'

He explained about Moncrieff using Erin as a bank messenger. It seemed he'd stashed away thousands of pounds, probably in fifty-pound notes.

'Do you believe her?'

'We're checking it out. Can you think of places he might have used in his bedroom? Only now's the time . . . '

Hilary pondered the question, then shook her head.

'That room was his kingdom,' she said. 'We were allowed in to attend to him but that was pretty much it. He could have found places anywhere. Surely your people have the means . . . '

'Of course. If the money's still there, we'll find it.'

'Where else might it be?'

Suttle didn't reply. He wanted to know about Neil's new laptop. 'He showed me a receipt. We're talking more than two thousand pounds.'

'You think Neil took the money?'

'I'm asking where he got it from. Did he have money of his own?'

'Not to my knowledge. He was as poor as a church mouse. Not that it ever seemed to bother him.'

'What about cameras? For shooting material?'

'He's got a couple. A biggish one, I think it's a Canon. That's what he was using on Saturday for the concert. He bought another one recently, much smaller. He's been doing a project on birds on the estuary. I don't know anything about the technology but you can plug this little thing into the mains and leave it running for ever. There's also a way you can watch the pictures through a mobile. Don't ask me how. He showed me once but I've forgotten.'

'How much was this new camera?'

'I've no idea. It wouldn't have been cheap.'

Suttle scribbled himself a note then looked up again. 'Do you think your father might have given him the money?'

'I doubt it. It might have made Neil happy.'

'So you're suggesting Neil helped himself?'

'God knows. I've never had Neil down as a thief, but Pa certainly had to leave the bedroom from time to time. He was a creature of habit. We always knew when he'd be in the shower.' She frowned. 'But he'd surely have missed a sum like that?'

'You'd think so.' Suttle hesitated a moment, then tried to warm the atmosphere with a smile. 'Some good news. We've found your mystery guest.'

'The African gentleman?'

'The very same.'

Suttle described the chain of events that had taken him to St David's station, and then to Plymouth. En route, he'd paid his way with fifty-pound notes. Not once but twice.

'That's great,' she said.

'About the money?'

'About the African guy. Be honest. You were

starting to doubt us.'

'Not at all.'

'Yes, you were.' At last a smile. 'You people are paid to be sceptical. I can see it in your eyes. Even the young one. Luke?'

'Luke's an angel. Like we all are.'

'That I doubt. Have you found this man?'

'Not yet. But we will.'

'Have you got a name for him?'

'No.'

Suttle went back to her father's stash. He wanted to know whether the African might have lifted the money, and if so whether he might have done it with Moncrieff's blessing.

'That's certainly possible. Pa loved dramatic gestures. He was reckless that way. And the two of them spent days and days together.'

'Have you checked his credit cards? Made sure they're all there?'

'I haven't. Should I?'

'Yes, please.'

She got to her feet. Some of her father's effects were upstairs, carefully stored in the room she used as an office. When she returned, she had a handful of cards.

'There's a debit card missing,' she said, 'the one that links to his current account.'

'Do you happen to know how much is in it?'

'Just over six thousand pounds. I checked the balance on the Internet yesterday.'

'Try again.'

She left the room. Suttle heard footsteps overhead, same room. Then she was back with a sheet of paper.

'It's down to five thousand, four hundred. There was one ATM withdrawal yesterday, another this morning.'

'Where?'

'Plymouth.'

'You've got the details?'

'Here. Take it.' Suttle was looking at a printout of transactions over the last month. Apart from direct debits, there'd been no withdrawals on the account for the past three weeks. Before that, against a five-figure balance, there were three cheque debits within a single week. Suttle totalled them quickly in his head. Nearly four thousand pounds.

'These would have gone to Erin?'

'Probably. I can check.'

'And then come back to him?'

'So she says.'

Suttle's eyes went to the 'Paid in' column. On 6 November the account was richer by £3,447. On the 17th by another £1,934. He showed Hilary.

'They come from feeder accounts. Stock dividends, regular pension payments, lots of other income streams.' She nodded at the printout. 'That's the tip of the iceberg, believe me. Pa was a very rich man.'

'Which makes this whole thing bizarre, no?'

'Yes. Live with it long enough, it becomes normal. Doesn't everyone get tormented by their relatives? Isn't that how life's really supposed to work?'

The bitterness was back in her voice, a sharpness that spoke of years of resentment.

Suttle asked about the correspondence with the estate agent that the Scenes of Crime team had found on Moncrieff's desk. Was he really planning to sell up?

'Probably not. That was another game he played.'

'Game?'

'Yes.' She nodded. 'He knew we both loved the place. And he knew we both had nowhere else to live. He liked keeping us on our toes.'

'Take nothing for granted?'

'Exactly.'

'Nice.'

'I'm glad you think so.'

Suttle took the conversation back to Neil. The last thing he wanted was to make an enemy of this woman. Not yet, at any rate. 'Tell me he's not going to do something silly,' he said. 'That house of Roz's is only yards from the sea.'

'He won't. Not that way, at least. The thing about water goes way back. The one you ought to talk to is Olly. Ask him about the day Pa tried to teach Neil to swim.'

'Who's Olly?'

'Neil's younger brother. There's two years between them.'

'I never knew Neil had a brother.'

'Is that my fault?'

Suttle shook his head. He felt suddenly very stupid. Amazing how the best investigations can miss the obvious.

'So where is this Olly? Does he live locally?'

'Absolutely not.'

'Where, then?'

'West Africa. Accra.' The smile was back again. 'That's in Ghana, if you're asking.'

★ ★ ★

Nandy erupted at the news. He'd corralled both Suttle and Golding in their office. He'd wanted Wendy Atkins there too, but she was paying Neil Moncrieff yet another visit.

'So how come we never knew?'

'We never asked, sir.'

'Why on earth not?'

Suttle was trying very hard to rerun the story of the last twenty-four hours: the conversations he'd had, the impressions he'd formed, the lines of enquiry he'd explored, the investigative pathways that seemed to show real promise. Nowhere among this mountain of evidence had he once suspected the existence of another son, someone else who might have had good reason to bring Moncrieff's life to a violent end.

'And you're telling me he works at the High Commission in Accra?'

'That's right, sir. That's what Hilary told me, and that's what the FCO confirm. He works as an Entry Clearance Officer.'

'Issuing visas?'

'I assume so.'

'And he's there now?'

'Yes.'

'Jesus. So we have a prime suspect on the run. A guy we assume is from one of the francophone countries. That puts him in West Africa. The visa people work a hub system. I've been this way before. Accra probably handles applications from Christ knows how many countries. Including the francophone lot.'

'That's right, sir. I asked. Only Nigeria is different. They have their own set-up.'

'So this Olly may well be sitting at a desk in Accra dishing out visas to the likes of the man we still can't find.'

'Yes, sir.'

'And just by chance this guy happens to turn up at Olly's family house.'

'Yes, sir.'

Half a lifetime in major crime had taught Nandy a great deal about the likelihood of this kind of coincidence. With a bit of savvy, plus the obvious question, they could have been onto Olly Moncrieff twenty-four hours earlier.

Nandy was glaring at both of them. Over the last six hours he'd flooded an area of Plymouth with detectives and uniformed officers to no great effect. Now he had someone to blame.

'Anything else? With regard to this Olly?'

The Nandy glower went from face to face.

'Look on the bright side, sir.' It was Golding. 'I doubt he was in Topsham on Saturday night.'

6

Late afternoon, with her editor's blessing, Lizzie cleared her desk in the newsroom, packed what little remained into a cardboard box, said her goodbyes and headed downstairs to the car park. The only colleague to express any real interest in what had prompted this sudden spell of extended leave was Gill Reynolds, her best mate. Lizzie had phoned her earlier. Too busy to go into details on the phone, Gill had insisted on a celebratory drink. Five o'clock felt a bit early to be hitting the café-bars downtown, so Lizzie opted for a half of Peroni at the pub up the road.

The pub wasn't to Gill's taste. Her lip curled at the smell of stale beer and the scatter of peaceable afternoon drunks nodding over the paper's early City edition.

'Get a life, my love. If this is all you can manage I'd stick to the day job.'

Lizzie ignored the dig. She'd already ordered the drinks. The barman was trying to find a slice of lime to cheer up his attempt at a mojito.

They headed for a table in the corner. Lizzie spelled out the deal she'd done with Mark Boulton. Gill wasn't the least surprised.

'Exclusive serial rights? Our little rag? At some knock-down price? He always was a greedy bastard.'

128

She wanted to know whether Lizzie's agent approved. Lizzie said yes.

'Then he's mad.'

'I told him it was a deal breaker.'

'For who?'

'Me.'

'Why?'

'Because I want my job back at the end of it.'

'Then you're mad too. Get this book right and you'll be able to work anywhere you like. You might even try somewhere real. Like London.'

'So why aren't you up there?'

'What makes you think I haven't tried?'

It was true. Lizzie had lost count of the number of times she'd fielded tearful phone calls from Gill begging for reassurance that the latest rejection was their loss and not hers. As features editor, she'd given Lizzie all the scope in the world. She had a pushiness that had become legendary in the newsroom. She could recognise a promising story at a thousand miles, and her looks coupled with raw nerve had blagged some serious access for her tiny stable of writers. But when it came to the sharp end, to putting the stuff down on paper, she had a rare knack of burying any story under a swamp of clichés.

'Cheers . . . ' The mojito had arrived. 'Here's to good times. And to Grace.'

Even a month ago Lizzie wouldn't have been able to handle a toast like this. Now she simply reached for her glass. Maybe it was meeting Jo Dillon, she thought. Maybe it paid to give everyone a decent listen. Maybe her sainted publisher was right to stress the importance of POV.

Gill wanted to know about Jimmy. She'd always had a soft spot for Suttle, and there'd been moments over the last few years when Lizzie had wondered whether she'd ever make a play for him. Gill had always found it difficult to keep her hands off certain kinds of men, and Jimmy — with his sleepy eyes and blaze of curls — ticked most of the boxes. He'd also been a decent athlete in his time, turning out for some serious football teams, and Gill adored fit men.

'So have you told him? About all this?'

'No.'

'Are you going to?'

'Of course I am. At some point.'

'And what do you think he'll say?'

'I'm not sure. Like I told the publisher, it's a detective story.'

'So he might feel threatened? Is that what you're telling me?'

Lizzie thought about the question. Just the merest hint of confrontation always did it for Gill, but the possibility of her and Jimmy at each other's throats seemed remote. He might think the world of the idea. He might not. Either way, Lizzie wasn't sure it really mattered.

'We don't talk much,' she said. 'That's the strange thing about grief. You think it'll bring you closer but it doesn't. In fact it does the reverse. You end up in a bubble of your own making. You don't trust anyone, not even your husband. You've just killed the one good thing you ever did with your life, and that takes you

130

somewhere very out of reach. Phone calls? Meets? Conversation? Forget it. You're better off banged up in the bubble. Or at least you think you are.'

For once Gill appeared to be listening. 'You never put it that way before. Not to me at least.'

'Not to anyone else either. Least of all Jimmy. He's got his own demons, I know he has.'

'And his own way of coping with them?'

'Yeah.' Lizzie reached for her glass again. 'Maybe.'

★ ★ ★

When Lizzie left the pub, close to seven, Jimmy Suttle was still on the phone to the duty uniformed Inspector at Charles Cross, the city-centre nick in Plymouth. Carole Houghton had asked him to keep tabs on the hunt for *Amber*'s prime suspect, and now Suttle wanted to know how it was going.

The Inspector explained that the search was targeted on an area called Greenbank, a maze of narrow streets beyond one of the big main roads that flanked the university. Private landlords had brought up terrace after terrace, subdividing the houses and letting them to students, many of them foreign. Greenbank was also home to a small army of benefit vagrants barely keeping themselves afloat, as well as the city's quota of asylum seekers awaiting permission to stay. The latter, many of whom came from sub-Saharan Africa, occupied specific addresses controlled by outsourcing companies retained by the Home

Office. According to the duty Inspector, Greenbank was awash with black faces, and if you were an African looking for somewhere an hour from Exeter to submerge in, then a ticket to Plymouth would be a logical choice.

Suttle, who knew surprisingly little about Plymouth, was busy writing notes. A squad of *Amber* detectives armed with photo-fits, supplemented by half a dozen uniforms the duty Inspector had managed to scrounge from elsewhere, had been knocking on doors the entire afternoon. To date, despite their best efforts, they'd yet to raise a decent lead.

'The place is a warren,' the Inspector was saying. 'Think occupied Paris during the war. If you're organised, and this guy sounds pretty handy to me, then you're going to be tucked up somewhere safe. Maybe not Greenbank at all. Maybe Mutley. Maybe somewhere else. This city is full of fat white girls just begging for brown babies. It wouldn't take a lot.'

Suttle was trying to put himself in the head of the fugitive African. You've probably seen your photo in the paper or on the laptop you've nicked. It might not be an exact resemblance but it's close enough. You have an urgent need to make yourself invisible and for whatever reason you head for Plymouth. Has this man got African mates who might be studying there? Might Moncrieff have contacts he could put to good use? Either way, in Suttle's view, you'd need some kind of prior contact, somewhere you could touch down ahead of the men in blue.

It was the duty Inspector who voiced the

132

obvious question: 'I understand there might be issues with this guy's visa. Do we have any more on that?'

Suttle said no. Nandy had tasked one of his most experienced D/Cs to make contact through the immigration people with the Visa Application Service in the Accra High Commission. To take *Amber* in the right direction, he needed to know who the man in the photofit might be. A copy had already made its way to Ghana. He was still awaiting some kind of response.

'So we plod on? Is that what you're saying?'

'Afraid so. Keep me briefed?'

'No problem. But don't hold your breath.'

Suttle ended the call and checked his watch. He had strict instructions from Luke Golding to get to the bar in a local arts venue called the Phoenix by half seven. Oona would be there with the tickets. A card and a birthday drink would be more than welcome. Over and out.

Suttle put his head round the SIO's door but the office was empty. No sign of either Nandy or Carole Houghton in the Incident Room. The regular squad meet had come and gone, and most of *Amber*'s detectives had dispersed. Suttle logged out and headed for the car park. A date with a stranger, he thought. Absolutely the last thing I need.

Parking around the Phoenix was a nightmare. Suttle stowed his Impreza in the multi-storey down the road and walked back. To his surprise, the bar was packed. It was a moment or two before he spotted Oona and Luke Golding.

'Stella's off,' Golding said at once. 'Try the

133

San Miguel. Mine's a Kronenbourg.'

Suttle ignored him. He'd picked up a bottle of cava from the Tesco Express on the corner. Oona opened the carrier bag and peered in.

'You've got glasses too?'

'Later. Happy birthday.' He gave her a hug. 'Tell me about tonight.'

'There. On the table.'

Suttle picked up one of the leaflets. The Telling Room offered an evening of words and music in aid of Refugee Support. Tickets were a fiver each, and there'd be a collection afterwards. Beyond that, no clues.

Refugee Support? Suttle was resigned now. He made for the bar but Golding had beaten him to it. Back in the spare seat beside Oona, Suttle checked his mobile. Still nothing from Plymouth.

'So where's my date?' He was looking around.

'Be patient, my sweet one. Everything in God's good time.'

'It's a wind-up, right? You just wanted a bottle of decent fizz.'

'In which case you'd have bought me Moët.' She gave him a kiss. 'Cheapskate.'

Golding returned with the drinks. Suttle took a long pull. He was looking at the leaflet again.

'Music?'

'Yeah. The real thing. Refugee music. Roots music. You're going to love it.'

Moments later a bell sounded and the crowd around the bar began to thin as people drifted into the auditorium. Suttle took another gulp of San Miguel and stood up.

134

'No panico, skip. We can take the drinks in. No one seems to care.'

'You've been here recently?'

'Last week. Similar gig but without the words. The music's going to blow you away. That's why we're here.'

The auditorium was full by the time they finally went in. By some sleight of hand, Golding had secured three seats in the front row. Suttle sank into one of them. The San Miguel had settled nicely. Leaning lightly against Oona, he resisted the temptation to check his mobile again.

'I'm losing track,' he said. 'Is she in the audience, this woman?'

Oona didn't answer. Afterwards they were all going to a Lebanese place in the nearby student area. It served hummus and tagines to die for and you could take your own booze. The cava would be perfect for starters.

'Look me in the eye,' Suttle murmured. 'You said *all*.'

'I did.'

'How many of us in the restaurant?'

'Four.'

'No clues?'

'None.'

The lights went down. The stage was hidden by a fall of black curtain. From beyond came simple chords in a slow, lazy rhythm, then came a tune Suttle seemed to recognise picked out on an acoustic guitar. He'd heard this music before. He knew he had.

Next, a woman's voice, deep, plaintive, then

135

abruptly soaring. This was Gypsy music but with a difference. Music that told of fate and passion and loss. Music from the heart of long-ago Portugal.

'That's fado,' he said.

'You're right, my sweet boy.' Oona reached for his hand and gave it a squeeze.

Suttle was staring at the curtains as they began to part. On the bareness of the stage, lit by spotlights, were two women. One of them was playing the guitar. The other, perched on a high stool, was singing. She was tall, commanding and very black. A loose dress in a million colours enveloped her figure. She swayed with the music, very slowly, and her eyes were closed. She hadn't bothered with a microphone, yet her voice — soaring and swooping — filled every corner of this space.

'*Tenho janela do peito,*' she sang. '*Aberta para o passado.*'

Suttle was transfixed. The last time he'd seen this woman she'd been on the other side of the table in an interview suite in Torquay police station. Her name was Nicinha. She was Angolan. She'd got herself involved with a confused white man who played brilliant guitar and later died in a hail of bullets on the staircase at Chantry Cottage.

The song came to an end. Nicinha bowed. There were whoops and then a storm of applause. Even Suttle was on his feet. He couldn't take his eyes off her.

'So where's my date?' he managed at last.

Oona was standing beside him, still clapping.

'Up there.' Nicinha had settled herself on the high stool. 'Enjoy.'

* * *

Lizzie was back at her mother's house by early evening. On Mondays her mum attended a French conversation class down in Southsea, a brave bid to coax a little Gallic sunshine into the depths of a Pompey winter. The class was important to her, not least because her circle of older friends had begun to shrink, and Lizzie was surprised to find her mother's Clio parked at the kerbside.

She found her in the tiny kitchen-diner sitting at the table staring at a plate of curling pasta. There was a bottle of oloroso sherry at her elbow and an empty glass. When she looked up, shiny-eyed, Lizzie knew at once that she was drunk. Her mother very rarely touched alcohol. Even a glass of Lizzie's wine with the roast on Sundays was a big ask.

Lizzie examined the bottle. A third had gone. 'Mum?'

Her mother blinked, visibly embarrassed. She was a small woman, almost bird-like, and lately she'd begun to wear the kind of cardigan Lizzie had always associated with someone much older. Even a year ago her mother would never have given house room to a garment like this. Now her wardrobe was awash with beige. Food stains next, she thought. Then handwritten reminders to put the milk bottles out.

Lizzie shed her coat and gave her mum a hug.

On the way home she'd been planning to break the news about taking leave from her job. Her mother had never been great at negotiating the sharper bends in life's road, and the twists and turns of Lizzie's troubled marriage had stretched her to the limit. Then had come the real prospect of reconciliation, a brand-new start, before the thunderclouds gathered once more. Oddly enough, she seemed to have weathered the events of the summer, partly — Lizzie suspected — because it gave her a role to play. With Grace gone, Lizzie in bits and her son-in-law back in Devon, she'd become a proper mum once again. And Lizzie had been truly grateful.

'Cheers . . . ' Lizzie had found herself a glass. 'Why no French class?'

'I couldn't face it.'

'Why not?'

She stared at Lizzie for a long moment then shook her head. There were tears in her eyes, and she turned her head away when Lizzie fetched a box of Kleenex before turning the radio off. She couldn't stand *The Archers*.

'What's the matter, Mum? What's happened?'

'Nothing's happened. Maybe that's the point.'

'I don't understand.'

'I don't want you to. It's nothing.'

She sounded angry at herself. Appearances had always been important, and now, thought Lizzie, she thinks she's let herself down.

'It doesn't matter, Mum.' Lizzie put her arms around her. 'Whatever it is.'

They clung together for a moment, then Lizzie disengaged and got rid of the cold pasta. Back at the table, she topped up both glasses.

'I don't want it.'

'It's not an option, Mum. What are we toasting?'

The question brought more tears. Finally, her eyes dry again, she raised her glass. 'It's my wedding anniversary,' she said, 'if you really want to know.'

Lizzie blinked. Her mother had not once celebrated her wedding anniversary in living memory, not since her husband walked out of the marital home fifteen years ago. Since then, after a couple of awkward weekends in his bare Southsea rental with Lizzie and her teenage sister, he'd vanished without trace. So how come the sherry? And the tears?

'I don't know. If you want the truth, I think it's a bit of an indulgence. I was feeling sorry for myself. I wanted a bit of a weep. December the 9th? What better excuse.'

'He hasn't been in touch? Nothing like that?'

'God, no. He might be dead.'

'Do you care?'

'Not at all. I loved him once. We got married really quickly. Did I ever tell you that? My parents were horrified, your gran and grandpa. They tried to change the date but we weren't having it. I thought he was a lovely man. He was all I ever wanted.'

'And then we came along.'

'That's right. That's something else that couldn't wait.'

'And wrecked it all?'

She shook her head and reached for her glass.

'Don't say that.' She wiped her lips.

'But is it true?'

'No. Life changes. That's certainly true. But I suppose we must have wanted a family otherwise it wouldn't have happened, would it?'

Lizzie was staring at her. This was her mother. Angela. The stern-faced maths teacher who'd always tidied up every corner of her life with an energy that verged on mania. The woman whose sudden passion for the Baptist Church had been the talk of the staffroom. The mother who had — alone — steered two pretty teenage daughters through late adolescence with a fiercely protective awareness of just how many things could go wrong. Was it possible that she'd once been as wayward as her daughter? A woman adrift on a rising tide of hormones?

'I think we ganged up on him in the end,' she murmured. 'He found himself in a house full of women. Which was never part of the plan.'

'So he walked out? Just like that?'

'Yes.'

'Was there someone else in his life?'

'Not to my knowledge.'

'Would you have known?'

'Probably not.' She was fingering the glass again, reflective, swamped by memories. Her head came up. 'That's an admission, isn't it? Living with your husband and not having a clue who he really was?' She frowned. 'You know what happens, Elizabeth? What *really* happens? You turn people into who you want them to be. You've got a little place reserved for them and you want them to fit properly. No fuss. No

140

bother. No complaints. It's very selfish, and it's very wrong, and actually it's pretty pointless as well because in the end it doesn't work. We are who we are. He was what he was. And so he went.'

Lizzie nodded, impressed by this small truth. She'd never seen her mother like this, so candid, so rueful and so wise. She and Jimmy had camped on exactly the same spot. With horrible consequences.

'We got it wrong too, Mum. Me and Jimmy.'

'I know. I'd begun to think it was genetic'

'It's not. It's life.'

'You really think so? That sounds like an excuse to me. We should be bigger. I should have learned how to *listen*. It's amazing how deaf you can be when it suits you.'

'You blame yourself?'

'Almost entirely.'

'That must be hard.'

'It is.' She was looking at the bottle. 'Mostly at this time of year I just blank it all out, pretend he — we — never happened. But sometimes that's impossible.'

'Like now?'

'Yes.'

'Why?'

'Because . . . ' She shrugged, a gesture Lizzie interpreted as hopelessness. She put an arm around her mother again.

'Because what, Mum?'

'Because of this, of Grace, of everything. There shouldn't be that much pain in the world, but there is. That little scrap. What happened in the

141

end — I just can't get it out of my mind.' She turned into Lizzie and buried her head in her chest. Her shoulders were heaving. Lizzie rocked her to and fro, much the way she used to comfort Grace. Then the sobbing began to ease and her mother's head came up.

'I'm a foolish old woman.' She swallowed hard. 'Ignore me.'

Lizzie held her at arm's length for a moment and then shook her head and drew her in again.

'You're not, Mum. And don't worry.' She kissed her on the forehead. 'I've got a plan.'

★ ★ ★

It was a couple of minutes before Suttle realised that Oona and Golding had gone. The three of them had walked to the restaurant after the event at the Phoenix. Nicinha was due to join them as soon as she was through with selling her stack of CDs to an impressive queue of fans. She'd appeared three quarters of an hour later, turning heads as she made her way between the tightly packed tables.

By now Golding had confessed all: how he'd taken a call weeks back from Nicinha, how she'd seen all the press stuff about Grace in the summer and had been wanting to make contact, how the Phoenix had invited her down for a gig, and what a good opportunity that would be for her and Suttle to meet up.

Golding, after talking it over with Oona, had offered to arrange a meeting. His skipper, he'd told Nicinha, had gone into denial about everything that had happened. He'd blanked off whole sections of his life and — in Golding's view — he was half the bloke he'd once been. He needed to get out from under the rock. He needed to feel better about himself. And he needed, above all, to have a few laughs.

Nicinha, listening, hadn't been sure what she could do in the way of laughs but thought she might bring something else to the table. Exactly what was anyone's guess, but if all else failed, in Oona's view, Suttle could ask her to sing. A woman with a voice like that, she said, could stop the traffic in O'Connell Street.

O'Connell Street? Waiting for Nicinha in the restaurant, Suttle had been touched by Golding's concern. Sharing a meal with a key witness in an investigation as high profile as last year's job was deeply inappropriate but he didn't care. Across the interview table in Torquay nick he'd been impressed by this woman's honesty and her quiet sense of self-worth. Her own story had taken her from the chaos of Angola to a new start a trillion miles away, and she'd coped with everything an equally chaotic society could throw at her. Golding was right: if there was anyone who'd understand where Suttle now found himself, it might well be her.

They were looking at each other across the table.

'They won't come back.' Nicinha nodded at the door which led to the toilets.

'How do you know?'

'Because Luke told me on the phone. I get him to a restaurant. I sit him down. I make sure

143

he has something to drink. And then we go.'

'Him?'

'You.' Her smile warmed the space between them. She had a big face, full lips, no make-up, a single silver stud high up in her left ear. Also a small scar under her left eye that he couldn't recall from the last time they'd met. 'You liked the music?'

'I loved the music.'

'I was singing for you.' She shook her head. 'Not you. Not you yourself. For all of you.' She shaped a space between them with her hands. With the gesture came a jangle of silver bracelets.

'All of me?' Suttle was confused.

'Your life. Your little girl. Your wife. All of you. Everything.'

Suttle nodded. Something was snagging in his memory, a detail buried in the notes he'd made in the interview room. This woman was a fortune-teller. She communed with the spirits. Maybe that was what had whetted Golding's interest. Counselling with a twist.

'So how's it going?' he asked. 'Still living in Paignton?'

'Bristol.'

She'd left Paignton, she said, after everything had gone bad. *Gone bad* was an arresting phrase. In the space of a month or so Nicinha had lost the man in her life, another guy called Ian who'd been her ex-lover and — probably most important of all — her partner's child, whom she was still looking after. The first two had died, both violently, while the child had been

144

returned to his natural mother, a scriptwriter who'd scored a big contract in Hollywood and returned to lavish the proceeds on a new start with her infant son.

'Is the boy OK? Have you heard anything about him?'

'Nothing. I know where they live, the mother and this man she married. When it was really bad I once took the train there. To Salisbury. They have a house near the cathedral. A big house.' The hands again, open wide, showing the scale of the place. 'Really I want to go knock on their door, ask to see Leo, see if he remembers me, but I can't do that, no way, so I sat all afternoon outside, just waiting in case she takes Leo for a walk. Just to see him. That would be enough.'

'And did he come? Did it happen?'

'No. In the end I go back to the station and go home. Three hours. Three hours on the train for nothing. After that I tried to stop thinking about him.'

'Did it work?'

'No.'

Suttle reached for the menu. This woman had lost a child too, and he wondered whether it would be more painful to know that he was still alive yet for ever out of reach. He tried to put the thought into words. She saved him the trouble.

'It's different,' she said. 'Everyone's story is different. Only you know about your pain. Me? I still think about Leo. He'll be bigger now, and different. In two years' time, three years' time, ten years' time, different again. Money will make

145

him different. His mother will make him different. And so the Leo I miss is my Leo, still a baby nearly, just learning to walk, cheeky, a nice, nice boy. And that's the way he'll always be.'

'Like he'd died?'

'Exactly.' She nodded. 'Like he'd died.'

The waiter arrived. Nicinha wanted hummus with pitta bread. Suttle settled for chicken. To his surprise, he found himself looking at a newly opened bottle of cava.

'Your friends left it,' the waiter said. 'Happy birthday.'

'It's your birthday?' Nicinha was beaming.

'No. It's a private joke.' He poured two glasses. 'Good to see you.'

He asked her about Bristol. She said she was sharing a house with four other people. She didn't offer any details, but he got the impression she didn't much like it. It was in the Jamaican area of the city. Very noisy. Big problem with drugs. Everyone knowing everyone else's business.

'Would you ever go back to Africa? Back to Angola?'

'You have a very good memory.'

'It comes with the job.' He paused. 'Am I hearing a no?'

'To Angola? You're right. Your life is a movie. Never run it backwards. For me Angola is like Leo, something that doesn't belong to me any more. The future will be full of blessings. All we have to do is wait.'

This, to Suttle, was a vote for blind faith. Did she mean it? Was she that confident that life would be kind to her?

'Life is up here.' She tapped her head. 'Life is me, what I make it. I have a problem with Bristol? I move. My songs work OK tonight? I learn some more, make them even better. I turn on the TV in the summertime and I see you and your wife with the police, hurting, hurting, no daughter, no Grace, what do I do? I say to myself one day I will try and help, God willing.'

'And here you are.'

'And here I am. So trust me. Tell me. How was it?'

How was it? The simplicity of the question took him by surprise. He'd done his very best to avoid a conversation like this since the day Grace disappeared. For a while — at least a month — the world had seemed full of people who wanted to offer him some kind of counselling, people who felt for him, people who shared his pain.

Some of them, like the FLO assigned by Hantspol, ticked boxes. Others, like Carole Houghton, were genuinely worried. She had a professional stake in the man she saw so changed, so inwardly damaged, and she'd done her best to get him help. Suttle had been grateful, and told her so, but even when he'd seen the disappointment on her face, he hadn't changed his mind. One day, he told himself, the worst would pass. And after that he'd be up for a proper conversation.

Now he sensed this might be it. This was a woman who'd lost most of everything in Angola's civil war. The way she'd told it in the

147

interview room, the Unita rebels had robbed her of most of her family and all of what little wealth they'd possessed. Mercifully, she was still physically intact. She hadn't been raped or tortured, or lost a limb to a landmine. But she'd found herself at the very bottom of the anthill that was Luanda, the teeming capital city on the coast, and it had taken a great deal of effort — and luck — to make it out to Europe. She'd gone to Lisbon first, and afterwards to the UK. She had nothing in the world but her voice.

So how was it?

'It was hard,' he said, 'and it was something I never expected. I'd been a copper most of my life. I'd deal with stuff every moment of my working day. People out there. People who fuck up. People who *get* fucked up. But losing a *child*? Your own kid? Because you were looking the other way? Because you didn't try hard enough? Because you thought everything was so sweet with the world that nothing could go wrong? That's a killer, believe me.'

'Sweet? I don't understand.'

'My wife and I — her name's Lizzie . . . '

'The one with you on TV? A pretty woman?'

'Yes. We had a bit of an upset.'

He briefly described leaving Pompey and heading west. Grace was still very young. The cottage was remote. His wife had loathed it. Other stuff had happened, lots of other stuff, and in the end she'd gone back to her mum.

'You weren't living together? When I met you?'

'No.'

'You were living alone?'

'No.'

'Another woman?'

'No.'

She raised an eyebrow, and Suttle wondered whether to tell her about his lodger, Eamonn Lenahan, the wild Irishman who'd brought so much laughter to his life, but decided against it. Lenahan too had died, plunging the cottage into darkness. A bitter foretaste of what was to come.

'By the time Grace went missing,' he said, 'Lizzie and I were back together again. It was definitely working and we both knew it. I'd be over in Pompey whenever I could. We were a family again.' He paused. 'You want the details? About what happened?'

'Yes.'

Suttle shot her a look, then reached for the bottle. This was very definitely a novel development: Nicinha bossing the interview, himself on the receiving end. Open Account, he thought. Followed by the Challenge Phase.

'It was a Saturday,' he said. 'We all got up late. We were staying at Lizzie's mum's. She'd gone to do the shopping. We had breakfast and then decided what to do. Lizzie had seen a piece in the paper about a kite festival on Southsea Common. It happens every year. It was a lovely day so we decided to give it a try.'

They packed some toys and a blanket in the car, drove to a local supermarket, bought the makings of a picnic and drove down to Southsea Common at the bottom of the island. By the time they got there, the sky was a mass of colour, hundreds of kites.

'Grace loved it. I'd got her some balloons in the supermarket and I tied a couple to a piece of string and she was dancing around like a mad thing.'

It was hot on the common. He and Lizzie spread the blanket, and while Lizzie prepared the food, he played with Grace. The whole vibe, he said, was just so relaxed: the kites, the crowd, mellow 60s music from a band on a makeshift stage, yachts out on the Solent, ferries coming and going, even — at one stage — a hot-air balloon.

'We had the picnic around lunchtime. Just baguettes and pâté and fruit and crisps and stuff. We'd bought some beers and bottle of wine as well. After that lot we were pretty mellow too.'

'So what happened?'

Suttle hesitated. The next three hours, the next four months, were imprinted on his brain. None of this was easy.

He reached for the bottle again. Nicinha shook her head. He refilled his own glass.

'It was Lizzie who sussed that Grace had gone. She'd met some other kids earlier. We thought she must be with them. We weren't worried or anything. We just needed to find her.'

Lizzie went first. She was back within minutes. She'd found the other kids but no Grace. For the first time Suttle started to concentrate.

'We asked each other where she could have gone. There was a big crowd by now. She could have been anywhere.'

They got a neighbouring couple to keep an eye on their things while they started a proper search. Lizzie kept looking in ever-bigger circles while Suttle set out to find the organisers.

'They were in a camper van up by the stage. They were really helpful. They had a tannoy arrangement, basically a couple of speakers for the music, so they stopped the band and made an announcement. Little girl called Grace. Four years old. Pink sandals. Pretty dress with blue flowers. Probably carrying two balloons. Definitely lost.'

Lost.

The word caught in his throat. He covered his mouth, ducked his head, aware of the prickle of tears. For the second time that day the world was a blur.

Nicinha reached out across the table. Her hand was warm in his.

'Lost,' she repeated.

'Yeah. Hard to believe, eh? Broad daylight? Hundreds of people? A nice day like that? Takes some doing, eh? To lose your own kid?'

'You didn't lose her.' Nicinha was shaking her head. 'She was taken away.'

'But that makes it even worse. It was down to me to make sure that never happened. The world is full of evil people. I'm a cop, for God's sake. I know about this stuff. That's what I do for a living. It's my job to put these numpties away. If anyone should have wised-up about what a horrible world it is, it should have been me. Yet there I was, flat out on my blanket, belly full of Stella, sky full of kites, happy as Larry, thinking of absolutely fuck all. That's when she went. That's when she was taken.'

'You blame yourself?'

'Of course I blame myself. Who else should I blame? I'm her dad. Whatever you say, whichever way you cut it, the death of that little girl is down to me. That little girl was my daughter. And now she's gone.'

It felt like a confession and it was. Suttle liked this woman, admired her, but he knew he couldn't stay here a moment longer, not if he was to retain a shred of self-respect. He pushed his plate away and got to his feet. When he asked for the bill at the counter, the owner said his friends had left a credit card. The treat was on them.

'Happy birthday, sir . . . ' The man extended a hand.

Suttle stared at him, not understanding a word, then made for the door. Dimly he was aware of Nicinha getting to her feet. Outside it was raining. He looked left, then right, then set off towards the railway station, running fast, stepping into the road to avoid couples coming his way. Lungfuls of freezing air muted the voices in his head. By the time he got to the station, fighting for breath, he realised that his mobile was ringing.

He ducked into the shelter of the platform canopy. It was the duty Inspector at Plymouth. He was at home, his shift over, but he'd just got word from the Search Coordinator.

'A bloke's come forward with information,' he said. 'Apparently he met your guy this afternoon. The bloke's already been interviewed but you might like to take a second look.'

Suttle thanked him. He checked his watch: 23.17. It was too late to drive down to Plymouth and in any case he didn't want to. Instead he belled Luke. The phone rang and rang. Finally it was Oona who answered. She sounded sleepy.

Suttle asked for Luke. Oona wanted to know how he was getting on.

'I'm not,' he said. 'Just tell Luke I'll pick him up first thing.'

7

TUESDAY, 10 DECEMBER 2013

Suttle woke early, five to six, tugged into consciousness by a huge thump from the flat above. The flat was rented by the young Polish couple whose dog he walked every Sunday. Tadeusz was a decent carpenter with regular work on the building sites and his girlfriend Klaudia was heavily pregnant. Suttle lay still for a moment, then heard a cry for help — Klaudia's voice — followed by the sound of bedsprings and the urgent pad of feet across the floor above his head.

Suttle got out of bed and reached for his jeans. He'd no idea what had happened, but this was no time for a pregnant woman to have a fall and he knew for a fact that they didn't have access to a car. Moments later he was up the stairs and outside their flat. Klaudia sounded hysterical and the dog had started to bark.

Tadeusz opened the door. He was a big man, young, with an open face and a shock of blond hair. Suttle could see Klaudia on the floor behind him.

'Fell over.' Tadeusz rolled his eyes. 'She wake you up?'

Suttle said it didn't matter. If he needed an ambulance, Suttle would make the call. Alternatively, he could drive them to hospital.

154

'Ambulance? Hospital?'

'Check-up? Baby?' Suttle was never certain about Tadeusz' English.

'Baby fine. Klaudia fine. Thank you. Thank you.'

Suttle shot him a look, then shrugged and stepped away. He'd be downstairs for a bit if they needed him. Sorry to intrude.

Tadeusz nodded. With Klaudia, as far as other men were concerned, he was always fiercely protective. No problem. Thank you. Baby fine. Have a nice day.

★ ★ ★

Oona was still in bed when Suttle rapped on the door to pick up Golding. He was demolishing three Weetabix in the kitchen while checking out the Premier League table on his iPad. Man U, under their new manager, had hit a rough patch, blowing the title race wide open. Just now, pre-Xmas, any of half a dozen clubs had a decent shout come the end of the season. One of them was Southampton, Suttle's home team. He'd watched their game against Man City in an Exmouth pub on Saturday afternoon, toasting Danny Osvaldo's equaliser with a third pint of Stella before making his way home. Now he was tapping his watch.

'I've belled Nandy,' Suttle said. 'We're in Plymouth for half nine.'

'Why?'

'They've raised a lead on chummy from Topsham. Some bloke who seems to know where he's gone. Be sad not to ruin his day.'

'Sure . . . ' Golding dropped his bowl into the brimming sink. 'And what about last night? Do the biz, did she?'

'Nice try.' Suttle was already heading for the door. 'I'm grateful.'

★ ★ ★

The guy the Plymouth officers had flushed out was called Musamba. He lived in one of the streets straggling up the hill towards the edges of Greenbank. According to the Charles Cross station interview log, already pinged to the *Amber* MIR, Musamba had come forward of his own volition, approaching one of the search teams on the street. He had information on the man in the photofit and for a share of the reward money he'd be only too happy to share it.

'Reward money?' This was news to Golding.

Suttle had brought the Impreza to a halt in front of an address in Waterloo Street. A sagging wooden porch was barely attached to damp-stained stucco while an ancient mattress was leaking yellow sponge stuffing onto a tiny scrap of front garden.

'That's what our guys asked him yesterday. He'd been talking to his mates. They all think we live in the Wild West. Reward for capture. Dead or alive.'

Suttle got out of the car and waited for Golding. The terraced house looked forbidding. Someone had taped newspaper to the inside of the front windows on the ground floor. Water was still dripping from holes in the guttering after the overnight rain, and Golding caught sight of a dead rat as they stepped round a NO PARKING bollard where the front gate used to be.

'Nice,' he said. 'Welcome to England.'

It was Musamba who came to the door. He was small and slight, probably still in his twenties. His feet were bare beneath the stained grey trackie bottoms, though the Disneyland Paris T-shirt looked new. According to the duty Inspector, Musamba's street name — Fat Georges — was the locals' tribute to the asylo diet.

'You police?' He was squinting at Suttle's warrant card. He had broken teeth, heavily tobacco-stained.

He asked them inside. The hall, surprisingly warm, smelled of cooking oil and roasted spices. Close your eyes, thought Suttle, and you could be in some souk or other, looking for a bargain among the leather goods and the knock-off iPhones.

Musamba's room was at the back, under-furnished but immaculately clean: single bed, a trestle table that served as a desk and long planks supported on bricks laden with paperbacks. On a clothes line stretched tight across the back wall hung a small selection of clothes, mainly jeans and T-shirts, and Suttle counted four pairs of designer runners neatly stored beneath, all brand new. On the wall over the desk hung a photo of the Twin Towers silhouetted against a flaring Manhattan sunset. Quite what part this image played in Musamba's political credo was unclear, though Suttle imagined some of the eager souls from MI5 might form a view.

Musamba was waiting to see what happened next. He sat on the bed, his toes curling on the bare floorboards. Tucked under the bed, barely visible, was a Londis bag bulging with goodies. The only chair in the room belonged to the desk and seemed to be the property of the Red Cross.

'Is this the man you met yesterday?' Suttle had a copy of the photofit.

'Yes.' Musamba barely spared it a glance.

'You're sure it was him?'

'Yes.'

'What was he wearing?'

Musamba made an effort of memory. Jeans. White T-shirt. Leather jacket. Nice bag.

Suttle nodded. Spot on.

'Did he have a laptop?'

'No.'

'You told us he came here to this house.'

'That's right.'

'Why would he do that?'

'He said he had a friend who lived here. He was lying.'

'How do you know?'

'Because the people who live here are Somalis. Somalis and Sudanese. The man he wanted to see came from Senegal.'

'Then maybe he was mistaken.'

'Sure.' He shrugged. 'Why not?'

Musamba spoke excellent English. According to the duty Inspector, who'd talked to the Diversity guys, he was one of the area's longest-surviving asylum seekers. To date he'd managed to fend off the authorities for no less than nine years while he awaited permission to remain. On a number of occasions he'd been pressed for his country of origin but had always refused to impart either his nationality or even his date of birth. His excuse, which he was only too willing to share, was simple: if no one knew where he'd come from then there was no way he could ever be sent back. This chronic attack of statelessness had so far earned him a two-year prison sentence for refusing to cooperate, but eighteen months inside had simply hardened his resolve.

'So what did this guy say?' Suttle asked.

'He wanted to know about his friend. I didn't know his friend. I couldn't help him.'

'Did the other people here see him?'

'No. Just me. They were at the mosque.'

'Did he say where he'd come from?'

'No. Except that something had gone wrong.'

'Wrong? How?'

'He wouldn't say.'

'Did he give you a name?'

'Yes. In case his friend came to look for him. Everyone knows this address.'

'Why?'

'Because I have many friends.'

It was true. The duty Inspector, with a hint of admiration, had described Musamba as a home-grown intellectual. This was a guy, he said, who haunted the café-bars on the university campus and had acquired a circle of like-minded fellow lefties, both black and white, with whom he'd meet three or four times a week to thrash out the shape of the socialist paradise to come. He also dealt quality cannabis on the side, supplementing the five quid a day he got from the state.

Golding had produced a pad. He wanted Musamba to write down the stranger's name.

'Dominique,' he said.

'Dominique what?'

'I don't know.'

'What else did he say?'

'He said he wanted to get to Birmingham. He had a lot of money. He showed it to me. He wanted to pay someone to drive him.'

'Why didn't he take a train? Or a coach?'

'I don't know. I asked him but he wouldn't say. Maybe because of that.' He nodded at the photofit.

'So did you find someone for him? Someone who'd drive him up there?'

'Yes.'

'And this person has a name?'

'That's what they asked me yesterday.'

'And?'

'I said I didn't know.'

'That has to be a lie.'

'It is a lie.'

'Then tell us.'

'I can't. This person would be in trouble. I can't do that.'

'You can, my friend. Otherwise we might have to arrest you.'

Musamba shrugged. Then he grinned and extended both wrists.

Suttle hid a smile. He'd been checking out the books on the makeshift shelves. A lot of the authors he'd never heard of, but Karl Marx, Dostoyevsky, Kafka and George Orwell certainly rang bells. He rather liked this man. He seemed impervious to pressure. Arrest me if you want to. Put me on trial. Send me away. See if it makes the slightest difference to this life of mine.

Golding looked briefly lost. If this had been chess, he'd be looking at stalemate.

'So you think this man . . . Dominique . . . has gone to Birmingham?'

'Yes.'

'When?'

'Yesterday.'

'You *know* that?'

'Yes.'

'How come?'

'My friend . . . she came here last night, very late, and told me.'

'Why didn't she text? Or phone?'

'Because she wanted to see me. Face to face.'

'Your friend has a name?'

'Of course.'

'What is it?'

A shake of the head again, almost apologetic. Then a smile and the skinny wrists held out again.

⋆　⋆　⋆

Minutes afterwards, in the car, Golding was angry.

'He's lying, skip. He has to be. The stuff about

161

the girl is bollocks. We could check a phone call or a text. He knows that. She doesn't exist. He's taking the piss.'

'So what's the real story?'

'Fuck knows. Maybe he believed there really was a reward. Or maybe he gets his kicks from winding us up. Either way we should pull him. Perverting the course of justice.'

'Where would that take us?'

'To court. Where we might even get a result. Then they could send him home.'

'But no one knows where home is.' He told Golding about Musamba's long dance with the immigration ninjas. 'The guy's got it sussed. A week inside costs us nearly a grand. A week in his little room costs us fuck all. The accountants are in charge. No way do they want him back on B Wing.'

Golding looked chastened. Then he noticed the route Suttle was taking, quartering the area street by street. Finally Suttle found what he was after.

'What's this about, skip?'

He got out of the car and followed Suttle across the road to a Londis corner shop. Inside, the counter was manned by a harassed-looking Sikh. Suttle flashed his warrant card. He wanted to know whether Fat Georges had been in recently.

'Musamba?' The Sikh glanced at his watch. 'An hour ago.'

'What did he buy?'

The Sikh frowned a moment, then tallied the purchases. Bread. Long-life milk. Sugar. Ground coffee. Lentils. Onions. Ghee. A jar of prawn balichow. Five packs of rolling tobacco plus some Rizlas.

'Was that usual?'

'Never. The guy lives on nothing.'

'So how did he pay?'

'Ah . . . ' The Sikh was smiling now. 'Excellent question, my friend. Here. Take a look.'

He opened his till and lifted the coin tray. Underneath, among the nest of tired fivers, was a single fifty-pound note. He took it out. Exhibit one.

'Brand new,' he said. 'A beauty.'

★ ★ ★

Suttle and Golding were at Middlemoor by late morning. Carole Houghton, juggling two phones in the Incident Room, signalled for them to join Nandy in her office.

Nandy was eyeing a plate of custard creams. Crumbs on his lap suggested he'd already made a start. He wanted to know more about Musamba. Suttle had already shared the guts of the interview on the phone from the car. How Musamba had said he'd had a meet with the guy from Topsham. And how they couldn't place any reliance on his account.

'You think this guy's still around? In Plymouth?'

'I doubt it. The one thing we know he has is money. Moncrieff's money. In that kind of community money will buy you anything. In his shoes I'd have done exactly what Musamba

163

suggested: I'd have found myself a man with a van.'

Nandy nodded. Scenes of Crime, he said, had now finished with the ground floor at the Topsham property. After a phone call from Houghton they'd returned to the master bedroom and torn it apart in search of places where Moncrieff might have stashed his money. They'd found a number of likely hidey-holes — a loose floorboard, a biscuit tin hidden at the back of a drawer, an old radio with an empty battery compartment — but in every case there'd been no sign of money.

'You think our man robbed him, sir?' This from Golding.

'We've no way of knowing.' He turned to Suttle. 'Jimmy?'

'I doubt it. The way I read it, this thing begins and ends in that house. Understand the relationships, the dynamic, and we'll find a way through.'

'I'm asking you about the money.'

'Moncrieff gave most of it to our man, sir.'

'Why?'

'Because he liked him. Because they got on. Because he wanted to do a number on his own kids. And because — bottom line — he couldn't care a fuck. Moncrieff had been reckless all his life. He also enjoyed hurting people, especially his own family. A couple of grand? More? It would have been nothing to him. Drop in the ocean. The guy was a recreational sadist. You heard it here first.'

Recreational sadist put a brief smile on

164

Nandy's face. He took the conversation back to *Amber*'s elusive prime suspect. 'He won't have gone to Birmingham?'

'Obviously not, sir. My guess is he bunged Musamba money to put us off the scent. Tear that house apart and we'll find the other notes.'

'Action that. And when the money turns up, nick him.'

'Really, sir?'

'Really.'

Suttle wasn't convinced. Arresting Musumba, in his view, would achieve nothing. Better to put him under surveillance.

'But you're telling me the guy's already gone.'

'Sure. But he may have other associates in the area. I'm suggesting he knew Musamba already. That's why he turned up in the first place. Start to map Musamba's world and that might give us a lead or two. Like a name, for starters.'

Mention of a firm ID for Moncrieff's mystery guest drew a nod from Nandy. He'd taken a call from the Foreign Office only minutes ago. They'd at last had a response from the Entry Clearance people in Accra. The photofit matched a Senegalese man who'd been issued a visa a couple of weeks ago. He'd been living on a residence permit in Accra for the best part of a year.

'And his name, sir?'

'Here . . . ' He'd written it down. 'We need to develop this quick-time.'

Suttle glanced at the name. Ousmane Ndiaye. Not Dominique at all. Nandy had Ousmane's travel plans from his visa application. A Turkish

Airlines flight arriving on Monday, 2 December. A hotel address in London.

'How long is the visa valid?' Suttle asked.

'Six months. He comes in as a tourist and has to leave before his time is up.'

'He had a return ticket?'

'Yes.' Nandy nodded at the door. 'Get it sorted, yeah?'

Suttle got to his feet. One more thing. 'Who processed the visa?'

'That isn't clear. We need to get out there. I'll be talking to the High Commission this morning.'

'We, sir?'

'You and me, Jimmy. Check out the jabs you'll need.'

★   ★   ★

Suttle found himself a desk in the Incident Room. He asked Golding to make the check calls to Turkish Airlines and the London hotel and to press the Border Agency for entry details. Golding had at last secured a contact and a private phone number within the agency, a helpful young thing called Grenadine with a Croydon accent and a passion for swim dancing. Golding hadn't a clue about swim dancing but already fancied a trip to the Border Agency for a case conference.

Houghton was at last off both her phones. She beckoned Suttle across. He updated her on Musamba while she monitored incoming emails out of the corner of one eye.

166

'Did Nandy tell you about the people in Accra?' she asked

'He did.'

'Then you ought to know about Moncrieff's earlier visitors.'

Suttle nodded, remembering the lead Moncrieff's masseuse had offered about the African couple who'd paid the old man a visit back in May. He'd fed the information into the machine only yesterday but already it felt like ancient history.

'We actioned it?'

'Of course we did. They stayed at the George and Dragon just the one night. The night manager remembered them because he kept getting calls he had to put through to their room.'

'From where?'

'Accra. He had quite a conversation with these people. The man, the younger of the two, turns out to be an academic at Accra University. He's written some book or other and he'd come to England for a conference. The night manager was clueless about the details but we've confirmed the university connection. His name's . . . ' she leafed back through her notepad ' . . . Josiah Wambote.'

'And the woman?'

'His mother. Salome. Seriously old, according to our guy.'

'So what were they doing at Moncrieff's place?'

'No idea.' She paused, her gaze returning to the notepad. 'We checked out the London conference, though.' She looked up. 'How much do you know about the Mau Mau?'

* * *

Lizzie finally tracked down Steve Dalgety. She'd been phoning all morning, trying the mobile number she'd got from Jo Dillon. Every time she dialled, the number was engaged. Now, at last, there was a voice at the other end. Pompey. Rough. Wanting to know her name.

'Lizzie,' she said. 'Lizzie Hodson.'

'Friend of Jo's?'

'That's right.' Lizzie skipped any kind of explanation. Claire's mum had obviously been through all this already.

'I can do a meet if you can get round here sharpish.'

'Where's here?'

He gave her an address in Gunwharf. Then he had second thoughts and said he'd meet her at the residents' entrance on the ferry side of the development. That way she could blag free parking in the undercroft.

Lizzie was out of the house in minutes. Of her mother there was no sign. Maybe shopping, she thought. Maybe a walk out towards the bird reserve at Farlington. Either way, Lizzie hoped she felt better after her tearful evening on the sherry.

Dalgety, as promised, was waiting at the entrance to the Gunwharf Quays apartment blocks, a newish development that had quickly become one of Pompey's prime addresses. A small wiry figure, he was underdressed for the chill of the wind off the nearby harbour. Bouncing up and down, one leg to the other, he was trying to keep himself warm as Lizzie rolled to a stop. He opened the passenger door and slid in. He had a savage razor cut and cheeky eyes. He hadn't shaved for at least three days, but the stubble failed to mask a sizeable scar along the line of his jawbone. As he turned his face to hers, Lizzie saw the blue tatt on his neck: 6.57. A one-time football hooligan.

Dalgety directed her through the development and down into the open mouth of the underground car park. The last time Lizzie had been here was with her husband, years ago, when Paul Winter had invited them round to take a look at his holiday vids. She'd tried to get in touch with Winter when Grace died but without any luck. The number she had didn't work any more and a long letter to his address in Belgrade had been returned.

Dalgety had a ground-floor apartment in the Vulcan Building: high ceilings, long thin rooms and overwhelmingly male decor. A poster featuring Stevie Claridge dominated one wall of the living room and there was an open copy of Harry Redknapp's autobiography on the carpet beside the new-looking rocker. A biro lay beside the book and Lizzie stole a look at a scrawled comment in the margin of the open page. Tosser.

Dalgety returned with two coffees.

'New espresso machine,' he told her. 'Italian. Proper job.'

Lizzie had caught sight of a pile of car magazines beside the audio stack. Jo had mentioned that Dalgety was in second-hand motors but had been vague about the details.

'You buy and sell cars? Have I got that right?'

Dalgety was finding a couple of coasters for the mugs. He wanted to know what that had to do with Claire Dillon.

'Nothing. I'm just curious.'

Dalgety shot her a look and then settled in the rocker.

He'd been in the motor trade most of his life, he said, buying and selling as stuff came along. The last couple of years, thanks to a mate with connections in London, he'd happened on the market for top-end motors involved in accidents. Written off by the insurers, he bought these cars for a song and shipped them over to a trading estate on the Isle of Sheppey where a couple of mechanics, mates of his mate, put them back together again. One of them, he said, had done an apprenticeship with Porsche, the full nine yards, while the other — a total geek — had taught himself everything worth knowing about Ferraris.

Happily, an unbelievable number of quality motors were bought by spoiled rich kids dying to show off. They normally lasted a month or two before they overcooked it on some corner. The ones who survived claimed on the insurance, shrugged off the new premium and simply bought another one. Good news for Ferrari, the insurance company, and — most important of all — his genius rebuild merchants on the Isle of Sheppey.

'There's a market for these rebuilds?'

'Like you wouldn't believe. A new top-end Porsche, you're looking at ninety grand. After buying the write-off and paying my guys, I can do you the same motor for half the price. These cars sell themselves, either word of mouth or on the Internet. I even fucking deliver. Claire loved it. Turning up in a Ferrari California? All the trimmings? Couldn't get enough of it. Any time you fancy a real motor, give me a ring.'

He paused to take a gulp of coffee. Lizzie had been looking for any evidence of Claire in this man's apartment. Nothing.

'So how did you two get together?'

'At her parents' place first off. Years back. She was still at school. I'd been going out with her sister for a couple of months. Anna was a sweet woman, game as you like, but the old man hated me. I think that turned Anna on for a bit, but then she went off to university, way up in fucking Scotland, and that was a whole new gig. I think Glasgow was the old man's idea, anything to get her away from me. Tosser.'

Lizzie smiled. It wasn't hard to imagine the ripples that Steve Dalgety would have made in Selsey Avenue. Not only did he have the wrong accent and way too much attitude, but his kind of raw energy — for the father at least — would have been deeply alarming.

'Were you still 6.57 then?' Lizzie was trying to work out his age.

'No. This was 2007, 2008, the time of the crash. The 6.57 was long gone. You were either dead or rich or inside, or just bumping along like I was.'

Lizzie nodded. The 6.57 had been town-speak for a small army of football hooligans who took one of the first trains out whenever Pompey were playing away. For years and years they battled rival firms at stadiums up and down the country, shedding blood for each other and for their precious team. Hence, Lizzie supposed, the scar on Dalgety's chin.

'So you and Claire finally got it on?'

'Yeah. She was working at a bar across the way there.' He jerked his head towards the window. 'I was in one night and I recognised her. This was years later. She'd always been a looker, always, and nothing had changed. At least I thought it hadn't.'

'So what was she like?'

'Like?' The question put a grin on his face. 'She was gorgeous, amazing, every department you couldn't fault the woman.'

'Hair?'

'Blonde. Real blonde. Never seen a bottle in her life. Legs to die for. Lovely smile. The rest? A picture. You'd hang that woman on your wall. I kid you not.'

That first night, as it happened, he'd been alone. They'd made conversation across the bar between customers, and when her shift finished he'd taken her back to his place for coffee.

'Here?'

'Yeah. Turned out she was living at home and having a shit time with her dad. Not hard to imagine.'

172

'So she stayed?'

'Yeah. In fact she moved in.'

'Just like that?'

'Yeah. There was no way I was gonna stop her but I didn't have to. Next morning she said she loved me and might be back with a few things. I thought she was taking the piss. Turned out she wasn't.'

By now, he said, he had the business revved up nicely. He was buying and selling on the Internet or on the phone and running the whole shebang from his sofa. He had a vehicle recovery company squared up to deliver the write-offs to his recovery ward on the Isle of Sheppey, and every time he took a call to say the next patient was ready for collection he'd take the train over and do the biz.

'This is some kind of code?' Lizzie loved the thought. 'Recovery ward? Patient?'

'It's a joke, love. We do funny in my trade.'

'Right. And Claire went with you? On these trips?'

'Yeah. That's when I started wondering. First off they'd given her the boot from the bar. That meant something. The people over there aren't horrible or nothing. They look after their staff. And when they said they'd done their best with her, I believed them.'

Lizzie nodded. Claire's mum had made exactly the same point. *They were good to her there*, she'd said, *but she was her own worst enemy*.

'So she was with you full time?'

'Yeah. And it wasn't a big deal or anything. It

was just nice — cool, no dramas, you know what I mean? Except . . . '

'Except what?'

'Except she was odd.'

'What does that mean?'

'It's difficult. Hard to explain. At first I didn't really notice it. We were shagging like rabbits, and it was hard to keep people from buying my motors and everything seemed sweet with the world, but then you begin to listen a bit harder, tune in like, and you start realising that a lot of it makes no fucking sense.'

'Like what?'

'Like that . . . ' He nodded at the Hoover parked in the corner. 'When we were at home, just talking, she kept putting it on. She wasn't doing the cleaning or nothing. The first couple of times I turned it off, like you would, but that freaked her out so in the end I just lived with it.'

'Did you ever ask why she needed it on?'

'Of course I fucking did.'

'And?'

'She said it was because they were listening.'

'Who?'

'The drug dealers in the roof space.' His eyes drifted up towards the ceiling. 'The people who were going to kick our door in and tear our heads off. That was a fantasy, of course. As it happens I know most of the dealers in this city and there's no way they'd come anywhere near this place. In fact most of them drive my motors. They're good guys. They're onside. They're family. But she wasn't having it. Only the Hoover would keep them away.'

'So what did you do?'

'Nothing. I liked her. We were good together. It sort of worked.'

'But what did you think?'

'The truth?'

'Yes, please.'

'I thought she was potty.'

'Ill?'

'Not at that stage, no. Just potty. To be honest, I haven't been around this kind of thing much. The blokes I used to knock around with could be pretty mad, especially when they'd had a toot or two, but this was different. She didn't do drugs. She didn't drink very much. She was just — ' he shrugged ' — different.'

His mobile rang. He glanced at it and then put it to his ear. A couple of grunts and the conversation was over. He checked his watch. A tiny frown.

'Is time a problem?'

'No, we're all right. I'll make some more coffee in a moment, but we've got to get one thing straight first. Yeah?'

'Sure.'

'That husband of yours was Filth, right?'

'Still is. He's down in Devon now.'

'But he was the one who nailed Bazza, yeah?'

'Yes.'

'Then you ought to know that Bazza was a very good mate of mine. In fact it was Bazza that bankrolled this lot.' He nodded down at the phone. 'Without him, I'd never have got the motors rolling. I paid him back, more than paid him back, but I owed that guy everything.'

Lizzie nodded. This was new territory. The jokiness had gone. Bazza Mackenzie had been Pompey's top face, a football hooligan who'd turned a fortune in cocaine dealing into a city-wide business empire. And Dalgety was right. Key to the operation that had brought him down was D/S Jimmy Suttle.

Dalgety hadn't finished.

'Killing him was totally out of order,' he said. 'I just want you to know that. We all think it, every one of us.'

'I'm sure you do. So why are you bothering with me?'

'Is that a serious question?'

'Yes.'

'Because Jo asked me to. And she was always the sanest woman in that house. Sanest and fairest. And because I owe it to Claire. She got monstered afterwards. It was all over the press, all over the telly, every-fucking-where. They said she was evil. And that was the purest bollocks.' A cold smile. 'We understand each other? Otherwise it might be early doors . . . '

8

Suttle paused for an update at lunchtime. One of the FLOs had shipped a pile of sandwiches over from the canteen and there was coffee from the kitchenette down the corridor from the Incident Room. Suttle drew a chair alongside Luke Golding. He wanted to know about progress on the airlines and the hotels. Then he could share what he'd wrung from the visa people in Accra.

Golding studied the litter of scribbles on his pad. Ousmane, he said, had travelled on an overnight Turkish Airlines flight out of Accra on Sunday, 1 December. The flight went via Istanbul but was significantly cheaper than anything else.

'How much?'

'Four hundred and fifty-five quid.'

'Return?'

'Yeah. That's cheap, believe me.'

'So when would he get to the UK?'

'Monday the 2nd, like we thought. The flight was due in at 10.25 in the morning. Heathrow.'

'That's the day he turned up at Moncrieff's place. According to Neil.'

'That's right. I cross-checked with his statement. Ousmane turned up mid-afternoon. Which means he must have come straight down from Heathrow.'

'Have you talked to Immigration?'

177

'I left the details with Grenadine.' There was a smile on his face. 'She's phoning back.'

'What about the return flight?'

'Turns out he's got an open ticket.'

'Is that what he put on the visa application?'

'Yeah.'

'What about a contact address in the UK?'

'He booked a hotel in London. Cheapie place near Victoria station.'

'You checked it out?'

'Yeah. He cancelled it.'

'How?'

'By phone from Heathrow. The afternoon he arrived.'

'He made the reservation on a card?'

'Yeah. I've got the details. It's a Visa credit card.'

'In his own name?'

'Yes. I've applied for drawings on the account. Should be here tomorrow or Thursday latest.'

Suttle nodded. Houghton had appeared across the room. She wanted both of them to join her in the office down the corridor.

Golding collected a handful of sandwiches from the tray beside the Statement Reader. For such a skinny guy, his appetite was legendary.

Houghton closed the door. Nandy, she said, was upstairs with the ACPO lot. He wanted a full briefing before the squad meet at six. 'So where are we with the people in Accra?' She was looking at Suttle.

Suttle had a mouthful of cheese and tomato. He took his time, trying to fix the chronology in his head.

178

'I talked to a guy called Perry Lonsdale,' he said finally. 'He's an ECM — Entry Clearance Manager. These people have a language of their own. I thought we were bad.'

'What did he say?' Houghton was showing signs of impatience. Suttle could see it in her eyes.

'He said the application under discussion — that means Ousmane — had arrived in early November. Everything seemed in order so he got the visa.'

'That's all he said?'

'Yes. I asked for more details but he said he couldn't help.'

'Did you ask who'd handled it?'

'Of course I did.'

'Did you mention this Olly person? Moncrieff's son?'

'Yes.'

'And?'

'He wouldn't say. Only that most applications never get to a face-to-face interview.'

'So this one was waved through?'

'That's what it looks like. Without actually being there it's hard to know how the system works. Face to face, it'll be much easier.'

Houghton nodded. One of the items on Nandy's agenda for the meeting upstairs was a bid for himself and D/S Suttle to pay the Accra High Commission a visit.

'You'll obviously be talking to our Professor, as well.'

'Of course, boss.'

'So it might be good to get yourself up to

179

speed with the background. We're talking Kenya in the 50s and early 60s. The Mau Mau were the bad guys.'

Suttle nodded. Neil, he said, had told him about Moncrieff's National Service days, acting as an interpreter between the British army and the locals. 'It's all in the statements, boss.'

'I know. I've read them.'

'And he was with the film people too, the Pathé lot. Which might be important.'

After his conversation with the ECM in Accra, Suttle had spent a couple of hours on the Internet exploring reasons why Josiah Wambote and his mother might have been visiting the UK in May, and he'd found the answer in a series of press cuttings.

Back in 2011 a bunch of Kenyans had gone to court in the UK, claiming damages for abuse and torture at the hands of the Brits during the Mau Mau uprising. The judge had found that a reasonable case could be made in their favour and had ordered the release of documents from the Foreign Office archives. The documents contained reports implicating British officers in atrocities against men and women suspected of being Mau Mau rebels. These included mass arrests, whipping, beating, starvation and systemised murder in holding camps containing thousands of detainees. The files also contained evidence of cover-ups at the highest level, including a quote which had caught Suttle's eye. Eric Griffiths-Jones, the colony's Attorney General, had written to the Governor, Sir Evelyn Baring, warning him of the need to hastily

180

rewrite local law in order to decriminalise hundreds of assaults. 'If we're going to sin . . . ' he'd written ' . . . we must sin quietly.'

'Sin *quietly*?' Houghton was impressed with Suttle's research. But she still needed to know what this had to do with Moncrieff's African visitors.

'Josiah Wambote is Professor of Modern African History at Accra University,' Suttle said. 'It seems he's written the definitive book on the Mau Mau business. You were right about the conference in London, boss. Most of the Kenyan guys had gone home but he met some journalists and a bunch of academics.'

'Is he Kenyan himself?'

'I think so. I'm not sure.'

'So what's he doing in West Africa?'

Suttle shrugged, said he didn't know.

It was Golding who came up with an answer. 'Kenya's not a place you want to be just now,' he said. 'Blowing up the Westgate Shopping Centre was just the tip of the iceberg. There's loads going on. Al-Shebab. Various splinter groups. We're talking proxy wars spilling down from the Horn of Africa. Nairobi's exploding. If you had any kind of choice you'd be living somewhere else.'

'And our Professor has that choice?'

'I can only assume so, boss.'

Suttle nodded. The breadth of Golding's knowledge never ceased to amaze him. Not only did he speak decent French and a smattering of Spanish but he seemed to have his pulse on a world growing more complex by the hour.

181

'Nice one,' he said quietly. 'I'll buy that.'

There was a moment's silence. Houghton's gaze strayed to her smartphone, then she was struck by another thought. 'What about the hood? The one we found in Moncrieff's bedroom?'

Suttle nodded. This too had featured in the press cuttings.

'The Brits used hoods to disguise informers when they held identity parades,' he said. 'They cut eye holes so these guys could see the Kukes and ID the ones to go off to the camps. If the informers were recognised they'd be down on the Kuke death lists.'

'Kukes?'

'Members of the Kikuyu lot. It's a tribal thing. The Kukes were the guys giving us all the grief.'

Houghton nodded and reached for a pen. Then the door opened and Nandy stepped into the office.

Suttle looked up at him. 'Accra, sir? Are we on?'

'We are, son.' The news didn't appear to please him. 'But first we need to know a great deal more about this Olly.'

★   ★   ★

It was Steve Dalgety's idea to continue the conversation with Lizzie over lunch. On certain days, for reasons he couldn't explain, he had a passion for fish and chips. A pub called The Old Customs House served a decent pint and offered cod and fries to go with it. It was a couple of minutes' stroll across the canal. And lunch was on the business.

'Yours or mine?'

They'd left the Vulcan Building and were heading for the café-bars, restaurants, designer outlets and miscellaneous shopping opportunities that had turned Gunwharf Quays into the smile on Pompey's face.

'Mine.' Dalgety exchanged nods with a passing security guard. 'You don't have a business.'

'Wrong, I'm a journalist.'

'That's what I meant. Since when did journalism produce anything worth having?'

For a millisecond Lizzie interpreted this as a direct challenge. Then she felt his arm curl around her shoulders and give her a squeeze. Wind-up, he was saying. Take it easy. Chill out.

The pub was filling up fast. Lizzie secured a quiet table by the window while Dalgety placed the order. They did a beer called Bengal Lancer. Dalgety turned up with two pints.

'Cheers,' he said, wiping his mouth. 'Happy Christmas.'

The conversation resumed. It was autumn by now, two whole years ago, and his relationship with Claire was beginning to mature. He'd learned to live with her funny little ways. He was happy to tolerate strangers in the roof space. He'd even managed to ignore the fucking Hoover. Then something she said had really got to him. They were coming back from delivering a Maserati to a wealthy scrap-metal merchant in Harrogate. They'd taken a local train down to Leeds and were waiting for the express to

183

London when Claire suddenly broke down.

'She was sobbing her heart out. And you know what? I hadn't got any fucking idea why.'

He'd looked around for clues — faces on the crowded platform, maybe something on the big widescreen TV — but could find nothing. He knew that she'd spent nearly three years in the city as a student and assumed that might have something to do with it, but try as he might he couldn't get a word of sense out of her.

'It was like she'd forgotten how to talk. Everything came out mangled, all the words in the wrong order, then she'd shake her head like some kind of dog trying to shift something inside. Weird.'

Over the next week, back at home, he'd kept a careful eye on her. By now he'd begun to recognise that she was ill rather than just potty, but this realisation hadn't helped at all.

'For starters she wasn't registered with a GP. I tried to get her to sign up with my bloke but she wouldn't hear of it. As far as she was concerned, there wasn't a problem. You went to a GP if there was something physically wrong with you. If you were hearing voices in your head, that was just company.'

'Voices?' Lizzie remembered Claire's French boyfriend up in Leeds. According to Jo Dillon, he'd said something similar.

'Yeah.' Dalgety nodded. 'She was hearing things, smelling things, imagining things. Some days she'd tell me she couldn't work out who she really was. Others she'd be sweet as pie. That was when I started keeping a little chart of what she was eating and drinking, just in case it was an allergy thing. You try anything, don't you? If someone matters to you?'

Lizzie nodded. This, she thought, spoke of someone who really cared. Under the tatts and the blizzard of oaths, the onetime Pompey scrapper was doing his level best to understand exactly what was going wrong. In this respect, thought Lizzie, Claire had been lucky.

'Was it any help? The food thing?'

'None. In any case her eating habits were all over the place. Some weeks she'd eat nothing but fruit. Other times we'd live on fry-ups. It all depended on the voices.'

'And that worried you?'

'Yeah. I'm a patient bloke, me, because you have to be in my trade. I don't take any shit, and people know that, but there's no harm giving people the benefit of the doubt sometimes because fuck knows none of us are perfect, but if you want the truth, the situation was starting to do my head in. Any minute now, I thought, I'll be the one hearing voices. So I knew I had to do something.'

In the end he went to an organisation he'd found on the Internet and thought might be able to help.

'And did they?'

'Yeah. Sort of. They sat me down and listened to what I had to say, but the problem was they couldn't really do anything without Claire's consent. She was always the beginning and the end of all this, and you can understand that, but without her say-so I was dead in the fucking

185

water. The closest I got was asking them what might be wrong.'

'You mean like measles? Or flu?'

'Yeah. Except in here.' He tapped his head. 'That wasn't a question they were happy about either. What they really needed, what we all fucking needed, was Claire to play along, maybe just for one session, but I knew that wasn't ever going to happen. I think in her own little way she was happy. And I mean that.'

The food arrived. Lizzie had settled for fish and chips too. She reached for her glass as Dalgety tore the ends off three sachets of brown sauce.

'Did she ever mention a child?' she asked.

'What child?'

'A child she might have wanted to keep? A child she might have had?'

His head came up. He licked brown sauce off one bitten fingernail.

'Never. What are you telling me?'

Lizzie wondered whether this conversation had limits, areas where it was best not to go. Then she thought of Grace.

'Claire had an abortion when she was younger,' she said. 'Her mum told me. Was that something you might have discussed?'

'Never,' he repeated. 'A baby? Fuck me.' He reached for his knife and fork and then had second thoughts. 'She definitely wanted a baby,' he said slowly. 'I remember that.'

'And you? Did you want one too?'

'No way. I've got two already. Both live with their mums. Proper handfuls. One's six. The other's eight. Both girls. Nightmare, since you're asking.'

'You still see them?'

'Of course I do.'

'Did they ever come round to the flat? While Claire was there?'

'No.'

'Why not?'

'Because I made fucking sure they didn't.'

'Why?'

He held Lizzie's gaze a moment, then started on the fish. Only after the third mouthful did he resume the conversation. 'You know something?' he said. 'You're fucking good at this.'

★   ★   ★

It was early afternoon when Suttle knocked on the door in Victoria Road. After a second knock, it was Roz who stood in the flaring sunlight, the Labrador between her legs.

'It's me,' Suttle said. 'The police guy.'

'I know.'

'How?'

'The knock at the door. Everyone's different. You have to listen very hard but it's true.'

'Is Neil in?'

'No. He should be back soon. Do you want to wait?'

She stepped aside to let him pass. The dog gave Suttle a precautionary sniff. Music was playing in the sitting room, an opera Suttle recognised at once, the overture from *Gianni Schicchi*. Lenahan, he thought at once. He saw

187

the little Irishman busy in the kitchen out in Chantry Cottage while Anna Netrebko revved herself up for the big number.

Roz was leaning forward to turn the music down.

'Puccini,' Suttle said. 'The best.'

'Really?' She sounded pleased. 'You don't mind?'

'Not at all. Leave it on.'

He told her about the first time he'd heard Netrebko sing 'O Mio Babbino Caro' and how amazed he'd been to secure this tiny foothold on the alp that was opera. Another thank you to wee Eamonn.

Roz offered to play the aria. Suttle said yes and watched her bend over the record player. He'd always had a passion for vinyl but he'd never seen a blind woman trying to find a cue point on a whirling disc. She seemed to do it by instinct, the fingertips of her left hand feeling for the edge of the record while her right guided the needle to touchdown. To Suttle's amazement, she hit the aria seconds before it started.

'O mio babbino caro,' the soprano sang, 'mi piace, è bello, bello. Vo'andare in Porta Rossa, a comperar l'anello!'

Roz wanted Suttle to guess who was singing.

'Maria Calks,' he said at once.

'You're looking at the sleeve.'

'You're right. I am.'

She laughed and gestured for him to sit down. Suttle let the rest of the aria play itself out, swamped by memories, then fumbled for his notepad.

'I need to find out about Neil's brother,' he said. 'Has Neil talked about him?'

'Olly? Yes.'

'What does he say?'

'Maybe he should tell you.'

'But I'm asking you, Roz.'

She nodded. For a moment the conversation threatened to become awkward. Then her hand found the volume control on the record player and the music became a whisper.

'Olly was the late arrival,' she said. 'Olly was fearless. Olly was Tigger. No one frightened Olly. Least of all his father.'

Olly, she said, was a couple of years younger than Neil. In every respect, from a very early age, he appeared to fulfil every one of his father's expectations. He was handsome and brave. There was no physical challenge he'd ever duck. If his father said jump a certain height, or wade across a stream up on Woodbury Common, or roll down a sand dune here in Exmouth, then Olly would do it. He was swimming like a fish by the age of five. On his eleventh birthday, with a trickle of tide, he swam the mile and a half down to Lympstone. Life, in short, was there for the taking.

'Tigger,' she said again. 'I can even picture him.'

Suttle could hear Neil's voice in her account. She must have got this stuff from him, he thought. There was no other way she'd have known so much of the detail.

'And Neil? Where was he in all this?'

'Neil was the also-ran. Neil haunted the

189

shadows. For protection he had Olly. Olly looked after him. That's the irony, the younger brother keeping watch over his elder sibling. Something that Neil found shaming.'

'What about their mother? Inge? Was Olly as close to her as Neil?'

'Never. You're right. Neil was Inge's boy, mummy's boy. Olly was closer to his dad. That's the way his father wanted to play it. Divide and rule. Never fails.' She hesitated. 'Did Neil ever tell you about the day they first went sailing?'

'No.'

'Then I will. Neil was fourteen, Olly twelve. Their father decided it was time to teach his boys to sail. Not just Olly but Neil too. Neil loved the river, he's always loved the river, he still loves the river. But he hates water.'

'So what happened?'

'They all set off in the dinghy. Neil says it was high tide. They went down the river to where it suddenly broadens. You know where I mean?'

Suttle was looking up at the black and white photo on the wall, the one Neil had taken from his father's garden. He knew exactly where she meant.

'Go on,' he said.

'So there they were, plumb in the middle of the channel, deep water, and the father suddenly tells Olly to jump in. It was a kind of test. Just to prove he could swim.'

'But he knew he could swim.'

'That wasn't the point. The point was to set an example.'

'For Neil?'

190

'Of course. Neil was terrified. He knew exactly what was coming next, and when his father told him to jump he just froze, just sat there.'

'He couldn't swim?'

'Not a stroke.'

'Was he wearing a life jacket?'

'No. His father had made him take it off.'

'So what happened?'

'His father told him again. Jump, he said. Neil didn't move, didn't argue, didn't say a word. Just sat there. So his father counted to five.'

'And then what?'

'He threw him overboard. Threw him in. Some men are like that. Sink or swim.'

Neil, she said, thrashed around. He hadn't got a clue what to do. Every time he reached for the safety of the boat, his father pushed him away. Then he started going under, and that just made him panic more, and the water got into his lungs, and after not very long he knew he was going to die.

'Neil said everything went green first. Then brown. Then black. Black is the colour of death, Mr Suttle. Unless you happen to be blind.'

It was Olly, his brother, who finally got him out.

'That boy saved Neil's life,' she said. 'So if you're after clues about how important he is then look no further.'

'And they're still close?'

'Like that.' She linked her two forefingers and pulled hard. 'Inseparable.'

'But Olly's in Africa.'

'You're right.'

191

'You're telling me they talk a lot?'

'All the time.'

'Still? Now?'

'Yes.'

'Have you talked to Olly yourself?'

'Yes.'

'And?'

'He sounds nice. He's not at all like his brother. He's cheerful. Jolly. Much *louder*.'

There was a long silence. Suttle wondered about another dose of Callas. She seemed to have unlocked a great deal. Then Roz stirred on the sofa. There was something else she needed to add.

'What's that?'

'It's about Neil. We're blaming all this on his father. That's not quite fair. Are you making notes, Mr Suttle?'

'No.'

'Are you recording this?'

'No.'

'Good. Because I'm afraid it's deeply personal. When I first met Neil, I took him at face value. He stepped into my life at a time of great need. I had this lovely tandem and no one to keep me company. He offered to do that. He said he was a keen cyclist himself, a real fan, and I was right to believe him because he is. But that's not where it ended.'

'No?'

'No. It turns out that he liked me, liked me from the start, liked me physically.'

'Fancied you?'

'Yes.' She nodded. 'And he fancied me

because he'd seen my photo in the paper. That's where it began for Neil. And the fact that I was blind made it possible for him.'

'Made what possible?'

'Made it possible for him to be with me, to get to know me, to start . . . you know . . . a proper relationship.'

'You mean a sexual relationship?'

'Yes. Women with eyes, women who can see him, terrify Neil, because of this . . . ' She touched her cheek, her forehead, the side of her neck.

'Because of his skin? The state of his face? Because he thinks they may reject him?'

'Exactly. He thought I'd never do that because I was blind, because I couldn't see him. That made me safe. He could open up. He could get close. I hate the phrase, and I'm sure you do too, but Neil had done the risk assessment. He'd be safe with me. I'd never reject him, never turn him away.'

Suttle nodded. He thought of this stick of a man with his cratered face and his inner anguish. This was probably the first woman he'd ever slept with, ever trusted with his ruined looks. Thank God, he thought, for Roz McIntyre.

'And it works?'

'Happily, yes.'

'Because you're blind?'

'Because we've fallen for each other. It's a rather wonderful thing. You know what they say about love? It's not looking into each other's eyes, it's looking in the same direction. That's what we do. And that's why it works for us.'

193

Suttle sat back. A shadow fell briefly over the window. Then came the scrape of a key in the door. Neil, he thought.

Roz had heard it too. She leaned forward, her hand on Suttle's knee, the lightest pressure.

'There's one other thing,' she said quietly. 'Blind people see with their fingertips. The moment I first kissed him I knew exactly what he looked like. And you know what?'

'It didn't matter.'

'Exactly.'

The door opened and Neil stepped in. He tried to mask the blush of anger in his face but failed completely.

'You again,' he said. 'Why can't you just leave us alone?'

★ ★ ★

Lizzie's plate was empty by the time Dalgety came to the end of his story. Claire, he'd decided, badly needed help. He'd made other calls, knocked on other doors, but the response was always the same. We need to see her. We need her to be here. But she'd always refused. So, in the end, he'd taken the only remaining option.

'Which was?'

'Lie.'

He'd gone to his own GP and told him that she was threatening to take her own life. It wasn't true, but Dalgety didn't much care. He wanted the cavalry on his side. He wanted to wake up to the sound of fucking *hooves* on the

194

cobblestones outside. He wanted someone to whisk her away and look after her, and bring her back the gem she'd once been. Fully restored. Great on the sharper corners. Much like the motors that would pay for their future together.

'And did it work?'

'No fucking way.'

The GP, he said, had been sympathetic and suggested that Dalgety bring Claire along to the surgery. When she refused, claiming there was nothing wrong with her, the GP consented to making a home visit.

'Claire wasn't going out much,' he said. 'That was easy to arrange.'

The GP turned up. He spent half an hour talking to Claire and went away convinced that Dalgety was right. She was delusional. She was ill. She needed psychiatric help.

'So what happened?'

'We got another visit, a different doctor, plus a psychiatrist and another guy — nice bloke, Irish accent. Mental Health Practitioner? Something like that. Real houseful, we had. Impressive, if you're asking.'

The psychiatrist, he said, seemed to be in charge. He wanted to do an assessment on Claire, a proper job, but when they got round to talking about suicide threats, she didn't want to know.

'That was fucking awkward,' he said, 'because I'd invented that bit. Just to get the doctor round.'

'But they still thought she was ill?'

'Big time. Claire had clammed up, wouldn't

say a word, just sat there wringing her hands. Nothing dramatic, but if you knew her like I did you could see she was upset. She hated people getting physically close to her. Asking her questions. Getting in her face. Except maybe me.'

'Maybe?'

'Yeah. Some days she'd be all over me. Other times she wouldn't want to know.'

The medics, he said, packed up after an hour or so and said they'd be in touch later in the day. The mental health guy gave me his mobile number. He told me to keep an eye on Claire, make sure she didn't wander off, but he said they'd definitely be back that afternoon. They wanted to take her in for a proper look, a proper assessment.'

'Take her in where?'

'St Francis'. The nuthouse. He told me there were a couple of special wards there where she'd be safe. Tree names, they had. Aspen and something else. Fucking bizarre, but there you go.'

He shook his head and pushed the empty plates away at the sight of the approaching waitress. Already Lizzie sensed he was talking about a stranger.

'How did she cope? When she went in?'

'She didn't. It never happened. She was clever, Claire. She knew exactly what was going down. She never let on, but there was no fucking way she was ever going into that place.'

Lizzie nodded. St Francis' Hospital lay on the edge of the city, a sprawling Victorian institution that had once housed hundreds of patients. She knew things had changed in mental health, but St Francis' still had a forbidding reputation among the locals.

'So what happened?'

'She did a runner. My fault, really.'

There'd been a problem, he said, with the alarm system in his Audi. The sensor had tripped, and the security people wanted him to get down to the undercroft and turn the fucking thing off before it deafened half of Gunwharf.

'I went down there and sorted it. Took maybe twenty minutes. By the time I got back, she'd gone. Packed a bag and done a runner. The harbour station's five minutes away. I went over there sharpish thinking that's where she might be, but there was no sign of her. I found out later she'd taken a cab from the rank.'

'She had money?'

'Yeah, and that was another thing. I always had moolah in the flat. It's a cash business. You're talking thousands of pounds. Claire knew where I kept it.'

'And helped herself?'

'Yeah.'

'How much?'

'Just over two and a half grand.'

'Did you tell the doctors? The mental health people?'

'Yeah. I explained about the alarm and said she'd gone. The mental health bloke didn't seem surprised.'

'What could they do about it?'

'Nothing. She wasn't a threat to anyone else,

not then, and when he pressed me on the suicide thing I told him I'd made it up. That meant she wasn't really a threat to herself either.'

'Just ill.'

'Yeah.'

'And the money? Did you go to the police?'

'No fucking way. The money was the least I owed her . . .'

His voice tailed off and he turned his head to gaze out of the window, and Lizzie realised where this story had taken him.

'That was it, wasn't it?' she said. 'That was the end of it.'

'Yeah.' He nodded.

'Because?'

'Because I didn't know her any more. I was out of my depth. Whatever I did seemed to upset her and just make things worse.' He looked at Lizzie. 'Would you go into a place like that?'

'Of course not. But then I'm not ill.'

'Yeah, you're right. Of course you're right. But that's it, isn't it? What she had wasn't something you could put a label on. Not something you could treat. If I'd known what was going to happen down the line, maybe it would have been different, but then I just told myself the thing was over. She could still function. She could still make decisions. She could still pack a bag and find a cab for fuck's sake. And with two and a half grand in her pocket she might make a new start. Maybe it was me making her crazy? Fuck knows.'

'Is that what you told yourself?'

'Yeah. It was.'

'And was that an excuse? To get you off the hook?'

'Yeah.' He looked her in the eye again. 'And you know something else? I ain't proud of it. Why? Because I bottled it. I should never have gone down to the fucking Audi. I should never have let her out of my sight. My fault. That was my fault.'

'And did you ever see her again?'

'No.'

'You didn't try and get in touch? No texts? No phone calls?'

'No.'

'Did you think about her at all? Where she might be? *How* she might be?'

'No.' He held her a gaze for a long moment. 'Crazy, eh?'

⋆ ⋆ ⋆

Suttle went looking for Carole Houghton the moment he got back to the MIR. He found her on the phone in her office, deep in conversation with someone at the local authority, talking about litter bins and refuse collection schedules. Finally the call came to an end.

'Nandy,' she said. 'He's starting to wonder about Neil Moncrieff's laptop. The cabbie who picked up Ousmane didn't see it and neither did your bloke down in Plymouth. A ZBook isn't small. It's something you'd notice.'

Suttle agreed. He'd been thinking along exactly the same lines. He was carrying a Co-op bag. He put it on the desk.

199

'What's that?' she said.

'Neil Moncrieff's cameras. I seized them this morning.'

'Why?'

Suttle explained about Roz. It turned out that the relationship was much closer than Moncrieff had ever admitted. His girlfriend was using the word love.

Houghton spotted the implications at once. 'But he told us he slept on the sofa on Saturday night,' she said.

'Exactly, boss.'

'Did you put that to him again?'

'I did.'

'And?'

'He insisted that was the case. I asked her too. She said they hadn't started sleeping together until the following night.'

'When he moved in?'

'Yes.'

'But that's only yesterday.'

'Exactly.'

'And you believe them?'

'No. I think they've been at it for weeks. Maybe longer. I think we need to tear that place apart, and I think we need to take a good look at this gear here.' He nodded at the cameras. 'Moncrieff is motive on legs. He hated his father. He's glad he's gone. He even admits it. If they're lying about Saturday night, and about Sunday morning, then he's definitely in the frame.'

'And Ousmane?'

'God knows.'

Ousmane's passport photo, she said, had been

emailed from the Accra High Commission. Circulated to forces nationwide, it had failed to raise any sightings. Either he'd gone to ground or fled the country. The latter, going against the flow of inbound immigrants, would have been all too possible in the back of someone's van. Security staff at the major ferry ports rarely checked vehicles heading for France.

'So we need to get out to Accra. Give the other son a shake.'

Houghton nodded. Nandy, she said, was talking to the Home Office about *Amber*'s latest line of enquiry. CID visits to non-European countries had to be channelled through Whitehall.

'It might take a week or two,' she said. 'Nandy has to file a full report. Nothing's as simple as you might think.'

Her hand was reaching for the phone again. If Scenes of Crime were to descend on Roz McIntyre's house, she had to run it past *Amber*'s SIO. Yet another decision for Det-Supt Nandy.

'There's another thing, Jimmy.' She'd abandoned the phone. 'That partner of Erin, Moncrieff's masseuse.'

'The mechanic guy?'

'Yeah. His name's Stone. Tim Stone. And it turns out he's on the radar.'

A couple of months ago, she said, he had a run-in with a bloke who'd sold him an old camper van. Stone had made the guy an offer, which he'd accepted, and he'd collected the camper van but never paid the balance after leaving a deposit.

'How much are we talking?'

'Peanuts. Four hundred quid. Matey who was owed the money kicked up a fuss and threatened him with a lawyer, but Stone just ignored him. Matey wouldn't give up. Kept phoning him, knocking on his door, all sorts. He even tried to get us involved.'

'And?'

'Stone lost it. Went round to his place with a hammer and threatened to kill him.'

'*Kill* him? For four hundred quid?'

'Exactly.'

'Was he pissed?'

'It seems not. Matey phoned us. Made a complaint. His girlfriend was a witness. He said that Stone was a dangerous man and should be locked up. We did the biz and Stone got a caution. We also made other enquiries.'

'And?'

'It turns out Matey was right. Mr Stone is partial to a fight. And he's also very jealous.'

'About?'

'His partner.' She smiled. 'Erin.'

9

Lizzie phoned Jo Dillon from the pub in Gunwharf. Dalgety had given her a peck on the cheek and departed. It was time, he'd said, to get back to real life. He had a stack of punters lined up for a rather nice Bentley he was due to collect and was currently conducting an auction on his smartphone. The bidding, last time he'd looked, had just hit sixty-three grand. Happy days.

Jo answered on the first ring. She wanted to know how Lizzie was getting on. 'Was Steve OK?'

'He was sweet. Really helpful. I liked him.'

Lizzie was tempted to go further, to explore her growing realisation that mental illness was infinitely more complex and challenging than she'd ever anticipated, but she resisted. At this point, she told herself, she needed to gather the evidence, not to come to any premature conclusions but to find out exactly what had happened. No one ended up killing someone else's child by accident. There had to be a reason, a thread of event and circumstance that had plucked Claire Dillon from the comforts of Selsey Avenue and put her on the front page of every newspaper in the country.

'Steve mentioned a mental health guy he'd met. Irish accent.'

'Billy McTierney,' Jo said at once. 'These people call themselves AMHPs. Ask him what it stands for. I can never remember.'

She gave Lizzie a number. She thought he was a manager up at St Francis' Hospital. He'd interested himself in Claire's case after she'd fled from Gunwharf and come round a couple of times for coffee. When Claire resurfaced, McTierney had been the first in Portsmouth to know.

'So where did she go?'

'Leeds. It was obvious really. That was the only other place she could ever call home.'

* * *

Suttle took the cameras to the Scenes of Crime office at Heavitree nick. The Crime Scene Manager attached to *Amber* was bent over his PC, finishing a report. Suttle explained where the kit had come from. One Canon EOS 7D. One GoPro Hero3.

The CSM logged both of them in. 'Are we looking for prints here? DNA?'

'That's your call.'

'Right. So what do you want me to do with them now?'

'I want to see what he's shot.'

The CSM nodded. He could dust for prints later. All he needed just now were the memory cards from both cameras.

They started with the Canon. According to the CSM, who was a camera buff, it was a top-of-the-range model, barely a year old, not a penny under sixteen hundred pounds. It shot stills plus HD video, had built-in GPS plus an assortment of other bells and whistles, and if all else failed you could probably cook your evening meal with it.

Suttle was making notes. Where on earth had Neil Moncrieff laid his hands on sixteen hundred quid?

The CSM had loaded the memory card into a laptop reserved for what he called evidential review. The first files dated from July 2013. Suttle bent to the screen. These were unedited sequences shot in the garden of the Topsham house. He recognised the low stone wall and the reed beds the other side of the river. The camera was hunting for close-ups of the teeming birdlife on the water. Suttle spotted widgeon, mallard and a gaggle of oyster catchers feasting on a mudbank. Then came a slow fly-past by a pair of swans, followed by an unsteady pan to a lone turnstone.

Suttle made a note. The CSM jumped onto the next file. More birds. File followed file, each one numbered, timed and dated. By November, with the rushes at an end, Neil Moncrieff would have been ready to start editing.

The CSM opened the next file. It was dated 7/12/2014, just two days ago. The opening shot, in poor light, showed the exterior of an unlovely red-brick building. A close-up offered a poster for a concert of music by Schubert, Vivaldi and J. S. E. Bach. The highlight was to be Schubert's *Death and the Maiden*. One of the string quartet at the heart of the evening's

205

entertainment was Hilary Moncrieff.

The next shots took Suttle inside the building. The hall was empty except for a semicircle of blue chairs around a performance space. Music stands had already been erected but the players had yet to arrive. The shot was rock steady, the camera anchored on a tripod, and Suttle watched a figure he recognised wander into shot trailing a couple of cables attached to microphones. Neil Moncrieff. Setting up for his big production.

Suttle asked the CSM to freeze the picture. Moncrieff was turning towards the camera. Jeans. Runners. And the white top Suttle remembered from the first of yesterday's interviews, the yellow symbol of the pilgrim route to Santiago de Compostela, souvenir of the trek he'd shared with his stepsister.

One of the unresolved mysteries surrounding the old man's death was the issue of the killer's clothing. Half an hour ago, mentally reviewing the weight of circumstantial evidence piling up around Neil Moncrieff, Suttle had acknowledged that he had the potential to be *Amber*'s prime suspect. Yet anyone who'd inflicted that kind of damage on another human being would be covered with blood. So how come that same Neil Moncrieff had appeared at Heavitree nick just hours later, wearing exactly the same gear? And how come neither Scenes of Crime nor the Territorial Aid Group had found any trace of bloodstained clothing?

He looked harder at the image on the screen. The jeans and the sweatshirt, to the best of his

206

memory, were identical to the clothes he'd been wearing on Sunday morning. The runners he couldn't be sure about. There'd have been mud on the cycle path after overnight rain. Maybe Moncrieff changed his runners before coming to Heavitree. Something else to check.

'You want to take a look at the other camera?'

Suttle nodded. He'd made notes on what he'd seen so far. He waited until the CSM swapped the two memory cards, then bent forward again. The GoPro camera was clearly an earlier purchase. The first file dated back to February last year, video again, a snowy scene in a corner of what looked like Moncrieff's garden. The shot was centred on a wooden bird table. Ten minutes of video, shot against an ever-darkening sky, brought a handful of sparrows and finches to the grease balls hanging over the table. More files, later in the month, showed exactly the same scene. Birds had become Neil Moncrieff's life, thought Suttle. Maybe they'd been a comfort for him, a form of solace, a way of escaping a life banged up with a father he loathed.

The coverage went on and on. A hard winter gave way to a late spring. By June the garden was a blaze of colours and the table had become second home for an impressive range of bigger birds. Then, without warning, it was winter again, rain puddling on the lawn, a distant skein of geese high above the reed beds across the river.

The CSM hit the Stop button. He was frowning. 'Someone's been cleaning up,' he said. 'Look.'

He rolled back to June. The file number was 134. Five months later, in late November, the file number was 152.

'You mean he's deleted stuff?'

'Someone has. Definitely. We'd need to evidence who's had access, but the numbers never lie. We're missing seventeen files.'

'Can you get them back?'

'Yes.' He was checking his watch. 'Give me half an hour, eh?'

★ ★ ★

Lizzie hadn't been in touch with her husband for more than a month. The last time they'd met, way back in early November, they'd shared a meal at a pub on the main road west of Wimborne. They'd been to the Coventry Arms before. It was as good a place to meet as any, a ninety-minute drive for Suttle, less for Lizzie. The food was good, and there were corners of the lounge bar where they could enjoy a little privacy. At the end of the meal Suttle had promised to give her a call. Since then nothing.

Now she felt they owed each other an update. Phoning during working hours had always been a no-no, but her meeting with Steve Dalgety had taken her to a place she'd never expected and she wanted to share this news with Jimmy.

To her surprise, he answered on the first ring. She asked whether he was busy.

'Always,' he said.

'Give me five minutes?'

'A pleasure.'

There was something new in his voice that she couldn't quite place. Then she had it. This husband of hers was excited. Something must have happened.

'Everything OK?' she said.

'Everything's fine. You?'

'Yeah . . .'

She told him about Sunday's meeting with the publisher. The news that the Devon book had fallen flat on its arse drew a sigh of relief from Suttle. The money she'd blagged for the commission was awesome, but he'd never been keen on sharing the kind of operational secrets the book needed with his wife. He knew that would leave a sour taste in his mouth, not least because she was also after a personal account of what it felt like to be taken hostage by a bunch of guys who'd already killed three men. He didn't mind reliving those hours in the intimacy of their own relationship but sharing it with the rest of the world didn't appeal at all.

'It's dead in the water? Gone? Finished?'

'Yep.'

'Thank Christ for that.'

She laughed, wondering what he'd make of its replacement. She outlined what the publisher wanted.

'And you've said yes?'

'I have.'

'Why?'

'Because we owe it to Grace.'

'We?'

'Me. I owe it to Grace. And maybe you do as well.'

209

'I'm part of this?'

'You were her father, my love. And we wouldn't want it to happen again. To anyone.'

There was a longish silence. She was making the call from the promenade beside the harbour in Gunwharf. The sun had gone in now and the wind was howling off the water. Even the gulls looked cold.

Suttle was back on the line. He wanted her to know exactly how many nutters there were out there.

'Hundreds,' he said. 'Thousands. Squillions. We see it in the Job every day. I was talking to a bloke in Torquay only last month, a custody sergeant. He thinks we've become the paramilitary arm of the social services. He reckons between 40 and 50 per cent of the people he deals with have issues. Visit a prison, it's the same story.'

'Issues?'

'Mental health issues. That's code for bonkers, in case you were wondering.'

'So is that a good reason for not trying? Not bothering? Is that what you're saying?'

'Bothering about what?'

'Bothering about trying to understand how our daughter ended up dead. Nothing can bring her back, I know that. But this is something different. Maybe it's me. I just need to track back, to find out how our paths could ever cross, ours and Claire's, and then . . . I dunno what happens.'

'You write a book.'

'Yes.'

'Is there money in it?'

'Yes. A lot of money, as it happens.'

'So is that why you're doing it?'

'Don't be offensive.'

'I'm not. I'm just asking.'

Lizzie was biting her lip. In arguments like these Suttle always bested her. He was so logical, so black and white. If only he could explore the places in between, she thought. If only he could glimpse the bits of human behaviour you could never rationally account for. Policemen, she'd concluded, lived in a world of forms. There was no form for Claire Dillon.

Suttle wanted to know whether she was really going ahead with this project.

'Of course I am. In fact I've started.' She told him briefly about Steve Dalgety.

'Little guy? In your face all the time?'

'That's him.'

'He used to run with the 6.57. Big mate of Bazza's.'

'I know. He told me.'

'And you're saying he was shacked up with that woman?'

'Absolutely.' Lizzie was heading for the shelter of a nearby café-bar. Strange how her husband still couldn't handle using Claire's name. 'They were together for a while. I think he did his best.'

'Yeah?' Suttle started saying something else, something about the kind of company a guy like Dalgety would be keeping, but then he broke off. Something had come up. He wished her luck. He had to go.

211

'Fine.' Lizzie tried to mask her anger. 'Another time, eh?'

★ ★ ★

Back in the Scenes of Crime office the CSM had disinterred the missing files from the memory card. Suttle enquired how but quickly lost track. Unless the card had been overwritten with fresh material, it seemed the latest software could restore anything.

The CSM had cued up the first of the missing files.

'You're going to love this,' he said. 'I'm sure he did.'

The picture stabilised and began to roll. Suttle was looking down at Rupert Moncrieff's bedroom. The lens was very wide, the room slightly distorted. Moncrieff was lying on his back, stark naked, his hands folded over the flatness of his stomach. Beside the bed, unpacking glass phials from a leather bag, was Erin. Suttle had last seen these phials in the Portakabin she used out at Woodbury. Body oils, he thought. Full service.

There was sound on the recording, excellent quality, and Suttle asked for more volume. The CSM obliged, a smile on his face. The CSI was back too, and Suttle began to wonder how many passing staff the office could comfortably hold. Maybe he should be charging for this, he thought. Reduced rate for the matinee performance. Full price later.

Erin was stepping out of the loose dress she'd

been wearing. According to the time and date stamp it was 16 July 15.07. Hot, Suttle thought.

Down to a thong, Erin began to oil Moncrieff's body. For a man in his mid-eighties he looked to be in remarkable shape. The brain cells might be popping but there wasn't an ounce of spare flesh on him.

Maybe he exercised. Maybe he tottered down to some gym or other. Anything to sweeten the pleasure to come.

Erin was telling Moncrieff about some friend who'd arrived out of nowhere and overstayed his welcome.

'He's driving my fella insane,' she said. 'He thinks the guy's got designs on me.'

'And has he?'

'Yeah, maybe he has. But how cool is it to have a big scene about it? My Tim's a child. He never left adolescence, never wanted to. I guess I should be flattered, but you've no idea how much that man winds me up.'

Moncrieff laughed. Looking at him, Suttle wasn't entirely sure he was following the conversation. It might have been the distorting effect of the lens, but there was something about his eyes that suggested the stroke that Neil had described.

Erin finished with his chest and shoulders and danced her fingers down his body. Moncrieff lifted his hands the way you might open a gate, and Suttle saw at once that there was nothing wrong with his todger. She curled her hand around it, ducked her head, gave it a kiss. There came a tiny groan from Moncrieff

213

as it grew in her hand.

She reached for more oil, playful now, telling him to behave himself, telling him to wait. They had a whole hour. First things first.

This is drama, Suttle told himself, probably the same script for session after session, Erin cast as the authority figure, stern-faced, teasing, the dominatrix with sole script rights, the stage manager who would — alone — decide when Moncrieff deserved the roll of drums, the grand finale, and — if he was exceptionally lucky — an encore.

Moncrieff was talking now, gravel-voiced, a little hesitantly, his head on the pillow, forever dabbing at his mouth with a handkerchief. Suttle wondered whether this was another message from a body that refused to obey its master's commands. A stroke, definitely.

Erin had slipped onto the bed, straddling Moncrieff's legs. She oiled the cleavage between her breasts, more theatre, making sure that Moncrieff had the best seat in the house. Then she rocked gently forward, slipping his penis between her breasts. Up and down, very slowly. Moncrieff had closed his eyes. The handkerchief had slipped from his hand. He was groaning again, a tiny animal whimper, lust softened by something close to gratitude. Then, without warning, Erin rolled off the bed and found her feet again, ducking her head to give him a kiss on the forehead. She moved with a natural grace. She was effortlessly beautiful in the kind of way that would drive any man insane. No wonder Tim Stone had a short fuse.

Suttle glanced at the CSM. 'Just where might

214

this camera have been?'

'Exactly my thought,' he said.

He fetched a diagram of the master bedroom and compared it with the picture on the screen. The viewpoint appeared to be at the position and level of a bookshelf marked on the plan. You could hide the GoPro behind the books, leaving a gap for the lens. Knowing exactly when the old man summoned his masseuse, it would be child's play to position the camera and then collect it later.

'Could you monitor the pictures?'

'Easy.' The CSM reached for the GoPro. 'This little baby's got Wi-Fi. Download the right app and you could watch this stuff live on your smartphone. I expect he did. Wanker.'

Suttle wasn't so sure. If the CSM had it right, there were sixteen more of these files. Maybe they weren't all shot in Moncrieff's bedroom. Maybe there was other stuff.

'Do you mind checking?' he said. 'On the other files?'

The CSM zipped through the opening few seconds of each. They were all shot from exactly the same position, and they all featured Moncrieff and his busy masseuse. Summer slipped into autumn. Then it was November. In the last file Erin arrived in a faux fur coat, and what little dialogue Suttle caught was about the incessant rain.

Suttle hadn't got the time to watch any more. He reached for his phone and called a stored number. Luke Golding was on the line in seconds.

215

'Little treat for you, golden bollocks.' Suttle's gaze strayed back to the screen. 'Call it a thank you for last night.'

★ ★ ★

Lizzie drove out to St Francis' Hospital. She'd managed to contact Billy McTierney, and after a wary start to the conversation he'd worked out the link to Jo Dillon. It seemed she'd put in a call seconds before Lizzie had got through. Parking outside the low block of offices in the grounds of the looming hospital, she wondered what to buy Jo as a present. A bottle or two of nice wine? A new husband? She wasn't sure.

She'd caught McTierney at the end of his working day. He was behind a brimming desk, gazing at his smartphone. The office was stuffy and overheated and the glass coffee pot bubbling on the filing cabinet badly needed a good sluice.

'I didn't realise.' He waved at the empty chair.

'Didn't realise what?'

'Who you were. That should be *are*, right?'

He had a lovely smile. He was lean, medium height, jeans, white cotton shirt with the faintest hint of a blue stripe. He hadn't shaved for a while and it definitely suited him.

Lizzie refused coffee.

'Very wise. It's shite.' Soft vowels. Irish accent. Lovely voice. 'How can I help?'

Lizzie quickly outlined what she was about. Her brief conversation with her husband had wised her up. She had to be precise. She had to

216

be unemotional. Play the journalist, she told herself. Pretend that Grace was someone else's daughter.

McTierney followed her explanation with just a hint of a smile. He seemed to radiate patience spiked with something a little more direct, and she wondered whether the world of mental health bred many men like this.

'So your question is what? Exactly?'

'My question is simple. Claire Dillon left Portsmouth at the back end of 2011. Her mum says she went to Leeds. You were one of the last people to see her before she went. What happened next?'

'The short answer is I don't know, not the whole story. This is important to you?'

'Yes.'

'Why?'

'Because I need to fill the gap. She was back here by the middle of this summer. I know that for a fact.'

'To your cost.'

'Of course.' She held his gaze. Was he expecting something else? Tears? Anger? Recriminations? She couldn't tell.

'You're a journalist, right?'

'Yes.'

'Have you found that's helped? With all this?'

It was a good question, all the more intelligent because no one else had thought to ask it.

'It has, yes.'

'How?'

'When it happened, it gave me a bit of control. That's rare, believe me. The media can roll all over you. I wasn't having that. And I knew how to avoid it.'

'You were good. I read your stuff. I saw you on telly, caught you on the radio. Very cool. Very controlled. Almost *too* controlled.'

'It wasn't an audition.'

'I know it wasn't. I was thinking of you. Of you in here.' He tapped his head.

'That's very sweet of you. I'm flattered.'

'Don't be. It's what I do for a living. Something like that can take you to a very bad place. I've been there myself. I know about this stuff. Sometimes you need to let go.'

'Why do you think I didn't?'

'Because you're sitting there telling me something very different. You're telling me it hurt, sure, but you're also telling me that you're bigger than what happened.'

'No one's bigger than what happened. What happened was totally beyond anything I could possibly imagine. *Ever.*'

'Don't get angry. There's no need.'

'Of course there isn't. But you seem to be suggesting that I should emote more, have a bit of a wallow. I don't do wallows. Not then and not now. You understand what I'm trying to say?'

'Of course I do. More than you probably think. What happened in August was absolutely in my patch. It was a mess. It was horrible beyond description. That's why I followed it all on the media. That's why I stalked you, caught everything you did. For the record, I admire the way you coped. That's all I'm trying to say.'

Lizzie didn't know quite how to handle this.

She seemed to have touched a nerve or two. Time to stop? She thought not.

McTierney stole a look at his watch. Nearly half past five.

Lizzie leaned forward and grinned at him. 'I'd like to buy you a drink,' she said. 'Do you think you could handle that?'

★   ★   ★

She took him to a pub down the road, a stone's throw from Langstone Harbour. At this time in the evening it was empty. A sheepdog dozed by the fire. The barmaid was adding a bit of colour to a poster for the Christmas raffle. Lizzie insisted on buying the drinks while McTierney settled at the table beside the dog. He was drinking Guinness, just a half.

'So what brought you to mental health?'

'I fancied being a professional mountaineer. Bottled out on an ice wall in the Himalayas. So I ended up doing this.'

'You enjoy it?'

'Sometimes. It's like anything. If you're any good, you end up behind a desk sorting out the staff. I used to think the patients were the ones needing attention. How wrong can you be?'

Lizzie laughed. She liked this man. He had an easy wit and didn't seem to take himself too seriously. Rare, she thought.

He wanted to know about being a journalist. He followed her stuff in the paper, especially the profile pieces, which had become a bit of a speciality.

'How come you get these people to open up?'

'You learn to listen. It's a dying art, believe me. If people think you're genuine, if they think you care, they'll tell you anything.'

'And do you care?'

'Mostly, yes. Otherwise I pretend. You get to be good at that too.'

'Bit of an actress, then?'

'When I have to be, yes.' She studied him over her glass. 'And you?'

'I play the game, study the moves, tick the boxes. Mental health's like everything else. We're institutionalised. We think too hard about ourselves. We're terrified of making the big mistake, the one that makes it onto the evening news, the one that might put you in court.'

'Like Claire Dillon?'

'Yep. Exactly. And that means we take fewer and fewer risks, which is a pity because we're not talking any kind of exact science here.'

'We're not?'

'No way. I shouldn't be telling you this, but you've probably sussed it already. Nothing in my world is stuff you can really nail down. Some of it's guesswork, some of it's intuition, some of it might as well be witchcraft.'

'We're talking diagnosis?'

'Yeah. Someone rocks up. You're looking for the obvious markers, sleep patterns, issues to do with concentration. Can they read a book? Follow a TV programme? Finish a crossword? Are they hearing voices? Are they *afraid*?'

'That's a marker?'

'It is. Then you look for corroboration. Maybe

you talk to the neighbours, see what they think, then you go back to the patient. You probably know a lot more about them by now, but in some ways that makes them even stranger. These people can live entirely in a world of their own making. They can spot personal messages in a newspaper article or even a car registration plate. At first it feels weird, but after a while you realise there's a certain logic to it. They've reconfigured the world around them. They've reimagined it.'

'Why?'

'To keep themselves sane.'

'But they're not sane. They're mad.'

'Exactly. Catch-22. That's why it's still a job that gets me up in the mornings.'

Lizzie nodded. It was impossible not to put Claire Dillon in the middle of this craziness.

'Do you think Claire was afraid?'

'I know she was.'

'Is that something she told you? When Steve Dalgety called you in?'

'Not explicitly. Not in so many words. But body language tells you everything. Especially in a case like hers.'

He hugged himself and then rocked back and forth in the chair. The dog looked up, briefly interested, and then went to sleep again.

'She was terrified of us,' he said. 'She didn't want us anywhere near her. Her partner was crazy to leave her like that. I know he had to go down to the car, but it was obvious she wanted out.'

'So what would have happened had he stayed with her? What would you have done?'

'We'd have pulled her in here for a proper assessment.' He nodded at the window. 'We've got a couple of wards. Sycamore and Aspen.'

'But she'd have refused. She'd have said no.'

'Then we'd have detained her. Section 2, Mental Health Act. Twenty-eight days.'

'You've got that power? You can do that?'

'Yes. With police back-up if necessary.'

'And at the end of the assessment? What then?'

'The psychiatrist would make a diagnosis. He'd probably put her on meds.'

'Job done?'

'Never. You can take meds for the rest of your life. Meds can *become* the rest of your life.'

'But she'd be out? Living alone? By herself?'

'Probably. These people are hard to live with. Often they don't want company. We keep an eye on them, of course — CPNs, regular visits — but basically you're right: they're on their own.'

'And Claire? Once she'd left? Did no one try and find her?'

'Not to my knowledge. She'd done nothing criminal that we knew about. She wasn't a threat to other people. Her partner admitted making up the suicide stuff, so she was no threat to herself. She was just ill.'

Just ill. Lizzie stirred the dog with her foot, trying to imagine Claire's story through this man's eyes.

'You must see hundreds of Claires,' she said.

'That's true. Each one's different but the caseload is huge. No money. Shite resources. A & E turning patients away. The police picking them up and dumping them on us. We've got just seven emergency assessment beds for the whole of Hampshire. What do you do?'

Lizzie nodded. It was a good question. She could see Claire in the cab, fleeing a life she couldn't cope with.

'Nothing,' she said quietly.

★ ★ ★

Suttle was packing up to go home when Luke Golding appeared. Good news always sparked the broadest of grins.

'We need to talk to Nandy,' Golding said at once.

'He's gone down to Plymouth. Suss murder in Devonport. Bloke went off the top of a block of flats and Nandy doesn't think he jumped.'

'Houghton?'

'She's in her office.' Suttle put his briefcase down. 'Why?'

'I've been through all those video files. We need to talk.'

Houghton, as ever, was on the phone. Suttle and Golding waited for her to finish. The conversation was evidently private. She ended it with a muttered endearment and then looked up. Houghton was partnered with a lawyer called Jules. She worked in London but they shared a pretty cottage on the outskirts of Tavistock at weekends.

'Well?' Houghton looked from one face to the other.

Suttle briefed her on the material from the

cameras. The pictures from the concert on Saturday evening appeared to confirm important aspects of Neil Moncrieff's alibi, while the GoPro was offering them new insights into his father's private life.

'Tell me about the alibi.'

'He was definitely wearing the kit he turned up in on Sunday morning. Same sweatshirt, jeans, runners. There's no way he could have done that kind of damage and not got blood all over him.'

'So he didn't do it?'

'I can't see how it would have been possible.'

'Right.' Houghton nodded. 'So we're back with Ousmane? Is that what you're telling me?'

'Maybe. Except we have a clothing issue with him as well. Unless he was stark naked, he'd have needed to get rid of whatever he was wearing. So where did it go? Where did he put it?'

Houghton got to her feet and had a stretch. A long afternoon in front of the PC was wrecking her back.

'The council have isolated all the rubbish they collected from the street bins this morning. We've had blokes up at the landfill all morning. Nothing so far.'

Nandy, she said, had ordered a POLSA search of every garden in the immediate vicinity of Moncrieff's house. Tomorrow, in the absence of any result, he'd be extending the search to the paths and hedgerows south of the village.

'What about the river, boss?' This from Golding. 'Stuff the gear in a bin bag, weight it with a rock from the garden, job done.'

Houghton nodded. She'd put a bid in for the force specialist underwater search unit, currently on a job in a reservoir in mid-Devon. With luck they'd be available for tomorrow afternoon and most of Thursday, enough time to search the riverbed within chucking distance of Moncrieff's garden.

Suttle reminded her that seawater destroys DNA. Houghton shrugged. If a bin bag came to light there'd be other ways of tying it to the house. Batch manufacturing numbers. Sales receipts. Tear patterns. Ditto any clothing inside. Evidence like that, carefully marshalled, should be lawyer-proof in court.

'If we find it.'

'Yeah . . . '

Suttle turned to Golding. He'd yet to hear the results of his trawl through the rest of Neil Moncrieff's files.

'Top stuff, skip.' Golding flicked back through his notes. 'By August she's giving him full sex. She even arrives with a condom. He gets the oils first, then a massage, then she does the business. By the end of the hour he's normally asleep.'

Houghton stirred. For once she'd abandoned her PC screen.

'You asked her about all this before? Am I right?'

'Yes, boss.'

'And she denied having sex with him?'

'Yes, boss.'

Houghton wanted to know whether there was a soundtrack on the video files.

Golding nodded. 'That's where it gets really interesting,' he said. 'He treats her like a daughter. He wants to know what's going on in her life. This woman is really clever. She plays him like a fish.'

Houghton wanted to know more.

'Erin is having trouble with her partner. His business is losing money and she's trying to keep him afloat. To make the business fly, she says he needs new premises. The lease is about to run out on the barn he's using at the moment and anywhere else is going to cost a fortune.'

'So she's after money?'

'Yes.'

'Does she ask for it?'

'Yes. She's looking for twenty-five grand in the form of a loan. But here's the really interesting thing. Come September it turns out that Moncrieff has been having a think about his will. He's not been feeling too great lately and he thinks he might be due for another stroke. If it's a big one it might well kill him. So he's thinking about calling his solicitor in.'

'He *says* this? Spells it out?'

'Yeah.' Golding bent to his pad. '*Twenty-five thousand is nothing. If you want to make a business work you've got to put serious capital in. I could do that for you. It would only take a phone call.*' That's September the 8th.'

'Direct quote?'

'Horse's mouth. By the following week he's talked to his solicitor and set the loan in motion.'

'Interest?'

'That isn't clear.'

'How much was he offering?'

'Two hundred and fifty thousand. He's also started asking her about her other plans. Like whether she'll ever have children or not.'

'And what does she say?'

'She says she'd love to. She tells him it's her one big desire in life. She says she dreams of one day having a big family. That's when she stops turning up with a condom.'

'They go bareback?'

'Yeah. And when he can manage it, they do it twice. This is a story that tells itself, boss. The old boy knows he might peg out at any moment. He really fancies this woman. For whatever reason, he's not happy with the kids he's got. And so he ends up with a little fantasy of his own.'

'Her carrying his kid?'

'Exactly. By the end of the month, they're discussing names. Listen to this. September the 24th. *How do you feel about Ross for a boy? I had a friend called Ross. I thought the world of the man.*'

'And she says?'

'*Ross does it for me.*' Golding turned the page. '*What about a girl?*'

'And?'

'Daisy. He likes Daisy. And guess what? So does she.'

'Incredible. This is a soap opera.'

'Wait, boss. It gets better. By 15 November she's convinced she's pregnant. She's missed her period a couple of times and she's feeling like shit in the mornings and she's off to buy a testing kit at Boots. The next time she turns up she's bought the old boy a bottle of Moët. To wet the baby's head.'

'She's pregnant?'

'So she says.'

'But she's still sleeping with her partner?'

'That's what Moncrieff wants to know.'

'And?'

'She says not. She says she's had enough of him. Too controlling. Too volatile. Kicks off at the slightest excuse. No.' Golding grinned. 'Moncrieff's the man. And he loves it.'

'What about the solicitor? You're telling me Moncrieff's changed his will?'

'That isn't clear. He certainly wants to. Has it actually happened? We're trying to check.'

Houghton frowned then glanced across at Suttle. 'But we've no proof this woman's telling the truth,' she said. 'She could be leading him on. It could be a hoax.'

Suttle nodded.

'And if she *is* pregnant, the baby could be her partner's.'

'Sure.'

'But either way, she's trying to make herself rich.'

'Yes, boss. Which leads us to the key question.'

'Which is?' Houghton looked from face to face.

'Easy.' This from Golding. 'What the fuck was the camera doing there in the first place?'

★ ★ ★

228

Minutes later Houghton managed to make contact with Nandy. In her judgement the video evidence warranted a swift return to Middlemoor for *Amber's* SIO. Nandy, still in Plymouth, listened without comment then said he'd be back within a couple of hours. Houghton, putting the phone down, suggested Suttle and Golding take an early supper break.

Suttle had other ideas. By now it was nearly half six. He knew that Scenes of Crime were close to releasing the house by the river, and before that happened he wanted to spend a little time in the place, preferably alone. Lifting the phone, he put his request to the Crime Scene Manager.

'No problem. One of the CSIs still finishing up. I'll make sure he waits for you.'

Suttle drove down to Topsham. The CSI had readied a forensic suit and a spare set of keys. If Suttle could leave the keys with the scene guard when he was through, he'd be grateful. In the meantime, help yourself.

'What are you after?' he added as an afterthought.

It was a good question. Suttle said he didn't know, not exactly, but interviews over the last couple of days had wised him up about just how dysfunctional this family had become, and there were maybe ways in which the house could tell him more.

The CSI seemed to understand.

'The place is spooked,' he said. 'You'd never want to live here.'

You'd never want to live here. Suttle waited

229

for him to leave, then slipped into the suit under the eyes of the uniformed officer acting as scene guard. The front door was still open, and the house lay in darkness beyond. Suttle stepped inside and pulled the door shut behind him. The acrid scent of forensic chemicals hung in the chill air and Suttle stood motionless for a full minute before feeling for the light switch in the hall.

At first he could hear nothing but the mad chatter of dozens of clocks, then, very faint, came the call of a curlew from the mudflats beyond the garden wall. For Suttle the curlew had always been a special bird. Its long liquid burble spoke of solitude, of loss, of something beyond sadness, and Suttle found himself wondering whether Neil felt the same way. Was this the company he kept on long winter nights? The soundtrack to the anguish of his years beside the river? Banged up with a father he hated? Trying to revive a novel the old man had so casually trashed? Plotting video ambushes as some kind of revenge?

Suttle's gloved fingers found the light switch. The life-size carving of a human figure, ebony black, made him jump. He stared at it for a long moment, surprised he hadn't registered it on his first visit. The eyes, crudely carved, seemed to be watching him as he edged slowly past. He spared it a nod and then a smile. *You'd never want to live here.* Too right.

The sheer weight of the old man's past pressed heavily on the house. Across the hall was a flight of stairs. Native masks hung from the panelled walls of the staircase — more eyes, another tap on the shoulder from the African bush — and as Suttle rounded the turn that took him to the first floor he found himself looking at a framed photograph.

It was black and white, the corners creased beneath the glass. A young white officer was standing in front of a line of African troops. He was lean, clad in khaki shorts and a carefully ironed shirt. His feet were planted half a yard apart, his hands were on his hips, and he was eyeing his charges with an air of faint amusement. Even sixty years later there was no mistaking the jut of his chin and the hint of aggression in his stance.

This was Moncrieff in his prime. He owned those men, Suttle thought. Just like he owned the house, and his marriages, and the litter of children — acknowledged and otherwise — he'd doubtless left behind him. Suttle lingered a moment longer, marvelling at the confidence and the sheer self-belief that must have powered this man's journey through life. Up like a rocket, he thought. Down like a stick.

Upstairs the Scenes of Crime team had put yellow Post-it notes on the bedroom doors, each scribbled with a name. Neil's was the first on the left. Suttle stepped in and switched on the light. The room was smaller than he'd expected: a single unmade bed, Ikea bookshelves cluttered with bits of camera gear, a flat-pack wardrobe, a scatter of clothes across the floor and a desk beneath the window. There was a poster for a steam fair Blu-tacked to the wall above the bed;

231

one of the top corners had come adrift. A single cable trailed across the desk, disappearing to a printer on the floor below, and a small pile of post awaited Neil's return. The post, evidently left by one of the SOC team, was the only hint of order in the room. The rest of it could have belonged to a student or a passing dosser, evidence of a life broken into tiny fragments by neglect or bad luck or simple indifference. Even here, Suttle thought, Neil Moncrieff wasn't entirely sure who he was.

Beside the window, hanging on a nail driven into the plaster, was an RSPB calendar. It was at eye level if you were sitting at the desk, and Suttle bent to inspect it. Not much had happened to Neil over the passage of the year, nothing in the way of social engagements that might merit an entry, but then Suttle's interest was attracted to a series of marks. They started in late September with a carefully circled question mark. Three days later, the same pen, the question mark had become a single tick. The ticks recurred every three or four days. By mid-October some entries had earned a double or even treble tick. Then came a single exclamation mark.

Suttle slipped into the chair, still gazing at the grid of December dates, wondering what had been so special about Tuesday the 3rd. Then his eye strayed to the photo above and he smiled. After month after month of lapwings, buzzards, Dartford warblers and November's nightjar, he was looking — of all birds — at a curlew.

Hilary's room was next door, bigger than her

stepbrother's, and the moment Suttle stepped inside he sensed the care she must have taken to make it her own. Sea-green walls. A splash of red duvet on the double bed. A beautiful kelim on the polished wooden floor. Plus a substantial chest of drawers of a size and weight he'd last seen in one of the pricier Topsham antique shops. After the mustiness of the rest of the house, here was a carefully furnished space brightened by a woman's touch, a place of retreat and perhaps solace: somewhere she could truly call her own.

On the bedside table, beside the vase of wilting flowers, was a small framed photograph. Suttle peered at it. Two men were sitting at a table on a cafe terrace. One of them was Rupert Moncrieff, the other someone barely in his twenties. The old man had his arm around his companion, giving him a playful hug, and the grin on his face coupled with the empty carafe at his elbow suggested they'd shared a drink or two.

Suttle stared at the photo for a long moment. Both men were heavily tanned. A palm tree in the background and the blueness of the sea beyond spoke of a Mediterranean setting — Italy perhaps, or maybe Spain — but what really drew Suttle's attention was the hint of family resemblance in the set of the young man's face. He wore his blond hair long, tied at the back with a twist of green ribbon, revealing his face. As well as the old man's bone structure, he seemed to have the same poise, a confidence buried deep in the Moncrieff gene pool, and there was more than a hint of mischief in the warmth of the smile.

It was a lovely shot to have at your bedside, a peal of laughter to launch each new day, and Suttle realised for the first time that there must have been a great deal more to Rupert Moncrieff than either Hilary or Neil had ever let on. How else had this man amassed a fortune? Won countless women's hearts? Ended up in a house like this? Moncrieff had been a control freak, for sure. And he was plainly someone with limited patience for his weaker brethren. But his raw animal magnetism, his sheer appetite for life, was there in the photo, unblunted by his recent stroke, and for the first time Suttle felt a tiny flicker of sympathy for the way he'd met his end.

Suttle took a final glance at the photo, committing the young face to memory, then headed for the door.

10

Billy McTierney invited Lizzie back to his place. They'd spent a couple of hours in the pub, scarcely touching their drinks, and she loved the way he made the invitation so natural. Their conversation had barely started, barely touched the outer reaches of each other's lives. If she could stomach the prospect of grilled sardines and a light salad, it would be his pleasure to make it happen. He also had a bottle of decent white he'd been saving for months. Christmas, he told her with a smile, had come early for once.

He had a house in Copnor, an unlovely suburb a mile or two north of the hospital. Lizzie found herself body-checking around a serious-looking bike in the narrow hall. The kitchen-diner was at the back. Through the rear window Lizzie could see a line of washing.

'It's been raining most of the day,' she said. 'Do you want me to get that lot in?'

He shrugged, said it was up to her. She wasn't here to sort out his domestic life but so what?

Lizzie wrestled the soaking garments off the line. Billy McTierney had a thing about Lee Cooper jeans. Back in the kitchen he was shaking the sardines into a grill pan. He'd already put the wine in the freezer and now he wiped his hands

235

and slipped a CD into the audio stack. The music was irresistibly upbeat. She'd never heard of Caravan Palace.

'You mind if I dance?'

The question seemed to amuse him. *Like I would?*

She cleared herself a tiny space between the sofa and a table brimming with books and began to move with the music, her eyes closed. When the beat picked up on the next track she started to spin, her hands high above her head. She couldn't remember when she'd last felt like this — so buoyant, so pleased with herself, so relaxed. With any other man she'd be infinitely more cautious, aware of the dangers of misread signals. Billy McTierney, on the other hand, she already had down as one of life's accomplices, a fellow spirit with the rare gift of knowing exactly who he was. After an eternity of Friday nights in some bar with Gill or sat in front of the TV with her mum, this felt like party time.

'Dance with me?'

'No.' He shook his head. 'Watching's all I need.'

'Am I that crap?'

'You're lovely.'

He stepped across and kissed her on the lips. Then he held her for a moment, moving sweetly in time with the music.

'That's called dancing.' She put her arms around his neck. 'Who else lives here?'

'No one.'

'Just you?'

'Yes.'

'The whole house?'

'Yes.'

'I don't believe you.'

He led her out of the room. Upstairs there were three bedrooms. He opened each door for no more than a few seconds. The first one was empty: bare boards, no furniture at all. The second was where he slept. In the light from the street outside she glimpsed a tangle of sheets and a duvet. Over the big double bed was a black and white print she seemed to have seen somewhere else, a mass of faces on a beach in high summer, everyone in bathing gear, hundreds of thousands of pale white bodies, not an ounce of fat anywhere.

'Coney Island,' he said. 'Nineteen forty.'

She stepped back into the hall. The third room was smaller than the rest. For the first time he turned on a light. There were huge posters on the wall: mountains, snow, valleys in deep shadow, rags of cloud spooling off the highest peaks. He pointed to them one by one: Piz Badile, the Eiger, the Matterhorn.

'You've done all these? Climbed them?'

'Yes.'

'Alone?'

'No. I had a friend. More than a friend. His name was Jacques. He was French.'

'Was?'

'He died.'

'*Died?*'

'Yes.'

She looked at him a moment, wanting more,

but he shook his head and made for the door. From downstairs came the smell of burning sardines. In the kitchen the air was blue. Lizzie opened the back door and grabbed a cloth, fanning the smoke into the darkness beyond. When most of it had gone, she turned back into the kitchen. McTierney was examining the remains of the charred sardines. He wanted to know what else went with Chablis.

Lizzie closed the door. 'Me.'

★ ★ ★

They drank the bottle, decanted into waxed-paper mugs, in bed. It felt like a picnic, something you'd improvise if the sun was shining and you were in the right mood. He must have done this a thousand times, she told herself, on countless climbs. Maybe a decent bottle to toast a summit. Maybe a cup of something warmer on the way up.

'Tell me more about your friend.'

'Jacques? I met him in the Alps. He had a reputation even then but he was still really young. He'd grown up in the mountains. He treated them like old friends. We did a couple of climbs together and we just knew it worked. My French is shite and his English wasn't much better but that never mattered. You speak another language in the mountains. Or maybe the mountains speak to you.'

'Very profound.' She was running her fingertips along the line of his mouth. He caught her hand and kissed it.

'It's true,' he said. 'The mountains turn you into someone else.'

'Someone better?'

'Someone different. They put you to the test. Pass or fail. That doesn't happen much in real life. Not in any sense that matters.'

Jacques, he said, was heading for stardom. French TV had fallen in love with him and he'd become a poster boy for extreme climbing. He'd featured in a series on France 2, syndicated worldwide, and he'd written a book.

'It got published?'

'Yes.'

The book, he said, had been very Jacques, an exotic mix of climbing diary, technical detail, the odd swipe at this regulatory body or that, plus intermittent helpings of poetry and the kind of hallucinatory metaphysics that can only come with extreme altitude and a dodgy oxygen valve.

'He called it *Vertige*. He thought of the title before he wrote a single word. *Vertige* means vertigo, dizziness. It's what you feel sometimes when you're up beyond the eight-thousand-metre line in the Himalayas and your oxygen isn't working properly. It's like tripping without the acid. You're on the roof of the world and you think you can do anything. Fly. Levitate. Defy gravity. Whatever. It's all out there waiting for you. You feel weightless. It's second cousin to insanity. It's really dangerous. And really nice.'

'*Vertige*?'

'Yes. You become someone else. And when that happens, literally anything seems possible. Not only possible but *right*.'

239

Jacques, he said, had made himself a lot of money with the films and then the book. He'd lived with an Austrian ski champion called Birgitte for a while, but their relationship hadn't survived the demands of their separate passions and by the time Billy came along he was rich and single.

'We went everywhere together. After a tough climb we'd take time out on the beach. Guadeloupe was a favourite. We were really close. We were like brothers. *Frère Jacques.* Nice, eh?'

'You make it sound like a love affair.'

'It was. That's exactly what it was. I knew every inch of that man's body, and he mine. No secrets. We made each other very happy.' He paused. 'This house really belongs to him. It was his money that bought it. *Chez Jacques.*' He grinned at her. 'Should I really be telling you this?'

'I'm glad you are.'

'Why?'

'I don't know. Curiosity? Admiration? Some people have it. Just a tiny handful.'

'Have what?'

Good question. Lizzie gulped the last of her wine and then rolled on top of him. Her face was very close to his. His eyes glistened with the wine. She felt him beginning to stir beneath her. Second cousin to insanity, she thought. What a perfect description.

'*Vertige,*' she murmured. 'And you've got it in spades.'

★ ★ ★

240

Nandy was at Middlemoor by eight o'clock. Carole Houghton showed him a sample file from the bedroom coverage on Neil Moncrieff's camera. Nandy watched it for less than a minute, listened to her account of the conversations between Erin and the old man and then summoned *Amber*'s key players to an impromptu conference.

The Crime Scene Manager, stuck in a late traffic jam en route home, performed a neat U-turn and sped back to Middlemoor. A uniformed sergeant from the Tactical Aid Group was there in case of forced entry. As was the FLO, Wendy Atkins, and the adviser charged with framing an interview strategy. Golding was perched on a desk in the Incident Room, and Suttle, newly returned from Topsham, was the last to arrive. Operation *Amber* was at last gathering speed.

Nandy wanted to know where Erin and her partner lived. Golding glanced at his notes and supplied an address in Woodbury, a rented ex-council house on an estate on the northern edge of the village. As far as he knew there was no one else in the property though he'd noticed a dog bowl and tins of Chum in the Portakabin she used as business premises.

Nandy was looking at the uniformed sergeant from the TAG. He wanted Erin and Tim Stone arrested at 06.00 tomorrow morning. He also wanted the business premises secured on the farm, both the Portakabin and the barn Stone used as a workshop. He needed a POLSA team standing by at first light for a full search of the

241

surrounding area, plus Scenes of Crimes operations at both addresses.

'What are we after, sir?' This from the CSM.

'Bloodstained clothing. Ashes. A bin bag. Whatever.'

He turned to the interview adviser. After arrest Erin and her partner should be taken to separate police stations. He wanted two interview teams briefed and standing by. After the booking-in procedures and a meet with their lawyers, Erin and Stone should be ready for interview by late morning. On no account did he want early disclosure of the content of the video files. The first session would establish whether or not Erin was sticking to the story she'd told Suttle and Golding. If she was still insisting that her dealings with Moncrieff never went beyond therapeutic massage, the woman would be in deep shit.

'What about Stone, sir?' This from Suttle. 'Are we assuming he was in the know?'

'We're assuming nothing. It might be a conspiracy. They might still be sleeping together. She might be pregnant. It might be his baby. It might be Moncrieff's. And by this time tomorrow — ' he offered Suttle a thin smile ' — we might be a whole lot wiser.'

Suttle nodded. He still needed to contact the family solicitor to check out the situation on Moncrieff's will.

'Chase that, Jimmy. Quick-time, yeah?'

'Yes, sir.'

Nandy returned to the CSM. He wanted a separate operation at Roz McIntyre's flat in

Exmouth. Evidence of bloodstained clothing again, plus the ZBook laptop Neil Moncrieff claimed to have lost. He'd been deleting evidence. His account of Erin's dealings with his father was far from complete. Why had he withheld the truth about what went on in the bedroom? Why hadn't he pointed the finger at Erin? And Stone? The answers to all these questions, in Nandy's view, might well lie in the laptop. Recovery of the ZBook was now a top priority.

Suttle caught his eye. He'd been thinking about the money Neil would have needed for the laptop and the cameras.

'The old man was hiding his money away, sir. Neil would have known that. He'd have seen it happening on the video.'

'You're suggesting he helped himself?'

'Yeah, I am. The old boy's memory wasn't what it was. Who says he'd miss a grand or two?'

Nandy nodded, said nothing.

The FLO had raised a hand. 'You're arresting Neil Moncrieff, sir?'

'Yes.'

'What about Roz? The girlfriend?'

'No. Not at this point.'

Nandy was looking at Carole Houghton. He wanted to know the status of the multiple phone billings they'd requested.

'Should be here tomorrow, sir. Vodafone and Orange.'

'What time?'

'I've asked for midday latest. They're normally pretty helpful.'

Nandy had paused for breath. Carole Houghton quickly tallied the actions she needed sorting at once. When she got to the end of the list, it was Luke Golding's hand that went up.

'So where is Ousmane in all this?' he asked. 'Our African friend?'

★ ★ ★

The same question bothered Suttle on his drive home. By now it was nearly half past ten and pouring with rain. He'd stayed in the Incident Room for a while to bring the interview adviser up to speed before he conferenced with Nandy and Houghton to frame a strategy for tomorrow's interviews. He knew already that he and Golding would be talking to Erin, a gesture of thanks from Nandy for disinterring the video files from the bedroom, but he was starting to wonder about the real extent of the woman's involvement.

He could understand her bid to get her hands on the family's money. But had that clever piece of hands-on manipulation really extended to murder? The more he thought about the proposition, the less he was inclined to believe it. Ousmane's presence in the house and the circumstances of his sudden disappearance still had to be the key to *Amber*'s door. Either that, or they were looking at a coincidence beyond rational belief. The thought made him smile. Nothing warmed him more quickly than a complex investigation with a million possible outcomes. Life, as he knew only too well, could take you by surprise.

Suttle parked his Impreza behind the flats and made his way upstairs. After the clamour and excitement of the last couple of hours, there was something infinitely depressing in coming home. He'd kept the squirly carpet and the battered chintz because he was no more than a squatter in this flat. In his heart he knew it still belonged to the previous tenant, the old lady who'd died. This was still her place — her decor, her wallpaper, her crap lighting, even her smell — and the knowledge that he was only a passer-by was oddly comforting. He loved the view in the morning, and the light that poured in through the big bay windows, but he could ghost himself out of here at half a day's notice and the world would barely know he'd gone. No ties, he thought. Not a single hint of commitment.

That was fine. But there came moments, like now, when it would have been nice to walk into a hug and a conversation and the offer of a glass of wine. He'd never been a solitary. He'd always had mates and girlfriends, people he could rely on, people who'd make him laugh. Meeting Lizzie had been an extension of that, and back in Pompey, before Grace had arrived, they'd had a brilliant time. Then he'd left the city and gone west for the new job and everything had fallen apart. Hiding away in the depths of rural Devon had never been a career move Lizzie had anticipated and on reflection Suttle blamed himself for not realising how deeply it had wounded her. Everything that had happened thereafter was enough to bring most marriages

245

to an end, but happily they'd started to repair the damage. Then, back in August, the lights went out again. This time for good.

He settled at the table in the bay window, staring out at the dark. He'd collected the morning's post from the mat beneath the front door, and he went through it. Bills, more bills, begging letters from a couple of charities, dross. He shook his head, pushing the post to one side, and he was about to sort himself a can of Stella from the fridge when his phone rang. It was Oona.

'You're home?' she said.

'I am.'

'So where's my fucking man?'

'No idea. Are you checking up?'

'Of course I am. A girl takes nothing for granted.' To Suttle's surprise, she wasn't laughing. 'We're talking unfinished business, by the way.'

'What does that mean?'

'Look out of the window.'

Suttle got to his feet. Apart from the street lights, all he could see was rain.

'What am I after?'

'A Ford Capri. It's white. You're into all that classic car shit. You can't miss it.'

Suttle grinned to himself. This woman never failed to cheer him up. The Ford Capri was a car from his youth: long bonnet, sleek styling, big engine, dodgy on sharp bends. His brother had owned one.

'Got it.' The Capri was parked across the road.

'There's yer woman inside. She's been there a

while, asked me to give you a ring.'

'Yer woman?'

'Nicinha. The goddess from last night.'

'And what does she want?'

'You, my sweet boy.' A mirthless bark of laughter. 'You're supposed to be a detective, remember?'

Suttle stood in the window for a long moment, staring down. He'd been meaning to phone Nicinha all day but hadn't got her number. Her contact details would have been on the system but events had got the better of him. He needed to apologise for what had happened at the restaurant. This unexpected visit might save him the call.

He went downstairs and crossed the road. Nicinha was sitting behind the wheel of the Capri. She wound down the window, looked up. 'I hope you don't mind,' she said. 'I got your friend to ring, just in case.'

'No problem. You want to come up?'

'Yes, please. This won't take long, I promise you.'

Suttle stared at her, then shrugged. He led the way back to the flat. She stood in the living room, gazing around.

'This is your mum's place? Your granny?'

'It's mine. You want a drink?'

She asked for water. By the time Suttle was back with the glass, and a tinny for himself, she was standing in the bay window.

Suttle wanted to know about the car. She said it belonged to her new partner. He was a pastor at a Pentecostal church in Bristol. He also played the drums in a rock group recently featured on the local community radio station.

'You sing with this band?'

'No.' She was still looking around. 'It's not my kind of music.' She crossed the room and inspected one of the pictures on the wall. The drawing, in crayon, was crude enough to have been done by a child. A big yellow sun. Cartoon seagulls. A donkey on a beach. Splashy blue waves.

'Your daughter did this? Grace?'

'No. I don't know who did it. It belonged to the previous tenant.'

She nodded. She thought it was nice. She said it brought colour to the flat. And warmth.

'You're happy here?'

'As happy as I'd be anywhere else.'

'You get lonely?'

'Sometimes, yes.'

She nodded, said nothing. She was carrying a black leather shoulder bag. She looked at the table then asked whether Suttle minded if she lit a candle.

'Not at all. Go ahead.'

She had the candle in the bag. It was red, already much used, the wax beginning to curl in towards the wick. She found a box of matches and asked for a saucer. Suttle fetched one from the kitchen. She put the candle on the saucer and then placed it on the table in the bay window. The candle lit, the room began to smell of something pungent, something a world away from a wet night in Exmouth. Watching, Suttle thought immediately of Ousmane.

Nicinha had switched the lights off. As she returned to the table, her body threw a long flickering shadow over the patterned carpet.

'Come,' she said. 'Sit down.'

She'd arranged two chairs side by side. Suttle did her bidding. From the depths of the bag she produced a carefully folded square of black cloth. She spread it on the table and then her hand was back in the bag. This time Suttle found himself looking at a much smaller pouch, brown leather, tied with a drawstring. The leather was scuffed. It looked much travelled, and when she put the pouch on the table there was a *clunk-clunk* from inside. Dice? Scrabble letters?

'Give me your hand,' she said.

'What is this?' Suttle didn't move.

'I want to help you. It's nothing bad. I promise.'

'Help me how?'

'Help you with your future. Help you understand.'

He gazed at her for a moment. The candlelight was dancing in her eyes. Only last night he'd remembered a detail from the first long interview he'd done with her in the Torquay interview room. In Angola she'd learned how to commune with the spirits, how to tell fortunes. She'd brought this gift to England along with the handful of possessions she'd managed to stuff into a single suitcase, and it had given her the beginnings of a living.

Suttle wasn't sure he believed in fortune-tellers but just now he didn't much care. Better the company of this woman, he thought, than the rest of the evening staring at the walls.

'Your hand?'

This time he offered it. The touch of her flesh felt warm. She gave his hand the lightest squeeze, as if in reassurance.

'Now close your eyes.'

Suttle did what he was told. Then came her voice, the same voice he'd heard in the Phoenix last night, soaring, plaintive, intoning the same phrase time and again. He tried to make sense of it, tried to pick out the words, but it was a language he'd never heard in his life. He tried to relax, telling himself that this strange encounter might help loosen the knots inside himself, that this woman might indeed be in tune with the spirits. Lately, after refusing Houghton's offer of therapeutic counselling, he'd been wondering about some kind of alternative therapy. Maybe this was it.

The chanting came to an end. Then Nicinha released his hand and he heard a rattling and the fall of something onto the table.

'Open your eyes.'

Suttle did her bidding. Tiny pebbles were scattered on the square of black cloth. They were polished. They looked like ivory. Nicinha was studying them with intense concentration. Then she spread her open hands above them, palms down, as if seeking warmth on a cold night. She moved her hands around and then the chant returned, a different key this time, less sad, less uncertain. Finally she relaxed back in the chair.

'The spirits have spoken,' she said.

Suttle stared at her. He wanted to know what

these objects were and what they'd told her.

'These are knuckle bones,' she said. 'They come from children in the forest. Children the spirits have taken away.'

'They're yours?'

'Yes.'

'You've had them a long time?'

'For ever. When I die they'll come with me.'

'Where to?'

'Back to the forest. To the spirits.' She was smiling now. 'It's true, but you don't have to believe me. Belief isn't necessary.'

'Necessary for what?'

'For the bones to be true.'

'So what do they say? What are they telling you?' He was gazing down at the bones. The pattern looked random, like stars in the night sky. He hadn't the least idea what any of this stuff meant.

'There will be another child in your life,' she said. 'A little baby. A girl. And a woman too.'

'The baby belongs to the woman?'

'No. But you already know this woman.'

'I do?'

'Yes. And it will be difficult. It will be hard for you. And hard for everyone. But just say yes to her, do what she wants, don't be frightened, don't think what you're doing is wrong. It isn't wrong. It won't be wrong. And one day you'll be glad.'

'This is something permanent? Like long term?'

'No. But something very important. You have to give something of yourself to her. You have to make *room*.'

251

She gathered the bones together and dropped them back into the leather bag. She tied the drawstring with a double knot and emptied her glass. The visit seemed to be over. Job done.

'You're going home now? Back to Bristol?'

'Yes. You can always phone if you need me again.'

She scribbled a number on one of the envelopes Suttle had left on the table. She might have been a visiting nurse, Suttle thought, an itinerant professional with a stack of calls to fill her busy life.

Nicinha got to her feet. He didn't quite know what to say. Thank you seemed somehow inadequate. He walked her through to the front door, then remembered the candle.

'Keep it,' she said. 'Light it again when the woman comes.'

'When will that be?'

'When the spirits wish it.'

'And does this woman have a name?'

She studied him for a moment, then extended a hand. Suttle shook it.

'Well?' he asked.

'You'll know her when she comes.' She was smiling now. 'Just let it happen.'

Just let it happen. Suttle watched her from the window as she crossed the road. The Capri had a dodgy starter motor. At last the engine turned and caught, and she disappeared in a cloud of blue exhaust.

Just let it happen. Suttle emptied the can of Stella, thought about another and decided against it. He needed something to eat.

Tomorrow, at the very least, deserved a clear head.

He was stirring the pasta when he heard the knock at the door. By now, against his better judgement, he'd decided that Nicinha was well intentioned but full of bullshit. She'd felt sorry for him. She'd watched the reports on TV, read the papers, tried to put herself in his shoes. She'd never met Lizzie and she'd doubtless felt deeply for her as well, but her real connection had been with the Detective Sergeant who'd given her a decent hearing in the interview room back last year. It was, Suttle decided, a debt of gratitude repaid in full. And for that he was thankful. Nice woman. Nice gesture. Nice candle too.

He turned the gas down and went to the door. It was Tadeusz, the big Pole from upstairs. He looked wrecked and for a moment Suttle thought he might have been drinking.

'My friend — ' Tadeusz extended a meaty hand ' — I must thank you.'

'For what?'

'This morning.' He jerked his head towards the flat above. 'You were right. It was a big fall. Too big.'

Klaudia, he said, had gone to work as usual. She worked in the convenience store down the road. Mid-morning she'd felt terrible pains. Her boss, the man who owned the store, had phoned for an ambulance. Less than an hour later she gave birth in A & E.

'You're telling me she's OK?' Suttle was staring at him. 'Klaudia?'

'She's fine.'

'And the baby?'

'Six weeks early. But the doctors say she'll be OK too.' He crossed his fingers. 'We hope, yes?'

'Sure.' Suttle felt the first prickle of something close to shock. 'And the baby? A boy or a girl?'

Tadeusz was grinning now. 'A girl. And beautiful.'

11

Erin Maguire and Tim Stone were arrested at ten minutes past six in the morning. Erin was taken to Heavitree police station while Stone was booked in at the Torquay custody suite. Their Alsatian, who'd done his best to delay the arrests, was collected by the dog-handling team and shipped across to the RSPCA. The dog's name was Zipper, which seemed to amuse Luke Golding.

Half an hour later Neil Moncrieff was also arrested. According to the FLO, who was present when Moncrieff opened the door, he seemed less than surprised. When Roz asked whether she could come with him to wherever he was going, Wendy Atkins said no. Scenes of Crime were about to search her flat and garden. The search would take most of the day. Should she sort out somewhere for Roz and the Labrador to stay, or did she have a particular friend who might be able to help out?

Scenes of Crime searches began the moment the suspects had vacated their properties. Nandy was eager to have as much as possible to use once the interviews started. The video files from Moncrieff's GoPro were an undoubted windfall but there might be more to come. Bloodied clothing would have been a

255

clincher. As might Moncrieff's laptop.

By late morning the search teams had been through the obvious hiding places inside both properties and drawn a blank. They'd yet to make a start on the farm where Stone had his workshop but the Crime Scene Manager wasn't holding his breath. In a text to Carole Houghton he asked her to press Nandy for reinforcements. Another couple of CSIs, he said, would make all the difference. Houghton, who was only too aware of the force-wide demands on ever-decreasing resources, texted him back: 'No breath left to hold. We'll do our best.'

Suttle was sitting in the Incident Room, waiting for the summons to Heavitree nick. Erin had asked for the duty brief, a much-married woman from a criminal practice with a great deal of experience. Her name was Helen Doherty and Suttle knew she'd pull every trick in the book to make the coming hours as difficult as possible.

He was telling Golding about Nicinha's visit — what had happened when she threw the bones and consulted the spirits. The bit about the baby, he said, was especially spooky. Within less than an hour it seemed to have come true.

'What else did she say?'

'She said I was on for a nice surprise. Some woman or other was coming my way. Nothing specific but we live in hope. At the time I thought she was being kind. Now I'm not so sure.'

'Did she give you a name? Any clues?'

'Nothing. Except I'd know her.'

'Might be the wife then.'

'Lizzie?' He shook his head. 'I doubt it.'

★   ★   ★

Lizzie made a late breakfast. She'd no idea how Billy McTierney could suddenly take most of the morning off but she wasn't complaining. He was upstairs on the phone. By the time he came down, he had names and a number for her in Leeds. These were colleagues in the local mental health services he'd talked to in the aftermath of Grace's death. Like Lizzie, he'd made it his business to try and understand exactly where the life she'd led in Leeds had taken her.

'The key woman is Ellie Constanz. She probably had more to do with Claire than anyone else up there. She's a psychiatrist, and fingers crossed she'll be happy to talk to you.'

'Why don't you just tell me yourself?'

'Because you need to tease this stuff out face to face. You're bloody good at it and I should know. You'll probably find out more than I ever did.' He was reaching for his anorak. 'Good luck, eh?'

Lizzie stared up at him. After the last twelve hours this felt hopelessly abrupt.

'Are you married by any chance?'

'Christ, no.'

'Partnered?'

'No.'

'So do we ever get to meet again?' she asked. 'Or is that it?'

He studied her a moment, amused by the questions, then looked around for his car keys.

'Give me a ring tonight,' he said. 'Tell me how you got on.'

★ ★ ★

The interview with Erin Maguire began at 11.56. Limited disclosure to her lawyer, Helen Doherty, had simply established that further enquiries had led investigating officers to question the veracity of the statement she'd earlier given to Suttle and Golding. Suttle suspected that this would prompt Doherty to advise her client to go No Comment. Resting her case strictly on the facts she'd previously disclosed might limit further damage.

Erin was wearing the clothes she'd plucked from the bedroom floor during the dawn arrest: jeans, plus a scarlet fleece over an I LOVE GOA T-shirt. Given the circumstances, she looked remarkably perky. According to the turnkey in the custody suite, she'd devoured microwaved scrambled eggs on a white bap and two slices of toast. There was a part of her, thought Suttle, that might even be enjoying this. More attention. Another chance to be centre stage, hogging the spotlight.

Golding was running through her earlier version of events. She'd been seeing Moncrieff on a regular basis for more than six months. She'd been recommended by a mutual friend. She'd assessed Moncrieff as someone who could benefit from regular massage. After his stroke, she'd said, he had problems with the right side of his body, a lack of coordination she might be able to ease. She'd paid him regular visits, sometimes as many as three times a week. Each session lasted approximately one hour, and for this she charged him eighty or ninety pounds.

Each of these checks drew a nod from Erin. Initially she'd said, 'No comment,' but the phrase was no more than a gesture to her lawyer. What she really meant was yes.

Suttle took over. He wanted to explore the issue of the cheques she'd cashed on Moncrieff's account. A review of Neil's video files had confirmed that each session began with an exchange of notes. Moncrieff had often written her cheques for sums in excess of a thousand pounds, and Erin would perch on the side of the bed, extract her fee and count out the rest. Moncrieff would gather up the notes and put them under his pillow. After her departure he'd fold the notes, secure them with an elastic band and secrete them in a variety of hiding places. SOC had since revisited the bedroom to double-check these places. No notes.

Suttle wanted to know whether Moncrieff had ever offered her loans of any kind. Erin's gaze sought out her lawyer. The answer was plainly yes but Erin did her bidding.

'No comment.'

'Did you take advantage of these offers?'

'No comment.'

'Did the loans ever happen?'

'No comment.'

'Did Mr Moncrieff demonstrate any kind of interest in your private life?'

'No comment.'

'Did you ever tell him about financial problems your partner might have been having?'

'No comment.'

The drumbeat of responses went on and on. Erin was getting visibly anxious, stiffening in her chair as the questions piled up around her, sensing that something deeply unwelcome must have prompted this kind of detail. Finally it was Luke Golding who took the crowbar to her defence.

'You told us your services with respect to Mr Moncrieff never went as far as sex.'

'That's right.'

'Because he was impotent. Because he couldn't get an erection.'

'That's true.'

'Did you have any sexual contact with him at all?'

'Never. He was eighty-something. You wouldn't.'

Her lawyer shot Erin a look. Her fingers drummed on the table. She, like her client, recognised the baiting of the trap. When all else fails, go No Comment. Never respond. Never deny. Never affirm. Rarely fails.

Golding stopped the recording and left the room with Suttle to confer with the adviser monitoring the interview. Earlier the adviser had selected the most graphic of the video files and copied it to a laptop. It was November and Erin had arrived with the news that she was definitely pregnant. Moncrieff celebrated by asking her for a blow job. She complied with a smile and had afterwards confirmed that no way could the baby be her partner's. This news had put an even bigger smile on Moncrieff's face. Another conquest. Another chance to put himself at the head of the pecking order. Watching the pictures, Suttle thought of a phrase Neil had used only days ago: *He wanted to hurt me. Because that's the kind of animal he was.*

Returning to the interview room, Suttle lowered the blinds, stationed the laptop on the table, restarted the recording and announced the second session. Erin had frozen. She couldn't take her eyes off the laptop. Her lawyer sat silently beside her.

Golding hit the Play button and the screen came to life. A roll of fifty-pound notes was already lying on the pillow. Moncrieff counted the money while Erin fiddled with the thermostat on the radiator and then stripped to her thong before hopping onto the bed and straddling his belly. She leaned forward, kissing him on the lips, her breasts settling lightly on his chest.

'You want to hear my news,' she murmured, 'before we get going?'

Erin sat back in the interview room. She said she didn't want to see any more. What was coming next had happened barely three weeks ago. She'd remember every last detail.

'You want to know what happened? What really went down?'

Golding was looking at her lawyer. This was a woman who recognised a nightmare when she saw one. She asked for a break.

Erin shook her head. 'I don't want a break. I want to tell you how it really was.'

261

The lawyer shrugged and pulled her pad towards her. The best she could do under the circumstances was keep a tally of the damage.

Moncrieff, said Erin, had come on to her during one of the early sessions. It happened a lot in her business, especially with older men. They watched way too much porn and got carried away.

Neither Suttle nor Golding moved a muscle. Then Suttle gestured for her to carry on.

'He wanted sex. He was very blatant about it. He'd pay me extra. He'd pay me whatever I normally charged. I thought that was a bit of an insult. Who the fuck did he think I was?'

On that occasion she'd said no. Golding nodded. It happened to be true. But then came more persistent attempts on Moncrieff's part. She was a woman of the world. She had a lovely body. There were ways he could make the experience unforgettable. And so she complied.

The faintest nod from Golding told Suttle this was also true. Ninety quid a session, she said, became two hundred and fifty. He wasn't very demanding and she insisted he wore a condom, and — to be frank — there seemed no harm in it. The old man was nearing the end of his life and it was her pleasure to make that journey all the sweeter. Then had come the offer of money for her partner's business, a capital sum to set him up properly, and after discussing it with Tim she'd said yes.

Suttle wanted to know whether this was to be a loan.

'Yes. We'd pay it back when we could.'

'No time limit?'

'Not that we discussed.'

'Interest?'

'We didn't discuss that either.'

'And the sum involved?'

'Two hundred and fifty thousand pounds.'

Another nod from Golding. So far she was keeping to the script of the movies he'd watched.

'So did you ever get this money? Was it paid over?'

'No. He had to put it all through his solicitor. We never saw a penny.'

'Why was that?'

'I don't know. These things always take a while. Whenever I asked, he always said it would happen in the end. We just had to be patient.'

Suttle made himself a note. He wanted to know about Tim. Had her partner been curious about all this money Moncrieff was suddenly trying to lavish on them?

For the first time Erin laughed.

'Did he ask me whether I was shagging the guy?'

'Yes.'

'Of course he did.' She nodded. 'It was the first thing that came into his little head.'

'And?'

'I said I wasn't.'

'Did he believe you?'

'I don't know. He might have done.'

'Was he pissed off?'

'He's always pissed off. It was hard to tell.'

'Is he jealous about you? In general?'

'Very. Another bloke even looks at me,

sometimes Tim just loses it.'

'Was that why you denied having sex with Moncrieff?'

'Yes.'

'So he kept an eye on you?'

'Always. Still does. That's why the baby thing was always so important. Tim wanted a baby. He thought being a mother would lock me up.'

'So you were trying?'

'Yeah.'

'And nothing happened?'

'No.' She looked from one face to the other. 'And do you want to know why?'

Suttle nodded. She was leaning forward now, her hands plaited over the table. Tim, she said, had taken some tests. He had a very low sperm count. Pregnancy, according to the specialist at the hospital, was very unlikely.

'He was gutted. You can imagine. News like that just did it for Tim. He stopped talking to me for weeks on end. Like it was my fault.'

'But he still wanted a baby?'

'Yeah, I think he did. Yeah, definitely. He wanted me in the house, like a good little mum.'

'And you?'

'I thought it was a neat idea.' She paused. 'Especially because it wouldn't be Tim's.'

'You didn't want his baby?'

'I wasn't sure I wanted him.'

'So what did you do?'

'I started finding out about donor sperm. There are lots of ways you can do stuff like this, but the paperwork is beyond belief. Then it occurred to me there was a much easier answer.'

'Moncrieff?'

'Yes. Here was a rich old guy always telling me how horny he was, how many kids he'd had — '

'In wedlock? Kids he acknowledged?' This from Golding.

'Three from his marriages. And loads of others, African kids mostly, little half-castes he left behind him. The way he told it, half of Kenya was down to him. He was really proud of himself. Mr Super Sperm. That was when I started thinking about having his baby.'

Moncrieff, she said, thought it was a wonderful idea. Suttle wanted to know why.

'I don't think he liked his own kids much, especially not the ones he lived with. The woman, Hilary, was too prim. The son, Neil, was a weed. There's another one, Olly, he liked a lot more, but he was out in Africa so he didn't count, really. Then he had a grandchild, Hilary's boy Kennan.'

Kennan, she said, was Moncrieff's favourite. He said he had guts. He loved the music he played. He used to send him money, out in Spain, where he was trying to make it with his songs.

'Kennan was the one,' she said. 'Kennan was a bit of a wild child. He didn't want anything to do with his mum or dad. When their marriage broke down he was just coming out of university so he went abroad. Moncrieff didn't blame him. He thought it was a great decision. He wanted another little Kennan.'

Golding was about to ask another question, but Suttle put a hand on his arm. This was the

265

figure at the café table, he was sure of it. This was the grin at Hilary's bedside.

'Did you ever see a photo of this lad?'

'Yes. Mr Moncrieff had loads on his smartphone.'

'Describe him.'

'Moncrieff?'

'Kennan.'

Erin laughed and then apologised. Kennan, she said, was a hippy — long blond hair, twist of ribbon, good eyes.

'And he's living in Spain?'

'Yes.'

'Whereabouts?'

'A place called Bedar. He showed me pictures of that too. I haven't a clue where it is but Mr Moncrieff had a house near there, a bit inland, up in the mountains. That's where Kennan lives. Even now.'

'And money? He earns a living, this boy?'

'Bits and pieces, the way Mr Moncrieff told it. Cheap airport runs for the expats. Bit of gardening. Plus whatever he can scrape from the music. But without Mr Moncrieff's money, I don't think he'd make it.' She smiled. 'He wanted me to go out there and meet him. He said we'd really get on. I think he saw me as a prospect.'

'Another baby?'

'Whatever.' She shrugged. 'This Kennan sounded a nice boy.'

'And Tim? Was he part of this invitation?'

'No way. I don't think Mr Moncrieff had much time for Tim.'

'Competition?'

'Hardly. Tim's a loser. And he can be crazy too. Deep down I've always thought he had one of those borderline mental things. Bipolar? Schizophrenic? God knows.'

'Right.' Suttle nodded, glancing quickly through his notes, trying to tease a story from the jottings. 'So Tim never knew about you and Moncrieff trying to make babies? Is that what you're telling us?'

'Yeah.' She nodded. 'Until last week. Then he went bonkers. Nuts. Came storming across. I had a client in my little Portakabin. He just kicked the door open and barged in. It was really embarrassing.'

'What was the problem?'

'He wouldn't say. Not exactly. I'd just come back from the ashram. I felt really spaced, really floaty, and it wasn't just jet lag. I'd been in touch with myself, really in touch, and there he was mouthing off about what a whore I was. He said he wanted to kill me. And he said it would be my fault.'

'*Kill* you?'

'Yes. Nice, eh?'

'So what did you say?'

'I told him to shut it. Then I pushed him outside and told him to fuck off. I'd had enough. If he was going to treat me like that then he could find someone else to disappoint.'

'What did you mean?'

'In bed. Any-fucking-where.'

'You *said* that?'

'I did, yeah. I've got a temper too, when it matters.'

Suttle sat back and pushed his pad away. He was wondering about another break to take stock but knew they had to keep pushing while the door was still open.

'Did you talk about it afterwards? Later in the day?'

'No, he disappeared. I haven't a clue where he went and to be honest I didn't really look very hard. I didn't need another conversation like that, no way.'

'And what day was this? Exactly?'

'Saturday.'

'So what do you think triggered all this?'

'I don't know.' Her eyes strayed back to the laptop. 'Maybe he saw that.'

★ ★ ★

Suttle called the break. Nandy answered on the first ring. Suttle outlined the interview to date. He needed an update from the Crime Scene Manager out at Woodbury. He should be looking for a laptop or a PC or maybe an iPad. Anything that would support the video files from Moncrieff's bedroom. Nandy asked why. Suttle explained.

'She didn't go No Comment, then?'

'No, sir. She went off-piste. Big time.'

'Well done, son.'

Nandy was on another phone now. Suttle could hear him trying to raise the CSM on the landline. Then came a muttered conversation before Nandy was back on the mobile. The CSM had already seized a PC and an iPad.

'What was the date again?'

'Saturday, sir. The morning of the 7th. Or maybe some time the previous day.'

'Right. He'll take a look now. I'll call you back.'

Suttle grinned. He wanted to know how it was going with Tim Stone over in Torquay.

'No Comment.' A bark of laughter from Nandy. 'Early days though, eh?'

Ten minutes later Suttle's mobile rang. Nandy again.

'Three separate video files from the bedroom,' he said, 'and we're talking graphic.'

'This is on the partner's laptop? Tim Stone?'

'Yes. They came as email attachments.'

'So who sent them?'

'We're working on that. For my money it has to be Neil Moncrieff, but we need to nail it down. You'll be the first to know, son.'

* * *

Suttle moved the interview on to Saturday night. In her first statement Erin had been suffering from jet lag. She'd spent the night tucked up with Tim Stone.

'So when did you get back from India? Exactly?'

Erin looked at her brief. Helen Doherty muttered something in her ear. This stuff could be checked. Might as well tell him.

'Friday. The flight landed early in the morning. I got a coach down. By Saturday night I was still knackered.'

'You said you slept with Tim that night.'

'I did, yes.'

'Is that true?'

Erin glanced at her brief again. Doherty shook her head.

'No comment,' Erin said.

'But you probably didn't. Not after a scene like that. In the Portakabin.'

'No comment.'

'So where *did* you sleep?'

'No comment.'

'And where did Tim sleep?'

Erin was about to stonewall again but something held her back. Instead she looked Suttle in the eye. 'I haven't a clue.'

12

Suttle and Golding snatched a sandwich lunch in the Incident Room at Middlemoor. By now word had come from the Crime Scene Manager out at Woodbury that — in all probability — the bedroom movies had been sent from Neil Moncrieff's laptop. According to documents recovered in the search of his bedroom in the house by the river, he had two email accounts, but the vids had come from Mallard@btinternet.com, an address which was definitely registered to Neil Moncrieff.

'So what does that tell us, son?' Nandy was in an expansive mood, sprawled in a chair by the window examining the contents of a beef salad wrap. Suttle sensed that some of the pressure was off.

'Dunno, sir. Obviously Neil knew Moncrieff was screwing his masseuse. He must have picked up about the money, the loan, the little extras he was bunging her. Then comes the news she's pregnant, or *says* she's pregnant. If you're looking to inherit, and the old man's none too well, this would be a wake-up call.'

'To do what?'

'To stir a little action from Mr Jealous.'

Golding agreed. Neil Moncrieff would have pinged the video files to Stone in the hope that

271

he'd pay the old man a visit. A guy three times his age had been banging his lovely partner. Not just that but she'd fallen pregnant in a flash.

'Imagine you're Stone,' he said. 'You've seen the vid, you know what she's up to, you might even know she's starting to feel evil in the mornings. This is a violent guy. We can evidence that. So off he goes down to Topsham to settle an account or two.'

Nandy nodded. He'd asked Suttle to get Erin's consent to a second pregnancy test and Houghton had a police doctor standing by for mid-afternoon. Now he wanted to know how Stone might have got into the house.

'He either knocked at the door or went in through the back entrance in the garage,' Golding said. 'Erin would know the combination. Bound to.'

'And tell him?'

'More than possible. For my money, sir, she's still lying about the Saturday night. It would suit her very nicely to have both these guys out of her life. Now she's screwed his alibi he's got a lot of questions to answer.'

Nandy nodded. Tim Stone was still steadfastly going No Comment and — unlike his partner — showed no inclination to help. The Scenes of Crime team at the Woodbury farm had collected samples of his DNA and were busy sorting out possible matches from material collected at the house by the river. Suttle had phoned Hilary and asked her whether to her knowledge Tim Stone had ever paid the house a visit, but she seemed pretty certain that the answer was no. Any DNA match, therefore, would be a clincher.

Suttle stirred. He wanted to know about Neil Moncrieff. That interview was being conducted in another of the Heavitree suites and had started late. So far, according to the adviser, the interviewing team was concentrating on Ousmane's relationship with his father and on Neil's movements on Saturday night and Sunday morning. They were saving the deleted video files for a second session in the afternoon.

'Is he still saying he slept on the sofa that night? All by himself?'

'Yes.' Nandy nodded. 'He insists they hadn't started sleeping together. That came the following night when he moved in properly.'

'Neat.'

'Exactly.'

'What about neighbours?' Suttle was looking at Carole Houghton.

'The two girls upstairs were dead to the world. They say they didn't get up until midday. One of the houses next door is empty. The other one belongs to a builder and his missus. They sleep in as well.'

'The houses behind? The houses across the road?'

'We're knocking on doors as we speak, sir. Four PCs from Exmouth. Neil's bike was in the back garden. There's access to the road at the rear of these properties. Someone may have seen something. People walk their dogs first thing around there. Even in the dark.'

Suttle nodded. If Neil Moncrieff had left much earlier than he'd claimed, then his alibi too would also begin to unravel. So many motives, he thought. So many suspects.

Nandy was struck by another thought. He dropped the remains of the wrap in the bin and reached for his coffee. 'Apparently Neil's worried about something else that's gone missing,' he said. 'The interview adviser picked it up. I've passed it on to the CSM.'

Suttle wanted more detail.

The missing object, said Nandy, was called a spinthariscope. It looked like the brass eyepiece from an old-fashioned microscope and on the side was engraved *W Crookes, 1903*. He was reading from notes he'd made on the phone to the interview adviser.

Golding wanted to know what it was, what it did. Nandy was still peering at his notes. His handwriting was legendary. He should have been a GP.

'It's got a little speck of radium inside,' he said at last. 'This stuff's radioactive. You look in through the lens at one end and you see little flashes of light shooting out into the surrounding darkness. It belonged to the old man but it turns out that Neil had wanted it for ever.'

'He killed him for *that*?'

Even Nandy laughed. 'I haven't a clue, son. All we know is that he fancied it and that it's gone missing.'

'Is this thing valuable?'

'No idea. It certainly is to Neil.'

Golding and Suttle exchanged glances.

'Ousmane?' Golding queried. Suttle shrugged. Given developments over the last twenty-four hours, Ousmane was rapidly becoming history. Except he'd been there in the house. And he'd probably know what had happened.

Mention of his name brought Carole Houghton's head up. The first of the billings on Neil Moncrieff's mobile had just arrived on her PC and she was scrolling through the list of calls he'd made over the last four weeks. He'd phoned one number at least a dozen times over the past nine days, a torrent of conversation from a self-confessed sociopath.

Nandy wanted to know the number.

'It's international, sir. The prefix is 00 233.' She started to do a Google search but Suttle saved her the trouble. He'd dialled this code only yesterday.

'It's Ghana,' he said. 'Accra.'

★ ★ ★

The information went straight to the interview adviser. He wanted Suttle and Golding to monitor the second interview with Neil Moncrieff before they started on Erin Maguire again. The Scenes of Crime search at Roz's place had yet to yield anything worthwhile, and in his view they were nowhere close to a confession, but sight of the deleted files he'd sent Tim Stone might well loosen Neil Moncrieff's tongue, and then would be an excellent opportunity to feed in the new intel about the Accra number.

Suttle and Golding wedged themselves in the tiny monitoring room. The shot on the single monitor showed Neil and his lawyer sitting opposite two experienced D/Cs for whom Suttle had a great deal of respect.

One of them, Rosie Tremayne, was a vicar's wife. The quiet smile and gentle manner masked a steely determination to get at the truth, and she'd recently acquired a number of important scalps in the interviewing room. In her spare time she trained with a bunch of serious runners and had recently posted a personal best in a twenty-five-K endurance race across Dartmoor. Luke Golding thought she was awesome.

Simon Maffett was older, a bluff Cornishman, slightly overweight. He coached rugby with kids from the rougher areas of the city and had a season ticket for the Exeter Chiefs. In his mid-forties, he always reminded Suttle of Paul Winter, the Pompey D/C who'd taught him everything worthwhile about the darker arts of CID work: same MO, same matey charm, same talent for putting a smile on the face of the guy he was about to bury.

Neil Moncrieff, after the first session, appeared to be surprisingly relaxed. Even when Tremayne came in with a laptop and stationed it between them on the table, he barely spared it a second glance.

Maffett started the recording cassette and announced the time. Then he beamed at Moncrieff. He wanted to know about his interest in photography, specifically video. Moncrieff thought about the question, then explained that it was an extension of his bid to write a novel. Language, he said, was difficult stuff. Better — and certainly easier — to tell a story in pictures.

276

'What kind of stuff do you shoot, Mr Moncrieff?'

'Birds. A lot. We're spoiled for birds. I've put a couple of videos together. I try and tell the story of the seasons on the river through the birds.' He paused for thought. 'Then there was the concert the other day. Hils and her friends.'

'It's your own equipment? The cameras? The editing software?'

'Yes.'

Rosie Tremayne asked about the cost of the cameras. Suttle recognised the receipts she had at her elbow: £1,650 for the Canon, £270 for the GoPro, £2,078 for the ZBook. In all, nearly four thousand pounds.

'So where did this money come from, Mr Moncrieff?'

'My father gave it to me.'

'When?'

'Over the last year or so.'

'He *gave* it to you?'

'Yes.'

'You're sure about that?'

'Yes.'

'And did you ever lend the equipment out? Let someone else use it?'

For the first time Moncrieff faltered. He seemed suddenly nervous, uncertain.

'Why would I do that?' he asked at last.

'I've no idea. Perhaps you can answer the question. Was it just you using these cameras? Or was someone else involved?'

Another pause. Then a shake of the head. 'Just me.'

Tremayne and Simon Maffett exchanged glances. Then Maffett reached for the laptop.

'We have some video we'd like to watch, Mr Moncrieff. We retrieved it from the memory card inside one of your cameras. Here it is.'

He started the sequence. Neil was staring at the screen, his face suddenly pale. Erin Maguire stepped into his father's bedroom. Minutes later, having sorted the money, she was stripping for action. Neil watched his father beckoning her closer. He loved fondling her breasts.

Maffett froze the picture as Erin eased herself down onto Moncrieff's erection. No condom.

'There are seventeen of these files, Mr Moncrieff. Was it you who put the camera in the bedroom?'

Moncrieff couldn't take his eyes off the screen. 'Yes.' It was a whisper, his voice barely audible.

'Speak up, please.'

'Yes. It was me.'

'Why?'

Moncrieff closed his eyes. He wanted this nightmare over. He wanted to be anywhere but here, in this airless office, watching his father taking yet another scalp. The silence stretched and stretched.

Finally it was Rosie Tremayne who offered a suggestion: 'Did you do it for pleasure? Kicks?'

'Of course I didn't.'

'Why, then?'

'Because I needed to know. Because I needed to prove it.'

'Prove what?'

'That she was after our money. My father

wasn't the man he used to be. He was forgetful. He was losing his memory. I had a duty. A duty of care. That's why I did it. To protect us all.'

'Us?'

'Me. Hils. Olly. We've lived with this man all our lives, me in particular. He owed us. It was our money.'

He was defiant now, staring at them across the table, challenging them to disagree. They hadn't been there. They didn't know what life in that house had been like. The least his father owed them was a decent inheritance.

'But it was his money, Neil, not yours.' Tremayne had softened her voice. One day, thought Suttle, she might take up hospital visiting, cheering up the sick and the afflicted.

Moncrieff shook his head. He'd run out of things to say. He'd done what he'd had to do. And just look at the results.

Maffett shifted his bulk in the chair. When it mattered he could do intimidation.

'Did you share this stuff with anyone else, Mr Moncrieff?'

'Yes.'

'Who?'

'Her partner. Stone. I expect you know that now. I got his email from his website.'

'So why did you send it?'

'I wanted him to know what kind of woman she was. And I wanted him to know that we knew.'

'Knew what?'

'About the money.'

'Meaning it would never happen?'

279

'Meaning we'd do our best to prevent it.'

He explained that he'd contacted the family solicitor to find out whether his father was serious about offering his pet masseuse a quarter-million-pound loan. When the answer was yes, he'd talked to Hils about getting power of attorney over his father's affairs. The stroke, he said, had robbed the old man of any sense of responsibility. He was making crazy decisions.

'And what did the solicitor say?'

'He said that his father had to agree. Unless a psychiatrist thought he was crazy.'

'And your father?'

'My father thought he was perfectly sane.'

'So he refused to concede power of attorney?'

'Yes.'

'Meaning he could do what he liked?'

'Yes.'

In the monitoring room Suttle glanced at the interview adviser. This was true. A phone call to the family's solicitor had established that the family were at odds with Moncrieff over the loan. The solicitor was taking his time preparing the necessary paperwork in the hope that some resolution could be found, but in the end it was Moncrieff who still called the shots.

Suttle's gaze was back on the monitor. Simon Maffett wanted to know about the will.

'Did he have any plans to change it?'

'I'm sure he did.'

'In whose favour?'

'Hers.' He nodded at the screen. 'My father was crazy. He always has been. He did what he pleased. And she pleased him.'

'A reward?'

'More than that. He hated us. Especially me and Hils. Anything he could do to make us suffer, to make us *hurt*. Money was only one way. He was very inventive, my father.'

Maffett nodded. He seemed to understand. He nodded at the laptop. 'Do you think he knew about the camera in the bedroom?'

Neil blinked. It seemed he'd never thought of this possibility. Neither had Suttle. Clever question.

'I don't know . . . ' Neil was frowning now. 'I suppose he might have done. But you know something? That wouldn't have made the slightest difference. In fact he'd have loved it. He'd be sending us a message. He'd be showing off, celebrating, telling us who was really boss. My money. My woman. My choice. Fuck off, the pair of you.'

He was close to tears. Tremayne leaned forward, extended a comforting hand. 'And the will?'

'I don't know about the will. I'm sure he would have changed it, but even if he didn't — ' he gestured at the screen ' — she'd still be carrying his baby.'

Maffett took him back to Erin's partner. 'You sent him the pictures on Friday? Am I right?'

'Yes.'

'From your laptop? The ZBook?'

'Yes.'

'Which has now disappeared?'

'Yes.'

'So what did you think Mr Stone might do?'

'I've no idea.'

'He was a violent man. Did you know that?'

'No.'

'Really?'

'I didn't know.'

'Did you watch these pictures live? Through your smartphone?' Tremayne again.

'No.'

'Did you watch them afterwards? Once you'd got the camera back?'

'Sometimes.'

Tremayne nodded, then sat back and played with her pencil. Maffett took up the questioning. Time to crank up the pressure.

'I don't believe you, Mr Moncrieff,' he said. 'You've told us you had a sense of duty as far as yourself and Hilary are concerned. You went to great lengths to find out what was happening between Erin Maguire and your father. You're really suggesting it never occurred to you there might not be consequences?'

'Consequences?'

'For your father. For the man who was going to rob you of your inheritance.'

Maffett was in Neil's face now, leaning forward over the table.

'This woman told your father about her partner, didn't she? She told him how jealous Tim was, how easily he'd kick off. That's the truth, isn't it? And that's why you sent him the pictures? Because that's the reaction you wanted. You wanted the partner round to sort things out. You wanted him round on a night when you happened not to be there. That would have suited you very nicely, wouldn't it?'

Something had happened deep in Neil Moncrieff's brain. Suttle could see it on the monitor. The tiny tilt of the head. Even the suspicion of a smile.

'Yes,' he said softly, 'I suppose it would.'

★ ★ ★

The break came shortly afterwards. Suttle and Golding went downstairs with the interview adviser. Carole Houghton was sitting in a borrowed office in the Heavitree custody suite. The news from Torbay wasn't good. The interview team had been feeding Tim Stone the revelations from Erin about their difficulties conceiving a baby. References to donor sperm had made Stone visibly uncomfortable, and there'd come moments when the interview adviser had sensed a chink in his armour. Yet nothing they could throw at him had provoked anything but another muttered 'No comment.' Fine, he seemed to be saying. If you think I killed that old guy then all you have to do is prove it.

To date, as Houghton was the first to admit, they couldn't. No bloodied clothing. No conclusive DNA. Only at the very end of the first session did the team break the news that Stone could no longer rely on his partner for an alibi on Saturday night. She'd claimed first that they'd slept together. Now she hadn't a clue where he'd been.

'So the bitch lies?' Stone had rolled his eyes. 'Big fucking deal.'

Simon Maffett appeared from the interview room above. Neil Moncrieff's solicitor, he said, had requested a much longer break than usual. His client was complaining of stomach pains. Houghton nodded. A hospital doctor was due any minute to supervise another pregnancy test on Erin Maguire. She'd take a look at Moncrieff as well.

Suttle and Golding returned to the ground-floor interview room where Erin was waiting for them. After the preliminaries were over it became obvious that she'd been having a serious tête-à-tête with her lawyer. This time her lips were sealed. She said 'No comment' as if she really meant it, and no amount of persuasion from the likes of Suttle and Golding was going to make her lower her guard. She didn't want to talk about her partner, her love life or the small print of what might have happened on Saturday night. Her earnings from Moncrieff would — at least for the time being — remain a mystery. Asked to speculate about whether her partner's threats to nail this person or that were more than bluster, she simply shrugged. She'd given them a great deal of information, she seemed to be saying, and now they were on their own.

After half an hour Suttle brought the session to an end. Erin was led from the room to supply a urine sample for the police doctor, who reappeared within minutes with her verdict. Subject to a confirmatory test, Erin Maguire was very definitely pregnant. An hour and a half later, after an examination by the police doctor, the news brought a small gasp from Neil Moncrieff. From the monitoring room Suttle could see the set of his face had changed.

He was angry now. There must have been a part of him, Suttle thought, that had simply disbelieved what he was hearing from the bedroom. The girl was faking it. She'd had his father in the palm of her hand. She'd picked up every clue, every moment of confusion, every shred of evidence that another stroke might kill him. She'd recognised as well that he really wanted one last shot at conception, one last proof that he could still do it, one last opportunity to make a new baby. She'd been happy to oblige, and because it made the old man sweet Neil had assumed she'd pretended he'd hit the bullseye. Wrong. In the shape of the police doctor, he now knew that this woman really was carrying his half-brother or half-sister, that all his attempts to head off this disaster had come to nothing, that his father, as ever, had won the day.

'So how do you feel about that, Neil?' The question came from Tremayne.

Neil Moncrieff shook his head. He didn't want to say. For three brief days his father had been history. Now this.

Maffet wanted to know about the calls on his phone to Accra.

'Olly,' he said at once. 'I was talking to Olly.'

'Tell me about Olly.'

'You know already.'

'Do we?'

'Yes. One of your colleagues asked Roz. His name's Suttle. I understand she told him everything.' There was an unmistakable edge of accusation in his voice.

'Everything?' Maffett queried.

'About the way we were together. About the way Olly fought my corner, protected me. Even the swimming thing when my father chucked me in the river as a kid. Don't bother denying it. She told you that too.'

'She did.' Tremayne offered a nod of ackowledgement. 'I've read her account. Is that a problem, Neil?'

'Of course it is. Your Mr Suttle had no right. Roz is blind. She trusts people, and that's because she has to trust people. Christ, I think she even likes the man. And so he took advantage. I find that totally inexcusable.'

In the monitoring room, Golding raised an eyebrow. 'Top stuff, skip,' he murmured. 'You really got under his skin.'

Suttle ignored him.

On the monitor Maffett was back in charge. 'This is a murder investigation, Mr Moncrieff,' he said. 'We have a duty to ask questions.'

'Then ask me. Not her. Leave her alone, will you? Do I make myself clear?'

His vehemence took Suttle by surprise. Not a question but a command. My woman. My turf. Was this a leftover from the Moncrieff gene pool? A brief flicker of defiance from the runt of the litter?

Maffett let the moment pass. Then he asked about Olly again. Did he always phone him a dozen times in barely a week?

'We're close,' he said. 'We talk a lot.'

'That wasn't my question. I'm asking you whether you called him more often over the last few days than usual. If you like, we can check. It's very easy. Or you can just tell us.'

Moncrieff was biting his lip. His anger appeared to have deepened.

'Last week was exceptional,' he admitted.

'Why was that?'

'I don't know. Christmas coming? Maybe it was that. I can't remember.'

'So what did you talk about?'

'Everything. Life his end. What was happening to us.'

'Erin? Did you tell him about her? About the sex? The money?'

The silence went on and on. Maffett and Tremayne just looked at him.

'Well, Neil?' This from Tremayne.

'I did, yes.'

'And what did he say?'

Another silence, even longer. Then Neil pushed his chair back and tried to get up before his lawyer leaned across and restrained him.

Tremayne hadn't moved. 'Well, Neil?

'No go, I'm afraid.' He was shaking his head. 'I've told you everything I can. You'll have to ask him yourself.'

★ ★ ★

It was early evening in the Incident Room. The interview with Tim Stone had hit the buffers.

Nothing from Erin's partner, not the slightest indication that he was prepared to help them, and nothing remotely useful from the Scenes of Crime searches. The headline in the CSM's report was a cache of hard-core porn magazines discovered in a drawer of Stone's desk in the workshop. Beyond that, zilch. After twelve busy hours *Amber*'s case against Erin's partner was still largely conjecture.

Erin herself had been released on police bail pending further enquiries. After a thorough review of the interviews, Nandy had agreed that her involvement in Moncrieff's death was probably marginal. She'd undoubtedly provoked a situation that the family found extremely uncomfortable but she'd broken no law. The sex had been consensual and Moncrieff had paid her handsomely. She might have made the old man very happy indeed but they couldn't, in Golding's phrase, do her for that.

And Neil Moncrieff? Nandy, after some thought, had decided to detain him overnight. Like everyone else, he'd been very curious about Moncrieff's views on Suttle. There'd been something deeply personal about his determination to keep Suttle away from Roz, and if it was true that she'd taken a shine to *Amber*'s inquisitive D/S, then Nandy was determined to exploit it.

Roz's house had been released by Scenes of Crime after yet another fruitless search. Wendy Atkins had driven her back to Exmouth, and Nandy wanted Suttle to pay her another visit. He was to concentrate on the smallest print of her new relationship with Neil Moncrieff. If they could crack the sofa alibi, he said, then they might be back in the game.

'Thank Christ she can't see you, son,' he growled. 'It must be the voice.'

13

Lizzie lay beneath the duvet in a chilly B & B in the western suburbs of Leeds. She'd taken the train from Pompey in the late morning, crossed London and headed north on another train from King's Cross. Repeated calls on her mobile had failed to raise Ellie Constanz, the psychiatrist who evidently knew a great deal about Claire's months in Leeds, but a last try from the concourse at Leeds station had finally nailed her. She'd had a manic day but she was aware that Lizzie might be in touch. Tomorrow would be fine. She had an office at the Bellamy Centre, a psychiatric facility on the outskirts of the city. First thing, say nine, would give them a chance to talk this thing through.

Lizzie drew the duvet more tightly around her neck. She couldn't get the window to close properly, and the roar of rush-hour traffic along Cardigan Road filled the tiny bedroom. It was cold too, with a biting wind out in the street, and she began to wonder whether she was in bed, fully clothed, for the night.

She'd thought about Billy McTierney on the train, nodding in and out of sleep. They'd been awake most of the night, the way strangers do when the sex has been good and they decide to part the curtains a little. She'd told him about her marriage, about the early days, about Grace coming along and about the move west. The latter, she'd said, had been the worst decision she'd ever taken in her life, but on reflection she'd known that from the start, and in her heart she no longer blamed Jimmy. She should have said no. She should have thought the thing through. She should have realised that motherhood and non-stop rain were no substitute for a decent job in a biggish city with a story round every corner.

This admission seemed to amuse Billy. He'd grown up in Belfast but seized the first real opportunity to turn his back on the clamour and all the sectarian nonsense and get out of the place. A job across the water, he said, had taken him to a ski resort in the Cairngorms. The pay had been rubbish, but a girl working in one of the bars had taught him how to ski in his spare time and he'd loved it. Not just the skiing but the solitude and the silence of the mountains. That, in turn, had taken him to climbing, his first hesitant steps up a boulder-strewn hill near Glencoe, then reaching for his first handholds when he got to a near-vertical rock face and peered up at the scudding clouds beyond.

'You liked it?'

'Yeah. Big time. The guy I was with was very patient. He showed me all the moves. It's like anything. Once you crack the code, once you figure out your input, your responsibility, then it can only get better. Climbing's about balance and about trusting yourself. Fitness comes into it, and technique and all the rest, but balance is what matters. That's the raw ingredient. And it's not just physical.'

'Are we talking nerve here?'

'No. That's something else. That's got to do with risk. And the thing about risk is assessing it. That comes with experience. And you don't get that far without good balance.'

And it's not just physical. The phrase had pricked her interest. Exactly what did he mean?

'Balance is in here.' He'd tapped his head. 'You have to be sorted. You have to be steady. You have to know who the fuck you are. Not who you're supposed to be but who you *are*. That's tricky these days and it's getting worse. All the toys, all the noise, the social media, peer pressure, advertising, they all want a part of you. If you're sorted, there isn't a part of you left to give. That's why most good climbers live in their heads.'

Lizzie thought she understood. She certainly wanted to. So what happened after Scotland?

'I got ambitious. I knew I was a good climber. The guy who was keeping an eye on me thought I was a natural.'

'What does that mean?'

'I wanted to do it. Badly. And I wasn't into short cuts. Which means you listen.'

In the B & B she made another attempt to close the window but failed. Back in bed she thought again of Billy in Scotland. That first winter he'd worked at a pub called the Clachaig in Glencoe, climbing on his days off. The local winter walls and gullies, he'd told her, were supposed to be some of the world's toughest, attracting a handful of truly hard guys at the weekends. He'd listen to these men in the bar and he liked what he heard.

'They had it,' he said. 'For sure.'

'What?'

'Balance. They knew how to climb and they knew how to party and best of all they knew the difference. That matters, believe me.'

In Glencoe he met a girl called Yip. She was half Swedish and — like him — she was mad for the mountains. But she was also a qualified social worker, and he began to think about getting himself some kind of qualification.

'I applied to Sheffield. Hallam Uni. Three-year course.'

'Good?'

'Brilliant. We were out in the Peak District every weekend. Stanage Edge. High Tor at Matlock. The limestone cliffs at Stoney Middleton. There was something almost religious in it. I'm not a Catholic but it was like being confirmed. The bread and the wine and the mountains beyond. I was up there with the angels.'

Remembering the phrase, Lizzie found herself grinning. The three-year slog up the foothills of a degree in social work had evidently been incidental. What mattered was dangling on a rope with an ugly death three hundred feet beneath you. Last night she'd tried to voice the thought and drawn a brisk shake of the head.

'That's not it. It's like the circus. It might look dangerous, but it isn't. Not if you get it right. Not if you work out all the moves in advance.

Not if you're on top of the ropework and you're wearing the right kit and all the rest. The preparation is the challenge. You stand at the foot of the rock face and plot your route up and then treat yourself to a perfect climb. Some days it doesn't work. Some days there's extra stuff going on — weather, rockfalls, other people, whatever — you never factor in. That can be a pain but in general it won't kill you. Not if you've sorted everything else.'

After Sheffield he took a job in Barnsley for long enough to stash a few quid then bought himself a cheap ticket to Chamonix. Names came thick and fast, like battle honours in a regimental mess: summer climbs on the Aiguille du Midi, on the Bonatti Pillar on the Petit Dru, up the north face of the Grandes Jorrases. He began to pick up a decent smattering of French, enough to flesh out the gestural Esperanto shared by fellow *alpinistes*. Word went round. Impressed by his performance in the mountains, a local climbing school gave him a job. Then came winter and a taste of the six great north faces. His first took him to the summit of the Piz Badile, a terrifying axe head of ice-covered rock on the Swiss-Italian border.

'That climb changed my life,' he said.

'Again?'

'For real.'

'Why?'

'I met Jacques. He was climbing the same weekend. We had some beers afterwards. He'd been below us on the mountain and I think he was impressed. At least he said he was. Several years later.'

The two men bonded. More and more, they climbed together. Jacques already had his contract with a TV production company and was out on location for the rest of the winter, but he had clout with the TV people and got his new *mec* a job on successive shoots.

'I ended up doing some of the camera work. If you trust the ropes, if you make friends with the mountain, it's amazing how many hands you have free. On the really tough pitches, for the close-up stuff, Jacques always asked for me because the regular guy sometimes became a bit of a liability.'

'Meaning?'

'He bottled it. You don't need that. Not where we'd chosen to go.'

Where we'd chosen to go. Lizzie had nodded. She was beginning to understand. This was head space, not simply climbs that would look sensational on video. In the tight fraternity of the top climbers her new friend had won himself a space to pitch his bivvy bag.

He stayed in the Alps for two seasons. Jacques' TV series scored surprising audiences. The reach of the programmes became more ambitious: Mount McKinley in Alaska, Yosemite Valley for the big rock walls, Aconcagua in Argentina, even Mount Vinson in Antarctica.

'You went to *Antarctica*?'

'No. In the end we didn't. That was a stretch too far. And in any case we'd settled on the Himalayas by then.'

The Himalayas, he said, had been ringed for a whole series of their own. There were fourteen peaks over eight thousand metres. At that height the air is too thin to support human life for more than a couple of days. Steady acclimatisation could widen that window but the really big ask was to climb the lot without oxygen.

'You did it?'

'No chance.'

'You tried?'

'Not really.'

They'd chosen K2 as the first mountain. The weather, he said, was consistently shit. The logistics of putting climbs like these on broadcast video were awesome. But they set off nonetheless.

'Just you and Jacques?'

'For the last push, yes.'

Their fourth camp was at 7,876 metres, above them a huge overhang of ice. They'd studied it for weeks, read the literature, scoped endless galleries of pictures, looked at an animated fly-around on the web.

'We'd done everything we could. We'd prepped ourselves witless. We knew this was the big one, maybe the biggest one, and we'd left nothing to chance.'

Nothing to chance? Lizzie was starting to wonder where this story really led.

Billy, up on one elbow, his face in shadow, was reliving the day. Given the temperatures, they'd slept surprisingly well. They'd got up, made ready and set out.

'It was a beautiful day at last, and at that

296

altitude you just get blinded by the snow. You've got goggles, of course, but the real truth is that you shouldn't be there. No one should. Except we were. It was our mountain, our climb, and we were going to share it with this huge fucking audience.'

The producers, he said, had starting syndicating the series by then, selling it all over the world. This kind of material — men against the mountains — travelled really well. No need for subtitles. Just a minimal commentary, the odd muttered exchange on the soundtrack and the pictures. Always the pictures.

'We were good with that,' he said. 'We knew that when the Himalayan series came out mates we'd made all over the world would be seeing us on K2. And Lhotse. And Makalu. And Nanga Parbat. And Everest. So we had to do it right. For them. And for each other.'

After a latish start, five hours steady climbing took them to the top of K2. The sun was beginning to set, throwing the mountain's shadow deep into China. They took photographs of each other, Jacques wrapped in the Irish flag, Billy sporting the *tricolore*. The view out across the roof of the world, he'd said, was stupendous. Billy McTierney, the wee eejit from East Belfast, was in his element. Then they started the descent, hanging on their ice axes, nose to the mountain, crampons digging in.

'We were on this pitch. I had an idea for a shot. We knew each other so well by then I didn't have to explain it. I just made a gesture. And Jacques nodded.'

'What did it mean? The gesture?'

'I needed to get off the rope. And I needed him a few metres further on. It was a question of the background. Free climbing at twenty-seven thousand feet. Shot of the fucking century.'

Billy had unroped himself. He was steady on the ice, crampons, front pointing. He had a head camera and a tiny handheld. Jacques looked comfortable. He too had unroped. Billy gestured for him to take another step.

'Never settle for anything less than perfection,' he said. 'Big fucking mistake.'

The *serac* came out of nowhere. It swept Jacques off the ice wall before Billy had a chance to register what was going on. By the time he'd found his tumbling body in the viewfinder, it was no more than a dot.

'What's a *serac*?'

'It's ice that comes off a glacier. They can be big, small, whatever. They're totally random. The ice is always moving. Bits fall off.'

'So how did you feel?' The journalist's question.

'I felt nothing. It was unreal. It hadn't happened. It shouldn't have happened. You want the truth? I'd never felt so alone in my life.'

He had comms to the support team below. They alerted a search party, but at that altitude, given the fall, everyone knew there was no way Jacques could have survived. Billy, still clinging to the mountain, muttered a prayer for his best-ever mate. Better to die in the mountains on a day like this, he told himself, than grind down through the gears and end up a dribbler in a fucking wheelchair.

'So you binned it? The climbing?'

'I did. I got back down to the tent in one piece and stayed there that night. It was like I was sleeping with a ghost. In life there comes a moment when you have to get off the mountain.'

'You mean for ever?'

'Yes. For ever. There was no way I'd ever set foot on a mountain again. Not in earnest. Not without Jacques.'

He'd smiled at her in the half-darkness. Then he held her tight for a long moment.

'We did everything right on that mountain,' he muttered. 'We'd scoped the odds, we'd laid our plans, and nothing should have gone wrong.'

'But it did.'

'You're right. And that's the bit you never allow for because it's beyond rational calculation. Like I say, it should never have happened.'

'Grit in the machine?'

'Exactly.' He paused. 'You and Grace? Am I getting warm?'

The abrupt change of subject momentarily confused her. Then, very dimly, she began to understand.

'But we weren't on a mountain,' she said, 'and we weren't risking our lives.'

'And neither were we. Shit happens. And that's what killed him.'

'Right.' She frowned. 'So shit killed Grace? Is that what you're telling me? Wrong time? Wrong place?'

'Exactly. It could have been any child. It happened to be yours.'

'Or maybe no one's. If people had known about her, if she'd been taken care of . . . '

'We're talking Claire here?'

'Of course we are.'

'Right.' He nodded. 'Full circle. Ask me why I went into mental health.'

'I've no idea. To pay the mortgage? To save the world?'

'No. You get one more guess.'

'Pass.'

'Because most of the people I get to see have lost their bearings. They're unroped. They're all over the place. And that puts them in harm's way.'

'So what are they lacking? What can you give them?'

The smile again, and his hands cupping her face. 'Balance,' he said, 'if I'm lucky.'

★ ★ ★

Roz McIntyre was at home when Suttle appeared at her door. He'd phoned ahead and explained that he'd be grateful for another meet, and to his surprise she seemed to warm at the sound of his voice. Now she invited him in. To his relief, the Scenes of Crime boys had left the flat the way they'd found it.

'Would you like a drink?'

Suttle asked if she was having one. She said yes. He offered to get it but already she was out of the room. The dog, flat on its belly in front of the gas fire, seemed to recognise him. She was wagging her tail. Another friend.

Roz returned with a bottle of wine and a corkscrew. She gave them both to Suttle. 'Do you mind?'

'Not at all. My pleasure.'

'How's Neil?'

'He's fine.'

'Is he behaving himself?'

'He's fine.'

'You're not going to tell me?'

Suttle uncorked the wine. Roz had done something to her hair and he couldn't make out what. Then he realised the threads of grey had disappeared. Dye, he thought. She's been making a bit of an effort.

'Neil?' she repeated.

'I'm afraid I can't say, Mrs McIntyre.'

'Roz. Call me Roz.'

Suttle complied. Neil, he said, would probably be released tomorrow morning. In the meantime he had a couple of issues he needed to clear up.

'Issues? That sounds ominous. What do you want to know?'

On the drive down Suttle had been wondering quite how to broach this. In his experience very few people were prepared to discuss the minutiae of their private lives but in this case he saw no alternative.

'We need to know about you and Neil,' he began. 'To be candid, we're thinking you've probably been sleeping together for more than two nights.'

'Of course we have. Not sleeping together. Not staying over. But making love? Of course.'

'I beg your pardon?'

301

'We've been lovers for months. You should have asked earlier. It's no great secret.'

Suttle steadied himself. In every investigation there comes a moment of breakthrough, a moment when the door you least expect swings wide open, offering the view of your investigative dreams. Maybe this is it, he thought. Shame to be drinking this woman's wine when you're about to nail her lover.

'Tell me more,' he said carefully. 'Neil came knocking at your door.'

'No, he phoned first.'

'Offering you his services? On the front of the tandem?'

'That's right. And I said yes. Then we met and went for a spin, and then another and it became a regular thing. If you're blind you probably talk too much. Just like I'm doing now. Neil loved that. I could hear the excitement in his voice. Or maybe it was relief. Sometimes it's hard to tell the difference.'

'You mean he was shy?'

'Yes. I think I told you last time. He's someone who doesn't get out much, doesn't *communicate*, won't take the risk. And there we were.'

'So when was this?'

'September.'

'Still just friends?'

'Yes, but very much so. I've been married before. It might sound odd in my position but I can recognise — sense — a good relationship at a thousand yards. It's got nothing to do with looks, with appearance. All that's a distraction. It's in here — ' she touched her ear ' — and in

302

here.' Her hand briefly settled on her heart. 'Neil was made for me. He's got so much to say. He knows so much. He's so interesting. And once he lets you close he's so *trusting*. I once thought I was the first person he ever made love to, and that happens to be true, but I also know now that I'm the first person he's ever really talked to. I was virgin territory for him, and you've no idea how good that makes a woman feel. I'm privileged to know him, to love him. And I mean that.'

'So when did you start making love?'

'September the 23rd. It was my birthday. It's quite hard to buy a blind person something really nice, but he did very well.'

'Music?'

'Exactly. Brahms. *The Song of Destiny*. It's a beautiful piece of music. I adore it.'

She cooked for him that night, she explained. It was the first time she'd asked him to dinner and he turned up with a bottle of champagne.

'Another little gift. Very apt. But you know something strange? He wouldn't touch a drop. It was for me. My treat.'

'And . . . ?'

'We made love. Here in this room. To Brahms. Poor Neil hadn't a clue what to do. Not that it mattered. I loved his innocence. I remember telling him we had all the time in the world. It was a disaster, of course, but he was so nervous, poor lamb.'

'And he stayed the night?'

'No. He said he had to get back. He always had to get back. Which is why we always made

303

love during the day.'

'Why did he have to get back?'

'Because of his father.'

'But he hated his father.'

'I know. But that man dominated Neil's life. It's hard to explain. No matter how much he hated him he still had to be there through the night. Duty is a big thing in Neil's life. He has to do the right thing. He has to make sure.' She paused.

'Do you know how many times he checks to make sure the door is locked? Four. Four times. I've listened to him doing it. Here before we make love.' She nodded, reaching for her glass. 'Cheers, Mr Suttle. Here's to destiny.'

Suttle clinked glasses, wondering where this latest revelation led. Then he remembered the strangely random marks on Neil Moncrieff's calendar. Suttle couldn't be certain but he thought the first one, the question mark, was late September.

'Do you mind if I ask you another question?'

'Not at all.'

'How often did you make love?'

There was a brief silence. Then, over the hiss of the gas fire, came the sound of laughter. It was the softest sound in the world.

'Why do you want to know, Mr Suttle?'

'I'm just curious.'

'But why. Tell me why.'

Suttle said nothing. This was a cul-de-sac of his own making. Better to change the subject.

Roz had other ideas. 'Are you married, Mr Suttle?'

'I am. Yes.'

'So how often do you make love to your wife?'

'Very rarely. We're not together any more.'

'I'm sorry.'

'Don't be.'

'Do you have children?'

'We had one. A daughter.'

'And?'

'She died.'

'I see.'

Roz nodded, turning her head away. Suttle, expecting sympathy or some kind of apology for intruding, got neither. Instead Roz wanted to know whether he thought the death of the child had killed the marriage.

'Yes.' Suttle nodded. 'I think that's exactly what it did.'

'I'm not surprised. Grief is the ugliest emotion of all. None of us can cope with it. Not unless we have faith.' She turned back to him, her eyes invisible behind the dark glasses. 'Do you have faith?'

'No.'

'In anything?'

'No.'

'In yourself? Your job? Talking to people? Trying to get the truth out of them?'

'No.'

'That surprises me.'

'Why?'

'Because you're exceptionally good at it.'

'You think so?'

'I do, yes. You have the gift of listening. And that's more rare than you might believe.' She paused, her head cocked at a slight angle. Then she smiled at him. 'What else do you want to know about our sex life? If it's important, Neil got the hang of it very quickly. In fact he was extremely gifted. We make love often. It gets better and better.'

In spite of himself, Suttle smiled. Two ticks on the RSPB calendar, he thought. Then three. The expression on Roz's face told him she was enjoying these confessional moments and he was tempted to ask her why 3 December had earned itself an exclamation mark but thought better of it. He was here on a murder enquiry. Stick to the facts.

The first time Neil Moncrieff had stayed was the night his father met his death. A coincidence? Surely not.

'You told me earlier that Neil slept on the sofa on Saturday night,' he said. 'That can't have been true.'

'Wrong. That's exactly where he slept.'

'Why?'

'Do you want the details again? Do you really need to know?'

'I'm afraid I do.'

She nodded and asked for more wine. Suttle topped up her glass. She took a sip and then another, and then sat back. Neil, she explained, had turned up drunk. That was a first. That had never happened before. She'd opened another bottle to celebrate and later they'd gone to bed.

'Hopeless,' she said. 'He couldn't . . . you know . . . perform and it really upset him. I told him it didn't matter. I even told him my

306

ex-husband had exactly the same problem, but that only seemed to make it worse. In the end he got out of bed and slept here. I think he was embarrassed. Embarrassed and ashamed. Silly, really. It was the drink, not him at all.'

'So you didn't see him next morning?'

'No.'

'And you really didn't hear him leave?'

'Absolutely not. I was away with the fairies. The next time I heard from him was later that morning when he phoned with the news about his father.' She shook her head. 'So sad.'

Suttle gazed at her. He was as certain as he could be that this woman was telling the truth about Saturday night. Either Neil Moncrieff had retired pissed or she was an actress of genius.

He reached for his glass and thanked her for her time. She pulled a face, suggesting they finish the bottle, but he declined before getting to his feet.

'It's been a pleasure,' he said softly. And meant it.

14

Suttle was in the Incident Room by eight o'clock next morning. He found Det-Supt Nandy bent over a keyboard in the office he shared with Carole Houghton. Suttle began to tell him about his conversation with Roz last night but Nandy didn't look up.

'The Home Office have been on,' he muttered. 'I'm just sending them what they need.'

For reasons Nandy didn't fully understand, an invitation had arrived from Ghana for *Amber*'s SIO and another officer to get themselves to Accra as soon as they wished. His contact at the Home Office thought it might have to do with a Ghanaian trade delegation due in London tomorrow. They were interested in buying certain items connected with riot control. Some of this equipment was on a DTI blacklist, and a rapid response to *Amber*'s plea for access to police sources in Accra might help the Ghanaians' case. In any event, they wanted an outline of any potential Ghanaian involvement in *Amber* and a brief on Nandy's travel plans. Hence Nandy's furious attack on the keyboard.

'So when are we going, sir?'

'Tomorrow, son. Carole's sorting the tickets. You need to get yourself jabbed up. Yellow fever and a tetanus booster should do it. We're not going to be there for ever.'

Suttle nodded. He had a yellow fever certificate already.

'You want me to talk to the High Commission again, sir? Confirm we'll need a session with the visa people?'

'Do that. Olly Moncrieff is the issue. We need to track Ousmane's visa application back through the system. If Moncrieff was the issuing officer, it starts to look interesting.'

Interesting. Suttle hid a smile. After last night he knew he should see Hilary again. How much had she known about Erin and her father? Was she — like Neil — in regular contact with Olly Moncrieff? And where exactly did her son Kennan fit into her life?

He checked his watch. He thought Hilary was back in residence at the family home but he needed to be sure. When she answered the phone, she sounded remarkably upbeat.

'You again,' she said. 'What a surprise.'

★   ★   ★

Lizzie took a taxi to meet Ellie Constanz. The Bellamy Centre was an impressively new-looking complex beside one of the big arterial roads that funnelled traffic out of the city. According to Billy McTierney this was as close as the world of mental health got to showpiece provision: ninety beds for inpatients in single-sex wards, gym facilities, a therapy suite, a small army of specialist staff and a raft of programmes to ease service users back to a life they could call their own. Every city, said Billy, deserved a Bellamy Centre.

Lizzie reported at reception. Ellie Constanz came out to collect her. She was slight with wispy blonde hair and a ready smile. Her handshake had a slightly weightless feel, and she spoke with the faintest suggestion of a foreign accent. She led Lizzie through a succession of fire doors to an overheated office on the sunny side of the building. The sight of a poster for the Austrian Tyrol put a smile on Lizzie's face. *Vertige*, she thought. Where better to start?

Constanz had an open file on her desk. Years of investigative journalism had given Lizzie a talent for reading upside down. The file belonged to Claire Dillon.

'I have to say this is unusual,' Constanz said. 'We never discuss patients without their consent.'

'That would be difficult.'

'I know. I took the precaution of phoning Claire's mother last night. She's happy for me to go ahead.'

Constanz bent forward over the file. She wanted Lizzie to know that the Bellamy had done its best to assess Claire and get to the bottom of her problems. The file was extensive and included contributions from people who'd crossed Claire's path before she ended up in the hands of the police.

'Police?' This was news to Lizzie.

'Yes. We'll come to that in a minute. What I'm trying to explain is what we do here, our ethos if you like.'

There followed a brisk explanation of the

programmes on offer. Lizzie followed it as best she could, but it felt like the kind of jargon-fest that had engulfed every corner of the public realm. Talk of client responsibility and taking ownership. Emphasis on individualised treatment plans for the benefit of the whole person. The importance of mind wellness and recovery pathways. The tone was relentlessly optimistic, underscored by a brimming confidence, and Lizzie began to wonder whether mental issues might soon become a distant memory. Did madness stand any chance in the face of a regime like this?

Lizzie had abandoned her notepad. When Constanz paused for breath she asked about Claire.

'When did you first come across her?'

The question stopped the psychiatrist in her tracks. The beginnings of a smile suggested a degree of relief that the hard sell was over.

'We got a call from the police. They'd made a Section 136 arrest on her. That's not rare in this city, in *any* city, believe me.'

Section 136 of the Mental Health Act gave the police power to detain persons at risk of harming themselves or others.

Lizzie wanted to know why the arrest had taken place.

'You don't know?'

'No.'

'And you've no idea what Claire had been up to before the arrest?'

'No. That's why I'm here.'

'I see . . . ' The psychiatrist's eyes drifted down

311

to the file. 'Then maybe I should explain.'

Claire, she said, had reappeared in the city in the autumn of 2011. Over the coming winter she'd moved from address to address, sofa-surfing with friends she'd made at university. According to these friends, she appeared to have money.

'That's right.' Lizzie nodded. Steve Dalgety's stash. Over two and half grand in notes. 'So how was she?'

'Disturbed. One girlfriend said she could barely recognise her. She was hearing voices. She'd be awake all night then sleep during the day. She'd watch the same DVD countless times. This kind of behaviour, you can imagine the difficulties it presents.'

Lizzie asked about the DVD.

'You want the title?'

'Yes, please.'

Constanz flicked back through the file. '*Harry Potter and the Goblet of Fire*,' she said.

Lizzie at last made a note. Where did this belong in Claire's story?

Constanz hadn't finished. Claire's friends, she said, soon lost patience with their guest. Some of them tried to get her jobs. She still had her looks, and a couple of times she found work in bars and restaurants, but nothing ever lasted more than a week or two. This was someone, the psychiatrist said, who was too damaged to cope with any kind of responsibility.

'Did anyone try and help her?'

'A couple did. They suggested she went to the doctor or one of the walk-in clinics and get herself some meds, but she never listened. That's often the pattern with people like Claire. They think they're well, they think they're coping when the truth is they're not. They can be very very defensive. It's hard to break through.'

By the spring she'd ceased to function properly. She'd exhausted the list of friends prepared to put up with her and blown what remained of her money on a basement bedsit in one of the student areas. Constanz had never been there but she got the impression there was a problem with the drains. Hence the rats.

'She talked about the rats a lot. In fact once we got her in here, she was talking about everything. By this time she was very fearful, very afraid. She said the voices were telling her to hide. Then she started hearing one voice in particular, a man's voice . . . ' She frowned. 'Steve?'

'Steve Dalgety. He was her partner in Portsmouth.'

'Right. She never told us that, but it would make perfect sense. This is classic psychosis. This was a voice she really listened to, someone important in her life.'

'And what was he saying?'

'He was telling her she was at risk. Not just her but everyone. Especially kids.'

'What kind of kids?'

'Kids in general but especially young girls. Claire believed she could save them. No, she believed she *had* to save them.'

'Save them how?'

'Take them to a place of safety.'

A place of safety. Lizzie's blood iced. She thought of the footage sold to Sky News by the scrotes with the camera phones on Southsea Common. Flat 72. The one with the picture windows and the sun-trap balcony. A place of safety, she thought. If only.

'You're telling me she did it before?'

'Did what?'

'Took a child?'

Constanz nodded. Her finger found an entry in the file. It was 21 April 2012, a busy Saturday in the city's Eastgate shopping street. According to Claire, she was trying to find a job that day but everything was a mess. People were staring at her. She was finding it hard to concentrate, hard to get her thoughts in order, hard to even get through the crowds on the pavement. People thought she was on the vodka. She knew that's what they were thinking. She could see it in their eyes, in the way they looked at each other, in the way they gave her a wide berth. Then she saw this little girl. She could have been barely three. Her mum was with a mate. They had no time for her. They were going from shop to shop, interested only in buying stuff. The child was ignored, neglected. Claire watched the child, made eye contact, smiled, extended a hand. The little girl, she'd said, came running. And so off she went with her. Because the child needed someone to care about her. Because this little act of rescue was what had to happen.

Lizzie felt a brimming anger. All this scene needed was a sky full of kites and hot sunshine, and she and Jimmy sprawled on a blanket, not much bothered about Grace. She'd be fine. There were loads of people about. Peace and love. Never fails.

'So what happened?'

'The mother spotted Claire, saw what was going on.'

She came running after the child and grabbed her back before attacking Claire. A crowd formed. Someone called the police. Two officers were there in less than a minute. They arrested Claire and bundled her into a squad car.

'What did Claire say?'

'Nothing, according to the police. They'd sensed she was odd by now. That changes the picture.'

Rearrested under Section 136, they put a call through to the CRHT.

'The what?'

'Crisis Resolution and Home Treatment Team. They're our front-line troops. If you want a busy life, look no further.'

These people, she explained, would sort out what to do with Claire. It was a while before they turned up because they were out on another job. By this time Claire was in a custody cell.

'Alone?'

'Very.'

'It was early evening before the team arrived. With a psychiatrist was a social worker and a CPN.'

'CPN?'

'Community Psychiatric Nurse.'

These people were all experienced, she explained. They were used to dealing with extremes of human behaviour. By now the outraged mother had given a full account of what had happened and the police on the spot had taken further statements from a couple of witnesses.

'Was Claire charged?'

'No.'

'Why not?'

'Because the crisis team thought she needed further assessment.'

Under Section 2 of the Mental Health Act, she said, Claire was shipped across to the Bellamy, where she occupied a bed in one of the women's wards for the next month.

'Was this when you first met her?'

'Yes.'

'And what did you think?'

'I thought she was ill.'

'Is that why she was never charged?'

'Yes. It was our job to make her better. We needed to find out why she'd done this thing, but that was only a symptom. We knew there were underlying issues. There always are.'

A symptom? Trying to steal someone else's child?

For the next month Claire underwent intensive assessment. Life in the Bellamy, according to Constanz, terrified her. She hated being locked up. After the comforts of the bubble she'd been occupying all winter, this was horribly real. All she wanted to do was get out.

'So how did she respond?'

'She told us everything: the voices, the smells, the paranoia, the people who were watching her, the people who wanted to hurt her. She was a very damaged individual and that was painful to watch. We settled on a diagnosis early on, though, and after that we could start to treat her.'

The diagnosis was paranoid schizophrenia. The symptoms, Constanz said, varied from patient to patient, but in Claire's case they included delusions, hallucinations, disorganised speech and chaotic behaviours. Paranoid schizophrenics build a wall between themselves and reality. They normally sustain themselves by developing a story. The story is what keeps them going, it's their one slender hold on sanity.

'So what was her story?'

'It was about kids, about the vulnerable. She told herself she was there to protect them — to be their guardian, their keeper. That's what the voices told her. And she believed them. We call these command hallucinations. It's a common enough condition with schizophrenics but very few act on them. That made Claire extremely rare, if that's any comfort.'

It wasn't. Only months later Claire would be hearing the voices again with consequences too horrible to contemplate.

'You can treat schizophrenia?'

'Of course. Medication isn't perfect, but you'd be surprised what a difference it can make.'

Claire, she said, was prescribed a powerful anti-psychotic drug called risperidone. Towards the end of the second week the daily dose of two milligrams was increased to four and then eight. After twenty-eight days she was judged to be no longer a threat to herself or others.

'So what happened?'

'We discharged her.'

'Cured?'

'Stabilised. We got her assessed for ESA. Seventy-one pounds a week is a pittance to live on but we made sure she got housing and council tax benefits. With luck, she'd also qualify for DLA. We're not talking a fortune, but it was enough to keep her head above water.'

Lizzie scribbled herself a note. Employment and Support Allowance. Disability Living Allowance.

Constanz was consulting the file again. Claire, she said, had found herself a one-bedroom flat off the Kirkstall Road, an area near the canal. A CPN checked on her every fortnight, making sure she was still taking the meds. The outlook, while not entirely rosy, was promising.

'And the police?'

'They dropped charges. She was our responsibility now, not theirs.'

Lizzie nodded, trying to imagine Claire Dillon adrift with her risperidone prescriptions in the netherworld of Leeds. Strangers. Noise. And the constant possibility that the visiting CPN might revoke her modest freedoms and put her under lock and key again. Was this any way to lead a life?

'Have you the address? Of this flat of hers?'

'She's not there any more. As you well know.'

'Of course. I just want to take a look, try and picture her there.'

'Why?'

'It's hard to explain. You talk about the importance of a story. Just now Claire is my story.'

'But you know how it ends. I understand you were there.'

'I was. But it's not *how* it ends, is it? It's why it ends.'

The distinction drew the curtest of nods from Ellie Constanz. She checked the address in the file and wrote it out.

Lizzie sensed she'd overstayed her time but she didn't care. She hadn't finished yet.

'Claire had an abortion when she was sixteen,' she said slowly. 'Did she tell you that?'

'No, she didn't.'

'Her mother says she wasn't the same person afterwards. Is that possible?'

Constanz didn't like the question. Lizzie could see it on her face. 'You're looking for a life-changing event? Some kind of key to her psychosis?'

'I'm asking you whether losing a baby could account for all this.'

'Then I'll give you an answer. Of course it's possible.'

'So why didn't she tell you? Why didn't you find out?'

The question hung between them. The psychiatrist's patience was clearly at an end. Finally she closed the file and sat back.

'This is a therapeutic centre, Mrs Suttle, not a prison. We have to work within certain parameters. On the best available evidence we form opinions, make a diagnosis, chart a pathway forward. It's far from perfect but that's what we do.'

'And where did that leave Claire?'

'Better, in our view.'

'But she wasn't, was she?'

'Clearly not.' She paused. 'Don't think I'm unsympathetic. I'm not. That's why we've had this chat. What you've been through must have been unbearable. I hope this morning has been helpful.' She paused, her face softening. 'You're looking for answers, aren't you? You need to come up with an explanation?'

'Yes.'

'Very understandable.' She forced a smile. 'None of this is a science, I'm afraid, but you probably know that already.' She reached for her pen again and wrote another address. Then she looked up. 'A favour?'

'Of course.'

'If you find your answer write and tell me.' She slipped the envelope across the desk. 'Can you do that?'

★   ★   ★

Suttle was in Topsham by late morning. He found Hilary Moncrieff on her hands and knees in the garden of the house by the river. Her gloves were clotted with wet earth after the recent rain and she was attacking a sodden border with some vigour. Suttle looked out over the water. It was a still day, bright sunshine splintering the mirrored surface of the river, and a pair of swans was paddling slowly upstream against the falling tide. Hilary got up and joined him at the low wall.

'Hard to believe, isn't it?' she said. 'The peace of this place?'

Suttle wondered what to make of the remark. There was something in her voice that hinted of resentment. The last few days had ganged up on her and her family. If only she could turn the clock back: Moncrieff still alive, preparations for Christmas under way, maybe plans for a New Year's concert.

'You miss your father?'

'Of course I do. He was a monster, we all knew that, but at least he was *our* monster. No one would want an end like that.' She shook her head and turned away, kicking the mud off her wellies.

'And Neil? Do you think he misses him?'

'I've no idea. I expect that's one of the questions you're putting to him, isn't it? You're wasting your time, Mr Suttle. Neil could no more kill his father than fly.'

'What makes you think we've arrested him for murder?'

'You haven't?'

'No. We suspect him of withholding important evidence. There's a difference.'

He told her about the deleted video files.

Her eyes widened. Then she laughed. 'You're telling me he bugged the bedroom?'

'Yes. That's exactly what he did. You never knew?'

'Never. He told me that Pa was all over that girl, but I never imagined he had the proof.'

'So why would he do it?'

'God knows. He's a strange boy sometimes. I know he was worried about the money. So was I, to tell you the truth.'

'He told you about the loan? The one your father was offering the girl?'

'He did. He said Pa had mentioned it in conversation. That didn't sound likely because Pa didn't do conversation, but I checked with our solicitor and it turned out to be true.'

'So why didn't you mention it earlier?'

'I don't know. It didn't seem important. Pa's money was always his own to dispose of. He'd made that very clear indeed. All I could do was try and slow the paperwork down.'

'To what end?'

It was a clever question which Hilary acknowledged with a lift of an eyebrow. Not much gets past this woman, thought Suttle.

'You think we were hoping for another stroke? You think that might have resolved the issue?'

'Yes.'

'Then you're right. But a stroke isn't the same as murder, is it, Mr Suttle? As I'm sure Neil has pointed out.'

She invited him into the house. She'd been working for a couple of hours and wanted something to eat. The kitchen smelled of newly baked bread, and Suttle sensed that the oppressive sense of gloom he'd felt last night had lifted. Somebody had been out to buy wrapping paper for Christmas presents and there was even a bunch of mistletoe hanging on the back of the door. Who did the kissing in this house of shadows?

Suttle asked about Olly. Billing data suggested that he and Neil were close. Was that true?

'Yes. They've always been close, which is frankly a mystery to me. In some ways Olly is a clone of his father, and the older he gets the more you can see it. They share so much. The same impatience. The same physicality. The same recklessness. And then there's bloody Africa. The place obsesses Olly like it obsessed Pa. We'll never get him out of there.'

'You'd describe Neil and Olly as mates?'

'Brothers. For me that's where it begins and ends. Chalk and cheese the pair of them but a real kinship, a real blood thing. Olly would do anything for Neil, and Neil knows it.'

A real blood thing. Very slowly this richly dysfunctional family was beginning to slip into focus. Suttle had never had the chance to meet Rupert Moncrieff alive. Maybe this son of his would give him the clues he needed.

'You used the word reckless. Reckless, how?'

Hilary gave the question some thought. She was buttering a slice of the bread she'd just made. When she offered some to Suttle, he shook his head.

'Reckless, for me, is the badge of supreme confidence,' she said. 'You're reckless because you know you're right. You make reckless decisions because you know they'll work out. It never occurs to you that recklessness might have a darker side.'

'I'm not with you.'

'That something you do will make life tough for someone else. People like Olly have tunnel

vision. They don't live in a world of consequences. They do what they do because it serves
their purposes. That's why he's so much like Pa.'

'So is that a good thing to be?'

'Not at all, not to lesser mortals, not to the
likes of me and Neil. But that's the whole point.
If you're Olly, or Pa, you rise above all that
pettiness. You're living the big vision. The rest of
us are irrelevant.'

'Do you talk to Olly on the phone?'

'Very occasionally. I'm sure you'll check so I'd
better own up to a couple of calls recently, but
that's unusual. I had my hands full with Pa most
of the time. Two alpha males was a bit much for
me.'

'So why the calls?'

'I'm trying to remember.' She bit into the
bread, chewed and swallowed. 'The first one was
about Christmas. Olly normally organises a box
of wine for Pa. Pa was very particular about his
wine, and the people in the off licence needed a
couple of weeks to make sure they could get
their hands on it. But this year, for some reason,
he was going to give him something else.'

'Like what?'

'He said he hadn't made his mind up.'

Suttle nodded, fumbling for his pen. When he
couldn't find it, he decided to do without notes.

'And the other call?'

'Olly wanted advice. I think he's getting fed up
with issuing visas to our black brethren. He said
he'd met a South African businessman in Accra,
a white guy from Jo'burg. It's always been Olly's
dream to get into ecotourism. He thinks there

are opportunities in Botswana. There seems to be some kind of partnership on offer with the South African. He wanted my advice.'

'About what?'

'Money.'

'How much?'

'Half a million. He wanted me to talk to Pa.'

'And did you?'

'Of course I did.'

'And?'

'Pa said no.' She laughed again. 'Like he always said no.' Suttle nodded. 'Did he say no to everyone? Your father?'

'Yes. Unless they had something he wanted.'

'Like what?'

The bluntness of the question wiped the smile from her face. 'Are you talking business? What do you mean exactly?'

'You have a son, Kennan.'

'That's right.'

'He's living out in Spain.'

'Who told you that?'

'Erin. The masseuse.'

Suttle explained about the photos Moncrieff had shared. He didn't mention the shot on Hilary's bedside table.

'I get the impression your father had a soft spot for the lad.'

'That's true. Peas in a pod. Watch them together and you'd almost think Pa was a human being.'

'Did he send him money?'

'He may have done.'

'You monitored his accounts.'

'Then you're right. He did, yes. We're not talking huge sums, just enough to tide the boy over.'

'Does Kennan know your father was a rich man?'

'I imagine he must.' She was frowning now, the bread abandoned. 'Are we talking about an inheritance? Motive? Should I find myself a lawyer?'

Suttle shook his head. When he asked when Kennan had last paid Topsham a visit, she said she couldn't remember. Not this year, for sure. The state of his parents' marriage had spooked him, and the bitterness over the divorce had made it worse. 'To be frank, he hasn't got much time for either of us. I get the impression he's happy out there.'

'Impression? You don't talk?'

'Not really. I try from time to time, but leaving messages gets me nowhere.'

'He never replies?'

'No.'

'Never texts? Emails?'

'No.'

Suttle sat back, waiting for more, but Hilary had turned her head away. Suttle pictured the bedside photo again, the old man giving his precious grandson a hug.

'So what did your father want from the boy?' Suttle asked. 'In return for his money?'

For a moment Hilary said nothing. When she looked at Suttle again, her eyes were filmed with tears. 'Love,' she said. 'Like we all did.'

15

Suttle spent the afternoon at the Incident Room, preparing his files for the visit to Ghana. A lunchtime visit to his GP had won him a booster shot for tetanus, and a call to the High Commission in Accra had secured a brief conversation with the Deputy Head of Mission. She confirmed that arrangements had been made for a meeting with one of the top officers in the city's Criminal Investigation Department, and hinted that they'd started looking into Ousmane Ndiaye's past. Quite where these enquiries might have led them was anyone's guess, but she now had the arrival time for their flight and would have a driver meet them at the airport.

When Suttle reminded her that they'd also need a formal interview with both Olly Moncrieff and his supervisor, she said that wouldn't be a problem. She had alerted the visa section about the impending visit and was satisfied that arrangements were in hand. An office would be made available within the High Commission for Mr Nandy's use and accommodation had been booked in a hotel downtown. She looked forward to meeting them.

Before she hung up, Suttle had another thought. 'There's a Professor at the university.

327

Josiah Wambote. Has my boss mentioned him?'

'No.'

'I'm afraid he's a person of interest too. He visited the UK back in May. He came down here to the West Country. He paid Olly Moncrieff's father a visit.'

'You want me to fix a meeting?'

Suttle said yes. He gave her the name again. Professor of Modern African History. She said she'd chase it.

'That's not a pain?'

'Nothing's a pain here. Everyone knows everyone. Have a good flight, Mr Suttle.'

★ ★ ★

Late afternoon Suttle went hunting for Luke Golding. One of the data inputters, a pretty girl recovering from the wreckage of her second marriage, thought he'd been in earlier. She and Luke were meeting for a drink later. Was there any message she could pass on?

Suttle shook his head. The D/S in charge of Outside Enquiries, minutes later, confirmed that Golding had driven over to Heavitree after Maffett and Rosie Tremayne had failed to make any headway in their final interview with Neil Moncrieff.

Suttle had briefed them first thing on the real state of Neil's relationship with his blind friend, but when they'd sought confirmation that they'd been sleeping together since September, he'd refused to comment. The only thing he wanted to know was where this information came from.

Neither Tremayne nor Maffett had told him, after which — in the words of the D/S — the interview was history.

Suttle returned to his desk and phoned Tremayne. He wanted to know how Neil Moncrieff had been by the end of the interview.

'Angry. Spitting nails.'

'Why?'

'Because of Roz. He thinks someone's been talking to her.'

'He's right.'

'I know. When Luke turned up he thought it was him. Neil gave him a real mouthful. Completely out of character. We were amazed.'

Luke, she said, had been wounded. Not my fault. Blame someone else.

'So where is he now? Neil?'

'Luke drove him back to Exmouth.' She laughed. 'Think peace offering.'

Golding turned up at Middlemoor an hour later. Suttle was about to leave to pack a bag for tomorrow's flight. When Golding caught sight of him at the other end of the Incident Room he came over.

'Little present,' he said. 'Compliments of that nice Mr Moncrieff.'

Suttle found himself looking at the pen he'd been missing. 'I left it at Roz's place?'

'You did, skip. And Mr Moncrieff isn't best pleased.'

'Why not?'

'I've no idea. Except he's a very jealous man. He was on at me on the drive down. How you keep pestering Roz. How you won't leave her alone. How you took advantage last night when he wasn't there.'

'Advantage?'

'That's what he said, horse's mouth. This is a guy with very dark thoughts, skip. I put him right, of course. I told him there were good reasons we needed to ask his partner about their sex life, but I also told him you were a married man. No way would you ever stray.'

'And he believed you?'

'No.'

Luke paused to scan an email then gave the data inputter a little wave and tapped his watch. For reasons that Suttle had never fathomed, her squad nickname was Treasure.

'Fancy a wet, skip?' Across the Incident Room, Treasure was reaching for her coat. 'We're going into town.'

Suttle shook his head. The least he owed Olly Moncrieff was an early night.

'I'll pass,' he said. 'But behave yourself, right?'

★ ★ ★

It was dark by the time Lizzie found the flat Claire Dillon had used after her discharge from the Bellamy Centre. The street lamps threw long shadows across the steps that led down to the sagging front door. The dustbin hadn't been emptied for a while, and rubbish had spilled into the puddle beneath the overhang to the upstairs entrance. Lizzie looked at it. A pizza box. Other takeout containers. Onion peelings wrapped in soggy newsprint. And what looked like a couple of disposable nappies. Yuk.

She stepped across to the front door. Someone had tried to kick it in. The lower panels were splintered and there were gouge marks in the rotting timber frame around the lock.

Lizzie knocked and waited. From the depths of the flat came the sound of a baby crying. She knocked again. Footsteps. Then a face in the darkness. Pinched. White. Young. Angry.

'Yeah?' Thick Yorkshire accent. Plus a nose ring.

Lizzie explained she wanted a favour. A girl had lived here last year. Her name was Claire.

'Yeah. I know that Claire. She's dead, right? She were on the telly.' She stepped out of the light to get a better look at Lizzie's face. 'You from the social?'

'No.'

'The police?'

'No.'

'What's this about then? You'd better come in.'

The flat, to Lizzie's surprise, was warm, even cosy, scented with something that smelled like cinnamon. The furniture was falling apart and the carpets were cratered with cigarette burns, but this woman was making a definite effort. She'd found a scatter of rugs from somewhere and she'd hung the walls with cheap material from one of the Indian shops Lizzie had seen earlier. The pinks and greens were nicely subdued in the candlelight.

The girl was sharp. She clocked Lizzie's interest at once.

'You like my candles, yeah? I get them from

the market. Lovely fella. Sikh. The best. Honest as you like. Cheaper than the fucking electric. And warmer too. Four for a quid.' She cackled with laughter. 'D'you think he likes me?'

Lizzie laughed. The place was probably a fire hazard but Claire had lived here and she would have been equally volatile.

'You knew her? Claire?'

'Yeah. Gizza minute, will you?'

She disappeared down the corridor and returned with the baby. She'd swaddled it in a Rhinos shirt. It had stopped crying.

'Tinkabelle,' she said. 'Dad's a fucking nightmare. Paki kid. No manners on him.'

The baby was beautiful, melting eyes in the dark chubbiness of her face.

'What's her real name?'

'Tinkabelle. Like I said.'

'And the dad lives here too?'

'No way. I threw him out. Guy's a waste of space. Arrogant like you wouldn't believe. If he tells me again I'm lucky to have him I'll throttle the bastard. Eh, Tink?'

The baby gurgled. Mum took it as a sign of approval. She looked up at Lizzie again.

'You wanna know about Claire? Is that it?'

'Yes.'

'She were a sad case. We was living upstairs. I'm down here now because it's cheaper.'

'So you knew her?'

'I did, yeah. I weren't even pregnant then. My time was my own. I used to knock on her door some nights when it were hot in the summer. She'd keep it open to let the air in. She was in a right state, that girl, and you know the worst of it? She were fat.'

At first, she said, she hadn't got any idea that she had a problem but when they started talking it became obvious.

'She were putting on all this weight. She blamed the drugs she had to take. She had the shakes too, her hands especially, and she said she couldn't see properly because her eyesight was all blurred. She had these weird white chalky marks as well, just here — ' she touched the corner of her mouth ' — and she were forever dabbing at herself with bits of tissue. I felt right sorry for her. I did. She came up to my place a couple of times, but then she saw I had a big mirror in the main room and she didn't come up no more after that.'

'Did you try and help her?'

'I did, yeah. I said that stuff she were taking weren't doing her any good and maybe she should stop.'

'And did she?'

'Yeah. But then the voices were back, and she said that were worse.' Christmas came. She didn't see Claire for a fortnight. 'Then one morning I caught her coming out with this bag. She didn't even lock the door. She just went.'

'Do you know where?'

'No.'

'Did you ask her?'

'Yeah.'

'And what did she say?'

'She didn't say anything. I don't think she knew who I was. After a while a nurse came round. She'd been lots before. She were always checking up. She wanted to know where Claire had gone as well. I was carrying by this time and I were right mardy. So I couldn't help her.' She was staring at Lizzie as if she'd seen her for the first time. 'You were on telly afterwards, right?'

'Right.'

'You're her mum. That poor bloody child.'

'I was.' Lizzie tried to hold her gaze but had to turn away. 'Once.'

★ ★ ★

Lizzie sat on the bus back to Cardigan Road. Within eight short months of leaving her Leeds flat Claire Dillon would be patrolling Southsea Common, one eye on the kites, the other on any passing child who might need her protection. There'd been hundreds of kids there that afternoon. Why Grace?

The question had been haunting her since the summer. By now she could visualise the kind of life that Claire had been leading. As she slowly lost her grip on reality, she must have become a stranger to herself. Things she'd taken for granted — the company of friends, the excitements of a night out, the prospect of a relationship — had gone. The world was suddenly full of menace. She trusted no one, least of all herself. The only sure source of guidance were the voices in her head.

That would have been bad enough, but then had come the moment in Eastgate when all her nightmares came true. The outraged mother snatching back her child. The faces crowding around her. The cold snap of handcuffs around her thin wrists. The slam of the cell door in the Custody Suite. She'd suddenly become a ward of the state, judged to be dangerous. A month in the Bellamy Centre was designed to put that right. These people had nothing but her own welfare at heart, but the stuff they gave her, the tablets she had to take, pushed her down yet another path. Who was this stranger in the mirrors she was so desperate to avoid? Bloated? Dizzy? Hopelessly confused?

Getting off the bus, Lizzie paused at the kerbside. The radio had been warning of snow all day, and now the first flurries were caught in the street lights. She looked up, feeling the dampness in the cold night air. Maybe she ought to think of Claire Dillon as a prisoner of gravity on the daunting steepness of life's mountain, totally out of control, rolling downhill, gathering speed, getting bigger and bigger until finally she triggered an avalanche. That avalanche, as it turned out, had engulfed Lizzie's life, and try as she might, she still couldn't struggle free.

Crossing the road towards her B & B, she thought of Grace again, that sunny afternoon on Southsea Common, her face tilted up for a kiss, her grubby hands held out for a wipe before she danced away into the crowd and disappeared for ever. Moments like that changed your life. Like Claire, she'd never be the same person again. Was there any comfort in that knowledge? Were all her efforts to understand, and maybe forgive, doomed to failure? She shook her head, more confused than ever.

Gravity, she thought, and its terrifying consequences.

★ ★ ★

Suttle had finished packing when he heard the bell from the front door. He went to the window and looked down into the street. The forecast rain had arrived, and all he could see on the doorstep was an umbrella. The bell rang again. He headed for the door.

It was Oona. Suttle knew at once she'd been drinking. She gazed at him for a long moment, swaying uncertainly on her feet, then tried to take a step forward. He broke the worst of her fall, hauling her into the dry.

'How did you get here?'

'Taxi.' She nodded back towards the street. 'Nice guy.'

He helped her up to the flat, one stair at a time, supporting her weight. She'd never been there before.

The sight of Suttle's bag beside the door prompted a question: 'Going away?'

'Yeah.'

'Anywhere nice?'

'Africa. Didn't Luke tell you?'

'Fuck Luke.' Her face was very close. 'Can I come in?'

Suttle's heart sank. He'd been minutes away from getting his head down. The last thing he needed was a drunken Oona pouring her heart out.

'You want me to give him a ring? Let him know you're OK?'

'Luke? You think he'd fucking care?' She put her arms around him. 'You think I would?'

He led her through to the living room, lowered her into an armchair. Strong coffee, he thought. And maybe a couple of ibuprofen for tomorrow morning.

Oona was on her feet again. She wouldn't let him go. Now, she said. Just fuck me. Please.

Suttle shook his head. 'You're pissed,' he said. 'You've lost it.'

'Who says?'

'Me.'

'But who says I don't fancy you? Who says I haven't wanted to fuck you for weeks? Do a girl a favour? Let me have my way?'

There was something plaintive in her face, a real neediness, but she saw the funny side as well. Bladdered old Irish tart. There for the taking.

'Just a little fuck?' she murmured. 'Just the one?'

She'd stepped back now and was shedding her anorak. Then came a loose cotton top and the bra beneath. Suttle didn't move. Stepping out of her jeans, she was naked except for a pair of lacy knickers.

'Help yourself,' she said. 'Can a girl be fairer than that?'

She had a lovely body, lean and gently muscled. Suttle had always wondered whether she worked out. Now he knew. Despite himself, he was stirred.

337

'Coffee?' He was doing his best.

She tried to follow him into the kitchen but collided with the door jamb.

'Shit,' she said softly, rubbing her head.

Suttle busied himself with the kettle and a jar of Gold Blend. Golding had let Treasure get the better of him, he thought. He'd taken the civvy inputter to some bar or other, poured wine down her throat, lent a listening ear and offered hands-on counselling, probably at her place. Maybe he was still there. Or maybe he'd come home, reeking of Stella and recent sex. Either way he'd landed Suttle with a problem. Dickhead.

'Sugar?'

'You, my sweet one'

She swayed towards him, then knelt uncertainly at his feet. Suttle felt her fingers tugging at the belt on his jeans. He looked down at her. There were still drops of rain glistening on her hair. She was struggling with the rough denim of his jeans. Then came his Calvin Kleins. Her tongue began to explore him. Even pissed, she was an artist.

'You don't have to do this,' he said.

Her face looked briefly up at him. 'I know.'

'Is it revenge? Are you getting back at him?'

'Never.'

'What, then?'

'It is what it is. A pissed bog-Irish nurse having her way with you. Is that such a torment? Be honest.'

Suttle shook his head. He was beyond any kind of rational decision. Life and Luke Golding

338

had delivered this little surprise, and it was far too late to say stop. He leaned back against the worktop, wondering how long he could hold out.

'Why don't we go to bed?' he said. 'Do this thing properly?'

She shook her head and then peered up at him again. 'I've wanted to do this for weeks,' she said. 'Do you mind?'

Afterwards, he managed to get her into bed. Naked, she was asleep within seconds, her body curled around him, her head on his chest. Tomorrow, she'd mumbled, her shift started at eight. Maybe he could get her to the hospital. Otherwise she was happy to come to Africa.

Africa. The spirits in the Angolan forest. The hollowed remains of the candle still parked on his table in the front room. Suttle grinned in the darkness, his hand stroking the long splay of hair on his chest. Only now did he remember the whiteness of the bones against the black cloth. *You'll know her when she comes*, Nicinha had said. *Just let it happen.*

16

Suttle had never been to Africa before. The flight landed in Accra in mid-morning after a long smooth approach in flawless weather over hundreds of miles of bush. The promised driver from the High Commission was waiting for them at the exit from the Customs channel and shepherded them through crowds of relatives to the VIP car park outside. A light smog hung over the city, a brown smudge visible from the airport, and it was fiercely hot after the air-conditioned chill of the Arrivals hall.

Suttle and Nandy sat in the back of the Mercedes. Unlike Nandy, Suttle hadn't slept on the overnight flight, and ten hours in the near-darkness of the economy cabin had given him plenty of time to reflect on Oona's abrupt eruption into what passed for his private life. Yesterday morning, to his amazement, she'd woken without a trace of a hangover. She'd pleasured him again, just to warn him that she'd meant it first time round, and had ordered a taxi to get her to work. Later in the morning, poker-faced, Suttle had met Luke Golding for coffee.

'I hear you had a visitor,' Golding said. 'Help-yourself time, eh? Good fucking luck.'

Suttle hadn't known quite how to take this.

Neither, to his surprise, was he much bothered. Golding, as it turned out, had spent the night with his new friend Treasure and appeared to have no regrets about the wreckage of his relationship with Oona. Life, he seemed to be saying, could always take you by surprise. And thank Christ for that.

The High Commission lay in the administrative centre of Accra. Emerging from the traffic jams and clamour of downtown, Suttle found himself in a broad avenue planted with trees, a posse of gardeners bent over the flower beds on the verges. As the Mercedes turned and stopped at the checkpoint that guarded access to the High Commission, Suttle caught sight of a couple of joggers doing a careful set of stretches before testing themselves against the mid-morning heat.

The Deputy Head of Mission greeted them in the ground-floor reception area. After the brief walk from the Mercedes it was suddenly cooler again.

'Sophie Byers.' She extended a hand. 'Good flight?'

She led the way upstairs to an office overlooking the garden at the rear of the building. She was a tall woman with a ready smile and the kind of practised charm that suggests a busy social life. She was telling Nandy she hadn't had a UK cop in the building for ages. Suttle wondered whether their visit was entirely welcome.

Nandy opened the bidding. He understood she was responsible for security within the High

Commission. Did her jurisdiction reach as far as the staff who processed visa applications?

'Absolutely. I play sheriff. The buck stops with me.'

She quickly explained the way the visa hub system worked. Four offices served the whole of Africa. With the exception of Nigeria, anyone wanting a UK visa from West Africa had to apply through Accra. The applications came in by courier, hundreds a day. Most were processed without the need for a face-to-face interview, but when there was any kind of issue, applicants were invited to attend the High Commission in person.

'You've had a look at our Mr Ousmane?'

'We have, yes. His full name's Ousmane Ndiaye. You'll know that, of course. He's Senegalese, though it happens he's been living here in Accra for a while.'

'So did he come here for an interview?'

'Yes.' She opened the file on her desk and flicked through until she found the page she wanted. 'He was with us nearly three weeks ago. Thursday, 21 November.'

Suttle made a note of the date. Nandy wanted to know how incoming visa applications were sorted.

'In the first place they come to the Visa Applications Centre. We call it the VAC. We then sort them, prioritise them and allocate them to our ECOs.'

'ECOs?'

'Entry Clearance Officers.'

'How many have you got?'

342

'Twelve. Each of these guys will be probably be processing thirty to forty applications a day. Like I say, most of it's a paper exercise. As long as applicants meet our requirements, the visa will be granted.'

Nandy wanted to know what 'requirements' meant.

'We need to know that they have a current passport, that they can fund their travel and their accommodation. We need to know that they can sustain themselves in the UK so we need to see bank statements and some kind of asset history. If they've been to the UK before, of course, and got back in one piece, that counts in their favour.'

'And Ousmane?'

'He was an NPT.' She smiled. 'Non Previous Traveller.'

'Which sounded an alarm?'

'Not necessarily. We get lots of NPTs. And they normally get visas.'

'So what brought Mr Ousmane to your door?'

'I'm afraid you're going to have to ask one of our ECMs that question. With this level of detail I am, to be frank, uncomfortable.'

ECMs, she explained, were Entry Clearance Managers, with responsibility for oversight on all visa applications.

'They check each one?'

'No. Generally about 10 per cent get checked.'

'On a random basis?'

'You'll have to ask him that.'

'What's his name?'

'Perry Lonsdale.'

'And the ECO who dealt with Ousmane?'

'Oliver Moncrieff.'

It was an hour before Perry Lonsdale was able to join them. Sophie Byers was due at a meeting in the American Consulate and was happy to make her office available for Nandy and Suttle.

Lonsdale turned out to be ex-navy, a portly fifty-something who'd seen active service in the Falklands War and was contemplating imminent retirement in a village outside Peterborough. Over sandwiches and coffee he complained that the rules governing the Border Agency were changing by the minute, and the sheer grind of trying to keep up was becoming a pain in the arse. Even here, on the front line, morale was beginning to suffer.

Nandy offered his sympathies. Working in the Job, he said, had become an exercise in survival. Insanely deep budget cuts had savaged whole areas of policing and there was probably worse to come. Which put an ever-bigger premium on getting a quick result.

'Tell me about Oliver Moncrieff,' he said.

'He's one of our short-term guys. Interesting bloke. Good company. Parties hard. And *loves* Africa.'

'He's been here a while?'

'This is his third contract. He's into his second year.'

'How about his work?'

'Immaculate. This is a guy who can spot trouble before it even walks in through the door. He's in the wrong job. He can read these people like a book. He should be with you lot.'

'A bit of an asset then?'

'Totally. I have to write his end-of-tour report.' He reached into his jacket. 'Are you interested?'

Nandy shook his head. 'Just tell me,' he said. 'Tell me why you rate him.'

'Because the fella's dependable. He doesn't get pissed too often. He doesn't get homesick. He rattles through the paperwork. And like I say he has a real knack of spotting the duds. Plus he's a good guy to have around.' He looked from one face to the other. 'Are you telling me he's in the shit?'

'Not at all. I'm simply asking.'

Nandy changed direction. He wanted to know exactly how Ousmane's application landed on Moncrieff's desk.

'I'm not sure I understand you.'

'Who decides who looks at what?'

'Ah . . . right.' Visa applications, he said, were allocated either by the Office Manager or her asssistant.

'On what basis?'

'Complex stuff like settlement or student applications go to the long-term guys. They're the ones with experience. The short-term ECOs do tourism visas, family visits, sporting tours, that kind of thing.'

'So Ousmane's application would go to one of the short-termers? Is that what you're saying?'

'Yes.'

'And how many are there?'

'Four.'

Nandy nodded and scribbled himself a note. Lonsdale wanted to know when Moncrieff was wanted for interview. 'He's standing by now, if you need him.'

Nandy shook his head. 'Not yet. We need to talk to the locals first.'

★ ★ ★

Sophie Byers lifted the phone to police headquarters when she returned from her meeting. She'd yet to meet Chief Superintendent Kwasi Asare in the flesh, but everything she'd heard about him had impressed her. He was the coming force in Accra's Criminal Investigation Department. In six short years he'd emerged from the ranks and won himself a place at the top table. Even the Americans, who always reserved judgement, had become serious fans.

Nandy wanted to know whether he spoke English.

'Fluently.' She bent to the phone. The conversation was brief. 'He'll come and collect you at your hotel this afternoon.' She was checking her watch. 'I guess you guys might need a shower. I'll get the driver to drop you off.'

The hotel was a couple of blocks away. The High Commission had booked adjacent rooms on the fourth floor. From his window Suttle had a view of the hotel pool, a graceful blue comma fringed with palm trees. A woman was swimming lazy lengths on her back. She reached for the strokes without effort, her eyes closed, making barely a splash.

Suttle watched her for a moment, thinking of Oona's body curled beside his. He was tempted

346

to phone her but knew she'd probably be working, and in any case he wasn't entirely sure what to say. The long flight down to West Africa had lent the events of last night a bit of perspective. Had he been right to sense a relationship between them? Or was he — in Luke's phrase — just helping himself? Just taking advantage? Just providing a bit of TLC in Oona's hour of need? To these questions he knew he had no answers and just now he was too jet-lagged to even try for any. From the next room came the muffled sound of the BBC World Service. Nandy, he thought. Tuning in on his precious iPad.

Asare arrived within the hour. He was a small man, younger than Suttle had expected, impeccably uniformed. He waited in the big Toyota Land Cruiser with the window open while his driver escorted Nandy and Suttle from reception. His handshake was light and dry. He seemed to have no trouble with the heat.

They set off. Asare half-turned in the front passenger seat. He said he'd read the report forwarded from London and had made some enquiries. Before he took them to headquarters he needed to show them something.

'To do with Ousmane?' Nandy was staring out of the tinted windows.

'Of course.'

They drove out of the diplomatic quarter and plunged into the chaos of the market area. Behind the maze of street stalls, shack after shack climbed up a low hill. The driver pulled the Toyota off the road and got out to open the door for Suttle and Nandy.

Asare joined them. He was adjusting his cap. 'We walk from here.' He gestured towards the hill. 'It's not far.'

The heat in the market was brutal, yellow dust stirred by a thousand feet, stalls piled high with fruit and vegetables, clouds of flies swarming over huge joints of glistening meat. Asare led the way through the crowds of women drifting from stall to stall, heads turning at the sight of his uniform. There were kids everywhere, and they danced in front of Asare, pulling faces. The driver did his best to swat them aside, but Suttle sensed the Chief Superintendent enjoyed the attention. A rising star, Sophie Byers had said. Too right.

They emerged from the market and began to climb the hill. The streets were unsurfaced and little eddies of wind stirred the dust. The dust caught in Suttle's throat, caking in his mouth. He could feel the sweat trickling down inside his shirt, and he thought of the coolness of the hotel pool.

Near the top of the hill, at a gesture from Asare, they stopped. The house was single storey, breeze blocks painted an ochre red. The windows were unglazed, their wooden frames bleached a pale blue by the sun. A huge bird squatted on top of the roof, immobile, gazing down at them. Suttle thought it might be a vulture.

'He lived here, Ousmane Ndiaye. If you had come a couple of weeks ago he would have answered the door.'

Nandy was still getting his breath back after

the climb. He mopped his face with a handkerchief, looking down at the tumble of shacks below. He wanted to know more.

'You knew about this guy Ousmane?'

'We did, yes.'

'Why?'

'We share intelligence with our neighbours. In Senegal they are especially helpful.'

Nandy pushed him for more, but Asare shook his head. The flight, he said, was always a problem. Jet lag would tire anyone. Today was especially hot. Best to talk in the office.

Police headquarters was downtown, a ten-minute drive away. Asare had a suite on the first floor. He led Nandy and Suttle through an outer office and told his secretary to organise something to drink. Suttle, after a night without sleep, was beginning to feel slightly ill. The clamour and the dirt of the market. Everyone in your face. The smoke from the food stalls. The overpowering smell of broiling flesh.

Asare closed the door to his office and gestured at the circle of armchairs by the window. 'Please . . .'

He fetched a file from his desk. The first photo had to be recent because it was a clone of the mugshot that had accompanied Ousmane's visa application. The same high forehead. The same phony smile. The same eyes. Suttle turned the photo over. The stamp was in French: 'La Propriété du Départment de Justice, Dakar'.

Asare was watching Suttle. He missed nothing.

'Ousmane came here from Senegal last year,'

he said. 'He'd been arrested on suspicion of killing a couple of guys in some kind of vengeance attack. The evidence was poor. He had a good lawyer. They let him go.'

'And that's why he left the country?' Suttle was fumbling for his pad.

'Yes. We think so.'

The door opened and the secretary appeared with a tray of drinks. She poured iced mango juice into three glasses and left a dish of nuts on the table.

Nandy was studying another photo. This time Ousmane was sitting at a beachside bar beneath a roof of plaited coconut palms. His face was dark against the blaze of sunshine outside. He had a glass tilted to his lips. He wasn't looking at the camera. And he wasn't smiling.

'This is a surveillance shot?' Nandy held the photo up.

'Sure.' Asare nodded. 'We had a big operation on. Basically we're talking drugs. Ousmane was one of the suspects. We still think he was implicated, but cases like these take time to build. There was a lot money in it for him, millions of *cedi*. That house I showed you on the hill? We were about to wire it. No way did we think he was a flight risk.'

'Yet you allowed him to leave?'

'He left. It's not the same thing.'

Nandy held his gaze a moment, then nodded. Cop to cop, he understood. You can tie a man up in a million ways but still leave the key in the door.

'He wasn't on the database at the airport?'

'He was.'

'But they screwed up?'

'Yes.'

'So what else do you know about him?'

'He ran that bar on the beach, the one in the photo. It's called the Parakeet. You can eat there too. They do simple food, fresh fish. The expats love it.'

'He was selling the drugs from the bar? Hard currency?'

'That was the plan. We know they were expecting a big delivery, mainly cocaine. It ships in from Venezuela. We had a source on board. We knew the schedule, the distribution, everything. Ousmane leaving blew it. He must have known we were watching him. Shit happens, yeah?'

He voiced the thought with some regret and reached for his glass. Suttle suspected that some of the Passport Control guys at the airport would be looking for new jobs.

Nandy was eyeing the file. Were there any more photos?

Asare nodded. He was smiling now. After the humiliation of losing a prime suspect, here was the chance to save a little face.

'We took this one a month ago. You might find it useful.' He handed over another shot.

Suttle bent over the arm of Nandy's chair. A group of white faces around a table in the same bar. Suttle recognised the optics in the background and the board of trophy fishing photos nailed to one of the poles that supported the roof.

'So who are these guys?' Nandy nodded at the photo.

'Businessmen. People in the oil business. And diplomats. They go to the beach at weekends. Hang out together. Chill.'

Nandy nodded and bent to the photo again. Most of the glasses on the table were empty and a plate was stacked high with fish bones. Ousmane was kneeling beside one of the white guys, on the right. The man looked middle-aged and slightly overweight. He was wearing knee-length shorts and a black Iron Maiden T-shirt. His face was red from the sun and his hair was beginning to recede. He had his hand on Ousmane's shoulder and the two men seemed to be sharing a joke.

'You know who that is?' Asare asked.

'No. But I can guess.'

'So tell me.'

Nandy at last looked up. A rare smile. 'Oliver Moncrieff?' The smile widened. 'Am I right?'

★ ★ ★

Lizzie took the train back from Leeds on Saturday morning. She'd spent Friday trying to hunt down university friends of Claire's, culled from a list supplied by her mother. Most of them, it turned out, had left Leeds. On the phone they said that they remembered Claire and were sorry about what had happened to her, but they'd all somehow assumed that she'd get the help she so obviously needed. In most of these conversations Lizzie detected a reluctance to discuss their sick friend in any detail, certainly a reluctance to meet face to face, and in the end she decided there was no point pursuing these people any further. Their lives had moved on. Thank you and good night.

Only one lead, the French guy Alain, showed any real interest in trying to help. He was still in the city, working in a call centre selling mobile phones, and they met on Friday during his lunch break. He'd lived in the same student house as Claire when she was a student, a Gallic wolf among English lambs, and was happy to answer Lizzie's questions.

Yes, he'd started a relationship with Claire because she was beautiful and sometimes funny and seemed to need a man in her life. Yes, it had been fine to begin with, but very soon he'd met the other side of her and that, à vrai dire, had been scary. He didn't know about the symptoms — the voices, the delusions, the mad scamper of feet in the roof space — and had at first assumed that this was some weird form of role play, a theatrical tease designed to liven up cold nights in his upstairs bedroom. Only gradually had he realised that this stuff was for real, that la belle Claire — in a phrase he'd borrowed from one of his coarser mates — wasn't at all what it said on the label.

At this point in the conversation his time was up, but before he went back to work he was honest enough to admit that he should have done more. Claire had taught him a great deal about the fragility of appearances, about the judgements you should never make on the basis of a pretty face, and about the emptiness he now saw in so many strangers' eyes. At the time he'd sensed that his best interests lay in finding somewhere else to live, and he'd bailed out of Claire's life without a backward glance. Now, he said, it might be different.

'How?'

'I should have been more patient. I should have listened. I should have understood.'

'But you didn't.'

'No.' He'd buttoned his coat against the cold. 'And now, like always, it's too late.'

Like always. Claire had thought about this small admission on the train back to Portsmouth. Why do we give each other so little time? she thought. Why do we view each other in terms of our own wants, our own needs? Why aren't we more generous? Why, as people, aren't we *bigger*? There should have been a space for Claire Dillon that didn't have bars on the door. There should have been an alternative to the cudgel of risperidone. Salvation, she thought, always comes from relationships, from laughter, from other people.

Now, back in the little hutch in Anchorage Park, she tried to share her thoughts with her mother but could raise nothing beyond polite incomprehension. Her mum, as ever, was worried about the day job. Four months unpaid leave from the *News* was a reckless step to have taken. What if someone better came along? What if the paper, like the rest of the world, decided to downsize? Where would she be then?

Lizzie fended off these questions as best she could. She'd begun to suspect that the book she wanted to write would be a whole lot harder than she'd thought. Each tiny piece of Claire's jigsaw offered its own store of surprises, and she was certainly wiser about how easy it was to slip through the fraying safety net of mental health provision, but the question that had begun to obsess her was no easier to answer. Asked to name who'd killed her daughter, she still had no idea.

After supper, she phoned Billy McTierney. To her immense relief, he seemed pleased to hear from her. It was still early. Did he fancy a drink?

He did. He named a pub in Albert Road. Seconds before he rang off, she asked him about his contacts in the police.

'I thought that was your bag?' He was laughing. 'News reporter? Married to a cop?'

'Sure. But I need someone who understands.'

'Understands what?'

'The crazies.'

*　　*　　*

Suttle and Nandy were early for their appointment with Oliver Moncrieff. Sophie Byers had made an office available in the High Commission and asked Moncrieff to be there for seven o'clock. None of the ECOs, she said, worked on Saturdays, but Moncrieff had been happy to come in specially. Like many of the staff on solo postings, he appeared to be a man with a fixed routine. He'd scan the papers on the Internet, go to the beach, do his shopping and pay a late-afternoon visit to the gym down the road.

She was probably right about the gym. When

355

Moncrieff walked into the office his face was pink with exercise and his handshake was warm.

Nandy abandoned the sudoku he'd started on the plane and gestured at the waiting seat. 'Good to meet you,' he said. 'And our sympathies over your father.'

Moncrieff nodded, said nothing, and Suttle sensed at once that he had presence. His eyes were a startling shade of blue and had a gaze that showed nothing beyond a mild curiosity. He seemed nerveless, totally unflustered by the presence of two cops who'd flown four thousand miles to talk to him. The contrast with his elder brother couldn't have been more stark. Hilary was right: this was the old man in the flesh.

Nandy wanted to know when he'd got the news about his father.

'Hilary phoned me on Sunday. She told me what had happened. Not good.'

Nandy waited for more. Nothing. Not the slightest flicker of emotion. 'Were you upset?' he asked at last.

'Of course. Who wouldn't be?'

'Were you surprised?'

'*Surprised?* Dad hacked to death? Of course I was surprised. That's a call you don't want to wake up to on a Sunday morning, believe me.'

Suttle scribbled himself a note. Moncrieff made the news from Topsham sound like an inconvenience, he thought. A needless interruption to his precious weekend routine.

'Hilary thinks your father was a man who made enemies,' he said. 'Do you think that's true?'

356

Moncrieff thought about the question, then nodded.

'Yes.'

'How? How would he make enemies?'

'By the way he was. Dad never had much time for other people. He thought most of them were a waste of space and said so. That doesn't win you many friends.'

'Can you think of anyone in particular? Someone he might have really hurt?'

'You mean somebody who might have killed him?'

'Yes.'

'No, I can't. And it wasn't me, by the way, in case you were wondering. I was tucked up with a bottle of Black Label and a woman called Njeka. She's happy to talk to you. Here's her number.' He produced a folded note and tossed it across.

Nandy was less than amused. 'There's a man called Ousmane Ndiaye,' he said.

'I know. I gave him a visa.'

'He turned up at your father's house last Monday week.'

'I'm not surprised. I gave him Dad's address.'

'Why did you do that?'

'Because Dad would have loved him. The guy was a live wire. He was quick on his feet. He was a party guy. He was Dad's kind of African. The way I read it, Dad was in need of someone like Ousmane. Strokes don't happen by accident. England was getting to him.'

'How well did you know Ousmane?'

'As well as you know anyone who serves you drinks, cooks like an angel, makes you laugh,

357

makes you welcome. He's got a place on the beach. Weekends won't be the same until he comes back. Lovely man. Ask anyone.'

'You interviewed him for the visa, am I right?'

'Yes.'

'Why did you do that?'

'He hadn't been out of Africa before. I had to be sure about the financials. Some of this stuff is often a bit flaky. We have to see six months of bank statements, check them against salary slips, make sure they're kosher.'

'But you knew he had a regular job.'

'I knew he ran a bloody good bar. That's not necessarily the same thing.'

'So was it a coincidence his application landed on your desk?'

'I'm not with you.'

'You say you knew the guy already. And there he is suddenly in your office asking for a visa. Is that common practice?'

'We all know him, all the ECOs. We all use the Parakeet. It could have been any of us.'

Nandy nodded, said nothing. Moncrieff's punchiness was starting to have an effect. This man feared neither of them. He was bossing the interview.

Suttle leaned forward. There were indications, he said, that Ousmane might have a criminal past.

'Is that right?'

'Yes.'

'Who says?'

Suttle didn't answer.

Moncrieff was smiling. He had news to

358

impart. 'Accra is a village,' he said. 'Everyone knows everyone's business. It's the same here, in the High Commission. You arrived this morning, right? You'd already asked on email for time with the local police, yes? They'd have put you onto a guy called Kwasi Asare. I know that because someone told me. Asare is an ambitious man. One day he wants to be the Inspector General and after that I expect he'll go for the Presidency. This is a man in orbit. On the street they call him Mr Sunday. You know why? Because Christian names here are all linked to the day you were born. Kwasi was born on a Sunday. So that makes him gentle and sensitive and really shy. The locals love a joke. Kwasi Asare? Mr Super Cop? Gentle? Sensitive? *Shy?* You have to be kidding.'

Nandy didn't share the joke. 'I understand Ousmane is Senegalese,' he said stonily.

'That's true. He's here on a residence permit.'

'The Senegalese suspect him of killing a couple of guys.'

'Then why didn't they prove it? And lock him up?'

'You knew about this already?'

'Of course not. You think that's the way the conversations go on the beach? Africans are social people. You'll get to understand that if you spend more than a couple of minutes here. Ousmane is a social animal to his fingertips. That's why he does such good business.'

'So you knew nothing about what happened in Senegal?'

'Nothing.'

'And would it surprise you to know that he's suspected of drugs offences here? In Accra?'

'Ousmane?' He was laughing now. 'They want to do him for a bag or two of weed?'

'Cocaine. In bulk.'

'Who says? Mr Sunday?'

Nandy held his gaze. This interview was turning into a disaster and he knew it.

Suttle wanted to know about Moncrieff's long-term plans.

'I gather you're thinking of some kind of partnership in Botswana. Is that right?'

'Who told you that?'

'Hilary.'

'She's right. I am. Is that why you're here? You've come to talk to me about eco-safaris?'

'Among other things, yes.'

'Why?'

'Because we understand you asked your father for backing.'

'That's true.'

'Half a million pounds worth of backing.'

'That's true too.'

'So what happened?'

'I'm sure you know what happened. The old bastard said no. Was I surprised? Not in the slightest. Did I ever think he'd come across with *anything*? No. Was I angry enough to do something about it? Absolutely not. Just for the record, my dad was the tightest, meanest, most misanthropic bloke I ever met. Unless you stood up to him, he'd make your life a misery. Me? I quite liked him. And I quite liked him because he never bothered to hide who he really was.

360

With my dad you got the unfinished article, warts and all. And there were times when that was extremely refreshing. He loved Africa, by the way. Did anyone tell you that? And he was right too. This is a fucked-up continent, but the people are wonderful. And so are the animals. This is where the best of life started until us white guys turned up. Here — ' he nodded ' — in Africa.'

'So what happens to your project in Botswana?'

'It'll happen. One day.'

'You'll find the half-million?'

'Of course I will. The money's the least of it. That's why Dad got so rich. You only make real money if you can't be arsed to count it.'

Suttle glanced at Nandy. Nandy signalled for him to carry on.

'Tell me about Neil,' Suttle said.

'The guy's a wimp. Always was.'

'Are you close?'

'No.'

'But you were on the phone to him a lot over that last week.'

'Was I?'

'Yes. More than a dozen calls. That would be unusual, wouldn't it? Given that you have so little to talk about?'

Moncrieff shrugged. For the first time Suttle sensed a chink in his armour. He was looking out of the window now. Dusk came quickly this far south, and lights were on in the building across the road.

'Neil met someone,' he said at last. 'She happens to be blind, which is typical, but at least she's a woman. He worships her. He can't stop telling me about her. Apart from Hils she's the first woman in his life since Mum died. She's certainly the first woman he's ever slept with.'

'And that's why you've been on the phone to him?'

'Yes, partly. She's made him a human being. He's suddenly got the point of conversation. He's suddenly interested. She's pulled him out of his shell and given him a good shake. That woman deserves a medal.'

'So what did you talk about? Ousmane Ndiaye?'

'No. Ousmane was a present for Dad. I didn't even know whether he'd turn up.'

'So what did you talk about?'

Moncrieff ran a hand over his face. He badly needed a shave.

'The old days,' he said. 'This time of year Neil always gets in a state about Mum. I don't know whether anyone's told you, but she chucked herself off a ferry in the middle of the Channel. At least that's the assumption.'

'Do you know why that happened?'

'Yes.' He fingered a mend in his shorts. 'Dad drove her bonkers. Took up with another woman. That was the problem with the old goat. He could never get enough of it.'

'Did you blame him?'

'Me? I was thirteen. I didn't know sex from a jar of marmalade.'

'But did you blame him?'

'Yes, of course I did. He made her bloody unhappy. He used to belittle her. He used to taunt her. He used to make her life a misery. Towards the end she'd be in tears most of the time, even after they'd split up. In a way it was best she went the way she did.'

'Best for who?'

'Her. She couldn't cope. Just like Neil can't.'

'And you?'

'I cope. Always. I've got African blood pressure. That's why they love me here. The women, the men, everyone. For Dad Africa was a hot bath. Same for me. This place gives a man everything he could ever want. Space. Sunshine. Time to figure out who you really are. That's why the Botswana thing is perfect.'

'Your dad had made his massage lady pregnant. Did you know that?'

'Yeah. Neil told me.'

'Was that a problem?'

'Not for Dad. And maybe not for her either.'

'But for you?'

'No.' He shook his head. 'Like I said, I'm on African time. This place runs on fertility. This is where they really know how to make babies. Dad helping himself again? Enlarging the gene pool? Good luck to the old goat.' He glanced at his watch and yawned. 'You guys want a beer? The Parakeet's still open. We could go down to the beach.'

Suttle glanced at Nandy. He could murder a beer and a plate of fresh fish. Nandy hated finishing interviews on anyone's terms but his own, but in this case Suttle sensed he had no choice. Olly Moncrieff had steamrollered them. Just the way his father would have done.

Nandy and Suttle conferenced briefly in the office while Moncrieff departed to rustle up a taxi. He'd wait downstairs by the security gate.

Nandy got to his feet and went across to the window. He was convinced that Moncrieff had dispatched Ousmane on a mission.

'Mission to do what, sir?'

'Kill Moncrieff. This man has the motive. He needs the money and there's all the stuff about the mother. Those kinds of debts are often settled years later. Plus Olly knows from his brother that the massage woman is going to be helping herself. The family estate is leaking money and someone has to sort it.'

'Ousmane?'

'For sure. He's probably killed two men already. The old man was on a plate, just waiting for him. Saturday night? The house empty? No witnesses? This is a set-up. The only mystery is why he turned up so early, but that may account for all Neil's phone calls that week to his brother. Ideally, Ousmane should have walked in on the Saturday night, killed Moncrieff and done a runner. He's got a six-month visa in his pocket plus whatever Olly paid him. If he does the job right, he can stay in the UK for ever.'

'Olly didn't need to pay him anything, sir. The money was already there in the bedroom, and Neil would have known where to find it. Neat, the victim paying for his own execution. Nice twist.'

'You're right, son, but there's a problem, isn't there?'

'Evidence?'

'Exactly. So I suggest you take the man to the beach and pour beer down his throat. I think he likes you, and that's not a compliment.'

★　★　★

It was a five-minute drive to the beach. Moncrieff paid for the taxi and nodded towards the distant lights of the bar. The wind was stirring in the palm trees, and Suttle could see the dark shapes of a couple of men deep in conversation beside a line of wooden dugouts hauled up at the foot of the sand dunes. They paused to watch Suttle and Moncrieff walk by. One of them was smoking, a small red point of light in the darkness, and Suttle caught the bitter sweetness of weed on the night air. Away down the beach the whiteness of a breaking line of surf. It was much cooler now, and Suttle began to understand the tug of a place like this. Oona, he thought. A cheap flight and a rental near the ocean. Perfect.

The bar was packed. Moncrieff exchanged hugs with a handful of friends at the bar. One of them, a blonde with a perfect tan, asked for an introduction to his new friend.

'Jimmy.' Suttle's grin spared Moncrieff the embarrassment of not knowing his first name. 'And yours?'

'Adele. You're here on business?'

'Yeah.'

'Who are you with?'

Suttle was going to duck the question but Moncrieff had no intention of letting him off the hook. 'He's a cop. I thought he could be the evening's entertainment.'

'You're really a cop?' She sounded impressed.

'Afraid so.'

'On duty?'

'Always.'

'So how come you're with this guy?' She nodded at Moncrieff.

'We think he might have helped kill someone.'

'Really?' The woman's eyes were wide. 'This is true, Olly darling? Only you never told me.'

'I did but you weren't listening. Drink anyone?'

The evening developed into a party. Three guys on a makeshift stage played the kind of music Suttle had never heard before. Nicinha did plaintive. This band keyed a different mood: bright, upbeat, rich and very loud. Coshed by jet lag, Suttle let a succession of beers float him away. Fresh snapper from the barbecue appeared on a plate from nowhere with an ice-cold bottle of Sauvignon. He split the wine with his new blonde friend, and after he'd demolished the fish, they danced together. She wanted to know whether he was married. He said yes.

'Kids?' she shouted.

'No.'

'Won't or can't?'

'Neither.'

'I don't understand.'

'Nor do I.'

'But you're really a cop?'

'Yes.'

'That's good enough for me.'

The band slowed and she clung to him. Suttle wondered vaguely whether her husband's was one of the watching faces at the bar but realised he didn't care. Only Moncrieff's hand on his arm at the end of the set dragged him away.

'There's someone I want you to meet,' he said.

The woman was waiting further down the beach. Suttle was beyond exhaustion. He stood in the darkness, glad of the cool wind off the sea, looking up at the stars. So many, he thought. So bright. So distant.

'This is Ousmane's wife.' It was Moncrieff's voice, a thousand miles away.

'I'm glad to meet you.' Suttle thought he'd extended a hand but couldn't be sure. He fought to bring the face into focus. A big woman, handsome, long silver earrings. White teeth. French accent.

'You want a fuck?'

'No, thanks.'

'Cheap. Twenty dollars.'

'Sweet.'

'You want? Here? Now?'

'No.'

Suttle shook his head and turned away. He badly wanted to lie down on the warm sand. He could have slept for a thousand years and been perfectly happy. He found Moncrieff's face in the darkness. 'You're right,' he said. 'England sucks.'

'Good man.'

'But tell me something.'

'Anything.'

'Really?' Suttle looked at him very hard,

realising that Moncrieff too was pissed. 'Come here a moment.' He beckoned him closer. 'This is serious.'

'You're wrong. But it doesn't matter. What's the question?'

Suttle realised he'd forgotten. He frowned and then tried to find the woman. For reasons he didn't understand, she seemed to have gone. Was she really Ousmane's wife? Had he upset her by saying no? He hadn't a clue.

His arm was round Moncrieff's shoulders now.

A full bottle of wine dangled from Moncrieff's left hand. 'You want some?' He offered the bottle.

Suttle took it. He tipped the bottle to his lips. Wine dribbled everywhere. Moncrieff produced a serviette and dabbed clumsily at his chin.

'Thanks,' Suttle muttered. 'Appreciate it.'

They wandered off towards the breaking line of surf, zigzagging across the sand, supporting each other. Once Suttle stopped, looking around for the woman, but he couldn't find her. He was still vaguely troubled by the abruptness of his refusal. The bottle was half-empty now, the ocean closer. In the shallows Suttle tripped over a log. Only Moncrieff saved him.

Suttle steadied himself, grateful again. Then he remembered the question.

He held Moncrieff at arm's length, trying to keep his face in focus. He had the words lined up in roughly the right order. Now or never.

'Did you kill your dad?' he managed. 'Only I'm supposed to find out.'

Moncrieff roared with laughter, then hauled him a little deeper into the sea. The next wave caught Suttle in the crotch. He staggered back, one arm flailing, the other reaching for Moncrieff. He wanted an answer. He really did. He tried the question again but messed it up. Without Moncrieff, he knew he'd fall over.

'Is that a no? Did I hear a no? Just say it. Say no.'

He did his best to stand his ground, to play the cop, to resist the next wave and the wave after that, but Moncrieff was pulling him back now, away from the ocean, back towards the glistening beach. Then it was his turn to hold Suttle at arm's length. Suttle couldn't work out why he was laughing again.

Moncrieff pulled him close, his hand slipping down to Suttle's sodden jeans and loosening his belt. Then he kissed him on the lips.

'You know something?' he said. 'You'd make a fucking good African.'

17

SUNDAY, 15 DECEMBER 2013

Lizzie parked her car across the seafront from the hotel, zipping up her anorak against the first of the rain. Couples pushing buggies along the promenade were hurrying towards a nearby shelter. A plastic bag, ballooned by the wind, clung briefly to her leg.

'You're Lizzie, yes? I'm Dawn.'

Lizzie had never met D/C Dawn Ellis. She shook the out-stretched hand. Dawn Ellis was slight and pretty and looked younger than Lizzie had expected. On the phone, barely half an hour ago, Suttle had put her age at nearly forty. He'd worked with her on a number of jobs, including the morning he'd got himself stabbed when an attempt to arrest a local lowlife in Southsea had gone badly wrong. It was Dawn, he said, who'd summoned the cavalry, and it was probably down to her that he'd survived at all. He'd described her as shrewd and a bit troubled, a copper who thought too hard about the social issues for her own good. The news that she was now assisting the Force Lead on mental health issues had come as no surprise.

'Jimmy sends his love.' Lizzie paused at the kerb. 'Wanted me to say hi and Happy Christmas.'

They crossed the road towards the hotel. Lizzie

had made contact late last night, asking for a meet. Dawn had been happy to say yes but warned that she could only make Sunday morning. She was meeting a mate in the hotel for lunch. After that she was away until after Christmas.

The hotel lobby was full of young mums. Some of the other women were visibly pregnant. Dawn Ellis led the way through the crowd queueing at reception. Only as they reached the entrance to the hotel's coffee lounge did Lizzie spot the poster. YULETIDE BABY FAYRE, it read. ONE DAY ONLY.

She hesitated for a fraction of a second, long enough for Dawn to recognise the hint of panic in her eyes. Lizzie felt the pressure of Dawn's hand inside her elbow, steering her onwards.

'I'm really sorry,' Dawn murmured. 'I'd no idea this was on.'

'It doesn't matter. Really, it doesn't.'

Lizzie was angry with herself. She liked being around cops, always had, largely because most of them knew how to cope. Letting herself down like this was deeply pathetic.

Dawn found a table tucked out of sight of the crowded lobby. She wanted to know how Suttle was getting on.

'He's fine. He loves it down there. It's his kind of area, his kind of people. He was always a country boy at heart.'

'Really?' The news seemed to take Dawn by surprise. 'Do you see much of each other?'

'Not really.'

'And that's because of Grace? Of what happened?'

For the second time in less than a minute Lizzie found herself on the back foot. Dawn was an old mate of Jimmy's. Job gossip would have wised her up to the state of his marriage but what was so refreshing was her directness and her total lack of embarrassment. Like cops, journalists asked questions for a living. But seldom with such artless candour.

'What happened hasn't helped,' Lizzie said. 'These things are meant to bring you together. They don't.'

'That's a shame. Jimmy always struck me as a really laid-back guy. I'm surprised.'

'You shouldn't be. It's probably my fault. How come you got the mental health gig?'

'I put my hand up for it. The job's changing by the week. I always had the feeling we were social workers in uniform but it was hard to get anyone else to agree. Things are so bad now there isn't an option. Either we accept that we have to look out for these people or they go under.'

'These people?'

'The sick. The lame. The brain dead. The needy. The inadequates. In this city, believe me, you're spoiled for choice. Most of the trouble that comes in off the street needs a bit of care and attention. The last place we should take them is court.'

'You mean that?'

'Yeah. And I always have. I could bore you shitless with statistics, but you're a journalist so you'd know all this stuff already. On our side of the fence we've been a bit slow to react. And that's being kind.'

'But it's changing? Is that what you're telling me?'

'Yes.'

'Because . . . ?'

'Because it has to.' She signalled to the waitress. Lizzie settled for a latte. Dawn ordered a glass of sparkling water.

'Jimmy said you were a born-again veggie.'

'Jimmy's right. Except for the born-again bit. And vegan would be closer.' Dawn warmed the conversation with a smile. 'Tell me how I can help.'

Lizzie described the journey she'd made over the last couple of days, the people she'd talked to, the impression she'd begun to form. She'd tracked Claire Dillon through the last five years of her life and now she was close to its final chapter.

'Which happened down here, of course.'

'Exactly. And Billy McTierney gave me the impression you'd know pretty much what happened.'

'Billy's a good man. And he's tougher than he'd like you to believe.'

'Why doesn't that surprise me?'

'I've no idea. Be careful, though. This is a guy who doesn't need other people. It might be wise to bear that in mind.'

Lizzie smiled. On the phone Jimmy had told her that Dawn Ellis was one of the sharpest operators he'd ever seen in an interview room. This was a woman, he'd said, with a rare talent for understanding what made people tick. Too right, she thought.

Dawn clarified her own role in last summer's operation. Given the possibility that Grace had been snatched, the management had been thinking kidnap or nutter from the off. Hence her involvement.

'You were some kind of adviser?'

'Yeah. Riding shotgun, I was privy to pretty much everything. These jobs are mega-high profile, like you might expect. You've got a lot of people around the top table, and even more out at the sharp end, and you're constantly testing lines of enquiry until you can close them down. The one LOE we never closed down was my bit of the wood. There are nutters everywhere. Most of them are harmless. This one sadly wasn't.'

'Do you know that?'

'Yes. Your daughter died. Are you telling me different?'

Lizzie looked at her for a moment, slightly shocked at the bluntness of the question, then shook her head and gestured for Dawn to carry on.

Jimmy's 999, Dawn said, had been put through to the Control Room at Netley. The two beat officers closest to the kite festival were tasked to make contact while word was passed to the local duty Inspector.

Lizzie nodded. Jimmy, she knew, had given one of the attending PCs his mobile phone. He'd shot pictures of Grace only an hour ago, perfect for circulation if she didn't turn up.

'That was a bonus.' Dawn nodded. 'That got us off to a flying start.'

The Inspector, she said, had already declared

Grace a high-grade Misper. After Madeleine McCann's disappearance, both the media and the police understood the need to keep the next few hours under tight control. While the duty Inspector was flooding the immediate area with all the resources he could get his hands on, a Controller with five assistants was sorting data input at the Netley Control Room. By this time successive appeals to the crowd by the festival organisers had failed to raise any sightings of Grace.

Lizzie nodded and sat back, swamped by memories. The kite festival had taken place on the common less than a mile away. For the first hour or so she'd simply assumed that Grace was lost, that someone would stoop to the child to ask her why she was crying, that she'd emerge from the crowd in the hands of a stranger, that all would be well.

By five o'clock, though, she'd begun to succumb to quite another feeling. That something darker must have taken place. That Grace might have strayed onto the beach, gone into the water, had some kind of accident. She'd always been without fear. She had an appetite for physical risks. Had she waded in? Been taken by the passing wash of some boat or other? Lizzie had clung to this possibility for the next hour or so but in her heart she knew she was kidding herself. It was still a lovely day. There were still thousands of people around. No way would anyone let a four-year-old come to that kind of harm. So what else might have happened?

She closed her eyes, remembering the sour

taste of dread in her mouth as the crowds on the common drifted away, leaving acres of crisp packets and plastic bags tumbling in the wind. If only we'd have kept an eye on her, she thought. If only we'd known.

Dawn was looking alarmed.

'You want me to carry on? Only this can't be easy.'

'It isn't.'

'You want something in that coffee? Something stronger?'

'Christ, no.' Lizzie swallowed hard. 'Your guys are on it. It's five o'clock. Grace has been gone more than an hour. What next?'

★　★　★

Suttle ordered a cab for Accra University. It was mid-morning and the message from the High Commission tucked under his door confirmed that Professor Wambote would be pleased to meet him at half past eleven. He had an office in the Institute of African Studies on the main campus at Legon.

A cold shower and three more ibuprofen had stilled the thunder in his head by the time the phone rang to announce the cab. He knocked on Nandy's door to let him know he was off but there was no reply. Downstairs in the lobby he left a message for *Amber*'s SIO with the receptionist, glad to have avoided any kind of conversation. The last thing he needed just now was Nandy pushing for details of last night.

The university campus was a half-hour drive

out of Accra. Suttle sat in the back of the cab, trying to tease some sense from what little he remembered. Moncrieff, he knew, had been full of mischief. He recalled getting drunk. He thought he'd been propositioned by a black woman but he wasn't sure. After that he could only remember the beach and the waves and the scrape of Moncrieff's bristly kiss on his face. Even this morning his jeans were still soaking. Just what had the kiss meant? And what on earth was he supposed to say to Nandy?

The Institute of African Studies was a 1960s confection in rendered concrete and red tiles. Two storeys looked down on a neat garden of shrubs and eucalyptus. A couple of students sitting on the steps sharing a cigarette watched the cab roll to a halt. Suttle paid the driver and asked one of them for Professor Wambote.

He grinned at Suttle and jerked his thumb over his shoulder. 'First floor, man. Look for the name on the door.'

Suttle found it at the end of a corridor bathed in light. The breeze, laden with the rich scent of honeysuckle, flooded in through open windows. He paused, glimpsing bees in the garden, impossibly fat, drifting from one huge flower to another. Turning away, he knocked on the door.

Professor Wambote had the kind of African face Suttle found impossible to date. He might have been fifty. He might have been two decades older. He was a small man with curls of greying hair and a slight stoop. The paleness of his skin suggested mixed blood. Suttle loved the cardigan.

As a courtesy Suttle offered his warrant card, but Wambote waved it away. He wanted him to come in. He had juice, coffee, water. Later they could have lunch. But first he wanted Suttle to meet the woman in his life.

He said it with a sparkle in his eye. In a corner of the big office sat a woman even smaller than Wambote. She struggled to her feet and hobbled across. She was wearing woollen socks and leather slippers. There were tribal marks on the stretched leather of her face. What little hair she had was neatly gathered under a knotted scarf. She shook Suttle's outstretched hand.

'My mother,' Wambote said. 'Salome.'

Suttle thanked them both for their time. He'd try and keep this thing as brief as possible. Sunday was probably precious to them. He was sorry to interrupt their weekend.

Wambote wasn't having it. He'd taken the armchair beside his mother's, one hand on her arm.

'Please.' He gestured at the other armchair. 'You've come a long way.'

Suttle told them what had happened in the Topsham house by the river. He suspected they both might remember the property.

'Magharibi.' The word rolled around Wambote's mouth. 'Lovely views. Rather wasted though, don't you think?'

'On who?'

'On Mr Moncrieff.'

Suttle studied him for a moment, trying to gauge exactly what he meant. Erin had talked of raised voices, some kind of row.

'Did you know Mr Moncrieff?'

'Only by reputation.'

'May I ask you why?'

'Because he was a man with a history. And that, Mr Suttle, happens to be my field.'

He explained that he was Kenyan by birth, half Kikuyu, half something else.

'What?'

'British. My mother, my real mother, was raped by one of your soldiers. We called them Johnnies. Her name was Helen, Helen Muringo. She was a prisoner — I beg your pardon, a *detainee* — in one of your camps. It was called Kamiti. The regime was harsh. You wanted us, even the women, to see the error of our ways. You called it re-education. In my business I find that language can mask a thousand crimes. Re-education?' He seemed to savour the word. 'I think not.'

Wambote's lightness of touch, coupled with the warmth of his smile, hid a chilling precision. He was enumerating the various tortures inflicted by the British, ticking them off on his long fingers. This was a world of boots and fists and rifle butts. This was a regime where a woman suspected of the slightest infringement of camp rules would have scorching eggs stuffed into her vagina. His real mother, he said, had been forced to carry buckets brimming with shit in the heat of the sun. Her crime? Refusing to ferry dead babies, neatly tied in bundles of six, three kilometres to their collective grave.

'It was a shameful time,' he said, 'shameful for

you and shameful for us. My mother died. I never knew her.'

'I'm sorry.'

'That means nothing, young man. It wasn't your fault.'

'But Moncrieff? Was he the Johnny? Was he your father?'

'No. Soldiers help themselves in every war. It's a commonplace. There are many Kenyans like me — mixed blood, mixed race, relics of someone else's empire. No, what Mr Moncrieff did was infinitely worse.'

Suttle saw his hand tighten on Salome's skinny arm. There was a cloudiness in her eyes that reminded Suttle of Roz.

Her voice was low. 'I was a friend of Helen,' she said, 'in the camp. We were both in the black compound. The black compound was the worst. If you were lucky, if they liked you, one day you might go to *ng'ombe*.'

'To where?'

'The white compound,' said Wambote. 'The British called their system the Pipeline. You put shit in pipelines. You put water in pipelines. Never people. Not unless you want to humiliate them.'

Suttle nodded. He was still looking at Salome, inviting her to carry on.

'When Helen died,' she said, 'I looked after Josiah. He became my son. When I got out of the Pipeline, when they let me go, I took him back to my home village. My husband was a man called Atieno. He'd been in the Pipeline too, in a different camp. I told my husband the truth

— that my son was adopted, that he really belonged to someone else — but he didn't believe me. He thought I'd given myself to a white man, to a Johnny. He couldn't stand it. He couldn't stand the shame. In the end he killed himself. It happened a lot. Not just to my husband.'

After the British left, she said, she moved to Nairobi to work for one of the new companies that came with independence. What she wanted was the best education for Josiah. She moved from company to company, more money, better jobs.

'And you know what, Mr Suttle? My son won a scholarship. To Nairobi University.' She turned in her chair to pat Wambote on the arm as if it had happened only yesterday. 'And after that he became famous in all Africa.'

The word famous seemed to pain Wambote. The truth, he said, was that after he got his degree he left Kenya for West Africa. Nairobi, he said, was too noisy, too violent, and even after independence it was no place to have a Johnny in your gene pool. And so he found his way to Ghana, here to Accra, where he got a post as a lecturer and began work on a book.

Suttle knew the name of this book. *Land and Freedom* had become the definitive account of what the British had done in Kenya in the name of justice. It was the Kenyan view, the black view, of what had happened during the brutal years of the Mau Mau uprising. This was the book, according to the accounts Suttle had read on the Internet, that had taken Josiah Wambote to a

Professorship and made his name.

Suttle was still looking at Salome, trying to picture what she must have looked like during the years of struggle. 'You must have been proud,' he said.

'I am proud. I will always be proud.'

'But angry too.'

'Of course.'

'So is that why you came to England? Back in May?'

She seemed not to understand the question. Wambote answered it for her.

'The British have many files from those years,' he said. 'We historians knew about those files, but they'd never let us get anywhere near them. Then we took them to court and after that they *had* to release them.'

The files, he said, confirmed every accusation that Kikuyu survivors had made against the British.

'They called us Kukes,' he said. 'They wanted us to know our place and they wanted us to die without the world ever knowing the truth. That won't happen now. Thanks to the British courts.' He offered a polite nod of appreciation.

'Is that what you were doing in Britain? In May?'

'Yes.' Another nod. 'There was a conference. Whites. Blacks. Even half-Johnnies like me. We were celebrating our victory. It was a wonderful week.'

'But you went to Topsham too.'

'We did.'

'To see Moncrieff?'

'Of course.'

'Why?'

Wambote smiled and half-turned to his mother again. 'Tell him. Tell him what happened at Kamiti.'

★　★　★

At the Royal Trafalgar Dawn Ellis was still describing the opening hours of the search for Grace. By five o'clock, with the child still missing, the operation had been escalated to the Critical Incident Cadre under the duty Chief Inspector. A Detective Inspector from CID had been tasked to pull together an Intelligence Cell and searches had begun on the Violent and Sexual Offender Register. A dog team had arrived on Southsea Common and the Force Support Unit with specialist search skills was in transit from a job in Aldershot. Down the coast, at Shoreham Airport, a helicopter with infrared cameras was fuelled and ready to deploy.

Lizzie was genuinely impressed. She'd glimpsed a little of this gathering storm of activity, and Jimmy had done his best to fill in the gaps, but already she'd become aware that the police — despite the fact that Suttle was one of their own — were keeping them at arm's length. By now they'd had an officer assigned to them, a WPC who Jimmy happened to know, but however hard they pressed her she seemed to offer nothing but a box of tissues and the comforts of an encircling arm.

She tried to get a little of this frustration

across to Dawn, who simply nodded.

'Happens every time,' she said. 'At that point we treat you as suspects.'

'*Suspects?*'

'Of course. Most crimes are domestic. Most murders are committed by someone who knows the victim. The same with missing kids. You were no different. We bottomed it out pretty quickly, of course, took you out of the frame, but it's a process we have to go through.'

'How did you bottom it out?'

'Talked to a few people. Ran a few checks. Don't ask me for details because I won't tell you, but that's the deal, that's what happens.'

By now, she said, reinforcements were pouring into Pompey. Off-duty coppers from every corner of the county found themselves binning their Saturday nights and driving south. A Gold Command Group had been established at Fratton nick and begun the first of a series of meetings that would extend through the coming days. Without a Scene of Crime or any forensic evidence, the Gold Commander was forced to hypothesise.

'That means guess,' Lizzie said.

'You're right. But we're in the process of elimination now. So either she's in the sea. Or she's hiding with mates. Or she's been taken by a family member. Or she's been abducted.'

Abducted, Even the sound of the word made Lizzie shudder. What had this to do with poor Claire Dillon?

'So what did you think?'

'We didn't. We worked on each hypothesis. All

384

the guys coming in let us widen the search parameters. We started looking at the east of the island, at the area around Fort Cumberland, at Milton Ponds. We had unmarked cars on all the exits to the north of the island, checking out vehicles that might be of interest. We had officers at the stations. More at the hovercraft and the ferry terminals. The Intel guys were tagging hits on ANPR. The chopper was up that night. Body heat shows up on infrared.'

'Even dead?'

'Yeah. For several hours.'

Lizzie nodded. She'd heard the chatter of the helicopter as it circled the island. By mid-evening they were back at her mum's place at Anchorage Park, praying for the phone to ring. She remembered her mum digging out an old bottle of Ribena for them both, as if they were ill. Extra vitamin C. Bizarre.

'Media's absolutely key.' Dawn hadn't finished. 'We'd pinged out the pix from Jimmy's mobile already and flooded Facebook and Twitter. The story was national by now and Gold called a press conference for the Sunday morning. Overnight we were printing thousands of posters, using one of the phone images, and the Gold group was organising for house to house at first light.'

Many of these guys, she said, had worked with Jimmy and were only too happy to bend the rules. Certain addresses were prime targets, the occupants deemed to be dodgy when it came to young kids, and they got an earlier call than the rest. Anything to do a mate a favour. Anything to bust through the front door and find Grace in one piece.

'This happened?'

'Yes.'

'Legally?'

'Pass.'

Lizzie didn't know whether to be grateful or not. As a journalist she'd always been prickly about civil rights, but in her heart, when the chips were down, she knew she didn't care a fuck. Get my daughter back. Whatever it takes.

Dawn was talking about the press conference now. It had taken place at the Media Centre at Netley. The room had been packed with reporters and photographers. The guys from the nationals had no manners at all. Lizzie had watched them from the table on the raised dais she shared with Jimmy and the Gold Commander.

She and Jimmy had agreed to make a joint statement, and they'd both managed to get through it in one piece, but the questions afterwards had made her ashamed of her trade. Everyone, naturally, had wanted to know how she felt, how she was coping. She'd done her best to avoid the word devastated, but it was a question from a stringer working for one of the red tops that had nearly seen her off. This was a woman who was plainly disappointed at the lack of tears. 'Your daughter may be in the hands of a paedophile gang,' she'd suggested. 'How does that make you feel?' Lizzie remembered staring at her, shocked and affronted by the tackiness of the question. She'd been framing a brisk reply when Jimmy had stepped in, an act of kindness for which she'd be eternally grateful. 'How do you think it makes us feel?' he'd said, turning to the next raised hand.

Now Dawn wanted to know how she'd found the strength to get through the conference. She'd been at the back of the room, waiting to brief the Gold Commander on developments over the last half-hour, and like the rest of the nation she'd been astonished at the way both she and Jimmy had kept themselves together.

'I'd have been in bits,' she said. 'It would have been ugly.'

Lizzie permitted herself the ghost of a smile.

'I *was* in bits,' she said. 'And there are times when I still am.'

★　★　★

'Kamiti?' The old woman lifted her head towards the light. 'You want to know about Kamiti?'

'About Moncrieff,' Suttle said, 'if there's a difference.'

Wambote smiled and then offered Suttle a tiny nod of appreciation. 'I like that,' he murmured. 'I like that a lot.'

Salome was leaning forward in the armchair now, rocking slightly back and forth, and Suttle wondered how many times she'd told this story. At Kamiti, she said, the detainees received visits from Christian missionaries, who sometimes organised special 'cleansing' ceremonies. On one occasion the Archbishop of Mombasa turned up.

'His name was Beecher,' Wambote said. 'The

Reverend Leonard Beecher. And he'd come with a camera crew. They worked for Pathé. It was a big name at the time. Every cinema showed Pathé newsreels. This was before television.'

Suttle nodded. These were the people for whom Moncrieff had worked when he was doing National Service in Kenya. He'd translated for them, made himself useful, and much later, back in the UK after his discharge from the army, they'd opened the door to all the riches that followed.

'So what happened?'

The old woman was squinting at him. She had a gummy smile, which vanished as quickly as it had appeared.

'There were hundreds of us in the crowd,' she said. 'The missionary people talked and the Archbishop talked, and afterwards the man with the camera came over to us. He wanted to find someone to film. There was another man, younger, with him. He had a uniform on. He was a Johnny. He made all the decisions. The cameraman had gone to get more film. The Johnny went from face to face. In the end, I don't know why, he chose me. I had my little baby on my back. Little Josiah. His face was covered against the heat. It wasn't the picture he wanted. Then the cameraman came back, and the Johnny talked to the cameraman and he pointed at me and the cameraman nodded, and the Johnny came over and flicked the cloth back from my baby's face. Then he saw that my baby was a Johnny's baby, not a black baby at all, not a real black baby, and he leaned forward like

388

this — ' she beckoned Suttle closer ' — and blew me a kiss. I knew what the kiss meant. We all knew what the kiss meant. It meant that I was a whore. It meant that the Johnnies could do what they wanted with us. It meant that we were easy. And you know something? That kiss was worse than any rape.'

Suttle sat back in the chair. He was looking at Wambote. 'You know the name of the Johnny?'

'Yes.'

'How?'

'I traced the film. I traced the cameraman. The name was there in his location report.' The smile again, and the faintest sigh of regret. 'Your Mr Moncrieff.'

★ ★ ★

It was nearly lunchtime at the Royal Trafalgar Hotel before Dawn got to the end of her account. Over the course of the weekend the nation appeared to have taken the hunt for little Grace to its heart. Pictures of her from Suttle's mobile were all over the media, triggering an avalanche of crank calls to the Hantspol Control Room. Each of these calls was carefully sifted, yielding nothing of any evidential value while wasting hours of precious resource.

The Gold Commander, meanwhile, had extended the house-to-house parameters and was now knocking on doors city-wide. By Monday morning, said Dawn, Pompey mums — easily roused — were getting vocal. It was obvious to them that a killer paedo was on the loose. This, in turn, attracted the more predatory print reporters, who were only too happy to turn Grace's disappearance into a media shit storm.

Lizzie nodded. On the Monday morning, desperate for a change of scene, she'd left her mum's house and paid a visit to a local supermarket. The newspapers were racked by the door, and it was bizarre to see her daughter grinning back at her from every front page. BY THE GRACE OF GOD went one headline, a tasteless and probably confected quote from a Pompey mum who'd locked up her entire brood until the paedo was safely behind bars.

She shared the memory with Dawn, who wasn't the least surprised. Nearly twenty years in the Job, she said, had taught her a great deal about the darker reaches of human behaviour. Then, on the Monday afternoon, there came a 999 from a man named Neville Stockton.

Lizzie stiffened. 'This is the guy . . . ?'

'Yeah. We didn't know it at the time, but the woman who took the call had the sense to alert her controller. It sounded different. And it was.'

Neville Stockton appeared to be calm. He said he was calling from the corridor outside his apartment in St Martin's House on Clarence Parade. He'd just come back from a weekend in London. Like everyone else, he'd seen the pictures of young Grace. He'd let himself into his flat and found the little girl in the spare bedroom. She appeared to be asleep.

The woman handling the call had asked for more details. Was there anyone else at the address? Stockton had said yes. He had a lodger called Claire Dillon. And she had mental health issues.

Claire Dillon. Mental health issues. Grace asleep in the spare bedroom.

Lizzie was staring at Dawn. She knew a little of this. She knew the guy was a pensioner. She knew his address. She'd stood on Southsea Common and stared up at his balcony. But she'd never heard the story recounted in such detail, not even at the inquest.

Grace asleep in the spare bedroom.

'So what happened?'

'The call was escalated quick-time to the Gold Command Group. We have a vulnerable child in the same premises as the woman who may have snatched her. She has issues. That's problematic. She also, we assume, has access to weapons, certainly knives in the kitchen. That's going to put everyone at risk, certainly the guy who owns the flat and probably us.'

'And Grace?'

'Grace too. In these situations you always have options. Stockton was told not to re-enter the apartment. We sent a couple of cars to secure the block. Then Gold had to make a decision. If he thinks time's on his side, he can play the long game. That means covert surveillance, protracted negotiation, the whole nine yards. This stuff can go on for days and can be really messy. Plus it's going to turn into a circus. The media can't help themselves. They're the kids in the sweet shop.'

Lizzie nodded. The siege at Chantry Cottage last year had lasted barely four hours but

391

watching the gathering forces on live television had been an experience Lizzie never wanted to repeat. Dawn was right. Turning her daughter's fate into days of breaking news would have been close to unbearable.

'So that's why you decided to go straight in?'

'Yes. It wasn't a decision that Gold took lightly, but at the time it must have felt right. We have specialist officers on the Force Support Unit. We call it Dynamic Armed Entry. The guys train for stuff like this. They were standing by. It should have worked.'

'But it didn't.'

'No.'

Dawn extended a hand across the table. She'd taken the story as far as she could. Thanks to the media blitz, the hunt for Grace had narrowed to a single pensioner letting himself into his retirement flat. He'd recognised the face on the pillow. Made the call. Done the right thing. And the rest of the story, in Dawn's phrase, told itself.

Did this level of detail help? Lizzie wasn't sure. The first she and Jimmy had known of events at St Martin's House was a phone call minutes after the incident had come to an end. A CID mate on the inside, unaware of what had happened, had phoned to say that Grace had been found. Lizzie's mum had turned the TV on. News-gathering these days happened at the speed of light. Within minutes the broadcasters were pumping out footage from camera phones on the common. Horrible. Horrible beyond description.

Dawn's hand had closed on hers.

'All we can say is sorry,' she said.

'We?'

'Me.' She gave Lizzie's hand a squeeze. 'Tell Jimmy, yeah?'

18

East Devon. Mid-afternoon, with a curtain of rain pushing up the Exe estuary, a man was walking his dog across fields outside the village of Woodbury. His path home led him through a farm. One of the barns on the farm had been converted into a workshop specialising in camper vans. Tucked into a hedge nearby was an old Portakabin.

The dog ran towards the Portakabin and nosed at the gap under the door. Then it started barking. Its owner arrived and hauled the dog off, putting it on a lead, but the dog kept tugging him back to the door. Something was in there. Something not good. Even the man could smell it.

He tried the door. It seemed to be locked. He pushed harder, then gave it a kick. The door flew open. It was nearly dusk by now, the cold grey light draining from the surrounding fields, the first of the rain dimpling the puddles of standing water at the man's feet. Inside the smell was overpowering. Drains, the man thought. Or something worse.

He found a switch. The neon strip flickered into life, bathing the interior of the cabin in a harsh white glare. The dog was almost out of control, pawing at the floor, straining at the

394

leash. The man never fed the dog until sundown. It was hungry.

At the far end of the Portakabin was a long table, the kind you might see in a doctor's surgery. A woman's body lay on its back, legs splayed, naked except for a thin gold chain around her neck. There were savage slash marks across her face and breasts and her lower belly lay wide open, a glistening soup of entrails, rich yellows and mauves and a thick viscous black where the blood had coagulated. There was more blood on the floor, a dark trail of feathered splats that led to the door. Even in December there were flies.

The man hauled the dog outside into the gathering darkness. When he at last found his phone, he had to kick the dog into silence.

'Police,' he managed. 'Quick as you can.'

★ ★ ★

Suttle caught up with Nandy around four thirty. He'd returned to the hotel. Lunch with Wambote and his mother had made him feel immeasurably better. They'd eaten in the senior staff refectory at the university. Suttle had never had ostrich before. Wambote, who was a vegetarian, had toasted him with fresh lime juice and inspected his mother's fish to make sure there were no bones. Suttle liked to think they'd all parted friends.

Now he was sitting in Nandy's room while the Det-Supt took a shower.

'How did you get on, sir?' he shouted.

'Not well.'

Nandy emerged from the bathroom, towelling himself dry. Heat rash had exploded on his chest and belly, tiny scarlet eruptions. He'd been through Ousmane's visa application, line by line, with Perry Lonsdale, the Entry Clearance Manager. There was nothing out of line, nothing unusual, nothing to suggest that Moncrieff had given Ousmane a helping push towards the house by the river and a new life in Europe.

Ndiaye's bank statements checked out with his salary slips from the Parakeet café and from another job he had in a backstreet auto repair shop. Pulling the equivalent of about three hundred and seventy-five pounds a month, he'd saved enough to buy his Turkish Airlines open return and support himself in the UK. His visa ran from 1 December, the day before he landed at Heathrow, and lasted for six months. His hotel booking for his first night in London had been cancelled when he got to Heathrow but there was nothing suspicious in that. Ousmane Ndiaye's visa application, as far as the ECM was concerned, was 100 per cent kosher.

Suttle told Nandy about Wambote and his mum. Since the Professor's return from the UK in May, apart from one guest lecture in Nairobi, he'd not left Accra. His mother hadn't been well, he was hard at work on another book, and with great regret he'd ruled himself out of any involvement in Moncrieff's death.

His visit to the house by the river had, he seemed to suggest, been a private settling of accounts. He'd gone to let this man know exactly what kind of humiliation he'd inflicted on his mother in the name, he said, of colonial arrogance. Moncrieff had refused to recognise the accusation, a denial that Wambote had evidently expected. He'd had a number of black and white blow-ups printed from the frame of news film that had captured the moment when Moncrieff blew his mother that derisive kiss, and it had given him some satisfaction to leave one at his bedside.

'This is a man for whom other people have always been invisible,' he said quietly, 'but God is always watching.'

The news that the Almighty might have played some role in Moncrieff's death gave Nandy no satisfaction whatsoever. Wambote had also presented Suttle with a copy of the photo.

Still semi-naked, Nandy sat on his bed and studied it for a moment. Neither he nor Suttle could remember seeing this shot in the Scenes of Crime log. Where had it gone?

Nandy got dressed. He was due at the High Commission for drinks with the Head of Mission. He was still convinced that Olly Moncrieff had done a deal of some kind with Ousmane but he lacked the evidence that would justify further enquiries. Detailed analysis of Moncrieff's financial affairs and sight of mobile phone billings lay within the jurisdiction of the Ghanaian Police. So far the Chief Superintendent had been more than helpful, but the fact that these guys had let Ousmane slip out of the country didn't fill Nandy with confidence. Neither would the High Commission welcome a protracted investigation. Nandy wasn't in the business of accepting defeat, but even he had to admit that the case against Olly Moncrieff was looking pretty thin.

'So how was he last night?'

'Pissed.'

'What did he say?'

'Nothing we'd be interested in.'

Nandy nodded, holding Suttle's gaze. Then a smile ghosted over his face.

'Good night, was it?'

'Excellent, sir. Since you're asking.'

★ ★ ★

With Nandy en route to the High Commission, Suttle retired for a nap. He was asleep when the phone went. It was Moncrieff. He was down in the lobby. He wanted a word.

Suttle dressed and took the lift to the ground floor. Moncrieff, in shorts and a light cotton shirt, was deep in conversation with a black woman in the seating area beside reception. At first Suttle assumed the woman worked for the hotel. She was in her thirties, smartly dressed, a fold of silk scarf around her neck, extremely attractive. She turned to watch Suttle approach as Moncrieff got to his feet.

'Njeka.' He gestured down at the woman. 'My other half.'

Njeka was on her feet. She took Suttle's outstretched hand. Her English was perfect. 'I've heard so much about you.' She was still holding his hand. 'I'm glad you like our little town.'

'Do I?'

'So Olly says. I'm sorry I couldn't make last night. I was on duty.'

Moncrieff explained that Njeka was a casualty doctor in the city's biggest hospital. Suttle was looking hard at his face. He'd shaved since last night.

'So what can I do for you?'

Moncrieff nodded at a sofa on the other side of reception. He'd like a private word.

Njeka drifted off to inspect a line of gift cabinets while Suttle and Moncrieff settled on the sofa. Suttle wondered whether this was about last night, maybe some kind of apology, but he was wrong.

'I want to tell you about Kennan,' Moncrieff said. 'You guys shouldn't go home empty-handed.'

Kennan, he explained to Suttle, was Hilary's only son. The boy was barely a year out of university, some crap degree in drama and music, but he definitely had a mind of his own. He'd watched the end of his parents' marriage from a distance and after college had absolutely no interest in coming home. Like every other student in the country he was skint, but the old man still had a house out in Spain.

He was about to go into further detail but Suttle cut him short. He already knew about Kennan.

'Your father loved him. Have I got that right?'

'Absolutely. Kennan's a clever little tyke and he knew exactly how to play the old bastard.' He bent a little closer. Suttle could smell whisky on his breath. 'We had a conversation last night. You remember?'

'Go on.'

'You told me you'd never met such a fucked-up family in your life. You said Dad was a G28 waiting to happen.' He paused. 'G28?'

'It's a form we used when I was serving in Pompey. It's shorthand for murder.'

'Right.' Moncrieff looked delighted. 'You know something? You're dead right. That's why I got out. That's why Kennan got out. The Moncrieffs are the devil's spawn. Dad was a G28 waiting to happen.'

'So who killed him?'

'I've no idea.'

'Are you surprised he met his end that way?'

'Not in the least. Dad played the odds all his life. One day they'd bite him in the arse. Am I sad about it? Not really. Because, knowing him, he'd love all the attention. Better go out as a headline than some dribbler in a wheelchair.'

'Will you miss him?'

'Yes, in a way I will. Not personally, because we seldom met any more. But I'll miss the *idea* of him, sat in that house making everyone's life a misery. World class, my dad. World-class curmudgeon. Mr Impossible. Dying breed. Definitely.'

'Tell me about Neil.'

'You know about Neil. You've met him. All the clues are there. The guy's a shell, a husk of a man. Dad turned him upside down and gave him a shake. He did that time after time. He enjoyed it. My brother's so frightened that

400

sometimes he can't put two words together. Makes conversation on the phone really tricky. You can imagine.'

'Frightened or angry?'

'God knows. Maybe both. But that's for you to decide, isn't it?'

Suttle didn't answer. This man knew he was in the frame. He knew he was a suspect. Yet here he was, out of reach, quick on his feet, parrying every question with that tight little smile on his face. Forty years earlier this could have been Rupert Moncrieff. Like his dad, Olly regarded himself as weightless, invulnerable, not subject to the laws of gravity. Two cops had crossed a continent to get at him. And they'd found out nothing.

'About Kennan.' His hand was on Suttle's thigh. 'I phoned the boy in Spain this morning. He's in with some interesting people.' He gave Suttle's thigh a tiny squeeze. 'It might be wise to pay him a visit. I know he'll be happy to see you.'

* * *

The news of the killing in East Devon got to Accra in the early evening. Nandy was at a Chinese restaurant downtown with the Head of Mission and his wife. The Det-Supt was trying to explore what a more detailed investigation into Ousmane Ndiaye's visa application might involve when his phone rang. It was Carole Houghton.

Nandy mumbled an apology and took the call in the lobby.

'Sir? We've had a development.'

401

'When?'

'A couple of hours ago.' A body, she said, had been called in from Woodbury. A frenzied knife attack and a disembowelling.

'Man? Woman?'

'A woman. It's Erin Maguire, sir.'

She briefly filled in the details. Scenes of Crime were already on site. Her partner, Tim Stone, had been detained on suspicion of murder and would be interviewed very shortly. In the meantime someone else of interest had disappeared.

'Who?'

'Neil Moncrieff. Roz phoned an hour ago. She hasn't seen him since last night.'

Nandy grunted his thanks and brought the conversation to an end before putting a call through to Suttle. Then he returned to the table. Under the circumstances there seemed no point in leaving the meal unfinished. He was halfway through a plate of fresh lychees when his phone rang again. It was Suttle. Nandy didn't leave the table this time. He listened for a moment, checked his watch, then pocketed the mobile. When the Head of Mission enquired whether Olly Moncrieff should be alerted to the possibility of another interview, Nandy shook his head.

'We're on a flight out first thing tomorrow morning,' he said. 'I don't think we'll be bothering Mr Moncrieff for a while.'

19

Nandy and Suttle were in the Incident Room for an eight o'clock start. The flight from Ghana had been delayed several hours and it was gone midnight before they cleared customs at Heathrow. Houghton had sent a car to collect them, but they weren't back in Devon until three in the morning.

Nandy had kept himself updated by phone over the last twenty-four hours. Now he wanted the full picture.

Houghton looked almost as exhausted as they were. Tim Stone, she said at once, had been released without charge. He'd spent the weekend with mates in Bristol, and his alibi checked out. Not only that but he'd been pulled for speeding on the M5 on the way home on Sunday afternoon. No way could he have killed Erin Maguire.

'Which leaves Neil Moncrieff?'

'Yes, sir. That's the way it's looking. Ripping out a foetus is a pretty extreme thing to do but I suppose he'd have the motive.'

'That's what he did?'

'According to the pathologist, yes.'

'Protecting the family estate? That's insane.'

'Quite.'

Roz, Houghton said, had contacted Wendy

Atkins on Sunday afternoon. Neil, she said, had agreed to take her to church on Sunday morning but hadn't shown up. That had never happened before, but what was more troubling was the way he'd been when she'd last talked to him.

'Which was?'

'Saturday midday. She said he'd sounded really odd, very abrupt, not himself at all. She'd asked him what was the matter but he wouldn't tell her. Just said she knew already.'

'Knew what?'

'That was it. She hadn't got a clue. She said it was like she'd done something wrong. She couldn't make it out at all.'

Suttle wanted to know whether Hilary had been in the house over the weekend. Houghton said no. According to the FLO, Wendy Atkins, she was staying at her boyfriend's place in Exmouth.

'Leaving Neil in the house by himself?'

'That's the way it looks.'

'So where has he gone?'

Houghton said she'd no idea. She'd circulated his photo and details force-wide. She'd put out a media appeal. She'd arranged for extra overtime for uniformed beat officers in Exmouth. She'd organised checks on empty properties in the surrounding villages. So far, not a single sighting. This, she pointed out, was a man without friends and therefore without options. Yet he'd simply vanished.

'You think he might have topped himself?'

'It's a possibility. We're thinking of putting the chopper up.'

'Does Roz have friends he might be holed up with?'

'Not that she admits.'

'No note at the Topsham house?'

'Nothing. We started boshing the place again on Sunday night. The CSM still had a log of objects from Moncrieff's bedroom, which was helpful.'

'Why?'

'Because another of those machetes has gone missing.'

* * *

It was Dawn Ellis who slipped the address to Lizzie. Neville Stockton, she said, had put his apartment in St Martin's House on the market in the days following the death of Grace and Claire. To date, in a difficult market, it had yet to sell, but there was no way he'd ever set foot in the place again. Pressed for more details about Stockton, Dawn said she'd never met him. He'd failed to turn up at the inquest into Grace's death, pleading a nervous breakdown.

Now she understood he was living in a cheap rental in Wymering, a run-down area of ex-council housing in the north of the city. According to a Community Psychiatric Nurse who was keeping an eye on him, he'd gone to ground. A neighbour did most of his shopping and on the rare days he set foot outside the door, he hid behind dark glasses and a thick scarf.

Lizzie drove to Wymering. Third Avenue

descended from the busy main road that ran along the foot of Portsdown Hill. As a cub reporter Lizzie had known this area well. The maze of council houses had always been a reliable source of a certain kind of story. If you were looking for evidence that the glue holding society together was beginning to dissolve, this was a good place to start.

The address lay on the west side of the road. A neighbouring property was festooned with Christmas lights with a fat blow-up reindeer tethered in the scrap of front garden. Lizzie stepped in through the gate. Neville Stockton, according to Dawn, lived on the ground floor.

He came to the door on her third knock. He looked ill. His cardigan was threadbare at the elbows and his trousers were stained from a thousand food spills. This morning's shave had missed most of his chin, and the rest sported tiny wisps of cotton wool where he'd cut himself. He badly needed a haircut.

Lizzie stared at him. Barely a week ago she'd been looking at photos of Claire Dillon in late adolescence. She'd been a poster girl. She'd had the world at her feet. How come she'd ended up in this man's life?

Stockton wasn't at all clear who she was. Lizzie did her best to spell it out. The name Claire Dillon moistened his eyes.

'You'd better come in — ' he held the door open ' — before you freeze to death.'

The flat was cosier than Lizzie had expected. The radiators were on full blast and Stockton seemed to have found room for a cat in his life. It was a tabby, comfortably fat, and lay sprawled on the sofa.

'You want tea? I do tea.'

Without waiting for an answer, he disappeared. Lizzie heard the splash of water into a kettle. On a small occasional table, beside a carefully folded copy of the *Daily Telegraph*, there was a nest of photos. All of them showed a slightly younger Neville Stockton, and in most of them he had a woman his own age on his arm. In the later pictures she was beginning to put on weight but was still attractive.

'My wife, Jessie.' Stockton was back with the tea. 'Thank God she can't see me now.'

He put the tray down and tore the wrapping from a packet of biscuits. Jess, he said, had died a couple of years ago. Cancer. They'd been living on the seafront for a while by that time, and the real sadness was that she'd loved it so much.

'We both did,' he said. 'You can't beat a view like that.'

Lizzie was beginning to suspect this man was a lot less deranged than he had first appeared, although so far he didn't seem to have recognised her.

'I'm Grace's mum,' she said. 'In case you were wondering.'

'Baby Grace?'

'Baby Grace.'

He put the teapot down and stepped across and gave her a hug. He smelled unloved.

'And is that why you've come? To find out about Grace?'

'Yes.'

407

He studied her for a moment as if weighing up some private decision.

'Good,' he said at last. 'I'm glad.'

'Why?'

'Because I've never talked about it. Except to the police, and that doesn't count.'

★ ★ ★

It was late morning before Luke Golding joined Suttle in the Incident Room. Carole Houghton wanted them both to pay Hilary Moncrieff a visit to press her yet again on Neil. She wasn't convinced that she'd been telling the whole truth over the past week, and the brutality of what had happened to Erin, coupled with Neil's disappearance, might just prompt an admission or two.

Golding looked wrecked. On the drive down to Topsham Suttle enquired further. If Golding and Oona had kissed and made up, so be it. He'd apologise for looking after her and call it quits. No hard feelings. Blame the booze.

'So how's it going?' Suttle asked.

'How's what going?'

'Everything.'

'You mean me and Oona?'

'Yes.'

Golding shrugged, said he didn't want to talk about it. Suttle wondered whether to press him or not, but then Golding changed his mind. He kept checking the rear-view mirror, refusing to look Suttle in the face.

'If you want the fucking truth, skip, she's

missing you. In fact she talks of nothing else. Whatever you did to her definitely hit the spot. Don't get me wrong. I'm not giving you a hard time. Twat, me.'

'Didn't I tell you?'

'You did, skip.'

'And now?'

'I'm the baddest boy.'

'So what does that make me?'

'Lucky.' At last he looked Suttle in the eye. 'That Nicinha was right, wasn't she? About getting it on with someone you knew?'

'She was, yes.'

'So maybe I should have listened harder. Worked it out beforehand.'

'Yeah. Maybe you should. And maybe Treasure wasn't such a great idea either.'

Golding nodded, said nothing.

Suttle shot him a sideways glance. 'Was it only Treasure?'

'No.'

'And did Oona find out?'

'Yes.'

'When?'

'The last couple of days. She wanted the truth. Else . . .'

'Else what?'

'Else we'd be history.'

'And?'

'We're history. My call, in case you're wondering. She wanted an absolute guarantee that it would never happen again. That's fairyland and we both know it.'

The next mile sped by. Then Suttle asked

whether Golding blamed him for the break-up.

Golding shook his head. 'We were a car crash waiting to happen. She's a fantastic woman. She deserves someone who won't fuck her around. For the record, skip, I'm glad it's you. One day you might tell me how it's done.'

'How what's done?'

'Sticking with one woman. And meaning it.'

'You think I'm some kind of expert? With a marriage like mine?'

'I think you're in a pretty shit place.' Golding slowed for a bus. 'And I think you need someone like Oona to sort you out.'

★ ★ ★

They found Hilary Moncrieff in the kitchen at the house beside the river. This was the first time she'd returned in a couple of days, and once again she'd found the white SOC van in the drive. A lone CSI had been waiting to be let in, and now he was taking Neil's room apart.

'We need to find him,' Suttle emphasised, 'before this thing gets any worse.'

She nodded. She looked pale and drawn, and her hands were shaking as she decanted sugar into a bowl. Something's happened, Suttle told himself. Something very recent.

He asked her to sit down. He'd seen the Scenes of Crime shots from the Portakabin, Erin's torso slashed to ribbons, and in his mind there was little doubt about the two murders. They both spoke of anger and extreme violence. They both involved a blade of some kind. In

Moncrieff's case the weapon had been one of his own machetes. Now another one had gone missing.

'We have to be looking at Neil,' he said. 'And you'll understand why.'

Hilary nodded, said nothing.

Golding asked her how unstable she thought he might be.

'Unstable?'

'We get the impression he bottles things up.'

'That's true. He has done all his life.'

'That's what Olly said.' This from Suttle.

Hilary was staring at him. 'You've seen him, of course. You've been out there. To Africa.'

'Yes.'

'So what else did he say?'

'He said your father put himself in harm's way.'

'That's true too. Is that the same as deserving it?'

Suttle shrugged. If there was a case for a good murder, he said, it wasn't his job to make it. What interested him and his colleagues was who did it, when and how.

Hilary wanted to know more about Olly. Was he upset by what had happened? Was he coming back for the funeral?

'I doubt it.'

'On both counts?'

'Yes. Olly's nicely set up. He loves Africa exactly the way you told me, exactly the way his father did. He's turned his back on all this.' Suttle gestured around.

'On us, you mean.' Hilary was knotting her

411

hands. It was a small truth, perfectly phrased.

Suttle nodded. There was a long silence. On the other side of the river a train clattered south.

'Olly sent Ousmane, your mystery visitor, here,' he said softly. 'I'm guessing you knew that.'

Hilary's head came up. She looked suddenly old. 'You're right. We did.'

'And what was he supposed to do?'

'He was supposed to kill Pa.'

'Did you know that at the time?'

'Of course I didn't. It was a crazy idea. Totally lunatic.'

'So when did you find out?'

'This morning.'

'This *morning*? How?'

'Neil phoned me. He told me everything. He said Roz had a memory card. She'd never know what's on it, of course, but he didn't want to take the risk. That's why he phoned.'

'Where is he?'

'He wouldn't say. Except he's safe. A place where no one will ever find him.'

'And the memory card?'

'I picked it up from Roz this morning. She's in bits, poor thing.'

Suttle nodded. He wanted to get back to Ousmane. Why had he arrived early?

'No one knows.'

'Have you asked Olly?'

'Yes.' She nodded at the phone. 'I put a call through ten minutes ago. Just before you came.'

'And what did you say?'

'I asked him about Ousmane and this mad plan. He denied everything, of course, as he would. I expected nothing less. He said the man had been a friend. He said he'd issued a tourist visa in the normal way. When I asked him why he'd turned up five days early he said he hadn't a clue. He thought it was very African. He even laughed.'

'Was it a long conversation? With Olly?'

'Not really. He was at work. He was busy.'

'So what else did you tell him?'

'I told him about the memory card.'

'So what's on it?'

She seemed not to have heard the question. There came the chime of a single clock. Midday. The chant was taken up by the other clocks in the house, half a dozen of them, all chiming at once, a mad clamour. Hilary's head went down again, she buried her face in her hands, and she began to sob.

Golding left the room. Suttle tried to comfort her.

Then Golding was back. 'There's a laptop up in her room, skip. I think we ought to take a look.'

* * *

It was nearly lunchtime. Listening to Neville Stockton, Lizzie suddenly realised how hungry she was. After an hour of talking about his wife and kids, he'd yet to mention the other woman who'd stepped into his life.

'Tell me about Claire, Neville. Claire Dillon.'

'Claire?' He tried to brush the crumbs off his lap. 'I met her at that café by the tennis courts on the common. You know the one?'

Lizzie nodded. The courts had suddenly become popular among men and women of a certain age. They organised tournaments. There'd even been a tennis wedding. A fellow journalist had done a story on it way back in the early summer.

Claire, said Stockton, had been working behind the counter. He took a stroll down there most days, especially when the sun was out, and they'd got chatting. After a while, sensing a rapport, he'd asked her out for a drink.

'You were nearly three times her age, Neville.'

'That's true. But there was something about her — it's hard to put into words — something . . . I don't know . . . needy? She seemed lost to me. And she wasn't very good at the coffee either.'

Shortly afterwards, he said, she'd been called in by her boss. Some of the tennis players were complaining about the service and about her attitude.

'What does that mean?'

'She was in a world of her own. They'd make a joke and she wouldn't see it. They thought she was rude. Either that or stupid. Whatever the truth of it, she got the sack.'

She also turned out to be homeless. She'd been sleeping on friends' sofas. Evidently she never stayed long at one address.

'I had to drag this out of her. It wasn't easy. She kept insisting she could look after herself but it was obvious she couldn't.'

'Did you know she had family here?'

'No. I did ask, and she said no. She said her parents lived in Leeds.'

'Did you ever think of getting some kind of help for her?'

'Not really. To be honest I wouldn't have known where to start. I knew nothing about mental health. It had never come into our lives. Me and Jess.'

'So what did you do?'

'I offered her the spare room.'

'Did you ask for rent?'

'No. To be honest, she was company too. It could be lonely without Jess.'

Claire, he said, moved in towards the end of June. He remembered two things about that day. The first was her lack of baggage — just the single holdall — the other was the weather.

'It was such a beautiful day,' he said. 'Not a cloud in the sky from dawn till dusk. She arrived before lunch. I knew she was coming. I'd been out to Waitrose to get a little picnic — nice things, things I thought she'd like. I got a bottle of wine too. We ate on the balcony, overlooking the common. It was a wonderful start. She was never one for showing her emotions but she seemed really happy.'

Lizzie was wondering about the phantoms that had dogged Claire over the past couple of years. Was she hearing voices? Did she imagine other people in the room? Was she scanning the evening paper for private messages buried in some story or other?

Stockton wanted to shake his head, she knew he did, but she could see in his eyes that he'd known Claire was ill. It must have been hard, she thought, to make that admission to himself. It might have meant looking for outside help. That would have brought unwelcome visitors to his door. Worst case, she might have been sectioned again.

'That's what they do, isn't it?' he said. 'They take them away and lock them up. It's in the papers. You read about it.'

Lizzie nodded. She knew that this was Claire's nightmare as well. Twenty-eight days in the Bellamy Centre had told her everything she ever wanted to know about life inside. However well intentioned the care, the company of strangers had frightened her. So had there been some kind of compact between this odd couple? An unspoken acceptance that they'd keep each other's secrets for their mutual benefit? Claire to keep a roof over her head? Stockton to keep himself sane?

'Did you like her?' Lizzie asked.

'I did, yes, very much.'

'Because she needed you?'

'Because she trusted me. I know it sounds silly, but she became a kind of daughter. She never talked about her parents much but I got the impression she never got on with her father.'

Lizzie nodded, said nothing. She wanted to know about the weekend Stockton went off to London. Wasn't he worried about leaving Claire by herself?

'I was, yes. I left lots of food and some money and everything, but that wasn't it. What she needed was company.'

416

'You.'

'Yes.'

His real daughter, he said, had phoned on the Thursday. Her husband had left her and she was finding it hard to cope with the baby. She needed some kind of respite, someone to look after Sammy for an hour or two so she could get a little peace. The situation, she'd said, was tearing her apart. Please come, Dad. Please help.

'And so I did. Worst decision I ever made.'

He remembered himself and his daughter sitting in front of the TV all weekend, watching the drama unfold in Portsmouth. Little did he think the missing girl was tucked up with his new lodger.

'She'd never told you about trying to snatch the little girl in Leeds?'

'No.'

'About having an abortion when she was much younger?'

'No.'

'About the voices telling her to protect young children?'

'No.'

He shook his head and turned away, wanting the questions to stop. He was lying, she knew he was, but there seemed no point pursuing it any further. He'd tucked all this away in the furthest corner of his mind. It served no purpose to remember. That way lay nothing but pain.

The rest of the story Lizzie already knew. How he took the train back on the Monday. How he let himself into the flat. How he found Grace in Claire's bed in the spare room. And how he stole

417

out to share the news with the police.

'Was Claire there at the time?'

'Yes. She was watching television.'

'Did you ask her about the child in her bed? About Grace?'

'No.'

'Why not?'

'Because . . . ' His head tipped back. It was a question he appeared never to have asked himself. 'You want the truth?'

'Yes, please.'

'Because she frightened me. Seeing your daughter like that, your little Grace. Knowing what was going on. The number of people involved. It was scary.'

'And so you phoned 999?'

'I had to. I had no option. I realised we'd been living in a dream, Claire and I. That was my fault. Entirely my fault.' He looked around. 'I deserve all this. This is where I really belong.'

'Alone?'

'Yes.' He nodded.

My fault.

Lizzie gazed at him. Was this man what he looked? Was he really on the edge of madness or had he simply neglected himself? Let the silence grow heavier and heavier?

'I'm sorry,' he whispered at last. 'I'm really, really sorry. If you're looking for someone to blame, it's me. If there's anything I can do, just ask.'

Lizzie said nothing. She was thinking about the apartment in St Martin's House.

'Your flat's still for sale. Am I right?'

418

'Yes. No one wants it, not after what happened, and I'm not sure I blame them.'

Lizzie nodded. 'Do you still have a key?'

'Yes. Why?'

'I'd like to take a look.' She checked her watch. 'Would that be OK?'

★　★　★

Suttle followed Luke Golding upstairs to Hilary's bedroom. Hilary herself was still in the kitchen. As a precaution Suttle asked the CSI to accompany them. By now he had an inkling of what might follow. He needed someone from Scenes of Crime as a witness to whatever he and Luke might find. No way did he want to face any kind of challenge in court.

The laptop belonged to Hilary. She'd loaded the memory card into the SD slot. All Golding had to do was glide the mouse to the Play command. The screen came to life. The recording was dated 8/12/2013. The time 07.57.

They were suddenly in Moncrieff's bedroom. The old man appeared to be asleep. The camera angle was identical to the earlier sequences Golding had logged. Same camera, Suttle thought. Different memory card.

Neil Moncrieff stepped into the shot. He was wearing jeans and the top he'd bought on the pilgrim's route in Northern Spain. He took a brief look at his father then walked out of frame. When he returned, he was wearing rubber kitchen gloves and carrying the machete Suttle recognised from the Scenes of Crime photos. He

419

seemed to be talking to himself but it was impossible to tease any sense from what he was saying. The words disappeared into each other, utterly meaningless.

The old man jerked awake. He struggled upright in the bed, rubbing his eyes, watching this son of his taking practice sweeps with the machete. Then Neil crossed towards the bed and held the tip under his father's chin. His father stared at him for a moment and then started to laugh. Big mistake.

Neil took a tiny step backwards then slashed the machete backhand across the old man's face. At first Suttle thought the scream came from the old man. He was wrong. It came from Neil. He'd lost all control now. The sight of the blood pouring from his father's face sparked more violence. He slashed and jabbed with an eagerness Suttle found hard to associate with the shy, timid recluse he'd got to know.

This was a new Neil, a man reborn, taking his time and grunting with the effort of each blow. Moncrieff had collapsed back onto the scarlet pillow, his neck exposed. A final thrust severed the carotid artery. A fountain of blood soaked his son's sweatshirt.

Neil had stopped now. He hung over the bed, inspecting the wreckage of his father's face. From this angle it was impossible to see the expression on his face, but Suttle imagined a fierce delight in what he'd done. Revenge had been a long time coming. For most of his life he'd suffered countless torments at the hands of this man. Worse still, after acts of casual brutality

420

he could never forgive, Moncrieff had robbed him of his mother. But now the sins of the father had been repaid. In full.

Neil disappeared from the shot again. Then he was back with the hood. He shook it out, holding it at arm's length, getting the measure of this strange item, then he pulled it over Moncrieff's head, not bothering to feel for a pulse. He paused for a moment as if inspecting his handiwork before making a final adjustment to the hood. The crudeness of the eye holes stared back at him, unblinking. He stepped aside, throwing the camera a backward glance over his shoulder, making sure he wasn't spoiling the shot, and for several seconds he didn't move. Then he reached forward and took the hood off, laying it carefully on the pillow. Finally he turned and approached the camera. His face, his clothes, everything was covered in blood. Then he reached up towards the lens of the camera, and the picture cut suddenly to black.

Suttle found Hilary in the kitchen. She was still sitting at the table, her face a mask. He was studying her knotted hands. She wouldn't look up.

Suttle wanted to know about the sweatshirt. How come, barely an hour later, Neil had been wearing exactly the same shirt without a trace of blood on it?

Hilary appeared not to have heard the question. Suttle repeated it.

She stared at him, then she summoned a small cold smile. She and Neil had bought one each, exactly the same. Minutes before they arrived

421

she'd checked the drawer where she kept it. Her pilgrimage souvenir from Santiago de Compostela had gone.

★ ★ ★

Lizzie phoned Billy McTierney from her car. He took a while to answer.

'Me,' she said. 'After a favour.'

'What is it?'

She explained about Neville Stockton and the key to the flat on the seafront. She wanted to go up there for a look but she'd quite like someone to come with her, someone who knew, someone who understood.

'Like me?'

'Like you.'

Billy said he'd meet her outside the flats in fifteen. By the time Lizzie made it down to Southsea, delayed by traffic, the light was beginning to go. She parked and looked around. No Billy. She waited and waited, loath to chase him on the phone. Finally she gave up, crossed the road and used the key to open the door from the street.

She took the lift to the seventh floor. It took an age. She studied herself in the mirror, a small pale figure biting her lip. Was she really up for this? Wouldn't it be better to come back another day? When Billy had more time? Finally the lift juddered to a halt and she stepped out.

Stockton's flat was on the left. She stopped in front of the door, fumbling for the key, then let herself in. After long months lying empty, it

422

smelled stale and damp. From somewhere came the sound of a dripping tap. She switched on a light, then doused it again.

She went through to the living room and drew the curtains back. Sunset had come and gone, and dusk was beginning to fall. She bent to the handle on the glazed door, wondering how the lock on the slider worked, but managed to get it open. She pulled the door back and was about to step out onto the balcony when she had second thoughts. First she needed to see the bedroom where her daughter had slept.

It had to be the smaller of the two rooms. It was pink and powder blue, nursery colours, and standing in the open doorway Lizzie wondered whether Stockton had chosen the decor for his grandchild. Either way, she thought, it would have been perfect for Claire, the woman-child of the media's worst nightmare. She tried to picture the two of them in here, Claire and Grace, sharing the small double bed, maybe reading stories, maybe just keeping the world outside at bay.

Within hours of taking Grace away, she thought, Claire would have had a problem. Grace had loved strangers, loved anything in life that promised a treat and something new in her young life, but this abrupt change of scene would have been different. Where's my mummy? Where's my dad? No wonder Claire had panicked. No wonder she'd resorted to the blister packs of risperidone she'd been hiding away, the powerful psychotropic that had caused her so much torment. Samples taken at the post-mortem proved beyond doubt that Grace had died of a drug overdose. She'd died because Claire Dillon hadn't worked out how else to keep her quiet.

Lizzie stepped out of the room again, wondering what difference this discovery had made to Neville Stockton. The child in the spare bedroom hadn't been asleep at all; she'd been dead.

Out on the balcony Lizzie reached for the rail. The wind was cold off the sea, and across the darkening Solent she could make out the low black swell of the Isle of Wight. Much closer, the empty spaces of the common were bare in the late afternoon. A lone dog-walker. A mum with a buggy. A group of students still kicking a football in the last of the grey winter light.

She half-closed her eyes, trying to imagine this same scene in high summer: lots of people about, not a parking space to be had. Claire would be out here. Lizzie knew this. Neville had turned up from London and mysteriously disappeared again. She'd be alert. She'd sensed that danger was on its way, that people were coming to get her, that her days in this cave of a flat, this place of safety, were numbered.

Then she would have heard the sirens. Two marked cars to begin with, then, within minutes, the big white Mercedes Sprinter of the Force Support Unit. Figures in uniform staring up at her. Men in black jumpsuits pouring out of the van. An entry ram. Guns. Shields. Helmets. The horror film of her worst nightmare.

Out on the common the local scrotes had

424

gathered. Lizzie knew this for a fact. Many of them were on bikes. They had their phones out. They'd scented blood. They knew money was to be made. Down below, the uniforms, the jumpsuits, the men who'd come to get her, had disappeared into the building.

By this time Claire may have heard the thump of the lift coming to a stop. Footsteps down the corridor. Maybe voices at the door. By this time she'd been back to the bedroom. She'd scooped Grace out of the bed. Carried her through the flat, out to the balcony, out to the open air, out to the gathering crowd. Her job was nearly over. She was here to protect this little girl, to save her from the world below.

And so she'd clambered over the rail, steadied herself exactly the way all the phone footage had shown, hugged the little body just a little tighter, and jumped.

Mad, mad, mad, Lizzie thought. For a moment she stood there, staring down at the pavement, wondering just how easy it would be to jump. Then she felt a hand on her arm, easing her back.

'Don't,' said a voice.

She turned around, howling in her grief. Billy McTierney.

⋆ ⋆ ⋆

It was late, gone ten, when Oona turned up at Suttle's flat. She'd phoned earlier after a difficult shift and tried to explain about her and Luke splitting up, but Suttle had cut her short. I know

425

already, he'd said. Luke told me this morning.

'So how do you feel about it? Me and Luke?'

'You want the truth?'

'Yes, please.'

'Glad.'

Suttle had half-expected the trademark Oona laugh, but she'd been silent on the phone, and Suttle had wondered how much of herself she'd invested in her wayward detective boyfriend. Now, nearly an hour later, she was in the kitchen spooning a takeaway curry onto a plate Suttle had pre-warmed.

'He's a lovely boy,' she admitted. 'And I'll miss him.'

'So why not try to make it work?'

'Because I know it won't. Some men you can pin down. Lots of sex. Lots of potatoes. Football on Sky. Yer man ticks all those boxes, sure, but it's the rest I could never cope with.'

'Like?'

'Other women, obviously. Plus the fact he never bothered to cover his tracks. That's a double insult, in case you were wondering.'

Suttle nodded. Sex and potatoes and football on Sky, he thought. Not much of a future if you had an ounce of ambition.

'And me?' He couldn't resist the question. 'Us?'

'You're different.'

'How?'

'You're older, my sweet one. And a great deal wiser.'

'You're sure about that?'

'Of course not.' She offered him a spoonful of

steaming dhal. 'But I can't wait to find out.'

Suttle grinned back at her, opening his mouth for the dhal, then his mobile began to ring. He didn't recognise the number, nor — for a second or two — the voice on the other end. The tiny hesitations. The slight lisp. Then he had it.

'Neil,' he said. 'Neil Moncrieff.'

'That's right. How did you know?'

'It doesn't matter. Where are you?'

He wouldn't say. Oona had gone back to her takeaway. She wanted to know whether he was up for chicken jalfrezi.

He shook his head. Put his finger to his lips. Returned to the phone. Moncrieff was telling him they needed to meet.

'When?'

'Half an hour. You know the Geoneedle?'

Suttle had found a pen and was looking for a scrap of paper. The Geoneedle was an Exmouth cliff-top monument marking the start of the Jurassic Coast.

Moncrieff was giving him directions. Park at the end of the seafront. Take the zigzag to the top of the cliff. Then follow the footpath towards Budleigh. From the seafront it should take him no longer than five minutes.

'You'll need a torch,' he said. 'And make sure you're alone.'

He rang off. Suttle studied the number, wondering whether it was pay-as-you-go. Then he put a call through to Nandy. No way was he meeting Neil Moncrieff without backup.

Nandy was at his best in these situations.

'You think he means it?'

427

'I've no idea, sir.'

'OK. Leave it to me. I'll call back.'

Oona had gone through to the living room. Suttle found the torch beside his bed and slipped it into the pocket of his anorak. Then he was beside Oona, eyeing the food.

'Aren't you going to join me?'

Suttle shook his head. Something had come up, he said. He swallowed a spoonful of chicken and headed for the door.

Nandy rang back as he was on the way down to the Impreza on the hard standing at the back of the flats. The Det-Supt had raised two officers from Exmouth nick and had the force helicopter on standby. He'd be driving down with more bodies and should be up on the cliffs within forty minutes. The guys from Exmouth would meet him at the foot of the zigzag. On no account was Suttle to approach Moncrieff alone.

'We understand each other?'

'Yes, sir.'

Suttle rang off, thumbed the key fob for the Impreza and slipped in behind the wheel, replaying the call in his head. Why had Moncrieff suddenly broken cover? On the phone he'd sounded calm, not a trace of his usual timidity. After years of dither, he'd finally made a few decisions. First the old man. Then Erin. And now this.

Suttle stirred the engine into life and began to back towards the road, but the moment he turned the wheel he knew something was wrong. The car felt spongy under his fingers, and he could hear a grinding noise from one of the back wheels. He stopped and got out. It was raining again, and he put up the hood of his anorak. The rear offside tyre was flat, the rubber deformed against the hub.

He knelt beside it, already wondering about a taxi and fumbling for the torch. He thought he could see a tear in the tyre wall. He reached out, feeling the rough edges of the rent, then he heard a tiny movement behind him. Still on his haunches beside the wheel, he swung round, but he was too late. For a split second a tall thin figure was silhouetted against the street lights. Then Suttle's world exploded.

He came to seconds later. He was flat on his back, dizzy, sick, helpless. The world was still spinning. Everything was out of focus. Pain, he thought vaguely, tasted of chicken jalfrezi.

Slowly, he began to put the clues together. Neil Moncrieff was sitting on his chest. He appeared to be wearing a robe of some kind. It was black and enveloped his gaunt frame. With his back to the street lights, his face was a mask of darkness. He looked like the Angel of Death.

'Tell me about Rosalind.' The voice seemed to come from a million miles away. 'Tell me what you did with her.'

Rosalind? For the first time Suttle saw the machete. Moncrieff had the tip beneath his chin. He could feel the cold steel steady against his throat. Moncrieff had done exactly this to his father. Suttle shut his eyes, all too conscious of what might follow.

'We talked,' he said.

'What else?'

'Nothing.'

'You're a liar.'

'Ask her, then.'

'I did. She lied too.'

Suttle opened his eyes. He felt a little strength returning, a small flicker of hope. He knew he had to get out of this. He knew there was no way this man would listen to reason. He was crazy. Insane. A relay had tripped deep in his brain, and a voice in his head had taken over.

Suttle brought his knees up and twisted his body to one side, trying to throw Moncrieff off, but the grip of his knees around Suttle's chest simply tightened. Then he swung the machete backwards, slashing at Suttle's thigh, and Suttle felt the blade bite deep into his flesh. He screamed with surprise and pain. So quick, he thought. So deft. So strong. Moncrieff slashed again, lower this time, catching Suttle on the calf. Suttle felt the warmth of the blood coursing down his leg.

'Stop!' he yelled. 'For fuck's sake, stop. Just tell me what you want.'

'I want the truth. About Rosalind.'

'There is no truth. Nothing happened. It's in your head. *Nothing fucking happened, OK?*'

'I don't believe you.'

His hand was raised again. Suttle caught the flash of the street lights on the blade as it swung down. Moncrieff was going for his face this time. Suttle managed to half-turn, trying to avoid the blow, but the machete caught him on the side of the head. More blood.

'Just stop!' he gasped. 'We can talk this thing through. Yeah?'

It was hopeless, and Suttle knew it. Moncrieff wasn't listening. He was here to kill him. He was here to settle yet another debt. At his mercy was the man who'd taken the woman he loved. And he must suffer the consequences.

Moncrieff's arm was raised for another blow. He was going for the side of the neck this time, the blade of the machete poised in the rain. Suttle had no strength left to resist. His head was bursting, and the taste of vomit was rising in his throat. He tried to tuck his chin into his shoulder, picturing the blood that had fountained from the old man's severed artery. This, he knew, was what would kill him, a brief stab of pain followed by the hot sweet pumping gush of blood as he slipped away. What would a death like this feel like? What would await him beyond?

Suttle closed his eyes again. He thought of Lizzie the last time he'd seen her. He thought of his daughter, way out in deepest space. Would Grace be waiting for him? His little girl? He was limp now, not bothering to even try to protect himself. I've earned this, he told himself. This is my punishment, my due. Just do it. Just kill me. Good night and God bless.

For a second the weight of Moncrieff's body seemed to ease. Suttle's sudden compliance seemed to have taken him by surprise. Then came the rumble of an approaching car, the squeal of brakes as it slowed to turn and the sudden blaze of headlights on full beam. Suttle opened his eyes. Moncrieff's arm was still cocked above him. Then the blade came down, full force, and Suttle screamed in agony before the lights went out and darkness engulfed him. In the far distance he thought he heard a door open, footsteps, a man's voice, a language he didn't recognise. Then came the faintest cry. A baby, he thought vaguely. How strange.

Afterwards

Suttle spent the next week and a half in hospital in Exeter. Surgery had repaired the worst of the damage to his face and throat, and the wounds in his legs had begun to heal. He was in a four-bedded ward with a Sister brimming with Yuletide spirit, and once he was mobile he gave her a hand with the Christmas decorations.

Oona came up from time to time when the pressure was off in A & E. Suttle owed his life, she said, to the big Polish hunk on the top floor. He'd returned that night with his partner and new baby. He'd sat on Moncrieff, yelled for help and phoned for the police and an ambulance. Oona had come down from the flat and applied pressure to the worst of the bleeding.

Suttle, she said, was slipping in and out of consciousness and his pulse was beginning to weaken, but the paramedics had attended within minutes, and once they'd got him into the ambulance they managed to stabilise him. She'd crouched beside him on the fifteen-minute dash to A & E, telling him to hang in there, a journey she never wanted to repeat. He owed his survival, she said, to the surgical team that was waiting. A longer journey would have killed him.

Nandy swept into the ward a day later, towing Carole Houghton in his wake. Still shocked and slightly nauseous, Suttle wasn't sure he could do justice to the huge box of Devon fudge Nandy had brought with him but he appreciated the gesture. Nandy, who hated hospitals, didn't stay long, and it was Houghton who brought Suttle up to date.

Neil Moncrieff, she said, had gone to earth in the church behind the Beacon. He'd regularly accompanied Roz to Sunday morning services, and his knowledge of clocks had led to a conversation with the rector in charge. There were problems with the mechanism of the big timepiece in the church tower and visits from the engineer were costing the parish a fortune. Moncrieff had volunteered to take a look at it and had come up with a solution. The clock had performed faultlessly ever since, and the rector had been only too happy to make Moncrieff responsible for its maintenance. A key to a side door gave him unrestricted access. He could climb the tower and check the wretched thing out any time he fancied.

Suttle wanted to know more, but Houghton said he'd have to wait. She was sending Luke Golding along tomorrow. The Crime Scene Manager had videotaped what the SOC team had discovered up in the church tower, and Luke would be arriving with all the footage on a laptop.

Golding turned up the following afternoon, with a broad grin on his face. Nandy, for once, had been pleased with the passage of events and he was glad to report that Christmas had arrived early in the shape of a Czech vision called Eliska. He'd met her in an Exeter nightclub just a couple of nights ago. She was blonde and generous and extremely fit. He thought he might be in love.

'Again?' Suttle was trying not to grin. Grinning hurt.

'Yeah.' Golding was eyeing a passing nurse. 'Never fails.'

He opened the laptop and fired it up. Moncrieff, he said, had admitted both murders in a longish interview the morning after his arrest. Golding had been one of the two D/Cs in the interview room and had quickly concluded that the guy was bonkers.

'Should we have seen that, skip? Should we have known earlier?'

For the last two days Suttle had thought about little else. All the signs were there: the inwardness, the sudden flares of temper and the looming shadow of a father he loathed. This was a guy, he'd concluded, who could never rid himself of the past. Small wonder he'd finally cracked.

Suttle struggled upright in the bed and peered at the laptop. The Crime Scene Manager had started with an exterior view of the big handsome church behind the Beacon. The shot abruptly cut to a spiral staircase, dimly lit, rough stone walls. This, said Golding, offered access to the winding mechanism in the tower and the bells above. The CSM was still climbing the stairs. On a narrow planked landing he paused, and his torch found the golden mesh of wheels that had caused the vicar so much grief. This was what Moncrieff had volunteered to sort out for him. This was his passport to what lay above.

The climb resumed. More stairs winding ever upwards. Finally the CSM's torch settled on a narrow pair of wooden doors. A gloved hand reached forward, pushing them open, and suddenly Suttle found himself in a much bigger space. A silty daylight seeped in through a grille in the side of the tower. A wooden cage held the huge bell that struck the hours, and there were more bells, smaller, beside it.

'There, look . . . ' Golding was pointing at the screen as the CSM panned the camera left. He was inside the bell chamber now. Bits of old timber littered the floor but a narrow space had been tidied between the joists. Suttle could make out a sleeping bag and a clutter of possessions. Golding froze the shot.

Suttle wanted to know what else was up there.

'Candles, tinned food, water, a pair of binos, some books, bird books mainly, earplugs. It was weird. Truly weird. He'd been up there a couple of days. Maybe he'd moved in there for good. Fuck knows. It must have been noisy as hell. A bell that size? Every *hour*? No wonder the guy needed earplugs.'

Suttle lay back a moment. There was something that had been troubling him. 'Oona said he was wearing a cassock thing when he attacked me.'

'That's right. He'd nicked it from the vicar's robing room. Panto time.'

'Anything else?'

'Yeah. This.'

Golding had produced a square of paper. Suttle unfolded it. It was a copy of an old sepia

436

photo. A young squaddie was blowing a black woman a kiss. She had a child swaddled on her back. Moncrieff, he thought. Kamiti camp. Neil must have taken it from his father's bedroom, a trophy after spilling so much blood.

'Nandy says it's the key to everything. We found his laptop up there too. The ZBook.'

Suttle's gaze returned to the image on the screen.

'So Moncrieff spent all his time in this hole?'

'No. Watch.'

The video began again. Yet more stairs. Then, finally, the CSM pushed at a last door, and Suttle was out on the roof of the tower, back in the wash of thin grey light. The camera panned around. A lattice of metal girders secured the flagpole. A thin strip of lightning conductor circled the tower, tacked to the stonework. Through openings in the stonework Suttle caught glimpses of the estuary and the open sea. Then the camera panned left, and Suttle was looking at the back of the property that contained his own flat.

He must have been watching me, he thought. He knew from Roz that I lived on the Beacon and he knew my car because I'd given him a lift to Middlemoor to meet the photofit guy. He must have seen me coming home that night. He had my number. And so he chose his time, called my mobile, helped himself to the vicar's cassock and then lay in wait.

Next the camera panned down, and Suttle found himself viewing a mess of bloodied feathers and bones. They were everywhere. The

437

lead roof of the church tower was a crime scene.

'Peregrine falcon, skip. Moncrieff told us all about it. He loves the bird. He used to go up there in daylight to try and feed it. This is a bird that will eat anything — pigeons, seagulls, whatever. It takes them in midair and needs a place of safety to do the biz. And you know what birders call the place? People like Moncrieff?' He was grinning. 'The killing stone.'

Golding had frozen the picture again. Suttle gazed at the carnage. Me, he thought. That could have been me. The killing stone. Christ.

'So where is he now? Moncrieff?'

'Broadmoor. And I don't think he'll be out any time soon.'

'Does that make him crazy? Or just evil?'

'Mad. And very sick.'

'Did he cough to Erin?'

'He didn't have to. We found the foetus in a jam jar.'

'You mean her child?'

'Yes.'

'Where?'

'Up in the bell tower. Among the tinned food.'

★ ★ ★

After Golding had gone, Suttle had plenty of time to think. He found the ward routine oddly comforting — the brightness of the nurses, the gaggle of medical students who drifted from bed to bed listening to their consultant — and he'd made a kind of peace with himself by the time he looked up to find Lizzie at his bedside. Luke

Golding had been right to ask the question, he'd concluded. They should have sussed Neil Moncrieff far earlier. They should have clocked the symptoms that had pushed him over the edge. But madness wasn't an easy thing to understand.

Lizzie could only agree. It was a couple of days before Christmas Eve. Carole Houghton had made contact and offered her a bed for the night. Now she leaned over Suttle's still-swollen face and kissed the line of stitches across his forehead. When he insisted that time would heal everything, she gazed at him and then gave him a hug.

'Are we talking about this?' She nodded at his ruined face. 'Or the whole deal?'

Suttle didn't answer. Insanity, he'd concluded, was a wearying proposition. He knew Lizzie was trying to understand what had really happened in the summer and he did his best to feign interest in where her travels had taken her, but in his heart he'd had enough of the likes of Neil Moncrieff and Claire Dillon. At journey's end Lizzie claimed to have made a kind of peace with herself and he said he was glad.

'You don't believe me, do you?'

'I believe you've tried. Do I believe that any of it makes any sense?' He shook his head. 'No.'

It wasn't the answer she wanted — too male, too abrupt — but she was tactful enough not to revisit the moment when they'd watched their daughter's body tumble into oblivion on the evening news, and he was grateful for that.

Lizzie stayed an hour, talking about the book

she was going to start in a couple of days' time. She'd decided to see it through Claire's eyes, first person, a kind of mad travelogue scored for a woman who'd lost her bearings. The key, she told Suttle, was balance. Once that had gone, once you were alone on the rock face, you were probably doomed. She'd tried out the idea on Claire's mum. Interesting idea, she'd said. Go for it.

Suttle wasn't so sure.

'You think that will work? You really think you can get inside this woman's head?'

'Yes.' Lizzie was reaching for her coat. 'I've got all the clues. I've done all the detective work. The rest is down to me.' She'd stooped for a goodbye kiss. 'Get well soon, Jimmy Suttle. Take care.'

★ ★ ★

Suttle returned to work in late January. His face would be scarred for life, his legs too, but Oona claimed he was ahead of the curve. Scar tissue, she said, was the new tattoo. Her lovely man owed Neil Moncrieff a very big thank you. A collection of scars like that would soon cost a fortune. Suttle, jammy as ever, had got them for free.

Suttle wasn't so sure. Whenever he ducked his head in the bathroom to soap his face, he turned away from the mirror before applying the special ointment to soften the lividness of the healing tissue. He didn't much like who the mirror said he was, and there came a moment when he realised how crushing a disfigurement like this

440

could be. Maybe he should have devoted more thought to Neil Moncrieff's angst about his looks. Maybe his own scars were turning him inward, making him someone he found hard to live with.

Nandy, to his surprise, was sympathetic. Before he closed the file on *Amber* he wanted an interview with Kennan, Moncrieff's grandson. The Crown Prosecution Service had declined to pursue conspiracy charges against either Hilary or Olly Moncrieff. The outcome of any trial would be highly uncertain and — in Olly's case, given the nightmare of extradition — wildly expensive. Neither would they be mounting any kind of legal case against Roz McIntyre. She might have provided an alibi for her lover on the Saturday night but there was no way of proving it. Nor could a blind woman be expected to check the contents of a memory card. With respect to further prosecutions, the matter was therefore closed.

'So why Kennan, sir?' Suttle was lost.

'Because I need to complete the file. This is about the family. About what went wrong. There's no harm in getting the boy's account.'

Suttle nodded. He still had Kennan's mobile number. He'd sort a flight and get himself down there. A pleasure, sir. No problem.

Arrangements for the flight were Carole Houghton's responsibility. The fact that Suttle hadn't suspected a deeper motive on Nandy's part amused her.

'He thinks you could do with a bit of sunshine,' she said. 'Take someone you care

441

about. I'll sort your ticket. You pay for the other one.' She smiled. 'Deal?'

★ ★ ★

Oona was delighted. Working over Christmas, she said, had given her a whack of leave. She could talk to admin and be packed and ready within a couple of days. Was this bit of Spain south of the equator? Should a girl take her malaria pills?

Suttle tried to call Kennan. The first couple of times he didn't pick up but then Suttle got through. Light voice, soft. Wanted to know who was on the line.

'You're the cop?' The one Olly told me about? The guy he took to the Parakeet?'

Suttle wondered how much Olly had shared with his nephew. Necking in the shallows on an Accra beach wasn't the best introduction he'd ever had.

'I need to come out to talk to you,' he said woodenly. 'I'm thinking the day after tomorrow.'

'Friday? Good. Excellent. Where are you staying?'

'Not sure yet.'

'Leave it to me. You're flying to Murcia?'

'Almeria. We're picking up a car at the airport.'

'We?'

'A friend and I.'

'Even better.'

Kennan gave him directions. Drive north along the coastal motorway. Take the Mojacar exit. Turn left and head for the hills. Little village

442

called Bedar at the head of the valley. Can't miss it.

'When you get there, call me. Right?'

* * *

Two days later Suttle and Oona drove to Gatwick and joined the queue at the easyJet desk. By mid-afternoon, in bright sunshine, they'd picked up a mid-range Renault and were driving north through a grey lunar landscape largely spared the attentions of the developers. The coastal strip was shrouded in plastic, hundreds of acres of salad crops grown on an industrial scale, while inland the rocky foothills of the sierra were bare except for a handful of long-abandoned ruins.

An hour took them to the exit for Mojacar. The road to Bedar wound up the promised valley. On the outskirts of the village Suttle pulled over and made the call.

Kennan turned up within minutes on a battered trail bike. He was tall, nearly as tall as Neil, but he had a raw physical confidence absent in his uncle. He pumped Suttle's hand, shot Oona an admiring grin, then straddled the bike again and led them through the outskirts of the village, his long blond hair flying in the wind. Oona, already impressed, thought he looked like a Viking.

The narrow unsurfaced track dead-ended outside a long thin house built into the side of a cliff. This, said Kennan, belonged to a mate of a mate. Help yourself. Suttle, who was beginning

443

to wonder whether this trip was business or pleasure, wanted to know when they could talk.

'Sunday,' he said. 'We're gigging at a bar in the mountains. We'll have all the time in the world.'

Under normal circumstances Suttle would have pressed for an earlier meet. Revved up by the demands of *Amber*, he'd have been back at the airport within twenty-four hours, the statement already typed on his laptop, ready for the next assignment. But, as Houghton had pointed out only yesterday, *Amber* was largely history. Moncrieff's killer was safely tucked away, the team had dispersed to the far corners of Devon and Cornwall, and all that remained was a exploratory chat with the youngest member of the family who might — or might not — have something interesting to add to the file.

To Oona, who didn't begin to understand the cop mentality, Houghton's message was clear.

'Enjoy,' she murmured, unpacking the bottle of Bombay Sapphire she'd bought at the airport.

Suttle knew he had no choice. Saturday passed in a blur. The weather, if anything, was even better. They drove down to the coast, ogled the expats, inspected the ribbon of gritty grey sand and browsed the supermarket bulletin board. Ads for locksmiths and shutter security. A recipe for lumpy custard. A mobile app to help recognise the onset of skin cancer. Was this what had drawn young Kennan to Spain? Suttle thought not.

He found a sports bar down by the beach. They were showing the Arsenal-Coventry FA Cup game and he settled down to watch while

Oona prowled the local market. By the time she came back, Arsenal were 3–0 up and Suttle was on his fourth lager. When she slipped an arm around his shoulders, he told her he was starting to feel normal again.

'Booze and sunshine.' She gave him a sloppy kiss. 'Never fails.'

They went to bed early. Suttle woke in the middle of the night to the tinkle of goat bells in the valley. The patio of the house hung over the view. Swathed in a blanket, he stood by the rail staring out at the distant lights of the coast. A creamy moon hung in a cloudless sky, casting pale shadows over the craggy limestone, and it was cold up here in the mountains.

After a while he went back to bed, his mind wonderfully empty, a man at last untroubled by anything but the prospect of the next beer. Oona hadn't stirred.

By next morning Kennan had texted directions to the Bar El Pinal. Suttle and Oona were late getting up, and it was nearly midday before they got round to breakfast. Oona fried eggs she'd acquired from a smallholding down the road. They'd bought bread from the bakery in the village. The loaf — unleavened — reminded her of the soda bread at home as a kid. She made a huge pot of tea and produced a jar of Marmite she'd found in the supermarket. Convalescence, she told him, was an Irish invention, a lazy mash-up of indolence and gluttony.

Suttle could only agree. He was beginning to feel like an expat himself, one of the guys he'd seen ambling along the promenade, one of the

445

guys for whom time had ceased to have any real meaning. They set off for the Bar El Pinal in the early afternoon. By the time they found it the track outside was packed with cars. They got out. The sun was still warm. Already they could hear the music.

The bar was scruffy. A dog sprawled on the cracked tiles in the doorway, and the pool table had seen better days. Oona, who turned out to speak decent Spanish, ordered a San Miguel for Suttle and a large glass of Rioja for herself. The band had set up in the bar's backyard, an area of broken paving stones surrounded by a sagging wire fence. Beyond lay the mountains of the sierra.

A guy they'd met on the plane had described the area as the Wild West, and looking across the acres of mesquite and scrub Suttle could see what he'd meant. This was a landscape familiar from a thousand spaghetti westerns, the perfect backdrop if you fancied posing as Clint Eastwood for the rest of your life.

He shared the thought with Oona. She was already moving with the music. A dozen tables circled the band. Kennan was out front, chasing a song Suttle didn't recognise, while two other guys played rhythm and bass behind him. At the very back, partly hidden, was a drummer.

Oona had spotted two spare seats at a table. Suttle carried the drinks over. Most of the people were in their sixties or even older, and had obviously been partying all day. These were faces Suttle recognised from dozens of bars in Pompey: guys who'd got by on this and that but finally binned the motherland for a couple of acres in the back of the Spanish beyond. Everyone knew everyone. No traffic wardens. No rain. No grief about the mortgage or the gas bills. Just another winter afternoon in the mountains, scored for laughter, cheap lager and good weed.

He settled at the table. Kennan had clocked Suttle's arrival and offered a brief nod of welcome. Then he bent to the mike again, belting out the lyrics, his left hand dancing up and down the frets of his ukulele, his foot tapping to the beat. Face to face or on the phone, he had the lightest voice — thoughtful, reflective, someone intent on giving you space — but out here in the sunshine in front of his band that same voice had a rich, powerful, almost animal quality. The slight lisp Suttle had noticed earlier had gone. Cocooned by the music, he'd become someone else.

'Ain't no cheating the had times
Ain't no beating the way it was
Ain't no way out for any man
The night the past comes callin'.'

The set was coming to an end. Kennan turned to the rest of the band, and his nod signalled the big finish. These men had to be twice his age. Except for the drummer.

Suttle had a clear view now. He was staring at the drummer's face. He was black, skinny, high forehead, hooded eyes, big phony smile. The last time Suttle had seen this face was in Kwasi

447

Asare's office in downtown Accra. No doubt about it. The man in the mugshot: Ousmane Ndiaye.

The band were done. More drinks appeared. Kennan went from table to table, high-fiving the men, kissing the women, trading compliments and gossip. Finally he settled beside Suttle.

'You like the band?'

'Great.'

'And the song?'

'Brilliant. You wrote it yourself?'

'I did. It's about my grandpa.'

'That's what I thought. Drink?'

Oona went to the bar to fetch resupplies. Ousmane was still perched behind the drums, teasing the high hat.

'I know that guy,' Suttle said.

'I expect you do.'

'So what's he doing here?'

'Grandpa sent him, way before Christmas. He thought we might get on.'

'And?'

'We do. The man's a handful, no question, but he makes me laugh. Plus he needs to keep his head down. Which I guess you know already.'

Suttle nodded. He was trying to work out how Ousmane could have made it out of the country.

'How did he get here?'

'Back of a white van. If you have money it's no problem. Cash buys you the van and the driver and the ferry crossing. They're looking for guys coming the other way. No one cares if you're leaving.'

Suttle smiled. Simple, he thought.

448

Kennan was asking about the family. He still had a soft spot for his mum. How was she coping?

'OK.'

'Just OK?'

'Yeah. She was the one who found your grandpa that morning. I'm not sure you ever get over something like that. You ought to give her a ring some time. Have a chat. She misses you.'

'Yeah?' Kennan seemed unconvinced. He swallowed a mouthful of lager and wiped his mouth on the back of his hand. 'Mum was clueless when it came to men. Grandpa. My dad. She had a rough old deal.'

'And you?'

'I got out.' He nodded towards the stage. 'That was my salvation.'

'Music?'

'Yeah. Definitely. With the music you're never alone. It's always there, waiting for you. You can take it any place you want. A ukelele? The words in your head? No one can have that off you, ever.'

Ousmane had left the drums now. One of the band had bought him a drink, and he was carrying it across to their table.

Suttle fetched another chair. Extended a hand. 'The name's Jimmy,' he said.

'Ousmane.' He ignored Suttle's proffered hand. 'Is this your woman?'

'It is.'

The smile again. And the deep-set eyes gazing at Suttle's scars. He sat down. He had no interest in small talk.

449

'Kennan says you want to talk about Mr Moncrieff.'

'Kennan's right.'

'What do you want to know?' The heavy French accent softened the bluntness of his questions.

Suttle smiled. This was close to bizarre. No interview room. No recording machine. Just the sun sinking slowly towards the high sierra and the cackles of laughter from neighbouring tables as yet another San Miguel hit the spot.

'You came to visit him, right?'

'Yeah.'

'Straight from Heathrow?'

'Yeah. I had the address from Olly. You know Olly? Man, the thing is I was supposed to arrive later, like Mr *Invisible*, but this didn't sound like a good idea to me. I knew Mr Moncrieff. I knew him from Olly. He sounded a good guy, my kind of guy, a guy you can be around. And you know what? I was right. Maybe he's not as well as he used to be. Maybe that memory of his is fucked. But man, that guy knows Africa, my Africa. A pleasure to be with him.'

'But why did Olly send you?'

'Not your business. Not mine either, as it turned out. No way. *No fucking way.*' He beat the words out on the tabletop with his long bony fingers.

'No fucking way what?'

'No fucking way was I going to hurt the man. And he knew it.'

'Who knew it?'

'Neil. Mr Weird. Mr Tight-Arse. Up here . . . '

450

He put a finger to his temple. 'Finished. Gone. Totally A-one fucked.'

Suttle nodded and took a long pull at his lager. As it happened Ousmane was right. As Suttle had found to his cost.

'So what happened on the Sunday? The morning you left?'

'I don't know.'

'Yes, you do. You were there in the house when Neil came back. You must have been.'

'Sure, man, but I don't know what *happened*. Me and Mr Neil? We don't talk. We don't understand each other. And so we don't bother. He comes to me and says I've got to kill his father? I laugh in his face. He wants to know what's happened to all the money? Mr Moncrieff's money? I tell him it's mine. And I tell him it's mine because Mr Moncrieff gave it to me.'

'So what did he say?'

'Nothing. He cried. Like a baby.'

'Then what?'

'I went. I told him good luck. And leave Mr Moncrieff alone.'

'But he didn't.'

'Sure. You're blaming me?'

Suttle shook his head. Oona had beaten a tactful retreat and was deep in conversation with a seventy-something at a neighbouring table. The guy had tats and a greying ponytail and was already rolling Oona a joint.

Suttle turned to Kennan. 'You heard about the woman Neil killed?'

'Yeah. Excessive, I'd say.'

'Does it surprise you?'

'Not really. Neil was always on the edge. Olly said one push and he'd be over.'

'So who did the pushing?' Suttle was back with Ousmane. He wanted an answer.

Ousmane shook his head. 'Not me. Kill a man? *Jamais*. Never.'

'That's not what I asked. We know who killed the old man. He killed another woman too. And he nearly killed me. What I want to know is why.'

There was a long silence. Ousmane appeared to have lost interest in the conversation.

Then Kennan leaned forward. 'The guy lost it,' he said. 'Shit happens.'

'Two deaths? Nearly three?'

'Sure. This thing's irrational, like I say. You think you've got life nailed? That's when it falls apart. You know about his clocks? You know how self-controlled he was? Measuring out every little beat of his life, tucking it away somewhere safe, shutting the door on the world? Tick-tock? Tick-tock? Tick-tock?' He paused, suddenly intense. 'You know what happened to Neil? Roz happened to Neil. Sex happened to Neil. And after that the only question worth asking was whether he could handle it. He couldn't. He didn't. And the rest — ' Kennan shrugged ' — you know about.'

Ousmane was struggling with something in the pocket of his jeans. Eventually he got it out. It was inside a small plastic bag. He passed it across to Suttle.

'This is for you, my friend. A little present. *Un petit cadeau*.'

The plastic bag was heavy in Suttle's hand. He peered inside. Something made of brass. It looked like the end of a telescope.

'What is it?'

'It's for watching the stars, my friend. There's a whole universe in there. You want the answer to life? Just take a look.'

He leaned across and uncapped the lens. Suttle put it to his eye. At first he could see nothing.

Ousmane was laughing. 'Shut the other eye, man. Trust me.'

Suttle did what he was told. He could see nothing but darkness. But then came a tiny fizzing explosion of white light, then another, then a third. It reminded him of a firework display in miniature: delicate threads of light that hung in the darkness for a second and then faded into the blackness beyond. He tried counting between the little tiny eruptions, seeking a pattern, but they appeared to be completely random. Fizz. Then darkness. Then another fizz. Then nothing.

Hilary had mentioned this little toy, he remembered. It came from her father's study.

'It's radium inside,' Suttle said slowly. 'This belonged to Moncrieff.'

'Sure.' Ousmane was rolling himself a joint. 'And he gave it to me.'

'Why?'

'Because he thought I was the light. Because he knew no one could control me. Because he *knew* me.'

'And now?' Suttle was weighing it in his hand again.

'Now I'm giving it to you. Why? Because you need it, man. Because all the questions in the world won't give you the answer you want. Because life, in the end, is the way it happens in there.' He smiled. 'No pattern. No meaning. Pop. Pop. Pop. Gone.'

He leaned forward, his bony hand on Suttle's arm. He was looking at his scars again. Then he nodded at Oona at the neighbouring table. Something her new companion had said had just struck her as incredibly funny. She was laughing fit to bust. For once Ousmane's smile looked genuine. 'Show it to her, man,' he said. 'She'll understand.'

★　★　★

Suttle barely remembered the drive home. He had a headache from too much San Miguel and for some reason the wounds on his leg were incredibly painful. When they finally made it back to Bedar, Oona parked the car and then helped him limp up the flight of stone steps to the patio. He still had the present from Ousmane. And he still didn't know what to make of it.

He clung to the rail, gazing up at the stars. Where did Grace fit into all this? Where did Lizzie and her precious Claire? How could you ever explain a son slashing his father to shreds? Plunging his hands into a woman's belly? Sleeping in the company of a month-old foetus?

The thought of trying to voice these questions wearied him. Oona emerged from the house clad

454

in a blanket. She'd just had a text from Luke Golding. He wanted her to know that he'd moved his stuff out of the property they'd shared. If she fancied a new housemate, now's the time.

Now's the time?

Suttle rubbed his aching face and then reached out for her. She studied him in the half-darkness, then grinned.

'You're cold, you eejit,' she said. 'Come here.'

Acknowledgements

Sins of the Father, like all my other books, steps into worlds about which I knew nothing. In this case, the challenge was to penetrate and understand the inner workings of our Mental Health system, while getting to know a great deal about our colonial stewardship of Kenya during the Mau Mau Emergency. With the help of conversations with key players in both fields, I was shocked by what I found.

My sincere thanks to Waleed Abdullah, Adam Mandevu, Rupert Blomfield, Steve Carey, Scott Chiltern, Janet Gardiner, Huw Griffiths, Jack Hurley, Jim Mackie, Paul Netherton, Ali Pain, Bish Rourke, Jake Rourke, Oliver Todd, Peter Todd, Mary Tuckett and Kathy Whitehead. For readers wanting to know a great deal more about the scandal of the Mau Mau years, I can thoroughly recommend Caroline Elkins' *Imperial Reckoning: The Untold Story of Britain's Gulag in Kenya*. A fine, if disturbing, read.

I was lucky, once again, to have Hugh Davis as a copy editor and Diana Franklin to run her magnifying glass over the uncorrected proofs. This was my first book to be shepherded through the production process by my new in-house editor, Laura Gerrard, and it benefitted a great deal as a result. My thanks to my agent, Oli Munson, always a wise young head, and to my wife, Lin, the most ravishing (and consistent) critic any author could ever wish for.

We do hope that you have enjoyed reading
this large print book.

Did you know that all of our titles
are available for purchase?

We publish a wide range of high quality
large print books including:
Romances, Mysteries, Classics
General Fiction
Non Fiction and Westerns

Special interest titles available in
large print are:
The Little Oxford Dictionary
Music Book
Song Book
Hymn Book
Service Book

Also available from us courtesy of
Oxford University Press:
Young Readers' Dictionary
(large print edition)
Young Readers' Thesaurus
(large print edition)

For further information or a free
brochure, please contact us at:
Ulverscroft Large Print Books Ltd.,
The Green, Bradgate Road, Anstey,
Leicester, LE7 7FU, England.
Tel: (00 44) 0116 236 4325
Fax: (00 44) 0116 234 0205